Also available from Bloom Books

MEN OF THE WILDS

Crucible
Chrysalis

CHRYSALIS

B.B. REID

Bloom *books*

Published by Bloom Books, an imprint of Sourcebooks
1935 Brookdale RD, Naperville, IL 60563-2773
(630) 961-3900
sourcebooks.com

Cataloging-in-Publication data is on file with the Library of Congress.

The authorized representative in the EEA is Dorling Kindersley
Verlag GmbH. Arnulfstr. 124, 80636 Munich, Germany

Printed and bound in the UK by Clays and distributed
by Dorling Kindersley Limited, London
001-361021-Apr/26
10 9 8 7 6 5 4 3 2 1

FREE SETH.

CONTENT NOTE

This dark romance—like many—contains villains and villainous acts, so if at any point you find yourself uncomfortable or disturbed, remember where you are and that you can leave at any time.

You can find a full list of triggers on my website.

Enjoy!

PLAYLIST

ACT I

Dangerous—Sleep Token

you should see me in a crown—Billie Eilish

Flaws and All—Beyoncé

Change (In the House of Flies)—Deftones

Twisted—Mia Vaile

WE PRAY—Coldplay

Radioactive—Imagine Dragons (feat. Kendrick Lamar)

Bliss—Tyla

Dangerous Woman—Ariana Grande

Play with Fire—Sam Tinnesz (feat. Yacht Money)

Wicked Little Monster—Veda

Somewhere Over the Rainbow—Israel Kamakawiwo'ole

My Girl—The Temptations

I Was Made For Lovin' You—YUNGBLUD (feat. Dominic Lewis)

Apologize—Timbaland (feat. OneRepublic)

ACT II

Miss You—Aaliyah

Wrecking Ball—Miley Cyrus

Save the Hero—Beyoncé

Let the World Burn—Chris Grey
I am not a woman, I'm a god—Halsey
BODYGUARD—Beyoncé
Forgiveless—SZA (feat. Ol' Dirty Bastard)
Unstoppable—Sia

ACT I

ACT I

PROLOGUE

EZEKIEL

TWO YEARS BEFORE SETH.
FOURTEEN YEARS BEFORE AURELIA GEORGE...

"All right. Here it is," Thorin announces. He pans the laptop's camera around the sparsely furnished room. The line is silent as Khalil and I try to think of something to say that won't make Thorin regret signing away his life to the fucking Marines.

The dorm room is depressing as fuck and pretty much what you'd expect, but if you pictured the poverty line as the ocean's surface, Thorin and I are somewhere around where the *Titanic* sank. It's impossible to reach it without imploding. Needless to say, military barracks are a giant leap up.

At least now, he's guaranteed three meals a day and a roof over his head that he doesn't have to share with Annalise's smoker friends. It would get so bad at times that he'd come home from school and find that he'd have nowhere to sleep because the house, along with his room and his bed, had been loaned out for a fix. The three of us would usually run them off, but that would only solve his troubles on the surface and none of the ones that ran deep.

We have that in common—except Thorin can remember all the reasons why.

Khalil is the only one of us who came from a stable, loving home, and even though he's doing a better job masking his thoughts, his background inside the five-star hotel suite stands out in stark contrast to Thorin's. The cinder block walls of Thor's room remind me of the cells I spent a lot of time in as a kid along with the simple wooden twin bed, nightstand, desk, and four-drawer chest. He has a better view than I did though—a single window with a view of the neighboring barracks brick wall.

"It's um…bigger than I expected," Khalil lamely remarks.

"That's what she said." Khalil and Thorin groan at my even lamer attempt at humor while I peer into Thorin's background. "I don't see another bed. It's just you?"

"Yeah," he answers with a sigh as he takes a seat at his desk. "Most of the rooms are doubles, but I lucked out and got a single."

"That's pretty cool. You can jerk off whenever you want. I know how much you like your alone time."

Thorin flips me off.

Khalil laughs with his fist poised over his grinning mouth. He says something, but I only catch half of it.

On the path to become a boxing champ, his background is currently filled with the voices of his ever-growing entourage and groupies hoping to be chosen. When Thorin and I give him a questioning look, Khalil suddenly looks over his shoulder and snaps, "Can y'all shut the fuck up?"

The small but loud group that was standing nearest him moves away with mumbled apologies, but the rap music blasting from speakers still makes it hard to hear him, so he shakes his head in frustration before getting up and leaving the room.

The noise fades until he shuts himself inside another room.

"Sorry about that," he grumbles once he's alone. "I asked if the girl is cute, and if you hit it yet."

Thorin cocks his head with a deceptively innocent look. "What girl?"

"The one in charge of room assignments of course." *Lucked out my ass.* No way they were handing out single rooms to a grunt.

Khalil is showing all of his teeth when he sticks his face so close to the camera, I can count his nose hairs. "She clearly has a crush on you, my boy." He pulls back and waggles his brows. "So are you gonna fuck or what? What's her rank? Is she higher than you? Y'all gon' role play?"

"I don't know what you're talking about." Thorin dismisses Khalil's prying with a wave of his hand. "How's the shoulder?"

Khalil took a pretty nasty hit during his match tonight and still managed to knock out his opponent. I caught the whole thing on a friend's TV since I don't have cable.

Or power.

Or running water.

The only reason I'm even on the video call is because the girl I occasionally screw let me borrow her laptop and internet while she hangs out at her boyfriend's place.

Khalil's win is the reason for the celebration unfolding in his hotel suite, and even though I miss him more than I'll ever let on because Khalil will only feel guilty for leaving, I'm proud and happy for him. Khalil was living his dream—even if his dream took him far away from me.

Thorin too, except the Corps was no dream come true. It was an escape. But it also took him the farthest away, to Camp Lejeune in North Carolina.

I'd gone from being one-third of a pack to a lone wolf. Six Forks just wasn't the same without them, and even though Khalil's dad had given me a job at his construction company, it was still getting harder to find a reason to leave bed every morning.

I was happy for my best friends. Truly.

But some days, I lost the battle with the tiny seed of resentment over being left behind. It's been two years since we graduated from high school, and they've already figured out what the fuck they want out of life. Who does that?

It's unfair for me to feel this way. I know that. But knowing doesn't help it go away.

Thorin, Khalil, and I talk for an hour before there's a knock on Thor's door. He gets up to answer it, and when he returns, he isn't alone. Only half of the room is lit by a lamp, so I catch the silhouette of a woman as she shyly sits on the edge of his bed. She's short in stature with dark hair pulled back in a bun, a cute button nose, pouty pink lips, and a sergeant rank emblazoned on the front of her uniform. She clearly has a few years on Thorin too, appearing in her late twenties.

"One sec," he tells her before turning away to face the laptop. Thorin leans down so that he's eye level with the camera, blocking our view of the nervous girl.

"My boy," Khalil covertly praises with a grin.

Thorin winks. "Gotta go."

"Remember your safe words!"

"And wear a condom!" I shout just before his screen goes black.

Khalil and I are silent for several seconds before we erupt in a roar that lasts until I have a stitch in my side. For someone who acts like he's no good with charming women, Thorin sure works fast when he wants to. His Nordic features and those muscles he flaunts make him look like he's stepped straight out of a Viking romance. He's also mean as fuck, which…I guess some girls like too.

Once Khalil and I quiet, I notice a second too late that he's watching me with an assessing gaze that wasn't there before Thorin hung up. "So what's up, man? Everything cool over there? You good?"

"Yeah." My gaze shifts to the side as I rub the back of my neck. "Everything's…the same," I finish lamely because I can't even think of a lie worth telling when I spend my days on autopilot.

Khalil is quiet for a moment before he eyes me hesitantly, and I know what he's going to say before he even speaks. "You know my offer still stands. I've got a few months before my title fight. Say the word and I'll send you a plane ticket."

I laugh him off like I always do to keep from feeling like a total fucking loser.

My mom died when I was nine, and I barely remember her. My memories of my time with her are fragmented, inconsistent, and covered in rain clouds. There are pieces that whisper *terror* and others that promise love. But all those pieces have done is left me confused and torn—like I could split right in half—until I taught myself not to think about her at all. After she died, I was bounced around foster homes—when I wasn't in juvie—so I never stuck around in one place long enough for any of the countless faceless people who sheltered me to encourage me toward more. I can't blame it all on the broken system though. I stopped caring long before they did.

"You're just saying that because you feel guilty about leaving, and you *fucking shouldn't*," I tell Khalil. "I'm a grown man. Besides…" I force a smile as I wink at the screen. "We can't all be destined for greatness, and I have no interest in being your baggage." When Khalil says nothing and the silence stretches on, I realize all I've probably done is give him more reason to worry about me. "Look, I'll find my own thing," I promise softly. "You and Thorin did. I'm just a little slower to get off the stoop. That's all."

"Yeah, I hear you, man," he says unconvincingly before switching the subject. "How's work?"

I shrug noncommittally. "Fine."

Khalil's eyes narrow. "My pops told me you've been showing up late or not at all sometimes. What's up with that? You know he loves you like a son, but he *will* fire your ass, Zeke."

"You checking up on me?"

"Of course. You're my brother."

"Well, don't bother. I'm fine. I was just… I'm fine. Okay?"

"I know you are, man. It's just…" Khalil blows a breath and shakes his head but doesn't finish whatever he'd been about to say. Suddenly, he looks stressed and cornered, and now I'm the one worried.

"What?" I prod urgently.

His eyes flash with annoyance. "Has it even occurred to you that I'm offering to bring you with me because I fucking miss you too? Being on the road isn't all it's cracked up to be. I get homesick. I get lonely. It isn't just always about *you*."

"You literally have like fifty people in your hotel room right now."

An intense look of aggravation suddenly crossed Khalil's handsome face. "Man, I don't know them fucking people," he gripes.

I snorted. "Well, who invited them?"

"Gary."

I groan. "Dude, I told you making your cousin your manager was a mistake. He's a drunk. All he ever wants to do is party."

"Yeah, yeah. I know. I know. But he has a good head for business. Plus, if I fire him, my Aunt Cherise is going to kick my ass. Thanksgiving already be nothing but drama."

"Another reason why you shouldn't have hired him."

"I know, I know." He thinks about it for a little while and then adds, "I might have to fuck him up a little bit and then we'll be straight." Khalil yawns, and something that feels like panic spears through my chest. He's been so busy lately. This is our first time talking in two weeks. It was the same with Thorin, who had just finished his MOS training. His unit was getting ready to deploy, so there hadn't been any leave for him to come home before he had to report to his duty station either.

"Hey, uh…you want to call Thorin and see what he's up to?" I ask, scrambling for a reason to keep Khalil on the phone.

Just a few minutes more. I don't want to be alone.

Khalil shoots me a weird look. "You get hit on the head recently? He's fucking, remember?"

"Yeah, but I think I can hack into his account and turn the camera on." I'm already bringing up the web browser on Whitney's computer and typing in an address. "Trace showed me how."

"That's not at all disturbing," I hear Khalil say.

I'm already downloading the program Trace designed when I knowingly toss back, "So you don't want to watch?"

Khalil pretends to consider it for a moment before a slow smile takes over his face. "Nah, I definitely want to watch. Do it."

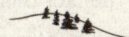

Later, when I'm walking home with my head down, hoodie up, and hands shoved in the pockets of my jeans, I'm staring at the ruptured sidewalk of my street like I always do, counting the cracks because it looks the way I feel inside.

Up ahead, I hear a bottle roll, and in this neighborhood, no matter the time of day, it always means something when you're not alone. I lift my head, but the red Porsche 911 parked on the street up ahead doesn't give me pause. It's not unusual to see a nice car creeping through here, someone looking to score. The true eyesore is the man leaning against it, sporting a Colgate smile, a thick wave of sandy brown hair, and Ray-Bans.

I keep my eyes on him as I dodge the deep gouges in the sidewalk like a rehearsed dance, and even behind the dark shades, I know the man is watching me back. His smile brightens with each step that brings me closer to him until I'm officially weirded out.

"If you're looking for Molly, that's two doors down," I tell him as I point. I don't wait for a response as I turn down the broken path with overgrown weeds sprouting through to the crumbling shack I once shared with my mother. It was a home she'd inherited from her grandmother, and the only reason it passed on to me was because it didn't.

I was squatting in my own home.

"I wondered if I'd know it was you," the man says mysteriously. I keep walking since I know better than to engage with anyone lurking around here. "You look just like your father!" he calls out when he realizes I'm not going to stop.

My foot pauses on the first broken step as I twist to look behind me. "What did you say?"

"Your father," he says. "You look just like him, Ezekiel."

Completely aside from the fact that he knows my name, he's wrong. I've never met my father, but I've seen pictures of my mother. I have flashes of her face in my head—sometimes contorted in rage and others smiling softly down at me. I have everything of hers except for her dark brown eyes. My green eyes I must have gotten from my father, who I hear has or *had* strong Italian ancestry. I still don't know if the bastard is alive or dead.

"I'm sorry... Who are you?" I ask rather than correct the stranger. It's clear this meeting was no accident, and I'm not telling him shit until I know why he's here.

Reaching up, the man removes his sunglasses and tucks them inside his shirt pocket. The shock of seeing my own green eyes staring back ripples through me, as does the wound that spreads into a spiderweb of cracks. It's not just the same color. It's a twin set—as if someone used a dropper tool to match the spring shade.

"I'm Isaac," he supplies casually. "I'm your brother."

CHAPTER ONE

EZEKIEL

PRESENT DAY...

I can't breathe.

Rolling over in the snow, I feel Thorin's presence more than see him as I inhale as much of the frigid air as I can. It's a soothing balm to the burn in my lungs. My ears are ringing, my fingers and toes are numb, and the rest of my body trembles violently. But the worst feeling of all is not remembering how I got this way.

Thorin doesn't crowd me, giving me a moment to sort out my shit. It always takes a while, especially when I almost end up buried alive.

Seth.

Fucking Seth.

This has him written all over it.

He'd bring the entire mountain down on our heads if it meant taking out Thorin and Khalil. I'd just be convenient collateral damage.

It's not his fault. Pain is the one thing I've never been able to hide from Seth, and it's not just the physical hurts that he feels he has to save me from. It's the ones that drive me to the edge of a cliff and make me want to leap.

The loose snow shifts and crunches, and I tense as someone moves behind me, inching closer. I assume it's Khalil until I hear him speak.

"Aurelia…wait."

Aurelia…

Who the hell is Aurelia?

I feel an insistent hand on my shoulder a moment later, too small to belong to Khalil, turning me around, and I don't fight it.

I barely get a glimpse of her.

No more than a glance at her brown eyes, long lashes, tear-tracked cheeks, and golden curls before she presses her full lips against mine. A charge voltaic enough to power a small city jolts through me and instinct has me reaching for her.

Suddenly ivory skin replaces brown, those golden curls lengthen and straighten to a curtain of raven black, and though her eyes are closed, I'm suddenly dreading seeing blue surrounding black pupils that I once mistook for warm and inviting like the waters in a tropical paradise.

Except this is hell, and Tatum isn't either of those things.

My heart rate spikes, and I feel Bane pressing against my skin the moment my mind speaks her name. The edges of my vision darken, and I know that I'm seconds from blacking out when I only just returned.

Confident that shit is about to go all the way left, I curl my fingers around the girl's arms and shove her away and into the snow. I watch her shock at my violent rejection and then her eyes raking over me, taking in every detail as if she's seeing me for the first time.

"Seth…" My gaze narrows at the name. The voice isn't the sharp whip of Tatum's either but rather soft and cajoling. "Baby, it's me. What's wrong?"

Suddenly, the image of Tatum fades away like it was never there, and I'm met with the face of the girl I'd mistaken for an angel. *Get a grip, Zeke. Thanatos isn't real, and she isn't one of his.*

"Goldilocks, don't. That's not—"

She's impatient and doesn't listen to Khalil, reaching out for me with lips chapped and blue from the cold. Or is it worry?

For me?

No.

For *Seth*.

I scramble away even as I ask through clenched teeth, "Who the fuck are you?"

The girl snatches back her hand with a blink of confusion. Her brown eyes once again scan my face and demeanor, but this time she doesn't dismiss the changes she sees, and understanding dawns.

The girl Thorin called Aurelia sighs. Her shoulders and the hand reaching out for me drop as if she's defeated, but my chest is still pinched tight as if she'll strike at any minute.

Does she have to be so close?

"You're not Seth," she surmises with no emotion. The gentle tone is gone, and I feel a spark of something green like envy.

What the fuck? "No. I'm not."

"Oh." Aurelia nods curtly and then avoids my gaze as she dusts off her hands and stands. "My mistake."

Her…*mistake*? Is that all finding out that I'm suddenly someone else is to her? If so, I say again… What *the fuck?* Exactly how much does she know?

I stand as well, but I still don't feel like I have the upper hand once I'm towering over her. Not with the way she's watching me closely like she's assessing and seeing if I measure up. What the hell did the others tell her about me?

"I'm Aurelia," she finally says. "You must be Ezekiel."

She starts to offer me her hand—a perfectly normal reaction

between strangers meeting for the first time—but then Khalil intercepts, wrapping his arm around her waist and pulling her safely out of my reach.

Aurelia looks up and over her shoulder at him, but he's watching me like…

Like I'm the threat. To *her*.

My chest tightens again, and Thorin clears his throat. It doesn't break any of the tension like he probably intended it to. "Obviously, we have a lot to talk about, but it'll have to wait until we get back to the cabin. It can't be here."

I look around one last time before Thorin helps me to my feet and we start looking for a way back to the cabin. It's not easy since there's snow everywhere and we're not geared up to traverse it at all. It's also spring now. I can tell by how warm the air feels rather than the bracing cold. The last time I remember being awake, it was still winter, if only for a few more weeks.

None of us speak as we walk back, and I keep waiting for the girl to go her own way but she follows us all the way back to the cabin. Thorin and Khalil also seem to be overly familiar with her, but all it does is send my anxiety through the fucking roof.

And I don't remember a thing.

Honestly, that surprises me. Seth is always a pissy bitch whenever I take my body back. Usually, I don't mind it, but this is the first time I've ever wanted to remember.

I have to.

I need to figure out what this girl is doing here and how to get her gone for good.

CHAPTER TWO

EZEKIEL

This is weird," Aurelia whispers. Her brown skin is still ashen from the avalanche, but most of the color has already returned to her cheeks and neck. I try to ignore the way they flush with heat each time our eyes accidentally meet. "I mean… This is *weird*, right?" she presses when no one else says a word.

Khalil, who is sitting between us like a barrier, grumbles something to her. Thorin sits on Aurelia's other side, and I wonder who those overbearing assholes are protecting: Her or me? Either possibility makes me want to roll my eyes.

Do they really think I'd hurt her? I'm not Bane.

Or do they think I'm so fucking fragile that I can't handle one girl?

The four of us are huddled in front of the wood-burning stove in our living room, trying to get warm. I'm pretty sure we're all past that now, but no one knows what to do. No one knows what to do about this. About us. About *me*.

It feels like I'm the outsider.

I've gotten used to waking from a split and having no idea what day it is or what's happening. It's still jarring as fuck, but it helps if it happens in a safe space, where I'm surrounded by familiar faces—neither of which happened today.

First of all, I'm pretty sure I died.

I place a hand over my chest to ensure my heart is still beating at a rhythm that won't trigger *them*.

Too fast and it wakes Seth.

Too slow…Bane.

I'm forever straddling that fine line, knowing my emotions rest on an explosive hair trigger.

Thorin and Khalil were vague on the details of what happened earlier, only explaining that we got caught in an avalanche before insisting we get back to the cabin.

Seth, what did you do? I ask the alter, reaching out with a mental probe.

Once again, he doesn't answer.

Radio fucking silent like a petulant fucking asshole because I woke up and ruined his fun.

I need him to tell me about her.

Aurelia.

Any hopes that she was a passerby were dashed when she followed us into our cabin, and from the looks of it, she's made herself pretty comfortable here.

What the fuck is going on? Why won't anyone tell me?

"How long was I out?" I finally demand when it's clear they won't offer the information on their own. Khalil and Thorin are probably hoping I'll just fall in line, but fat fucking chance of that happening. Exhaustion weighs down my voice, but the awkward silence makes it easy for them to hear me.

Thorin answers. "Couple of months," he grumbles.

The tightening of my skin—stretching impossibly as if I no longer fit—eases a little.

Two months isn't bad. Seth has been in control for much longer before, and the worn-down state I usually find Thorin and Khalil in after is never much better than my own. What scares the shit out of me is how much has changed in such a short time. Out of the corner of my eye, I catch Aurelia's shiver and Thorin pulling her closer, sharing his warmth with her while nuzzling her temple.

Thorin, soft and attentive? I'm in the fucking Twilight Zone.

"Zeke?"

"Yeah?"

"What do you remember?" Khalil asks with a caution that makes my skin prickle.

The better question is… What exactly don't they want me to remember?

"Nothing. Not a fucking thing. You know that."

The tension in the room heightens to a dangerous point since we all know my amnesia is temporary. It's not unusual for Seth to lock away some memories, though the memory loss is not always his doing. I don't know if the secrets he keeps are his way of punishing me for taking my body back or protecting me from further harm, but he always tucks the memories away just out of reach whenever he sleeps.

It's never bothered me before.

I've never been so tempted to go looking for them until now.

My gaze travels back to the girl because I can't help myself. She's leaning forward and staring back at me, too, with a mixture of curiosity and anguish. I have no idea what that's about, but it makes my teeth clench.

Seth…

Just like my last few attempts, he's eerily silent when I call for him. That space inside my head that Seth occupies is hauntingly hollow, and I'm left asking a terrifying question that would send me to my knees if I wasn't already sitting.

Can an alter die even if the body lives on?

A flare of unexpected panic seizes my muscles and sends my heart racing even as I reach for Seth again out of habit, grasping for the comfort he provides. My feelings toward Seth have always been complicated, but the dread wrapping itself around me like a barbed fist feels pretty fucking definitive. When all I feel is that emptiness again, I focus on trying to access his memories. It's a challenge for any of us to hide them all, especially from me. It's my head after all.

Wincing at the pounding in my skull when I probe for the ones of Aurelia—the memories Seth has locked down tighter than state secrets—I give up for now and absently rub my chest while staring into the flames. This ache right over my heart feels like my rib cage had been torn open recently. The last time I'd felt that way was when I learned of Tatum's betrayal.

My gaze flicks toward the girl again only to find her watching me.

Seriously, what the fuck is her problem?

Khalil hears my sharp inhale and then searches for the source, catching Aurelia gawking again. He leans and whispers something to her, but this time his voice carries enough over the crackling fire for me to make out the gentle order. "We need to talk to him. Go in the room and relax for me, Goldilocks. We got this."

Aurelia sighs heavily like she's annoyed about being shut out before pushing the blanket off her shoulders and standing to obey. I grit my teeth when I catch my brothers watching her like obsessed maniacs. Their eyes follow her out of the room and into Thorin's, but when she turns to close the door, it's my eyes she finds and holds as she quietly shuts it behind her.

It feels like she's hunting me, and I react like any cornered prey would. I do nothing while waiting for her pounce, to feel the sink of her claws and teeth bleeding me dry. The door closes, and even though I can't see her anymore, I'm locked inside my fear of this girl who watches me like she thinks I'm hers.

The moment she's gone Khalil swears and then places his hand on my back before instructing heavily, "Breathe, Zeke."

My lungs expand inside my chest, but I can't quite catch my breath. "Why is she here?" I choke out. "Who is she? What is she doing here? Why is she here?"

My heart is pounding dangerously fast by the time Khalil moves and wraps himself around me from behind for comfort as much as control in case I switch. "Shhh," he soothes with his bearded cheek pressed against the side of mine as he rocks us both from side to side. "It's okay, Zeke. She's not going to hurt you. Just breathe, man. Breathe."

I hold on to his promise even though I want to flee the cabin.

She won't hurt me. She won't hurt me. She won't hurt me.

I don't realize Thorin's left the room until he crouches in front of me with a pill in one hand and a glass of water in the other. I open my mouth, and Thorin places the pill on my tongue.

An image flashes in my mind of a smaller pill, a softer mouth, and…my hand placing the pill inside. The brown eyes staring up at me are resigned but grateful as I place the tiny pill on her tongue. Aurelia swallows it down, and the image is replaced by another.

She's now passed out in Khalil's bed, and I'm standing over her. She sleeps so soundly and peacefully while looking like she's been through hell.

The memory fades, and I'm left reeling. What the hell was that about?

Thorin hands me the glass of water, and I drink it because I know he won't stop watching me like a hawk until I do. When the glass is empty, he takes it from me and collapses next to me. I tap Khalil's hand, and he lets me go.

"She was in the plane crash, wasn't she?" I say, and they both stiffen. When neither of them respond, I growl out, "*Wasn't she?*"

"I thought you didn't remember anything?"

I shake my head that already feels heavy and let the lie leave my lips. "Nothing after finding her in Khalil's bed. Now stop dodging the question and answer me."

"Yes," Thorin answers.

"Isaac?"

Thorin shakes his head. "She's not with him. Far from it."

"Aurelia's a singer. A really good one," Khalil gushes, and I'm once again questioning if I've entered an alternate reality. "You should hear her sing sometime. She—"

"It's been two months," I interrupt. "If Aurelia was in that crash, why is she still here?"

They both fall quiet, and my heart plummets like a deadweight into the pit of my stomach.

I remember the morning she arrived.

We'd been in the middle of an argument that had nearly torn us apart when I caught sight of her plane engulfed in flames and flying dangerously low over our cabin like a shooting star.

And the argument *Aurelia* had unknowingly interrupted?

It was whether it was finally safe for us to go into town and find some local girls to seduce.

Seduce, not *kidnap*.

We definitely would have never brought them here. This cabin, these wilds, and this life were supposed to be ours and ours alone. Finding a woman for each of us would have been about fulfilling a need and nothing more. Nothing as serious or fucked-up as whatever the hell is happening with this singer who makes Khalil Poverly *gush*.

Staring at my brothers and wondering if I ever knew them at all, I scramble to my feet and back away with my hands clutching my hair and my vision blurring when they stand too. "What did you guys do?" I shout when my mind taunts me with horrifying possibilities. "What the *fuck* did you do?"

That argument ended with two against one and then *she* appeared, forcing us to shelve the discussion for now.

Or so I thought.

Only one thing is absolutely clear...

That poor girl's timing could not have been worse.

"Zeke—"

Thorin sighs. "Let's face it. We are never leaving this mountain. This is our home now. This is our life. This is how we stay together and keep each other safe."

Nothing of what he says surprises me because even though we've talked about leaving one day, none of us have ever believed it. "What the fuck does that have to do with her?"

"Everything," Khalil answers. "We finally have everything we've been needing."

My eyes rapidly flick between the two of them, and then I swear viciously. "What the fuck does that mean?"

"She's ours, Zeke."

"Ours." I echo the word, and it clangs around my psyche like a gong on D-day. "Does Aurelia know that?" *Aurelia*. It's my first time saying her name out loud.

"Of course."

"Tell me everything that happened," I demand. "Starting with the day she got here."

Thorin shrugs, but feigning indifference has never been a talent of his. The tension in his shoulders always gives him away. "Nothing to tell really. After you split, we questioned her to see if she was one of Isaac's, found out who she really is, and decided to keep her around for a while in case she was lying."

"And now that you know that she's not?"

Thorin's jaw clenches. "We told you. She wants to stay."

"Just like that?" I whisper sharply. Do they take me for a fool?

"It's complicated," Thorin sighs, "but it was her choice, Zeke. We didn't force her to make it."

But there it is…the quick look they give each other that leaves me pushing past the hurt of knowing my brothers are lying to me and focusing on getting the truth one way or another.

And if they won't tell me…

I'm on my feet and at Thorin's door before either of them can react.

"Where the fuck are you going?" Khalil barks.

I hear him rising to his feet, so I pause only long enough to say, "I'm going to ask her myself."

I push open the door of Thorin's room to their combined shouts. "Zeke!"

I don't consider the repercussions of barging into a room without knocking until I'm already inside. I throw my shoulder against the door to shut it just as the hard bodies of my best friends slam into it from the other side. Thorin and Khalil's chorus of pained groans filters through the door as I quickly lock it, but I immediately regret it when I turn to see one *very* naked girl staring back at me through equally surprised eyes.

"Fuck!" I slap my hand over my eyes and turn around to face the door again. "Shit. Sorry. Ah. Sorry. I didn't mean to…sorry."

Thorin and Khalil start pounding on the door—the rhythm in sync with my racing heart.

"That's okay," she says, sounding amused. "But do you mind telling me why those two sound like they're about to have a heart attack?"

I expected screaming and hysteria from my barging in. Instead, the light and lyrical sound of her giggling at my expense has me lowering my hand as I cautiously peek over my shoulder. Aurelia's covered now with a yellow silk robe that makes her glow that much brighter.

I look away again before I can get caught in a trance.

"Sorry about that," I say as I stare at the floor. "I should have knocked."

"Stop apologizing, Seth. It's nothing you haven't seen before."

My teeth clench a second before I correct her. "Zeke."

Aurelia winces, and I immediately feel like a dick. It wasn't a slight. She'll obviously need to acclimate to me being back. "Right…right. Sorry. I…I've never known anyone with DID before, and Seth is the only alter I've met so far. Please tell me there's a learning curve?" She bowls on, shaking off her fumble before I can reply. "Hi, Zeke. Nice to meet you…again. I'm Aurelia…again."

I peek at her curiously through the strands of my hair that Seth let get too long. He's usually more particular about his appearance, but haircuts are a sore spot for him. A few more inches and our hair will be long enough for those douchey topknots that Thorin wears. "So…you know about me? About…us?"

"Mm-hmm." She tucks her lips while nodding like she wants to say more but no longer trusts herself to say the right thing. "Yuuuup."

"And…" I frown. "You're not afraid?"

"Not to get competitive, but between the two of us I'm pretty sure I'm scarier." I take an involuntary step back, and she slaps her forehead with her palm. "*Fuck.* Zero for two." When I force myself to get a grip, she offers me a wobbly smile. "I keep putting my foot in my mouth, huh?"

I take a few moments to practice the breathing techniques Khalil helped me with until the worst of my anxiety passes and I no longer feel like fleeing. "It's not your fault, Aurelia." She winces at the sound of her name, but I don't fixate on why. "I should probably unclench."

"I didn't exactly leave you with a great first impression. And I'm sorry about that kiss earlier. If I'd known it was you…"

It was jarring as fuck. When was the last time I'd kissed a girl or even wanted to?

Tatum?

No. But she was the last time it meant something and that kiss from Aurelia earlier had certainly felt like it meant a lot to her. I just don't feel the same. Since I don't want Aurelia taking my rejection personally, I take a page from her book and choose not to remark on it. "So, you and Seth?" I ask instead.

"Uh-huh. Is that weird?"

I shrug even though I want to say yes. I don't know how far Seth has gotten with her, but it's possible I've already been inside her and I don't remember any of it.

Not. Important.

Aurelia makes a sound of distress, and then she's clutching her stomach and looking horrified. "I'm sorry. I just realized how that must make you feel." This strange and beautiful girl covers her face with her hands and groans. "God, you must feel so violated."

Yeah, they definitely had sex.

Nothing less would spark that kind of remorse and shame.

My lips twitch from the smile I keep at bay as I stare down at her. "It's okay. It's Seth's body too. He never really understood that, but I guess he finally found the right motivation."

I let my smirk fall when Aurelia slowly lowers her hands. She still has trouble meeting my eyes. "You're not mad?"

"I'd have to be blind," I mumble.

"What's that?"

"No."

"Oh. Good." She gathers the mass of her blond curls in her hands and a claw clip off Thorin's nightstand. The movement causes the gap in her robe to widen, and I'm momentarily distracted by the inner curves of her breasts while she twists and clips her curls. The natural brown roots are already starting to chase away the gold, creating an unintentional ombre that makes her skin look more bronzed.

When my gaze returns to her face, I find her arms by her side again as she silently contemplates me with a crestfallen look. "Are you okay?" I ask.

"Huh? Oh. Yeah. Honestly, today was nothing." She waves me off, misreading my concern. "You've missed a lot. There's been nothing but drama since I arrived." Sighing, she drops down onto Thorin's bed and leans back on her hands to consider her statement. "I'm pretty sure I am the drama."

"Aurelia…" There it is again. Her soft lips flatten, and that look like I'm breaking her heart by simply saying her name returns. I push past it again and focus on the reason I'm even in this room, ignoring the need to run away from her. "Do you need help?"

She sits up straight, bringing her hands into her lap before dropping them back to her sides to curl around the sheets like she doesn't quite know what to do with them. "Help?" she echoes quietly.

Thorin and Khalil are no longer pounding on the locked door. I hear them pacing outside though, and the words get stuck in my throat. The part of me that leans on them doesn't want to know the answer. I don't want to know if my best friends betrayed what I went through by holding someone else against their will. I feel like shit for even suggesting they're capable of doing that, but I can't ignore the way Aurelia's suddenly looking around the room like a cornered animal.

"Did my brothers hurt you?"

Aurelia's gaze snaps to mine, and she searches for something before quickly replying, "No."

Knowing Isaac would often trick me with kindness in order to break me down further, I don't let it go. "It's not a trick, Aurelia. Did they hurt you? You can tell me."

She blinks, seemingly regaining her composure and shedding some of her unease before she cocks her head and tightens the sash on her robe. "And then what?"

I'm stumped by her question for a moment, feeling my brows pulling down. "And then I get you out. I...I'll help you get home. I'll keep you safe from them. I promise you."

"Even if that means you all go to prison?"

My eyes fall shut.

I knew those pricks were lying to me.

I knew it the moment I tasted her lips, heard her speak, walked into this room and saw her body, and caught her scent.

She's ambrosia.

And we've been dying without her.

No way Thorin, Khalil, and *fucking Seth* would just let her go. They found her and they made her theirs like some twisted version of finders keepers.

"Zeke?" Aurelia calls softly when I don't speak for a long while.

I scrub a hand down my face—a hand that helped to shackle her and may have even harmed her—and then I force myself to open my eyes and face this beautiful girl who confuses and scares the shit out of me. "I have a better question for you, Aurelia. Why do you care what happens to us?"

"I don't," she says unevenly. She's all bluster. I caught her off her guard, and now she's trying to regain some control. "I just don't believe you."

Shame courses through me as I wonder again what we did to her. "You think this is a *test*?"

I feel like I've been punched in the gut when she gives the smallest nod without quite meeting my eyes. If I blinked, I would have missed it.

And suddenly, I realize how disorienting it must have been when I barged in here and flipped the script. Isaac did it often. He feigned mercy only to extinguish my hope in the most brutal way the moment it appeared.

All I've accomplished is convincing Aurelia that I'm just another monster.

Fuck.

"It's not a test," I assure her. "And as much as I wish I could convince you, I won't push for now, but this isn't over." I say it almost like an apology because I can't let it go—no matter how much she or my brothers might want me to.

"They're not so bad," she confesses with a small smile that I don't understand.

It eases some of the worry that my brothers did unspeakable things to her, but that smile only replaces those worries with new ones.

"You sure it's not the Stockholm talking?" I blurt. When the hearts in her eyes turn into sharp daggers, I feel like I'm finally getting a glimpse of the real her. "Right. Okay. Suit yourself. I'll leave you now. Good night."

Yanking the door open and barreling past Thorin and Khalil, I don't realize it's the middle of the day until I'm standing outside the cabin, bent over, hands braced on my knees, trying to convince myself of two things.

She's not Tatum.

And I'm not prey.

When I finally step back into the cabin thirty minutes later, Aurelia is stepping out of Thorin's room fully dressed. Our eyes meet briefly before she looks away and announces to no one in particular, "I'll get started on lunch."

CHAPTER THREE

AURELIA

The guys have gotten into the habit of hanging around the kitchen. They lend me a hand while I make us food or clean, but not today. Today, Khalil and Thorin sit around the kitchen table, discussing in low tones what to do about the dead bodies we left behind once the snow melts.

Ezekiel is nowhere to be found.

After I offered to make us food, he gave me a weird look like I'm a puzzle he can't figure out but wants no part of before disappearing. Intuition tells me that the more I try to make him like me, the less he'll trust me.

Of course, I can't take it personally, but it's easier said than done when he wears the face of the man I love. There are moments when he even sounds like Seth—though I suppose it's not hard to do when the differences in their cadence and tone are subtle.

Seth is loud and chaotic, his mirth spreading throughout the cabin and infecting us all.

Zeke is quiet and pensive, darkening the mood of everyone around him.

And then there's the moment in the dell earlier when Seth's

anger poked a sleeping Bane and the alter I hoped to never meet spoke in that terrifying rumble. *I know what you're doing.*

The mere memory raises the hair on my nape.

Khalil and Thorin are wrapping up their plans by the time I'm done whipping together our lunch. Thorin disappears to fetch Zeke, and I keep my gaze pinned to the table when they return to avoid looking at Zeke. *Even the way he walks is different.* I hear the hesitant shuffle of his steps behind Thorin's commanding stride.

I dare a peek when he passes Seth's usual chair directly across from mine and a guilty pit forms in my stomach when I glimpse the hard line of his mouth and the muscle in his cheek pulsing with unhappiness as he takes a seat at the far end of the table facing Khalil—as far away from me as possible.

There's no doubt in my mind that Zeke didn't come willingly, so I throw everything I have into the glare I pin Thorin with when he takes his usual seat next to me. The last thing I want is to force Ezekiel to accept me.

Thorin startles and winces when he notices my displeasure and then glances at Zeke, who drops down into the chair and crosses his arms, blatantly ignoring the plate of food I left at Seth's place.

Seth, who would have shoveled half of it down by now like there was a prize for finishing first.

Don't make comparisons, I scold the moment the thought manifests.

I clear my throat. "Um…so fair warning," I say jokingly to break the tension. "I have a lot of talents, but cooking isn't one of them. I'm awful at it."

My nervous chuckle dies an abrupt death when Zeke simply stares back at me.

"The trick is to avoid tasting the food while eating," Khalil says, coming to my rescue. "That's a mistake your stomach won't recover from."

When I cut my gaze at him, he flashes all of his teeth before lifting my hand to brush his lips over the back in apology. Suddenly, I'm desperate to feel his lips elsewhere, but Thorin speaks and breaks through that lustful fog. I reluctantly pull my hand away and banish all thoughts of Khalil's lips.

Right now is about making Zeke comfortable.

"Water to wash it down is also your friend." Thorin lifts his glass in the air in salute and takes a healthy gulp.

I snort out a laugh that isn't all for show, but Zeke still isn't buying what we're selling. His gaze was hostile when he first sat down, but it's the assessing look he levels at us that makes me squirm. Zeke's green eyes flick toward the untouched plate of food, but he still doesn't touch it.

Probably thinks I poisoned it.

The moment the thought forms, there's a demanding knock on the front door that threatens to break it down if we don't answer.

Naturally, the hackles of all three alpha males rise at the challenge.

"Shit," I blurt out at the same time Thorin pushes back his chair to answer the door. Thorin pauses, and three sets of eyes fly toward me, waiting for me to explain the expletive. "It's the sheriff," I confess without a trace of doubt, as if I'd personally invited him here. I can't believe I forgot about my encounter with him earlier— before Seth and the death squad and the avalanche.

"We know," Khalil answers.

Right. Because the sheriff is the only one who ever comes up here.

Still, Khalil's expression turns thoughtful as he wonders how *I* knew. His gaze flies to Thorin. "There's no way he found the bodies already. All that snow?" he asks rhetorically. "They'll be buried for a few more days at least, so what the fuck?"

Khalil and Thorin are frowning at each other, but I can feel Zeke's eyes on me when I finally speak. "It's my fault."

"Your fault…" Khalil echoes slowly.

"I'm so sorry. We crossed paths while I was out hunting." I look at Khalil. "H-he knows I'm not your cousin. I think he's here for me."

"If he knows who you are, why did he let you go?" Thorin questions.

"I…um…I might have told him I wasn't interested in being rescued, and when he refused to leave, I…persuaded him."

Khalil and Thorin swear at the same time. Zeke is silent—the weight of it falling over the room like a heavy blanket.

"Jesus, Aurelia." Thorin rubs at his brow and sighs heavily.

It's then I realize the sheriff is as likely here to arrest me as rescue me.

"So I guess hiding you isn't an option," Thor surmises.

I shake my head. "No."

"So, what do we do?" This time Khalil directs the question to Thorin, but it's Zeke who answers.

"We answer the door." His body is loose and a small smile plays at his lips now like he doesn't have a care in the world.

What did you expect, Aurelia? He offered to help you, to get you out… This is what Zeke wants.

"Fuck." Thorin shoves away from the table and stalks across the cabin.

I guess we're answering the door.

My heart is pounding, and I'm shifting nervously in my chair, eyeing the distance between the table and the stairs and wondering if I can make it to the den before it's too late. It's pointless to keep pretending I'm dead, but I don't see any other way out of this.

Unless we kill the sheriff.

A new bolt of panic seizes my muscles.

Oh, God… They're not actually going to kill him, are they?

My eyes slide to the side where Se—uh…Zeke—is sitting quietly, leaning back in his chair with his fingers laced on his abs and an unreadable look on his face and for the first time I'm happy that Seth isn't awake.

He would snuff the sheriff in a heartbeat to keep me.

Miserably, a pang of longing for the unhinged alter stabs at my heart, and I force myself to look away.

Zeke isn't Seth. And I'm pretty sure Zeke hates me.

The door opens, and I hear Thorin mumble something and then stand back to allow the sheriff and the two deputies by his side to enter the cabin. Khalil stands, but he doesn't move away from the table. He futilely angles his body at the head of the table to block me from view.

I hear a sharp inhale and follow the sound to see Zeke sitting forward, his knuckles white and the veins in the back of his hands bulging from how hard he's gripping the edge of the table.

He looks cornered…scared.

He looks ready to bolt.

I can't help reaching out a hand to comfort him, stretching my body to reach him at the other end of the table. "A-are you okay?" I whisper.

Those wide green eyes shoot to me and immediately narrow. He snatches his hand back and answers shortly, "I'm fine."

Okay then. The rejection stings a little, but Zeke doesn't owe me anything, so I shake it off and refocus in time to see the muscles in Khalil's back bunch and hear his bark.

"That's far enough, sheriff."

I peek around Khalil, and the knots in my stomach twist further when I see the sheriff making a beeline for the table.

For me.

There's a deputy stoically posted at the front door with his arms crossed while the other is a step ahead of the sheriff with his hand already on his gun and his uneasy gaze pinned on Khalil. My stomach bottoms out and it's fortunate that I haven't had the chance to eat or else my lunch would be all over the floor.

No, no, no, no, no, no, no.

I reach for Khalil as if I have any hope of removing him from the path of a speeding bullet.

I'm not the only one who notices the unspoken threat either.

"Sheriff," Thorin growls in a tone so menacing that as the hairs on my nape and arms rise, it dawns on me with a wind chill cold enough to rival Everest's that I haven't seen Thorin truly angry. Until now. "Get control of your fucking deputy before any goodwill between us dies and I remove him from my home out the back door."

We don't have a back—oh.

The cliff.

Thorin just threatened to throw an officer of the law off the cliff.

And his words fall on deaf ears as the nervous deputy continues to watch Khalil, who's standing perfectly still with his arms crossed and not saying a word. The sound of chair legs scraping across the floor breaks the tense silence, and in my peripheral vision, I see Zeke standing as if he seconds Thorin's warning.

Zeke may not like me, but he loves Khalil, which means that in this moment, he's just as unpredictable as Seth.

My heart is starting to thunder and I can no longer feel my fingers.

"Deputy!" Sheriff Kelly reprimands. "You will remove your hand from your firearm and contain yourself! I told you we are here in an unofficial capacity only."

I call bullshit.

The sheriff is bluffing. Otherwise, he would have come alone instead of bringing backup. I don't blame him though. Not even I know how my mountain men will react now that the cat's out of the bag.

I'm alive.

And I've been right under the sheriff's nose the entire time.

That's got to sting.

I think we all take a collective breath when the nervous deputy finally drops his hand and straightens. Khalil is angled just enough for me to see his profile and the smirk on his lips as he winks at the deputy.

My leg shoots out under the table, and I kick him in the shin. Grunting, he peers down at me over his shoulder and lifts a brow at my glare.

Don't taunt the trigger-happy police, fool.

Hearing my silent plea, he nods and schools his expression.

While all the men posture and dick measure, my mind starts turning over solutions. I hate myself the moment I think of my uncle. Marston George may be a piece of shit, but he's always been remarkably good at manipulating everyone around him—including me.

How would he spin and twist the truth into his favor?

How would he leverage the emotions, weaknesses, and temperaments of everyone in the room to get what he wanted?

The sheriff doesn't *want* to believe that his precious boys betrayed his trust. He *wants* to be absolved of letting his personal relationship with them get in the way of his duty. He *wants* to redeem himself by saving me—whether I want it or not.

My mountain men don't want to let me go. They want to protect and love me—to find a way for the four of us to live in seclusion and harmony until the end of our days, and I...

I just want to survive the day unscathed.

What I *don't* want is another person's blood on my hands.

Suddenly, the answer seems so obvious as I soak in all the testosterone and rage.

Thankfully, my guys remain silent once the sheriff unleashes his tirade of disappointment, anger, and betrayal on them. They stand like statues while he demands an explanation for their deception before launching into yet another chiding before my mountain men can even think to respond.

"*Ugghhhhhh*," I unintentionally groan out loud once I've had enough of listening to the sheriff rant like a wounded lover who caught his boys in bed with another sheriff.

I mean any other cop would have arrested them already, right? So why is he acting like their biggest crime was *hurting his feelings*?

My drawn-out groan causes the sheriff to sputter to a stop midsentence. Now that all eyes are on me once again, I rip off the Band-Aid and stand, nudging Khalil to the side with a dirty look when he tries to sidestep and keep me out of view.

Fucking really? We're way past that now.

When I get too close to the sheriff and his deputy for Khalil's liking, he grips the back of my shirt and yanks me back until I'm close enough to feel the heat emanating from his chest. He keeps me in front of him though, leaving me to face the sheriff.

"I think you might have amnesia, Gramps. I said I didn't need your help."

"Aurelia," Thorin warns.

The sheriff levels a look at me that makes it clear he's not amused by me like he was earlier. And here I thought he found me charming if not trying. "And as I told you, Ms. George. I cannot ignore the law."

"Even if it means killing me?"

Everyone's shock ripples across the room. My mountain men, of course, take it the wrong way, but there's no time to reassure them. The nervous deputy returns his hand to his gun, and the sheriff doesn't rebuke him for it this time. I just barely resist the urge to roll my eyes since this new web of lies will take delicate role-playing.

"There's no need to be afraid, Ms. George." He pauses to level a glare on Thorin, Khalil, and Zeke. "If you come with me now, I'll make sure you're safe." He holds out his hand, and I swear I hear a growl behind me that doesn't come from Khalil.

I almost ruin everything by peeking at Zeke to make sure it's still him.

"Well, see that's the thing. If I go back, I'm dead. I'm sorry, Sheriff, but you've got this whole thing all wrong."

The weathered lines around his mouth purse. "What the hell do you mean I've got it wrong?"

"Khalil, Thorin, and Se—Zeke," I say with the barest wince, "they didn't steal me, they saved me." I keep my gaze on the sheriff instead of letting my curiosity get the better of me and searching out each of my mountain men's gazes. I can *feel* their reaction to my words—wondering if I meant them or if it's just another part of the web I'm slowly trapping us inside.

"Save you? I don't understand. How so?"

I shrug as if learning that the man who raised me wanted me dead was no big deal.

"My uncle has been planning to have me killed for some time," I lie through my teeth. He probably has, but I sure as hell didn't know about it until this morning when he almost succeeded.

Focus.

Remembering what Finnegan confessed on that cliff, I spin and spin and spin my web of lies.

"Before I fled the States, I had more than suspicions. I had proof." It's a fucking bluff since I have jack shit but Finnegan's word to go on, and he's deader than dead.

I pray the sheriff won't call me on it, but why should he? He *wants* to believe that Thorin, Khalil, and Zeke are innocent, so I hold on to that lapse in his judgment and spin some more.

"My uncle hired those men to kill me *months ago*. He was just waiting for the right time to strike. I knew that if I didn't get away from him, he'd succeed, so I got as far away from him as I could. Obviously, I didn't count on my plane crashing and nearly doing his dirty work for him, but I survived and fought my way here. When Thorin, Khalil, and Zeke found me, they wanted to turn me in," I say, my tone inundated with desperation as if I was a fugitive on the lam and they were the good ole Boy Scouts the sheriff believes them to be.

"You gotta remember, Aurelia," my uncle schools. "There's the truth and then there's your version and theirs. Everyone enters the room with their own notions and what they are willing to believe. The trick isn't changing their minds. It's using it against them to get what you want."

So I turn the tables and I make the sheriff believe that *I* corrupted *them* instead of the other way around. Men have been blaming women for their troubles for centuries. It wasn't Khalil, Thorin, and Zeke's lust and frustration and loneliness that made them kidnap me and lie to the sheriff.

It was me.

After all, it was Eve who tempted Adam into eating the apple, right?

The sheriff isn't just searching for a truth he can believe. He's searching for a villain to blame, so I give him one. It's a role I know well.

"I told them what my uncle planned and begged them to help me hide until I could figure out how to stop him. I knew my uncle would send men to make sure I was gone, so they agreed to shelter and keep me safe until the coast was clear and they could get me home without alerting my uncle."

Once I'm done spinning my not-that-intricate web of lies that could unravel with a soft breeze, I exhale and wait for the verdict that will determine my mountain men's fate.

And mine.

The sheriff wants to believe.

"Miss George…" Sheriff Kelly removes his uniform hat and runs his fingers through his thinning gray hair with a sigh and shake of his head. My heart drops. "Forgive me if I have a hard time believing your story." He drops his hand and gives me a pointed look. "Especially since this is *not* what you told me earlier."

To their credit and mine, my mountain men nor I react, but I know it's coming later when we're in the clear and blissfully alone.

"Earlier, I didn't know if I could trust you." I make a point to narrow my eyes as if I still find him suspicious. "For all I knew, you were on my uncle's payroll since you're the one who led the assassins he hired right to me."

The sheriff reacts like a man with a guilty conscience, the fight leaving his body in an instant with his weathered cheeks reddening with shame.

I…feel like shit.

But I'd feel twice as bad if he died because I couldn't convince him to back off, so I shrug away my own guilt and search for the old Aurelia. The me who wouldn't give a shit about hurting anyone's feelings. I may not like her, but I can't deny she's useful.

"And if you still need proof, there are eight corpses buried under an avalanche that might clear some things up," I blurt.

Behind me, Khalil softly swears.

Telling the sheriff and his deputies where the bodies are buried is a risky move, but it's the only play we have left. They just have to trust me *like I trusted them* when I decided to stay.

"Is this true?" The sheriff's hopeful eyes bounce from Khalil to Zeke and then Thorin, waiting for one of them to confirm. I stop breathing when the crucial seconds that the sheriff's gullibility will last stretch and thin until his bushy brows are furrowing once more and I see doubt start to creep back in.

What the fuck?

I can't stop myself from searching them out this time, uncaring if it unravels my carefully fabricated lie. Why aren't they answering? The goal post is *right there*.

Thorin's shoulders are bowed, his gaze pinned to the floor so I can't see what he's thinking, but he must feel my attention because he suddenly looks up and…I stumble back a step, colliding with Khalil's chest at the sheer amount of regret swimming in his pale blue eyes.

It hasn't escaped my notice that they've been silent this entire time, but I just assumed they were following my lead for once.

But now…

Following a hunch, I glance behind me to see a tight jaw and brown eyes staring at nothing. Khalil feels me watching, his gaze dropping to mine, and he sucks in a sharp breath that expands his chest. The sorrow and apology in his eyes make my heart pound, and I know immediately that it isn't for the mistakes he made in the past but for the one he's about to make right now.

Khalil is *breaking*.

He's going to tell the sheriff what really happened.

He's going to tell him *everything*.

And all because he chooses now to wish he'd played the hero.

I'm not sure if it's desperation or instinct that makes me turn to my most unlikely ally for help.

Zeke.

He's leaning now against the wall between the kitchen and stairs with his foot propped up and his arms crossed. He seems perfectly content to let this life we've only begun to build crumble around us, and while it's no secret he wants me gone, I have to believe he doesn't feel the same about Thorin and Khalil.

Our eyes barely meet because he's already speaking, turning his head to address the sheriff before I can even figure out what to say to him.

"It's true," he says before Khalil can damn us all. Even though I'd hoped he would, it still shocks the fuck out of me that he's going along with my story.

"I see." The sheriff nods once, seemingly satisfied, and plops his hat back on his head before giving us all a hard look. "But until I can investigate the site and verify your claims, I'm going to need the four of you to come with me."

Fuck!

CHAPTER FOUR

KHALIL

After showing Sheriff Kelly the site where the bodies are buried, he ordered an excavation team up to our mountain to find them before marching the four of us into Hearth. The moment we reached the station, he threw Thorin, Zeke, and me in a holding cell together with a great amount of pleasure before escorting Aurelia into an interrogation room where they could talk.

That was an hour ago.

Obviously, he wants to see if her story will change now that she's safely out of our reach. Ironically, Zeke, the only one of us who isn't guilty, hasn't stopped pacing since she disappeared.

"That was pretty fucking brilliant," Zeke grumbles.

"What was?" I ask, even though I don't care.

"That bullshit story Aurelia told the sheriff. I never pegged us for the heroic types. Did you?"

Thorin winces, and I know I'm not alone in my guilt. I've been slowly drowning in it ever since Aurelia clawed her way into my heart, but it's been a hundred-foot wave battering me without a moment's reprieve ever since she stood in front of the sheriff—the one person who could rescue her—and chose to cover our sorry asses instead.

I guess that makes her our island—our only refuge in this storm we created.

But what if that means sinking herself in the process?

I can't let that happen. I *won't*.

If the sheriff doesn't buy her story, I'm coming clean. I'll spend a hundred lifetimes running before I drag my baby down with me. Hearing her alter the events of the night we found her taking shelter in our cabin—and all the ones that followed—had made me yearn to go back in time and be the man in the picture she painted. A man worthy of her protection, love, and loyalty.

In that moment, it felt as if the only way I could ever be that for her was to let her go.

But then Zeke stopped me, and at Aurelia's request—little do either of them know. He'd done it for her, and he's hated himself for the knee-jerk reaction ever since. Of course, he'll deny it and say it was to protect me. I'll try not to lord it over him too much since this soft spot he has for Aurelia isn't entirely his own. And it's not the first time Seth's or Bane's emotions have influenced Zeke's.

If only that were enough to prove Seth's alive.

Is it even possible for an alter to die?

Zeke's heart had stopped by the time we unburied him. What if Seth died in that avalanche?

I can't deny it's been a constant, unspoken fear, never straying far from my mind.

Disbelief floods my chest when I'm forced to admit—albeit to myself—that I'm actually worried for *Seth*. Less than three months ago, all I wanted was to figure out a way to rid Zeke of his alters for good, and now I find myself actually caring for Seth and not just because he's a part of Zeke.

I actually miss that asshole.

"It's not bullshit," Thorin retorts with his eyes closed. "Not all of it anyway. Her uncle really is trying to kill her."

"It doesn't concern you how pretty she lies?" Zeke plows on as if Thorin hasn't spoken. "The sheriff is a shrewd man, but it only took her minutes to have him eating out of the palm of her hand." He stops and gives us a pointed look. "Imagine what she could do with a few weeks."

Thorin groans and rests his head against the wall behind the bench he's sitting on. "Here we go. What are you saying, Zeke?"

"I'm saying you both need to stop thinking with your dicks. She's playing you."

"And why would she do that?" I ask with little concern.

"Revenge?"

"She had the perfect opportunity to do that hours ago. She could have turned us in, but she didn't."

"And you're so pussy-whipped, you haven't wondered why?"

"We trust her, Zeke." I hesitate a moment before adding, "So does Seth."

"Well, if Seth does," he tosses back sarcastically.

I scrub my hands down my face to keep from caving in his and then I watch him pace back and forth for a few moments before realization dawns and I feel my lips twitch. "What's interesting is how quickly she got under *your* skin."

"She's up to something," he says distractedly. Zeke abruptly stops his agitated pacing to white-knuckle the bars with both hands. He then tries to wedge his stubborn head through the narrow space and frantically searches the hall for her. "I know it."

Thorin and I share a look. *And I thought I was the paranoid one*, he seems to say with his eyes.

I grin, but my amusement is cut short when I remember the reason for this personality change.

Tatum.

Bitch did a number on him.

It had taken a long time before Zeke was even willing to talk about her, but when he did, it became painfully clear how much he loved her—so much that he ignored his gut when it warned him about Isaac. He refused to leave her behind, and it had cost him.

Zeke *loved* Tatum, and she betrayed him.

She used his feelings to trick him into staying just for Isaac to later torture him, and when the truth came out, he killed her.

Or rather, Bane did.

The pain of Tatum's betrayal was so heartrendingly, soul-crushingly great that it caused another identity to manifest. A particularly violent one that couldn't be reasoned with. And Zeke being unable to see the stark differences between Aurelia and Tatum makes my blood run cold as horror injects itself into my veins. It means that if Bane wakes up, Aurelia would not only be in grave danger…she'd be as good as dead.

Driven by rage and the horrifying memories of Zeke's suffering that started long before his brother's cult, Bane possesses the inhuman ability to completely ignore fear and pain. Disregarding the consequences, however, is a very human trait. Thorin and I decided, after too many broken limbs and scrapes with death, that it was too dangerous to take him on, even when it was two against one, so we resorted to tranquilizers to incapacitate him, but our first measure of defense was making sure that Zeke felt safe at all times.

It's the reason for Thorin's sudden shift when the possibility of what could happen occurs to him as well a moment later. "Ezekiel." The gentle tone and sound of his proper name makes Zeke stiffen, since the first time he heard that tone from us was after we found him malnourished, stripped, bleeding, delirious, and strapped to a metal table. Now it only ever seems to remind him of that dark period. "It's going to be okay. She's *not* Tatum. She's not going to hurt you. We would never let her near you if we thought for a moment that she would."

"I know that," he snaps as he turns to face us.

Leaning forward and resting my forearms on my thighs, I stare at him. I watch the restlessness return as he starts to pace again. "Do you?"

"You want me to trust her?" he challenges, his tone sharp like a whip. Zeke stops to stand by the back wall where he can face Thorin and me. "You can start by telling me everything that happened since the crash. Tell me that what she told the sheriff is true. Tell me that you kept her here to keep her safe and not because you *forced* her for some convenient, in-house pussy."

Thorin shoves his fingers through his hair and shakes his head. "We can't do that."

"Then I can't trust her," Zeke returns. "And for good fucking reason." Thorin starts to argue, but the burning glare Zeke throws him warns Thorin to save his breath. He won't be persuaded. His paranoia is embedded too deep and for good reason.

But there is loathing in that glance too—for Thorin and me. It's there and gone in an instant but impossible to miss. Zeke hates us for trapping an innocent woman here with us.

He hates himself too. For his part in it. Even if it wasn't really *him*.

"You don't have to worry though," he says after the silence becomes a heavy pall. "If Aurelia is out for revenge, I can't say that I blame her. And I won't stand in her way." Zeke seals his vow by turning his back on us and crossing his arms while he stares out of the window with an unobstructed view of the Cold Peaks in the distance. It feels like a line drawn in the sand, and for the first time, I realize that while Aurelia might have found it in herself to forgive us, Zeke is another story. "It won't erase what we've done, but at least you'll finally see the truth."

"About her?"

Zeke scoffs as he continues to glare out of the window. "About us. And whatever this is." He shakes his head. "One woman for all three of us? It won't work."

I stretch my legs and allow myself to finally relax on the bench opposite Thorin. "It's been working so far."

Zeke's smirk is almost cruel when he turns his head to meet my gaze. "*So far.*"

His words feel like a threat, and I don't feel my gaze narrowing until we hear a door slamming closed down the hall and it widens. That sound puts us all on alert as we listen to the footsteps growing closer.

Zeke even turns away from the window despite his promise to "distance" himself from this shit show.

He doesn't take a single breath, and neither do I. Thorin, on the other hand, looks half asleep as he lazily watches the cell door. It feels like forever before an officer finally comes into view. But he doesn't spare us a single glance as he keeps walking past our cell.

Thorin and I relax, but Zeke only grows more agitated.

"They've been in there for too long," he gripes with a tight jaw. "You don't think she's had a change of heart?"

"I think the sheriff is giving her every opportunity to do so," Thorin replies with his eyes closed. Clearly, he's not the least bit worried that she will. I've been wavering between wanting her to for her own good and praying that she doesn't. Thorin peeks an eye open to regard Zeke. "That means keeping her away from us as long as he's legally able."

Catching on, Zeke's olive skin drains of color as he looks around the holding cell. It may not be the dog cage that haunts his dreams, but it's a cage all the same. "He's going to keep us in here all night?" His voice is ragged now for a different reason.

"Of course not. Don't be silly." Shifting to lie on my back, I get even more comfortable as I take a page from Thorin's book and close my eyes with my hand resting on my abs. "We'll obviously be here all weekend."

"Bullshit," Zeke snaps. "He can only keep us in custody for twenty-four hours without formal charges."

Well, he'd know.

Zeke's file full of misdemeanors back home is as thick as my arm. The juvenile detention center was his second home, and sadly the only one he remembers fondly.

"It's Friday," Thorin informs Zeke. "The sheriff just lucked himself into an automatic extension. That means he has all weekend to decide if he's going to charge us or let us go."

And Aurelia has three days to decide if we're worth saving.

No one speaks as we let the knowledge that our fate is in the hands of someone who has every reason to burn us hang in the air.

Ten minutes pass before Zeke breaks the silence. "This might be a bad time to mention this, but I don't know if I can last three days. Something's off. I don't feel right."

"Well, you did die today," Thorin reminds him in a grave tone. "Even though it wasn't for long, we need to take that seriously and get you checked out as soon as we leave here."

I nod my agreement so that Zeke knows it's not up for discussion. He's never liked doctors, and that was before he was tortured by one.

Before his brother became a cult leader, Isaac was a psychologist who was under investigation after he was suspected of encouraging his patients' delusions and sometimes inciting them to commit suicide rather than treating them. There wasn't enough evidence to send Isaac to prison, but he lost his license. Subsequently, the stain on his reputation drove him from polite society, which left him free to found the Seeds of the Undying and continue his mental warfare on the vulnerable unchecked.

The fucker called Zeke his greatest symphony.

I feel my fingers flex with the urge to wrap them around Isaac's neck and *snap*.

"It's not just that. I feel…" Zeke absently rubs a hand over his chest where his heart beats underneath. "I don't know. Something's wrong," he repeats.

"What? You have heartburn?"

Zeke doesn't even notice my sarcasm as he continues to frown. "No. I mean that something is wrong with *Seth*."

Thorin's eyes fly open while I quickly sit up. "He's hurting you?"

In the past, tricking Zeke into feeling pain was a common tactic for Seth whenever he desperately wanted out.

"No." Zeke's frown deepens. "That's the thing…" He looks more than a little anxious when his green gaze meets mine. Before Aurelia, that look would have put Thorin and me on high alert because it meant that Seth was responsible, but now we're calm as we watch Zeke rub his chest. He drops his hand a moment later as his green gaze bounces between us, something like panic rising within those murky depths. "I-I can't…I can't feel Seth at all."

CHAPTER FIVE

AURELIA

The sheriff's strategy is pretty effective. By the fifth hour, I'm ready to crack.

He's just returned from his third coffee break after interrogating me for half an hour, and like the other times, he quietly reads over my written statement while taking slow sips of his coffee and once he's done, he sits back in his chair, folds his hands over his belly, and asks me to recount my story again from start to finish.

It's obvious that he's looking for holes or any small change in my story, but I'm media trained, so it never wavers.

"Okay, you're right. You got me. I was abducted, Sheriff Kelly." I wait until he straightens with a jerk, flips his notepad to a blank page, and plucks his pen from his shirt pocket, the ballpoint poised over the page in preparation to take my statement. "By aliens."

"*Ms. George…*" The sheriff sighs before dropping his pen and pushing his notepad to the side. "Refusing to cooperate will not help you or those boys. I also feel obligated to remind you that I'm still deciding whether or not to charge *you* with obstruction of justice. It's in your best interest to take this seriously and answer my questions honestly."

"I have answered you honestly. Several times. Your refusal to accept the truth is the only obstruction I see."

"Perhaps I should keep you here over the weekend. Give you time to consider what you remember before we speak again."

My blood runs hot as I study the sheriff silently. He waits patiently for me to decide my next course of action. "No," I finally answer. "We're done here. I'd like to call my lawyer now."

The sheriff is visibly startled before he nods in disappointment and stands from the table to leave. "I'll get you a phone."

He leaves and comes back immediately, carrying a landline inside and setting it in front of me along with a steaming cup of coffee before leaving the room again.

The door closes with a quiet snick, and even when the sound of his departing footsteps fades, I don't move. I stare at the black phone for ten solid minutes before I sigh and snatch up the receiver from the base.

As I dial, I draw forth the image of the tiny black numbers printed on the face of a crumpled business card. It was passed to me in secret nine years ago at one of the many industry parties my uncle dragged me to. I was newly eighteen and should have had control over my life, and apparently it had been obvious to all—or maybe just the shrewd and no-nonsense A&R rep at Savant—that I had *no* say, no autonomy, and certainly no control.

She'd slipped me her card and told me to use it when I grew a spine.

I remember thinking *what a bitch* and liking her immediately.

Still, I'd nearly thrown out her card right then and there—partly out of misplaced loyalty to my uncle but mostly out of fear. But *something* had stopped me, and whatever it was, I'm grateful for it now. Instead, I clung to her card over the years like a life raft while I drifted hopelessly in the endless sea of my uncle's tyranny.

This is the first time I've ever dared try to kick my feet and swim for the shore, and as the line rings and rings and rings, I squeeze my eyes closed and pray that I'm not too late. That she hasn't lost interest. I've never dialed the number—not even once. I have no idea if it still even works or if the music exec, who'd been my uncle's fiercest rival at the label, would even still deem me worthy.

Suddenly, the ringing stops, and I hold my breath as I wait to hear the recorded message for her voicemail.

A moment later, her voice comes through, but it's clear by the sound of her clicking heels in the background and the sharp bite of her rushed greeting that it isn't a recording. "Oni Sridhar and make it quick. Whoever this is, you get the first two minutes free and then I start billing for my time."

I pause twirling the coiled cord of the landline phone around my finger and snort. "Seriously? Are you that money hungry or is Bound paying you so little?"

The click-clack of the music exec's no doubt designer heels stops, and I hear her shaky exhales before she whispers uncertainly, "Aurelia?"

Feeling my eyes overflow with grateful tears that she not only answered but remembers me, I wipe them away and smile. The dam was broken when I almost lost Seth, and now I can't seem to stop. "Yeah… It's me."

After my phone call with Oni, the sheriff makes good on his promise and keeps me in custody. I also meet his wife, who is possibly the sweetest human I've ever met, and I've met Seth. She brings me a change of clothes, a hand-knitted blanket, and some of the lasagna she baked. The tiny woman really is too sweet for the gruff, overbearing sheriff, who I will only grudgingly admit in secret isn't so bad.

He doesn't throw me in a cell like I expected. Sheriff Kelly treats me like the victim he believes me to be, escorting me into a small private room with a single twin bed, a small table, and a window shielded behind blinds. The door doesn't even lock, but thanks to my mountain men, I know better than to think that means I can leave.

It dawns on me then that the sheriff isn't just being thorough.

He still believes what I confessed in the dell.

I have to put my game face on because I know he'll do whatever it takes to ease his conscience.

The night bleeds into the morning, but the sheriff doesn't question me again. Instead, he escorts me into a conference room where a woman wearing a pantsuit and blue-rimmed glasses with her hair styled in a sleek bun waits for me on a chair placed before an empty sofa.

"Hello," she greets cheerfully the moment we enter. Standing, she steps forward and offers a hand. "I'm Dr. Watts, and you must be Aurora."

At first, I assume she simply pronounced my name wrong until the sheriff catches my eye and he nods.

Okay, so he gave the doctor my alias the guys thought up for whenever I visit town, but why?

I look the doctor up and down like she's here to torture me rather than help me. "I'm not injured."

"Well, that's good to hear since I'm not that kind of doctor." Dr. Watts laughs like she told a hilarious joke.

Meanwhile, I feel a deep stab of betrayal and annoyance when I catch on to what kind of doctor she must be. The sheriff clears his throat and has the good sense to look guilty.

"I called her and arranged this appointment after our interview yesterday."

"You mean the interrogation?"

Ignoring that, he plows on. "Dr. Watts is a trauma counselor. I think she can help us both."

"Also, I'd like to make it clear that I'm not here to offer an official diagnosis, as I have explained to the sheriff here that I can't guarantee an accurate one within the strict timeframe I've been given." Her friendly mask drops a little, revealing some of her frustration at the time constraint, but then she recovers just as quickly and is back to beaming.

"Three sessions, *Aurora*," the sheriff pleads. "If you want me to send you back up that mountain, you'll give me three sessions. If you still want to go with them come Monday morning, I promise this will be the end of it."

"Sounds…fair."

After all, I don't *have* Stockholm syndrome, so what do I really have to fear?

"Please…sit." Dr. Watts reclaims her seat before waving toward the couch four feet away. Reluctantly, I sink onto the sofa, but the megawatt smile the good doctor flashes only serves to make my stomach roll. "Great!" When she leans in, I feel like I'm already under a microscope. "Let's get started."

Nodding, I suck in as much air as I can and slowly release it all in one shuddering breath. It feels like I'm going to war for them— Thorin, Khalil, and…*Zeth*.

But if war is what it will take, then so be it.

CHAPTER SIX

THORIN

Zeke isn't the only one ready to chew his own arm off to be free by the time Monday morning rolls around. This is the longest I've gone without seeing my wolf since the day we found her sleeping in Khalil's bed and it's all I can do not to reach between the bars and grab the sheriff by the throat when he finally shows his face some time around noon.

I don't hold his gaze for long before my attention drops to either side of him before looking behind him, searching for my fix of glowing brown skin, outrageous curves, and golden curls.

But she's not there.

She's *not fucking there*.

Flying off the hard bench that's been my bed for three nights and startling Khalil awake as I go, I wrap my hands around the bars instead of the sheriff's neck like I want to. "Where is she?" I demand before the sheriff can speak.

Ignoring me, he drones out, "It seems I owe you lot an apology," like he's being forced to read from a speech he didn't write and doesn't believe a word of. His expression and tone attempt to appear humble but it doesn't reach even the barest level of sincerity. "I should have never doubted you."

Ignoring him, since we all know we're guilty and deserve to rot in this cage *and* I couldn't give a shit about what the sheriff thinks of me in that moment, I say again, "Where. Is. She?"

"Gone."

My hands slip from the bars, and I stumble back an astonished step. "What the fuck are you talking about?"

"She left about an hour ago," he says shortly before unlocking the cage we spent the weekend inside and stepping back. "You're also free to go."

Seemingly satisfied with the blow he's dealt, the sheriff walks away, leaving the cell door wide open. Freedom is right there, but the three of us are too stunned to move.

"He's got to be fucking with us," Khalil reasons when I feel my entire body start to tremble. "She wouldn't leave without saying goodbye, go fuck yourself…something. That's not her style, man. You know that." I don't hear him stand or move in front of me, but then he's there, gripping my biceps. "Pull yourself together and let's go find our girl."

"Fuck," I exhale roughly when it feels like I can breathe again. I want to believe Khalil's right, but my head is swimming, and the ground feels unsteady. "Let's just go," I say with very little feeling in those three words.

Khalil's pace is fast as he leads us out of the holding cell, but Zeke is noticeably silent, and when I flick my gaze in his direction, even he seems confused and unsure as he follows us out. I don't know what to make of it, and at the moment, I couldn't care less.

The three of us leave the station and split up to search the town high and low for Aurelia. The sun is nearing the horizon when we finally admit defeat and leave Hearth. It takes us another couple hours to hike to the base of the trail where our truck is parked.

We usually avoid driving our truck up the mountain unless

we're hauling heavy loads, and even then we only dare traverse the trail during the spring and summer months since it's treacherous even during favorable conditions. The hidden trail is completely impassable during the winter, which is the reason we leave the truck parked by the main road leading into town.

Today, we don't have a choice but to risk it even though we haven't had a chance to verify that our secret path is free of the snow and ice that could send even the most confident driver careening over the side without warning.

"It's too bad we already swapped out the Ski-Doos for the ATVs," Khalil sighs before climbing inside the cab of the truck on the driver's side. He's our best chance of making it up Big Bear in one piece since he's the best driver out of the three of us.

Each year, before the last of the snow has a chance to melt, we bring down the Ski-Doos since driving them on bare ground could damage the engine, and we store them in the padlocked shed until the next snowfall. The ATVs would have been the best choice for navigating the tricky, thin trail leading up to the lonely cliff, but we drove them up a couple of weeks ago.

For a moment, I consider if plummeting to my death would be a better alternative than going back to that cabin without Aurelia before a horn blaring snaps me out of it and I see Khalil and Zeke staring at me through the windshield of the truck.

"Yo, Thor, you coming?" Zeke yells.

Shit. I climb into the back, and Khalil wastes no time speeding away. We travel for a few miles up the main trail until Khalil suddenly veers off and into the brush that conceals the hidden path. He doesn't slow down either, even when we leave behind the flat forested path, climbing higher and higher until the trail becomes bumpier, the curves sharper and more frequent, and the knot in my stomach tighter when we creep a little too close to the rocky edge.

"Khal, what the fuck, man?" Zeke scolds through gritted teeth. He's twisted in his seat to face Khalil, his back is to the door as he clutches the bar above his head with one hand while staring at Khalil like he's lost his mind.

Khalil executes a sharp U-turn on the switchback path without losing speed, and now the truck's engine is screaming, threatening to blow if we don't slow down as we climb higher and higher.

Khalil blocks out Zeke's and the truck's protests, his laser-sharp focus on the road ahead, and it takes me a second longer to realize the reason for his hurry.

"You think she's waiting for us at the cabin?"

Khalil risks turning his head to meet my gaze briefly before gripping the steering wheel tighter and accelerating. "Only one way to find out."

"Yeah, assuming we get there alive." Zeke scoffs.

"We really need to revisit our decision against giving her a radio," I say as I lean through the gap in the front seats to stare through the windshield. This mystery would have been so much simpler to solve if she had a radio.

Up ahead the path widens slightly. The rock wall of the mountain on our right becomes shorter until it gives way to trees once again.

We're nearly there.

Come on, come on, come on.

We drive for another mile before spotting our cabin up ahead at the edge of the cliff.

"The fuck?" Zeke mutters when we reach the clearing. Khalil stomps on the brakes, halting the truck abruptly when we notice the smoke coming out of the chimney.

Despite it being early May, it's a little chilly today, especially this high up, so a fire makes sense. And there's only one person who could have lit it.

Khalil, Zeke, and I stare at each other in the space of time it takes for us to all come to the same conclusion before the three of us rush out of the truck and to the front door. We reach it at the same time, and I'm not sure who throws it open, but it doesn't matter as none of us slow down long enough to file through one at a time. Our large bodies become wedged inside the too-narrow frame and after a lot of grunting, shoving, and wiggling, we finally burst through, collapsing into a pile in the foyer in an embarrassing display.

Aurelia, having a front seat to it all, pauses painting her toenails and looks up from her perch in the loft with her brows raised. She's freshly showered and dressed in Zeke's robe, and I can tell it doesn't go unnoticed by him when his nostrils flare. He looks away, biting back whatever vitriol is on the tip of his tongue when I shove him.

This side of Zeke is uncomfortably new—like navigating unknown terrain while constantly on the lookout for danger. He's been angry before, sure, but he's never been mean.

Tatum might haunt him, but I'll be damned if Aurelia pays the price for that bitch's treachery.

"Were you being chased?" she asks casually.

Khalil is the first to untangle his limbs from ours and climb to his feet. Instead of barreling for her like he did the entire drive here, he approaches her cautiously as if he fears—just as we all do—that she might change her mind about staying.

"You're here," he says once he reaches the edge of the living room, where he has to crane his neck to see her from her high perch.

Aurelia studies him for a moment before nodding once and echoing softly, "I'm here."

Khalil grabs her ankle and lifts her leg to kiss the bottom of her foot repeatedly in gratitude while staring at her through relieved eyes. "Why didn't you wait for us?"

Aurelia bites into her bottom lip before reclaiming her foot and shrugging. She glances at Zeke and me before going back to painting her toes with the red polish.

None of us quite know what to say or do since her body language is clearly screaming to give her some fucking space.

So we do.

I go into my room to shower while Khalil and Zeke disappear into the basement to do the same.

We can discuss what the fuck went down between her and the sheriff later.

CHAPTER SEVEN

EZEKIEL

My lungs and thighs burn as I push up the final hill, over the crest, and into the clearing. The snow is long gone, so our glade is green once again, and I can even smell the dew in the air. The air is still cool this high up, but it's a balm against my hot skin as I wipe the sweat from my brow.

When I see the cabin door, I slow my jogging pace until I'm walking and panting to catch my breath. I usually run every day—sometimes twice a day—but Seth didn't keep up my routine because I barely made it three miles before turning back.

I'm passing by the woodshed, where the framework of the unfinished bed Khalil's been building and the small garden that earns a glare from me sits unfinished, when I hear voices and stop walking as if I was caught somewhere I shouldn't be.

"Where does it go?" I hear Thorin's rough voice ask.

"Inside me."

A thud from the shed is followed by a high-pitched inhale in response.

"Where?"

"Inside me, Thorin. Please. I've been a good girl," she pleads in a voice that's too sweet for the thorns she wears like a crown. "Give it to me."

My jaw tightens when I hear Thorin's telling groan coming from the shed where he stores his kills. Losing control, he picks up his pace, the rhythmic pounding of their bodies colliding with complete abandon mingles with their cries, turning our clearing into some kind of salacious Eden.

I assume they're inside until I start walking again, eager to get away and pass the shed. Catching movement in my peripheral vision, I make the mistake of following the sound and seeing Aurelia pinned against the side of the shed, her legs and arms wrapped around Thorin as he drills into her.

Her hair is unbound and wild, and she's only wearing her yellow silk robe.

At least it's not mine this time.

The robe has fallen off her shoulders and hangs halfway down her arms, the panels open so that Thorin can use her body.

I quiet my steps as I sneak past, but I can't take my eyes off them. I know Thorin's aware of me. He's an apex predator. But if he has issues being watched, they aren't big enough for him to stop and run me off.

The muscles in his bare ass flex as he drives into Aurelia one last time. The divot between her brows deepens, and I tell myself to look away.

But I can't.

I know what he's doing to her. Thorin's had this kink for years. What I don't expect is for her to open her eyes—for them to find mine and hold my stare while my brother breeds her.

I'm frozen in place until they finish. Thorin sets her on her feet, and just as they both turn, I rush inside the cabin and slam the door behind me before leaning against it.

Now I feel like the creep.

It's been a few days since the avalanche, and while Aurelia and I have barely spoken and have seemingly agreed to steer clear of one another, I'm alarmed by how quickly I've become used to her presence. She sleeps in the loft, takes care of the cabin, asks a lot of fucking questions, and distracts my brothers...*a lot*. And when she's not doing that, Aurelia's watching me when she thinks I'm not paying attention, and I know what she's searching for.

Seth.

Don't get me wrong. I still want her gone, but I no longer have panic attacks when she walks into a room, so that's something. Now I only have them whenever she talks to me, looks at me, or gets too close. It should be a good thing that I'm getting used to her, but I'm worried about letting my guard down like my pussy-whipped brothers.

Thorin and Khalil haven't been subtle in their attempts to play matchmaker either. They can feel the connection between Aurelia and me—my wariness and her anguish weaving together into a rope that's quickly fraying at the edges.

But Aurelia doesn't want me.

She wants Seth.

And I don't know if my interest, however thin, is because Aurelia's a tempting and convenient hole or because she's just tempting. I can still enjoy a good fuck. It's the one thing Isaac didn't take away from me. After Thorin and Khalil rescued me from the compound, sex was the only thing that made me feel in control, so for a while, I used it like a torch to chase the darkness away...however briefly.

And then we came here, and there was no running from it, so the three of us welcomed the dark instead. We embraced who we truly were at our core, but alone up here, there was no one to unleash ourselves on. No one to unveil what lurked underneath.

And then Aurelia showed up, and I'm supposed to believe she's not looking for a way out?

Doesn't she know what we are?

Finding out from Khalil and Thorin that *Seth* and—by some fucked-up extension—me is head over heels in love with this perplexing and prickly girl is hard to swallow.

If only I could remember…

Unable to trust my own feelings, I've been spending a lot of time hiding out in my now empty room. I was planning to clear it out the day Aurelia's plane crashed, but those plans were derailed when I found her in Khalil's bed and Seth hijacked my head before I had a chance to even truly process her being there.

Some days I worry that Aurelia might be expecting more from me than I'm capable of giving, and others I hate myself for what she must be feeling. Maybe like having the rug pulled out from under her?

None of this is fair to her either, and my brothers have sacrificed too much for me already. I want to be strong for them. It's the least I can do now that they've found this slice of happiness for themselves.

Fleeing to the kitchen when I hear footsteps on the porch, I grab myself a glass of water.

Aurelia walks in a moment later looking flushed, with her robe tied, thankfully, and her golden curls slicked with sweat and pinned on top of her head.

Jesus.

I can see the fucking stubble burn Thorin left all over her neck.

The sheer amount of spontaneous fucking in and around this goddamn cabin is the only thing I haven't gotten used to. Thorin,

Khalil, and I have been monks for the last nine years, jerking off in private and silently wishing for better days.

Now those days are finally here, but there's only one problem.

I don't trust Aurelia George.

Startled when she heads for the sink where I'm leaning, I find a reason to escape to the other side of the island. Aurelia doesn't look at me though as she turns on the water, washes her hands, and splashes her face and neck. She then grabs one of the tin cups drying on the mat, and I start inching out as she fills it up with water and sips from it.

I'm clearing the edge of the island when her voice, soft and teasing, stops me in my tracks. "Are you running from me, Ezekiel?"

Feeling ridiculous since I'm nearly a foot taller and have at least fifty pounds on her, I force myself to face her. "I don't know what you're talking about."

"You're afraid of me," she says in that blunt way of hers.

Am I that fucking transparent? "Don't let it go to your head," I say. "These days I'm afraid of my own shadow." This is quite literally the longest we've spoken since the avalanche, and it's freaking me the fuck out.

"Having met one of them, I'd say it's not without reason."

My eyes narrow, and the easy banter between us dies a swift death. "You said Seth didn't hurt you."

Aurelia sighs like my concern is an inconvenience and then changes the subject. "Are you hungry? I can make you something to eat before I shower."

"No," I say tightly even though my stomach feels like it's touching my spine. And then I remember to at least *try* to be civil. "Thanks."

There's no way in hell I'm eating her damn food.

Aurelia quickly turns away from me like she's hiding her reaction and sets her cup in the sink. "I guess Seth must have warned you about my special stew."

I almost tell her that I haven't heard Seth since I woke up—not even to mock me as he's prone to do, but I hesitate at the hopeful look in her eyes before swallowing the words down.

She's searching for him.

In little ways. In whatever ways she can.

Aurelia probably thinks if she talks about Seth enough, he'll come back to her. Does she know the only way to him is through my pain? Would she care? I swallow when I feel my hands begin to shake.

She's not Tatum, I remind myself.

Aurelia isn't even close to being anything like my ex.

When I met Tatum, she was soft and sweet and never had an unkind word for anyone, but as it turned out, it was all a front to hide the fact that she had no soul.

And when I look at Aurelia? All I see is her heart and spirit. She quite literally glows from it shining through her with the brightness of a star and the force of the sun.

Sunshine.

My heart jolts from the shock of hearing Seth's voice after so many days of silence, but when I reach for him, I once again grasp onto nothing.

Seth?

Frustrated when he doesn't answer, not even to taunt me, I glance at Aurelia who isn't even trying to hide the fact that she's watching me, and a theory forms. The only way to know for sure is to test it.

"Are you okay?" she asks me before turning to the sink to wash out her cup.

"Actually, it was Thorin and Khalil who warned me to watch out for your stew," I say, responding to her earlier statement.

Looking at me over her shoulder, she flashes a sneaky smile, and it's the vengeful, unapologetic gleam in her eyes that oddly makes me relax. "It's an Aurelia George specialty. I call it Fuck Around and Find Out."

My amusement is earnest when I laugh, and like I theorized, images begin pushing themselves into the forefront of my mind.

It's the memory of a terrified Aurelia standing on the threshold of our cabin with the dark night like an impenetrable wall of black behind her. There's something surreal about the memory though. In my head, Aurelia glows—white light at first and then golden like the sun. Her torn milkmaid dress is wet and plastered to her body, and she's pleading with us not to let her go.

The memory ends, and I clench my teeth at Seth's attempt to manipulate me.

That's not what she meant, Seth, and you know it.

He's stubbornly silent again though, even after feeding me another memory. It's more than the crumbs he's usually willing to part with, but it's still not enough.

"You chose Khalil," I blurt once the rest of that night plays out in my mind. I shove the memory away once it shows me Aurelia naked in his bed and huddled under his sheets—waiting for him. I don't need Seth's memories to know what happened next. "Why?"

She stiffens at my question but then turns to face me instead of hiding away. Her nostrils flare, and then I worry if I'm making her relive something she doesn't want to. "Does it matter?"

"It will help me understand you."

She tilts her head curiously like I'm something to be examined and studied. "Why would you want to do that? You don't even like me."

My brow furrows when I realize she has a point. Except... "I don't hate you, Aurelia."

She watches me for a moment, and she doesn't just look sad. She looks vulnerable when our gazes connect. "No?" she whispers hopefully.

When I shake my head, Aurelia pushes away from the sink and stalks around the island, plucking a shiny red apple from the bowl as she goes. I will my feet to stay planted because I know she's testing me. And for some fucking reason, I want to pass. I stop breathing when Aurelia stops in front of me—so close I can smell the shampoo in her hair and Thorin on her skin.

"Prove it."

She holds out the harmless apple in offering.

My scoff is so sharp, she flinches.

It's a tiny movement that's barely perceptible, but it's there.

And like me, she's too stubborn to retreat. Aurelia stays put even if it means getting slammed with the full force of my ire.

"I don't hate you," I amend, "but I don't trust you either. I think you should know that. I don't know what the hell you did to my brothers and Seth, but I'm going to find out."

Aurelia's gaze is assessing before her wary expression morphs into a taunting one at my warning. "Then you might not want to run from the room every time I enter it," she says mockingly. Aurelia shoves the apple into my chest, and my fingers tangle with her softer ones as I move to catch it without thinking. "Start there, and if you're lucky, you'll find out *exactly* what I did to them."

What the—

My body is vibrating with the need to put distance between us even now, but I ignore it because being around Aurelia is the only time I can feel Seth. He's using his memories to push me toward Aurelia, and his scheming just might get me the answers I need.

I know the moment she's gone, he'll retreat to whatever dark pit he's crouching in, so I crack a smile that's as sharp as her tone. "I can't think of a better way to keep an eye on you, *princess*."

She pauses at the pet name, her eyes flaring with surprise.

Lifting the apple to my lips as I stalk from the kitchen, I sink my teeth into the forbidden fruit.

The next morning, I'm slouched in my seat at the kitchen table when Aurelia unceremoniously drops an empty plate in front of me. It clatters noisily on the table and wobbles like a spinning top until it finally settles. The plate is so clean I can see my reflection and the annoyed expression on my face.

Aurelia's already gliding away, completely in her element like a dance she's rehearsed. I watch through narrowed gaze as she lovingly sets Thorin's and Khalil's plates in front of them while dodging their groping hands with a wily grin. The table is a smorgasbord of breakfast foods that she spent half the morning making.

Thorin and Khalil wait for her to sit between them before heaping as much food on their plates as they can.

I don't get it.

I thought she was a terrible cook?

The food doesn't look bad at first glance, but the longer I study the dishes, I notice that the eggs are runny, the bacon is overcooked, the pancakes are miraculously flat and lumpy at the same time, and the toast is burnt.

I don't understand it until I see the look on Aurelia's face. She's not even eating because she's too busy swiveling her head back and forth to watch my brothers devour everything in sight.

She looks *pleased* and it makes her *radiant*.

As if they can't help themselves, Thorin and Khalil are sneaking glances at her too as they eat—as if her pleasure is all the sustenance they need to get through the day.

I'm going to fucking vomit.

Ignoring my growling stomach, I cross my arms and stubbornly sit there with an empty plate like I always do. I wouldn't even be at the table giving credence to this farce of a relationship, but Khalil threatened to knock my teeth out if I kept snubbing their girl, so here I sit. I also promised Aurelia I wouldn't run at the mere sight of her, and I can't have her winning this battle of wills between us.

I don't care how many bones Khalil or Thorin threaten to break though. I am not going to eat her fucking food.

It feels too…intimate.

I don't even know her. *They* barely even know her.

Thankfully, Khalil and Thorin never press the issue, and neither does Aurelia. She always just gives me an empty plate, in case I want to help myself, and walks away without a word.

It infuriates me.

Everything about this girl just pisses me off.

None more than the way she sets my fucking blood on fire.

My brothers are constantly following her every step with their dicks in hand and tongues hanging. They're so pussy-whipped, they can't see her for what she is. Well, I'll be keeping a closer eye on them after today.

From now on, where they go with her, *I* go.

Anything to keep them from slipping even further under her spell.

"You can eat the food, Ezekiel. I promise it's not poisoned," Aurelia teases as she plucks a piece of bacon from the platter. My eyes lower to watch her wrap her lips around the tip. Aurelia has this habit of sucking on her bacon for the flavor rather than biting it right away, and it drives me fucking crazy.

And by crazy, I mean *hard*.

I shift uncomfortably in my seat, my eyelids growing heavy as I zero in on her mouth. I don't even feel my hand creeping toward the bulge in my boxer shorts until Aurelia suddenly bites down on the bacon. It snaps me out of my trance.

She suddenly looks victorious, and I feel like flipping over the table.

I jerk my hand away, and it's all I can do not to abandon the table when I see her staring at me openly while chewing her bacon with a thoughtful look in her eyes.

I live in the wilds where death waits around every corner. I've been at the mercy of a psychopath and his cult. I have people living inside my head, neither of which I'm in complete control of and both of whom are willing to commit atrocities to protect me.

And still Aurelia George is the most terrifying thing I've ever seen.

Terrifying…and beautiful.

CHAPTER EIGHT

AURELIA

Seriously, I can't win with this guy.

Somehow, I make it through breakfast with Zeke scowling at me the entire time. He looks like he wants to bolt, but he doesn't. Was it because I dared him not to or did Thorin and Khalil threaten him? Both possibilities seem likely.

The moment they stand, Zeke does too, and I prepare myself to enjoy the solitude as they all go their separate ways. Thorin grabs his rifle by the door and leaves the cabin, Khalil goes downstairs to work on the repairs to Zeke's bedroom, and Zeke opens the sliding door to the upper deck and walks out.

The door closes behind him with a firm shut, as if to say, *keep away*. I pick up the book I brought to the table and open it up for some light reading before I clean up. An hour later, I'm halfway through the fifth chapter of the thriller when the sliding door opens again.

It's an effort not to look up.

I listen to the glass door slide closed again and his footsteps carry him around the living room. It feels like we're alone in the cabin even though I can hear Khalil hammering away downstairs. I'm so distracted by Zeke's quiet presence that I end up reading the same sentence over and over.

He stops by the shelves, and I cut my gaze toward the living room to see him perusing the books. My gaze flies back to my own when he turns toward the shelves that have him facing me now. He picks up a book, sets it down, and then picks up another. He does this again and again until he finally selects one.

My gaze becomes unfocused as he travels into the kitchen next. I listen as he opens a drawer, but I don't see whatever he grabs before he shuts it. He opens a cabinet next, and I hear the scrape of glass over the wood and the swish of liquid in a bottle.

Zeke starts walking again, and I assume he'll go back out onto the deck, but instead, he walks over to the table and slides into the seat in front of me.

In Seth's seat.

It's all I can do not to acknowledge his presence—to act as indifferent toward him as he is toward me. I turn the page even though I have no idea what is happening and try to focus on the words. Zeke sets the items he collected on the table, and I use the excuse of all the noise he's causing to finally look up and scowl at him.

"Do you mind? I'm trying to read."

"What's it about?"

God, I have no idea.

He swipes up the box of cards, thumbs the tab open, and empties the deck into his palm.

Even before he came in, I was having a hard time focusing because my mind never left breakfast. Zeke isn't eating, and no one seems to be concerned about that except me. It's only been a few days, but how much longer can he hold out?

"That's an incredibly rude question," I joke as I turn the page again.

"Do you play cards?" he asks as he riffle shuffles them.

"Yes."

"Would you like to play a round with me?"

I sigh and close the book in my hand that the chatterbox doesn't seem to notice I'm holding. Setting it down on the table, I sit back and stare at him. He also has a book resting near his elbow as if he's planning on staying. There's also a bottle of gin from Thorin's stash.

"Why would I play with you?" I ask.

"Call it an icebreaker."

"But I like the ice. It's kind of comforting."

"So that's it then?" His brows raise. "You've finally given up the nice act?"

"It wasn't an act. I was *genuinely* being nice to you, but then you turned out to be a dick, and now I'm over it. I've decided we don't need to be friends."

"Ouch." As if I hadn't insulted him, he splits the deck in half and starts dealing the cards. "One round," he pleads.

I sigh again, but I don't leave the table like I'm itching to do. Once all the cards are dealt, he slides the gin into the center, where it's easy for us both to reach. "What are we playing?"

"It's called War."

Fitting.

"We each flip one card over at the same time until one of us wins all the cards in the deck. The player with the higher card wins the hand. Whoever has the lower card has to take a drink." Zeke taps the bottle of gin with a fingernail. "That's where this comes in."

"It's barely noon," I point out. "And you haven't eaten."

"Are you worried about me?"

"No."

Zeke smiles, and it's not exactly friendly, but it's not *un*friendly either.

It's fucking beautiful.

My belly dips from the weight of my want when I realize he

has Seth's smile. The curve of it promises danger while drawing me in.

"Then there's no reason we can't play," Zeke decides before picking up his cards. He keeps them face down and pauses to regard me. "Unless you'd rather trade truths instead?"

"Pass."

Zeke smiles and licks his lips. And then he tips his chin toward my untouched half of the deck. "Ready?"

Wondering why he's doing this, I slowly claim my cards and keep them face down like he does. "Ready."

We both grab the top card in our hand and slam them down face up between us at the same time. Zeke swears when my queen of diamonds trumps his three of hearts.

I smile a little as I claim the cards while Zeke grabs the gin and takes a healthy swig before slamming it back down. "Beginner's luck," he says with his eyes on me.

We're still holding each other's gazes when we play two more cards. My seven of diamonds beats his six of spades. "You assume I've never played this before."

Zeke pauses to take another drink. "The game doesn't require any skill, *princess*."

"And yet you're losing."

We set down two more cards, and I win again, so I grab the platter of leftover bacon and push it toward him. "You might want to eat something," I taunt.

Zeke ignores the offer of food and sits back in his chair to study me with a drum of callused fingers on his un-played cards. "Alcohol poisoning or food poisoning… However will I choose?"

Something like anguish at the rejection lodges in my throat, but I swallow it back down. Zeke's a grown man. If he doesn't want to eat, he doesn't have to, but we both know this isn't about food.

He doesn't have to want you either, Aurelia.

"You're not what I expected," I blurt anyway.

Zeke is visibly startled by the admission, but he recovers fast, with his brows pulling low and his jaw twitching from clenching his teeth so hard. "Let me guess... My brothers told you that I was weak and damaged and afraid of my own shadow. They told you I wouldn't be able to handle your presence in the cabin."

It's my turn to study him and the resentment he tries and fails to hide at his own perceived weakness. "Trauma doesn't make you weak, Ezekiel." His green eyes are full of panic when they find mine again. "Being cruel does."

"Please don't call me that," he chokes out.

"What? Cruel?"

The knot in his throat works up and down as he decides whether to offer up a weakness to evil little me. "Ezekiel."

"Why?"

His body language screams *and that's enough of that.*

Zeke swears, straightens, and throws down another card.

King of hearts.

Something tells me this game, fueled by the alcohol, was meant to loosen *my* tongue, not his. I set a card down too, but mine is also a king—from the diamond suit.

Never having played this game before despite my bluff, I feel my eyes widen dramatically as I look to Zeke for answers. He's staring at the cards as if they mean something.

War, I discern when I remember the name of the game.

Two cards of equal value must mean war.

Suddenly, it doesn't feel like a simple card game. It feels like we're battling for the rights to Thorin and Khalil, who we both know will never be able to choose between us.

"What do we do now?"

"Now we drink." He snatches up the bottle and drinks before slamming it down hard enough to make me jump.

I'm not afraid.

I just haven't stopped being hyperaware of him since he first sat down. He's beautiful, tormented, and he hates me despite denying it.

Zeke pushes the bottle toward me, and I hesitantly accept it. I'm unable to look away from him as I tip the rim toward my mouth, barely letting it touch my lips as I take a small sip. The liquor is strong and not my drink of choice, so I immediately gag and pull the bottle away. Zeke presses his fingers to the bottom before I can set the bottle down, and he gently tips it back toward my lips until I feel the smooth rim.

Eyes on him, I obediently drink more.

After I gulp a healthy swallow, he finally takes the bottle back while I gasp for breath.

Once I recover, he pulls three cards from his deck, leaving them face down, and I mimic him. He then pulls a fourth, so I do too, and with our gazes locked, we turn the last drawn card over.

Zeke wins, claiming all the cards, making his pile much larger than mine.

I'm starting to regret not asking what the winner gets.

Or what the loser has to do.

I should know better by now. These men of mine never do anything without a purpose that extracts a heavy toll. Except Zeke isn't mine, so I have no idea what to expect, which makes me even more nervous.

I take a drink, and we keep playing, but the tides quickly turn after the first war is triggered with Zeke going on to win all of the cards in the deck.

"Heyyyy," I slur with a drunken smile. "You won. That was

fun." *Lie.* It was completely nerve-racking. I'm *soooo* glad I'm drunk. "We should do it again sometime."

"We're not done doing it now," he says with a small but amused smile. "I won. That means I get a prize."

"Riiiiight. Right, right, right, right, right." I smile again as I rest my cheek on my hand and stare at the blurry image of Zeke across the table. In Seth's seat. "Whaddayouwant?"

"You can either finish that," he says, referring to the last of the gin, which is about three shots' worth. My head and stomach immediately roil as I become dizzy. "Or you can answer one question for me honestly."

Why do I feel like he was getting me drunk and leading me blindly to this, the real game, all along?

Because of course he was.

I'm the fool for hoping he was finally coming around.

Oops.

"Orrrr I can make you a birthday cake."

The amused twinkle in Zeke's eyes winks out as he looks at me as if he's the one trapped in a...um...a trap...now. I'm *so* drunk. "What are you talking about?"

"Your birthday. I know it passed two days ago. Khalil told me. I wanted to bake you a cake," I blab as I run my finger over the surface of the table, "buuuut he said it probably wasn't a good idea." I pout since I had really been looking forward to cake.

"He's right. It's not a good idea. I don't have much of a sweet tooth anyway. That's Seth's thing."

"What do you like?" I let slip as I lean forward like I find him fascinating.

He is. He really is.

Zeke swipes up all the cards and begins to shuffle them again as he stares at me with a lazy look. "Sour things. Bitter things that burn."

"Wow… You must have really shitty taste in coffee then."

Zeke laughs, and it's deep, dark, and woefully short-lived. It falls quiet between us, and when my bare toes accidentally brush the rough hairs on his leg, we both startle like we were electrocuted. I can feel my toes tingling from that brief touch. That brief, sweet spark burning like an ember.

"Are you ever going to ask your question?"

"Do you really think you can be happy here, spending the rest of your life as a ghost?"

Ah. That. "Sure. Why not? It's better than the alternative."

"Which is?"

"Spending the rest of my life being what my uncle wants me to be."

Zeke studies me carefully. "And there's no third choice?"

For some reason I have trouble meeting his gaze as I answer. "None that I can see."

"Are you sure about that, Aurelia?"

I exhale a frustrated breath that reeks of gin. It feels like he's pushing me. "I believe that's four questions, but for your information I'm happy here, Zeke. I'm sure about *that*. What I think you should be asking is if you're willing to deny your friends something real just because it didn't work out for *you*." I stand and stagger away while I still can, but I swear I hear him grumble a warning as I pass.

"Nothing lasts, *princess*."

CHAPTER NINE

KHALIL

Ever since the sheriff came for us, things between Aurelia and me have been slightly off-kilter. Thanks to Thorin's constant fuckups, I've learned vicariously that Aurelia's way of dealing with her hurt feelings is to ice us out.

In this case, just *me* it seems.

Except she wasn't avoiding me, giving me the silent treatment, or picking a fight. Quite the opposite, actually. While she's had no trouble fucking me, any real sort of intimacy has been nonexistent.

She doesn't sleep in my bed.

She won't let me hold her.

She'll barely let me kiss her but will deepthroat my dick with an eagerness that makes my toes curl just thinking about it.

And we don't talk about everything and nothing like we used to.

She's taken away all the little things I didn't realize I craved until they were off the table.

I am starting to feel like a human vibrator, a toy, which is fucking rich because it's exactly what we tried to make her when she first arrived.

The thought that I've fucked up in some irreparable way has made me restless. Especially when it became obvious that nothing had changed between her and Thorin. I assumed Aurelia would get over whatever the hell was eating at her after a while, but after the first week passed, she was still rolling her fucking eyes at me whenever she thought I wouldn't notice.

I was even desperate enough to confide in Thorin and Zeke, who only snickered and cracked jokes over seeing me like this— chasing and pining for a girl.

Since my brothers were no fucking help, eventually, I caved and finally asked Aurelia what her fucking problem was, but she just smiled and said nothing before fucking me. After the best nut of my life—and two for her—she went right back to icing me out like it never happened.

It left me scratching my head until that confusion turned to dread when I was left to come up with my own conclusion.

Things between us only seemed to worsen after that because now we aren't even fucking, except this time it is my choice. I pretend to be asleep whenever she slips into my bed at night, and I leave the room anytime her gaze lingers in my direction.

Me.

Khalil Poverly.

Turning down sex.

I loved to fuck almost as much as I loved to fight. But with Aurelia, access to her body means nothing if I can't have her heart to go with it. I am a lover and a fighter, and Aurelia is about to find out exactly what that means.

Today, I decided to put an end to her silent warfare once and for all.

I asked Thorin to find a reason to take him away from the cabin this morning and to take Zeke with him. I didn't tell him my plan, but he seemed to know anyway and wished me luck before dragging Zeke out of bed. From the swollen cheek Thorin was sporting before he left the cabin, I'm guessing Zeke wasn't too happy about being forced out of bed so early.

Once I have everything ready, I search for Aurelia and find her outside in our glade. She's kneeling over her garden, grumbling to herself as she shoves a trowel into the ground inside the newly constructed raised bed. Oh, she tried to make them on her own but gave up after struggling for two hours to make one.

I'd gotten up early the next day and spent half the morning making several of different sizes since I didn't know what she needed them for, but did I get a thank-you?

Fuck no.

She grunted when I showed them to her, which I guess was better than ignoring me entirely, and then proceeded to do exactly that as she consulted her gardening book to figure out which size to use. I'd returned that excited, eager glint in her eyes, though, and I told myself it was enough. I even caught her humming when I stuck my head out of the cabin to check on her after.

Aurelia's back was to me now, so she didn't see or hear me coming as I silently approached, only to realize she was talking to herself.

"Fucking asshole," she grumbles. "Who the fuck does he think he is? My pussy not good enough now? Un-fucking-believable. I'm the one who's supposed to be mad." She shoves the trowel into the ground again with a growl. "Bitch ass. Stingy dick ass. Who needs you? I don't."

An unexpected grin splits the lower half of my face when I realize she's talking about me and the fact that I wouldn't fuck her last night. On the heels of my amusement is relief because at least now I know it isn't the end of us.

She still cares.

Aurelia's still talking shit when my shadow falls over her and she pauses mid-insult. A moment later, she goes right back to work and talking more shit even though she knows it's me and I can hear everything.

"How are you going to pretend to be asleep, knowing I want to make love, but forget that you snore like a bear in the woods? Who does that? Oh, I know. Bitch ass bitches. What's the matter, Khalil? Are you scared of my pussy now?"

"Got something you want to say to me, Goldilocks?"

"Fuck you," she immediately barks like I haven't spoken. She then huffs in frustration and throws down the trowel before sitting back on her heels.

My gaze passes over the garden bed that looks more like a dog dug a ton of holes after being let loose in the yard, and I realize belatedly what she was trying to do. "If you want to loosen the soil, that's not the tool you want to use. You need the hoe."

"Yes, I know," she snaps as she snatches off the gardening gloves and stands. "I couldn't find it."

Because I hid it, but I don't tell her that.

Last night, I overheard her tell Thorin that she was going to try planting the potatoes after their hunt today, so I snuck out to the shed and hid the hoe, hoping it would make her talk to me, but I overestimated her stubbornness. Apparently, she'd rather make her job three times harder than ask for my help. Whatever I'd done to piss her off, it must have been worse than I thought.

Aurelia turns around, but she doesn't meet my gaze as she walks past me.

"Aurelia." Of course, she ignores me and enters the cabin. I'm on her heels the entire time, so I easily catch her hand before she can get far, and I spin her around. "We need to talk."

"No thanks." She tries to walk away again, but my hands quickly snag her waist, and I lift her off the ground until she's eye level with me, and then I keep her suspended like this with her feet hovering off the ground. She wrinkles her nose at me. "Khalil, put me down."

"Not until we talk."

"So that's your plan? You really think you can hold me up that long?"

"Try me."

Her lips part with a smart retort, but then she eyes my arms and the huge muscles bulging beneath my skin and sighs. "Fine. I'll talk. Just… Put me down. I feel ridiculous, and you're pissing me off."

I gently set her down, and the moment I let her go, her lashes flutter in a telling way. Before she can roll her fucking eyes again, I grab her neck in a firm grip and trap her against the railing. "Roll your fucking eyes at me, and I swear to God, I'll pluck every last one of your eyelashes out. Do not test me, Aurelia."

I can tell she's getting ready to do just that when she suddenly switches tactics and lets her eyes roam over my bare chest and eight-pack. "What's wrong, Khalil?" I feel my grip on her neck weaken at the sudden switch in her tone. Every syllable is wrapped in sex now as she takes advantage of my loosened hold and pushes forward to cup my dick. "I think I know," she coos as she pets me. "You miss dipping this big stick in my hot honey, don't you?"

I know she's being crass to fuck with me, but my dick doesn't care. It twitches eagerly in my shorts under her palm, and Aurelia smiles knowingly as she rubs me. She molds the front of her body against mine, and I can't bring myself to care that she's finessing me. The fog of lust that demands I tear off her athletic shorts, throw her leg over my shoulder, and force my way inside swells along with my dick. The promise of pounding her warm, sweet pussy until she weeps for me threatens to derail my careful plans.

But then I feel it.

The pulsing vein in her neck that matches the rhythm of her heart. It reminds me of what I'm fighting for, and it's not her pussy. That part of her is clearly still mine even when *she* doesn't want to be anymore.

I have to know why.

"*Stop*." I swat her hand away before she can get it inside my shorts. My hand is still around her neck, and I tighten my hold before driving her back against the rail again. She makes a noise caught between a choke and a moan. "When I want your pussy, you'll know, and you'll give it up like a good girl. Now stop throwing it at me and *talk* to me. Tell me what's wrong. What did I do?"

She rolls her eyes despite my warning. "Big talk for a man who was willing to fold at the slightest wind two weeks ago."

So that's it.

I drop my hand to keep from strangling her and tuck my hand into my pocket. "Explain. And don't give me some smart-ass answer. I'm not with this cold-shoulder shit. Tell me what's up."

Her lips quiver as if everything she's been feeling these past couple of weeks is suddenly hammering against the dam she'd built. When Aurelia finally allows herself to meet my gaze, the levees crumble away and the tidal wave of her anger and hurt hits me like a jab to the gut.

"You were going to give me up."

"Goldilocks…" I shake my head in disappointment. Never did I think Aurelia would actually believe I *wanted* to let her go. I thought she knew I wouldn't walk away from this for any reason other than to keep her safe. "The sheriff knew who you were," I remind gently. "He knew he'd been played. What was I supposed to do, Goldilocks? Let you go down with us?"

"Yes!"

"*No.*"

Aurelia shoves at my chest, but I don't budge an inch. "It wasn't your decision."

"You're my girl. I'll protect you however the fuck I see fit."

"I don't need you to decide what's best for me. Other people have been deciding things for me for far too fucking long. It's *my* turn. I told you I wanted this. How many times do I have to prove I want to stay? How deep do I have to cut myself open before you accept that *I want to bleed*?"

"And when are you going to see that we don't doubt that?" I shake my head. "Not anymore. You are *owned*, but we belong to you too." Aurelia doesn't quite meet my gaze as her own glazes over, and I can tell she's overwhelmed. "The real issue," I say low and with a narrowed gaze, "is that you still don't know what that means."

She throws out her arms in exasperation. "Tell me."

"It means any one of us will fall on our sword for you without hesitation. And *without* apology."

"You're such a fucking asshole," she grumbles without any real conviction.

"Yours," I correct. Her eyes fly up to meet mine when I pinch and lift her chin. "I'm your asshole. I'm your very *loyal* asshole, Aurelia. You'll always come first."

"I don't want you sacrificing yourself for me, Khalil. I want us to work as a team."

"I'll try to keep that in mind," I say as I run my hands down her sides. "Now come on. We gotta go."

Aurelia looks curious when I take her hand and start walking toward the front door. "Where are we going?"

"It's a surprise."

"Wait." She tugs on my hand, and I glance over my shoulder when she stops walking. "I just need a few minutes. There's something I have to do." Before I can ask what, since she's already dressed for the occasion, Aurelia turns and rushes downstairs to the basement.

CHAPTER TEN

EZEKIEL

I curse Aurelia George's name once more while fighting a yawn.

It's because of her that I'm up before the sun.

It's because of her that my brothers are so blind and obsessed.

It's because of her that I can't seem to keep my thoughts straight. It doesn't matter if I'm near her or not. I can't stop fucking thinking about her.

"Zeke, goddamn it. Will you take the fucking shot already?" Thorin whispers from where he's lying next to me behind a fallen tree.

Forced out of my head, I watch the grazing doe through the sight of the rifle pointed downwind, but I can't bring myself to pull the trigger. Not when my mind is still overrun with thoughts of her.

Spitting out a curse, I lower the rifle. "What the fuck for? It's not like we need the food. We're out here because of *her*. What's the point in pretending otherwise."

Thorin cuts his gaze at me, and I feel the violence rolling off him before he shakes his head and stands with a growl. "Fuck this. I can't deal with your shit right now. I'm going to go take a piss."

Thorin vaults over the log, scaring off the doe and any chance at the game as he prowls away.

"Fuck you too," I grumble. Turning, I rest my back against the tree and set the rifle down.

All right, so maybe he has a point, I admit after ten minutes roll around and then twenty and Thorin still doesn't return. Maybe it isn't fair of me to sabotage their twisted little romance when they gave up so much for me. It's not even that I have a bad feeling about Aurelia. But that's exactly why I don't trust what I am feeling.

Isaac and Tatum's betrayal took me completely by surprise, so I obviously can't trust my judgment. I used to believe there wasn't a purer soul on this earth than Tatum, and yet every time I look at Aurelia, I see a halo of gold around her head.

I sure as shit never saw one around Tatum.

It doesn't make any sense. Tatum was cold, but she was polite, agreeable, soft-spoken, and never taunted anyone. Aurelia, on the other hand, is the complete opposite. She is spoiled, combative, temperamental, vain, and can stare right through like you aren't even there. And yet her presence—hell, the mere thought of her—fills me with a warmth that lingers even when she isn't around. That part of myself begs me to believe she would never do what Tatum did. That she would die before turning on Khalil and Thorin. Turning on Seth.

Turning on *me*.

And while I might have been wrong about a lot of people, I've never been wrong about my brothers. If Thorin and Khalil can trust her, put everything on the line for her, maybe I can too. It won't be easy, but I owe it to them to at least start *trying*.

I'm getting ready to stand and hunt Thorin down to apologize when the two-way radio he has tucked in his pack buzzes to life. At first, I ignore the static until a high-pitched whine follows that tells me someone is trying to use our frequency.

It's a public channel, so it's not impossible, but in the decade we've been here, it's never happened before.

"Sheriff?" a voice calls over the channel. The sound is muffled but unmistakably female. "Sheriff, are you there? Hello?" It crackles and hisses when the woman on the other end releases the receiver to wait for a response. Could she be hurt? She didn't sound in distress, but there was something familiar about the voice that was making my skin prickle with awareness. Whoever it was has to be close if we're picking up the signal. And Thorin and I aren't far from the cabin...

Cursing when realization dawns, I snatch up Thorin's pack.

Did something happen? Was Aurelia hurt? Was Khalil?

My heart is pounding as I search Thorin's pack for the radio. It feels like forever before I find it and yank it free. I'm getting ready to press on the receiver and ask her what's wrong when the sheriff's voice comes through loud and clear.

"Sheriff here," Kelly speaks gruffly. "You're early. Is there a problem?"

I'm frowning when the channel crackles again, and then it clears a moment later when Aurelia responds. "Not really," she says dryly like she'd rather not be talking at all. "Just sticking to our agreement."

"Our agreement was for the end of the day," the sheriff returns.

"Yeah, well, I can't really control when I'm at the cabin and when I'm not, so you're getting *this* call at the *start* of the day."

"Aurelia," the sheriff begins with a sigh like this is an argument they've had before. I never realized she and the lawman were so close. "This is for your own good. I just want to make sure you're safe."

"I'm safe *with them*," she snaps. "I told you that."

"Yes. Well, you've told me many stories, but none of them are adding up. Until they do, our deal stands. You are to check in with me every day. If you're late even once or miss a single day, I'll lock those boys up and throw away the key. Am I clear?"

"*Crystal*," she responds coldly. I feel goose bumps on my arm and fight the need to shiver.

"Good," the sheriff says as if he's unaware of her dark mood. "And, Aurelia?"

"What?"

"I still expect a call this evening before I leave the station. Is that understood?"

Aurelia doesn't answer, and it takes both the sheriff and me a while to realize she isn't going to. The amiable sheriff volleys a surprising string of curses sharp enough to make a pirate blush and then the channel goes dead.

Aurelia, I'm learning, tends to have that effect on people.

I'm not aware of my own rage building until I'm already moving. The radio flies from my hand and crashes into the tree before raining down to the ground in broken pieces.

Fooled yet a-fucking-gain.

I'm still sitting in the same spot when Thorin finally returns. His expression is relaxed until he sees the broken radio and my foul mood. "What the hell happened?" He quickly dismisses the radio and crouches in front of me. His blue eyes are filled with concern as he watches me. "Talk to me. What's wrong? What can I do, Zeke?"

I could tell him.

I could tell him everything I overheard between the sheriff and Aurelia and finally make him see the truth, but would he believe me? If he doesn't, it would shatter everything.

My trust in him and his trust in me.

And then there's the hurt.

The pain it would unleash on him to know it was all a lie.

It's been more than a decade, and I still remember it. God, I don't think I could ever forget. Could I really do that to Thor and Khalil? Could I really take it all away just because I can't let go? And what about Aurelia? Khalil, Thorin, and Seth are the ones who kidnapped her. She should have a way out if she needs it. *She's done nothing wrong*, I realize with a depressing twist of the knife in my back.

"Nothing," I whisper, sticking to my original plan. I reach for the hollowness inside my chest that is crying out for someone to fill it. "There's nothing you can do. It's what I have to do."

Thorin cocks his head. "And what's that?"

I look past him at the shattered pieces of the radio that could easily be my insides and exhale. "Try. I have to try."

CHAPTER ELEVEN

AURELIA

Khalil and I go to the lake a short hike away.

I eye the punching bag that's hanging from a low-hanging branch on the shore. Khalil drops his much larger pack before helping me out of mine and dropping it next to his.

"So, what are we doing here?" It obviously isn't to swim because we aren't wearing swimsuits. I'm not sure what I was expecting, but it wasn't for him to answer by attacking me.

Khalil tackles me from behind, and all the breath is knocked out of my lungs when I hit the ground. I only manage to flip onto my back before he seizes my wrists and pins them to the ground. I feel like it's exactly what he predicted I'd do.

"What the—what the hell are you doing? Get off me!"

"You want me off you? *Move me*."

I twist and shove and grunt to no avail. "I can't," I say when I'm out of breath and feeling weak. "You're too heavy."

"My weight has nothing to do with it. You're panicking. Focus."

"Okay, then. *I'm* not strong enough."

"Maybe. But your weakness isn't coming from your body," he says. "It's coming from here." He taps the side of my head. "You've already decided you've lost the fight without even trying."

"Okay, so tell me what I should have done and make it quick. It feels like a planet landed on me," I squeeze out. The bastard sits up until he's straddling me, and I realize he's much heavier than I thought. "Oh, God," I groan. "I can't breathe."

"Good. That should motivate you to listen, focus, and react quickly. Use your left leg to trap mine but make sure to keep your feet planted." Willing to do anything to get him off me quickly, I do what he says, hooking my ankle tightly around his to trap his right leg. Khalil demonstrates that he can't reposition himself now and my interest is immediately piqued. "Good girl. Now drive your hips forward like you're trying to throw me off." Khalil moves like he's about to grab my wrists again, and panic strikes a sharp chord within me. Instead of it freezing me in place this time, I buck my hips as hard as I can, and Khalil pitches forward, losing his balance.

He's still on top of me though, but I can breathe now and my heart is pumping wildly for a different reason.

"Perfect," he praises, and I immediately want more. "Now grab my right arm with your left hand. Always do this immediately after throwing your opponent off balance." I'm hanging onto his every word now, so I hook my elbow around his from the outside, and Khalil looks pleased but not all that surprised at my sudden eagerness.

It's like he knew this was exactly what I needed.

"That's it, Goldilocks. Very good." I'm preening from his praise and almost miss the move when he says, "Now you can use your right hand to go for the eyes or use your forearm to strike the face, throat, or chest. You want to get me off you, so we'll do the forearm strike. Use your arm, hip, and foot—essentially the entire right side of your body—to knock me off and gain the upper hand. Do it now."

It takes me three attempts to knock Khalil over. My foot slips the first time, so I don't have the traction to toss him off. The second time, I forget to use my hips, using only two-thirds of my power, which allowed Khalil to stay exactly where he was. It is my third attempt that lands Khalil flat on his back and me on top of him with my forearm to his throat, keeping him down.

"I did it!" I shrieked while grinning.

"Very good, Goldilocks, but there's another lesson you should know."

My frown snaps into place. "What?"

Khalil reaches up and yanks on my ponytail viciously enough to shock me into releasing him. I fall to the side to loosen his hold, and he lets me go and stands while I sit on my ass and rub my now sore scalp with a grimace. "Never drop your guard," he scolds. "You may have briefly gained the upper hand, but all you've done is make your enemy desperate. The fight isn't over until your opponent is truly incapacitated. Never. Stop. Attacking."

I sigh and shake off my frustration, knowing he's right. "Understood. What else?"

Khalil's pride is palpable as he wordlessly holds out his hand. His teachings are already sinking into my core though, so I hesitate, wondering if it might be another trap. "For the moment I'm just your man," he assures me. "This isn't a test." I take Khalil's hand, and he squeezes mine in a wordless apology for the hair pull before he hauls me to my feet.

"Follow me."

I trail Khalil over to the tree, and he instructs me to put my back to the trunk.

"Earlier, I had you pinned like this," he reminds me and then demonstrates by grabbing my throat and trapping me against the rough bark of the tree. "You didn't even try to break my hold. Why?"

"Because even though you're lucky to have me—*the* Aurelia George—as your girlfriend, *none* of you ungrateful assholes have thanked me yet by buying me jewelry. I've had to settle for the occasional hand necklace."

Khalil's mouth twitches and his brown eyes glow with amusement. "It's amazing how your sheer lack of humility still surprises me."

"You're welcome."

Khalil shakes his head, but then his humor is gone in a flash and he's wearing a stern "coach" expression again. "Why, Aurelia?"

"Um…I didn't know how?" That should be obvious, so why was he pushing?

"You also didn't try," Khalil scolds, "so you're going to now. How would you do it?"

I start to roll my eyes when Khalil's brows pull down in warning, and I gulp. I grab his wrist and tug with all my might, but he just stares at me. I claw at his arms, hoping the pain will make him release me, but he yawns like I've bored him. I try to knee him next, and he just sighs.

"Commendable effort but no."

"So what then?"

"Your hands are free, but you haven't even tried to hurt me yet."

"What do you mean? I scratched you." I indicate his arms where we both can see the long, jagged lines now. Some of them are even bleeding.

Khalil gives me a look as if to say, *get serious*. "You've clawed me harder than that when I'm deep inside you, Goldilocks. I mean *real* pain."

"You *want* me to hurt you," I say just to make sure we're on the same page.

"*Yes.*"

Remembering how he pulled my hair and his disappointment that I wasn't more aggressive in defending myself, I don't hesitate before I curl my fingers. My fist collides with his mouth, and the blow snaps his head to the side. His hand is still around my throat, but I notice his grip has loosened, so before he can recover, I punch him again and slap his hand off my neck at the same time.

Khalil actually stumbles away, but I don't fall for it this time. I keep my guard up, and when he recovers, he flashes me a red smile before turning his head and spitting out the blood pooling in his mouth and staining his teeth.

"You know how to punch and you're mean with it," he remarks rhetorically. "Good. That's good. It's a decent foundation to start with." Khalil walks over to his pack and tugs out two sets of boxing gloves. "Put these on," he orders after tossing a pair to me.

"What is this about?" I finally ask as I do what he says.

"It's about the fact that your uncle is trying to kill you and you don't have the first clue how to defend yourself. You got lucky the first time because we were there."

I pause. "You think he'll try again?"

"Most definitely. You need to be ready for it."

"But I have three big, strong, murderous boyfriends who apparently live to die for me." It sounds so ridiculous, but it's practically their motto.

"Boyfriends you refuse to listen to," Khalil retorts. "What happens if we're not there next time?"

"Hey, I listen," I argue. Under my breath, I grumble, "When I want to."

Hearing every word, Khalil tosses me an impatient look before snapping a mouth guard over his teeth. He has a new set for me, and I open my mouth to let him slip the guard in since I already have my boxing gloves on.

"Now what?"

"Now we work on your stamina," he says as he slips his gloves on. "When your enemy is bigger and stronger than you, exhausting them before they can finish their assault is the best tool in your arsenal. That means you need to be faster, and you need to build up your endurance."

"So what are the gloves for? Don't you want me to run laps around the lake or something?"

Khalil's smile is sharp as he regards me. "That will come later. First, I want to assess where you are. You're a stage performer and, from what I've heard, a really good one. I imagine it takes a lot of breath control to dance and sing at the same time."

"Sure, but I'm out of practice. I haven't toured in a couple of years and I was supposed to start rehearsals this summer for my upcoming tour, but I was in a plane crash and I've been held captive by three sex-starved mountain men for months so…" Khalil just stares at me. "All right. Fine." I throw up my hands. "So how do we do this?"

"I'm going to attack you, putting you on the defense. I want you to do your best to either evade me or free yourself from my hold using one of maneuvers I showed you. We're going to do this until you either knock me out or I can't continue."

"But that's impossible. You're in amazing shape. If this were a video game, you'd be this huge, scary boss, and your health bar would be a mile long."

Khalil looks surprised for a moment. "You play video games?"

"No, but I've seen videos of people playing online. It's fun to watch grown men cry when they lose to a computer."

Khalil chuckles. "All right. I guess that leaves option two."

"You really want me to knock you out?"

I'm rewarded with a lopsided smile that's equally boyish and cocky. It's infuriating that he just *knows* the chances are slim that I will. "If you can."

I totally can't, but even if I could...

I give him a wary look while wrapping my arms around myself. "I'm not sure I'm comfortable with that. We're kind of exposed out here. What if something happens?"

"Which is why I brought this." He reaches inside his pack again and pulls out my gingham headband. I watch him secure it on his wrist. "Get this off my arm and you win. Consider me knocked the fuck out."

I nod. "Okay."

"Ready?" he asks.

"I guess so."

I forget how scary Khalil is until the image of my boyfriend slips away and he immediately comes at me with a dark look in his eyes and no warning. Forgetting everything he taught me in an instant, I let out a terrifying squeal and run in the opposite fucking direction.

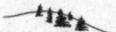

Two hours later, I'm lying on the ground. I'm groaning, panting, and sore all over after Khalil indeed made me run a couple of laps around the lake. He was right there with me, though, encouraging me to keep going, but it only made me hate him even more because being able to talk and run at the same time is definitely a flex.

I barely make it before collapsing into the dirt.

Khalil is crouched next to me with my head gently cradled in his palm as he makes me sip the cool water from his canteen.

Thorin and Ezekiel find us moments later.

"I take it training is going well?" Thorin asks like this was their evil plan all along.

Khalil pulls away, and I groan again, but the sound gets caught in my throat along with the last sip of water I'd been about to swallow. I spit it out when I catch sight of a shirtless Thorin carrying a doe on his shoulders. Blood runs down his sweat-slicked chest, and his hair is loose, probably a mistake since he rarely lets it down unless we're fucking.

He looks terrifyingly wild and untamable.

Zeke is walking next to him. He has a hoodie on despite the warm weather and the hood is up, shielding most of his devastatingly handsome face from view, but I can still feel the heat of his stare. He's *always* staring and sizing me up, so I pay it no mind this time.

Let him look.

"Yup," I answer with zero enthusiasm. "I'm kicking ass and taking names. In fact, I'm so badass, I don't need any more training today." My sore muscles twinge, and I quickly add, "Or ever."

Thorin heaves the dead deer off his shoulders and hoists it over the low-hanging branch. It looks like he already field dressed it, which explains all the blood. He then walks over to the lake and cleans up while I stare at the now-tanned skin of his back. He was really pale during winter, but now his skin has a golden, tawny hue that only defines his muscles even more.

Free of blood now, he stands and turns to face me. "Is that so? Well, then let's go. I want to see what you've learned."

"No more. Mercy." I weakly lift my hand and wave my middle finger in lieu of a white flag.

Of course the biggest red flag in history completely ignores it. "Come on, wolf. Show me what you got. Fuck me up."

I groan again and awkwardly climb to my feet. "You asked for it."

Thorin stands imposing and confident with his arms crossed while he waits for me to make a move. I take one step and stumble. He instantly rushes forward, reaching out to catch me. That's when

I right myself and snag his wrist, using his own momentum against him and yanking him forward until he's lying face-first in the dirt.

Khalil howls while I stare down at Thorin like the badass warrior goddess I am. He spits out a mouthful of dirt before regaining his feet with amazing speed.

"That was mean, wolf."

"You mean impressive? I agree." I hold out my canteen, which he accepts before taking a generous swig. His eyes never leave me as he swishes the water around his mouth to clean out what's left of the sand. The promise of swift retribution has me smiling and sinking my teeth into my lower lip.

"Very," Thorin finally answers. "Although I am wondering if you were like this in school."

"I was bullied in school," I reveal honestly. "I was an average student with average looks in a stable home. I wasn't smart enough or beautiful enough to make anyone feel inferior, and I was always well-fed and clean, so the reasons why are still a mystery to me."

"Is there ever really a good reason for bullying?" Khalil returns.

"True."

"Besides, one could hardly look at you and call you average, Goldilocks."

"True again," I say, making Thorin and Khalil groan. I can tell Zeke is listening but pretending not to. "But you didn't see me when I was thirteen. I was skinny with a too-large head. The boys in school would call me lollipop whenever I walked past. It…was an awkward phase for me. My glow up didn't come until I started putting on weight."

"Lucky us," Thorin murmurs distractedly while eyeing my tits.

I press my finger under his chin to lift his gaze. "When my dad was killed, it got worse instead of better after they heard how he died. The other kids liked to make up stories or repeat the gossip they heard from their parents about the reasons why. You'd think my father was Ted Bundy or something. I was never happier than when my uncle pulled me out of school. I guess that's what made it so easy for him to mold and control me. He took me away from my peers and isolated me in a world of adults before I ever learned how to stand up for myself. Funny how I didn't finally learn until my anger was at its highest peak. It was like I had this new superpower I didn't know how to control, and so it controlled me instead."

Thorin silently runs his knuckles down my arm, and I don't fight the urge to melt into him. It feels safe in his arms. Like a magnet being pulled, my gaze helplessly wanders over to Zeke, who is silent.

Seth would have at least gotten a kick out of me making Thorin eat dirt. Right now, Zeke is sitting on the shore of the lake with a handful of rocks. He tosses one, and it skips along the surface. I can only see his profile, but it's enough to know he's uncomfortable. The scowl on his face seems permanently etched, and I have a feeling I'm the one who put it there. It's been two weeks, and he still hasn't warmed up to me.

Khalil notices where my attention is and walks over to sit with him.

It feels suspiciously like Khalil and Thorin are working hard to split their time between us, making sure neither feels like the odd man out.

I clear my throat. "I assume this torture session has ended. Can we go home now?" I pull my drenched shirt away from my skin with a wrinkled nose. "Don't get me wrong. It's a beautiful day, and I'd like to stay out longer, but I can't stand the feeling of all this sweat sticking to my skin."

"There's a nice, cool lake full of fresh water just a few feet that way, songbird."

I eye the lake and dread pools in my stomach as I'm hit with the memories of falling through the ice. The low rumbling like rolling thunder charging toward me just before the ice gave way beneath my feet. The cutting cold burrowing into my veins and freezing my blood. My silent scream as water filled my lungs.

Endless dark.

No…not endless.

Because Thorin had been there in a flash, plunging into certain death and cutting through the water like a knife to pull me back to the surface. I remember Khalil frantically pulling me out of the frozen water and Seth desperately lending me his body heat.

I look away from the glistening blue surface of the lake and into Thorin's equally blue eyes. "Will you come with me?"

"I think the better question is, do you really think I'd let you go without me?"

Thorin and I are all smiles as we race to shed our clothes. Of course, he beats me since he wasn't wearing a shirt, and then he scoops me up bridal style before I can decide whether to shed my sports bra and panties too. Thorin runs full speed into the water while I squeal.

He keeps a tight grip on me when the water becomes too deep to stand in, but I push away from him, and he raises his brows just before I turn and dive underneath the surface.

The fresh water is indeed cool and surprisingly clear, but the deeper I swim, the less I can see. I can feel Thorin shadowing me like an anxious mother hen as I attempt to show off my swimming prowess. But the lake is dangerously deeper than I thought. It keeps going while my heart rate increases with each passing foot.

I feel Thorin grab my ankle a second later, a silent order to stop, and I obey. Immediately, I race for safety with Thorin's powerful strokes keeping him hot on my heels. I break the rippling surface with a gasp, and Thorin appears next to me a moment later.

"What the fuck was that?" he barks as he wipes the water from his scowling face.

I won't meet his gaze as I casually tread water. "What was what?"

"*Wolf.*"

I shrug as I continue to find interest in any- and everything except his probing eyes. "I was just curious."

"About?"

I sigh. "People die in lakes all the time, and sometimes their bodies are never found." This time I do meet his eyes as I remind him, "That could have been me."

"That will *never* be you. I won't allow it."

"*Run and we will let you die,*" I mock in a deep voice, while cutting him a scathing glare. "I believe it was you who said that."

"It was bullshit, songbird. All of it. We wanted you to stay. We would have done anything to keep you here. You must know that by now."

"Easy for you to say now that you love me. And rightfully so."

"Fuck, you're infuriating." Thorin tips his head back and closes his eyes like he's praying for patience.

"So you're saying you're not head over heels in love with me?"

"Ah." His eyes pop open, and he smirks at me. "So that is what this is about. You're fishing."

"I am *not.*"

He's full-blown grinning now, and what a beautiful smile it is. If I wasn't so enamored with his perfect face, I'd scratch it until it was in ribbons. "Come on," he says before swimming for the large, slanted rock shaped like a miniaturized version of Pride Rock.

How had I not noticed that before?

The rock is only a few feet from where Khalil and Zeke are

wrestling each other in the shallow end. I don't know what Khalil said to him, but Zeke is actually smiling now as the two try to best each other.

I trail Thorin across the lake, and we're nearly to the shore when Zeke manages to shove Khalil underwater. They've drifted a little farther out so Khalil doesn't immediately reappear, and Zeke's gaze narrows as he slowly turns, searching the glistening surface of the lake. His body is strung tight like he's expecting Khalil to pop up and strike.

Extremely likely.

But he's gone long enough for worry to gnaw at me.

"Is he—?" The words die on my tongue when Zeke suddenly pauses too, spotting something swimming past me underneath the water. "What—" His green gaze flies to mine and then he presses his fingers to his lips.

Um…okay?

I want to look and see whatever he does, but I'm too chicken-shit. I don't have a chance to second-guess his command before something jumps out of the water a few feet ahead of me.

I scream.

Thorin has already reached the rock and is reaching up to grab the pointed ledge to haul himself out of the water when Khalil suddenly wraps both arms around his middle and yanks him back in the water. There's a lot of splashing, thrashing, grunting, and growling as Thorin tries to break free of Khalil's hold.

The latter is holding on for dear life.

"Just out of curiosity," Zeke muses, "what exactly did you think was going to grab him?" It takes me a moment to realize the question was meant for me.

Zeke is making small talk with me. *Willingly.*

"I don't know. A crocodile? A bear? The Loch Ness monster? It really didn't matter. My heart would have given out regardless."

Zeke snorts and then glances at the massive lake behind us. "I mean, the bear is a possibility, but the rest are not even close to being likely."

"Come again? I thought it was trees bears can climb. You're telling me they can *swim too*?"

Ezekiel slowly nods while watching me carefully. "They're excellent swimmers, Aurelia."

I don't say another word. I just swim for land and pull myself out of the water. I don't have a towel to help me dry off, so I settle for my sweat-stained shirt to mop up the excess water.

"I'm sorry." Zeke says after following me. "I, uh…I didn't mean to scare you."

"No, no. It's okay. You didn't. I was ready to get out anyway. Really."

Zeke doesn't respond, and I busy myself repacking my bag. By the time I'm done, Thorin and Khalil are racing each other across the lake, which is a problem since I'm ready to go and they show no signs of winding down. I grumble at the delay and then I glance at the path home longingly.

I *really* want a shower.

"Come on," Zeke says, seemingly reading my mind. "I can walk you."

I glance back at the lake before meeting Zeke's gaze with my brows raised. "Shouldn't we wait for Thorin and Khalil?"

Zeke's lips flatten with displeasure. "Sure. If that makes you more comfortable."

"No," I answer quickly, realizing I probably offended him. I force a smile that only seems to put me even more on edge. "It's fine. Let's go."

CHAPTER TWELVE

EZEKIEL

A urelia and I walk in heavy silence for the first half of the long
trek back to the cabin.

Keep it together, man. She's just a girl.

A girl who has my brothers wrapped around her finger like a
Chinese finger trap. The more I pull, the tighter her hold becomes.
Even before we were forced to leave everything behind and isolate
ourselves, Khalil and Thorin were demanding and hard to reach
emotionally.

How did she do it? *Why* did she do it?

"So Khalil mentioned you're famous," I blurt to distract myself
from whatever nefarious plans she may or may not be hiding.

"Yeah. I am." She confirms it like it's a simple fact and not
anything worth noting.

Unfortunately, I don't know anything else about her, so I push
forward in my attempt to understand her. "Would I have heard
anything of yours?"

"That depends." She glances at me. "How often do you listen
to pop?"

"Not at all."

"R&B?"

I rub the back of my neck and wince. "Never?"

"Let me guess," she says as she stops to peer at me through the eyes of a musical savant. "You're broody and like to sulk in your feelings, but you don't strike me as a country music fan, so I'm guessing rock. Maybe a little metal?"

"You guessed correctly," I said while silently debating if I should be offended by the sulking part.

Aurelia smiles a little. "Who's your favorite band?"

I don't have to think about it for long before saying, "Bound." Aurelia's eyes flare briefly with recognition before she looks away quickly when I eye her skeptically. "Why? You've heard of them?" Bound wasn't huge when we left, but they were rising stars having just signed their first record deal. That was a decade ago though, so who knows.

"I might have," she answers coyly. A secretive smirk plays at the corner of her lips and I'm stuck wondering what it means and then not giving a damn when the far more tempting thought of what it would be like to lick her there presents itself. "So who was your favorite?"

"Huh?" My gaze snaps up from her lips and she giggles, the dulcet sound burning itself into my memory even as I turn my head away with a frown at being caught.

When she speaks again, her voice is no longer light and playful as we slip back into the wary distance we cling to like a life ring. "Your favorite band member?"

I flick my gaze toward her and remind myself why I insisted on talking in the first place. "Sure you don't want to guess?" I tease.

"Rich," she says without hesitation.

I trip a little but recover smoothly enough that she doesn't notice as she scans our surroundings. Thorin and Khalil haven't been fucking around with her training. "Nope," I lie because I don't know how I feel about her being able to read me so well. "Everill."

"I'm afraid I have terrible news," she retorts in a faux grave tone. "He's dead."

"I know," I confess with a laugh that isn't forced. "We don't have internet access up here, but there's a café in town with public computers and this thing called a newspaper." Like Everill, Aurelia was plastered all over them after her plane crashed, but I don't tell her that. I'm sure she's guessed as much.

"Wow…" Aurelia's gaze is unimpressed as she cocks her head to study me. "You're kind of mean when you're not trembling like a baby deer in my presence." I feel my cheeks warm as I scratch my nape. I'm about to apologize when she suddenly smiles. It's… radiant. "Keep it up, Cura. I have a feeling we're finally getting to the real you. So what about rap?" she asks, returning to the original thread of our conversation.

I wave my hand to indicate sometimes. Rap was Seth's thing. "Wait, you rap too? He didn't mention that."

"No." "I've only done a few features. It started with me providing backup vocals. There wasn't much notoriety or credit in it, but as my name grew, that changed to me singing the hooks and choruses."

"Which song was your favorite?" I hear myself ask before I even know the question is there in my mind.

"'I Know You Do,'" she states without hesitation. "It was one of the few projects I got to choose for myself. Before I became *Aurelia*."

"Is Aurelia a stage name?"

"No. It's the name my parents gave me. But it meant something different once stardom came. After that, I was *the* Aurelia to everyone and never just Aurelia to anyone."

"And that bothered you? Don't most people in your business want that?"

"Sure. At first. Until you realize you've never known true isolation until your face and name are known by everyone. I was constantly *on* all the time, guarding my feelings and measuring my words, knowing they'll be picked apart for entertainment between albums. There was no room for me in my life anymore. I was a celebrity all the time, even if I was just having breakfast."

"Sounds…" I grapple for a word. "Constricting."

"Some days it was unbearable. Others, it was just part of the job."

I consider everything Aurelia said and all the things she didn't before asking, "I take it something happened that you regret?"

"What I did to Tania was wrong," she says without context. I'm guessing it's a story I've heard before. It's one of the few times Aurelia slips up and forgets that I'm not Seth, so I don't fault her for it. I just listen. "I know that now, but what's the point of feeling remorse if no one gives a shit?"

"The point isn't that you regret your mistakes but that you learn from them. The only person who can offer you true absolution is yourself. Desiring more than that is a performance. It's theater, and people want to be entertained. Forgiving you just means the show ends. It seems cruel because it is, but don't you see the hypocrisy? You resent not being treated as a human being while begrudging others their human nature, just as they judge you for your public wrongs while burying the things they do in the dark."

"So you're saying we're all just hypocrites and it's hopeless?"

"There's always hope, princess."

The rest of the walk is made in reflective silence until our clearing comes into view, but I can't let it end there. "I'm sorry," I offer, wondering if my words had only done more harm than good to her. "I shouldn't have said—"

"No. I…" She sighs. "I needed to hear it. Thank you, Ezekiel."

"Zeke," I softly remind her. "Just Zeke." Aurelia gives me an inquisitive look. "You aren't the only one who feels as if their identity was stolen from them," I whisper. After another pause, I add, "My brother called me Ezekiel. He preferred formality when it suited him."

Tatum preferred my proper name too.

It literally *hurts* to hear Aurelia say my name, but sometimes, it feels healing too. Like the pain that briefly comes when you reset a broken bone or the stabbing, burning feeling of having your flesh sown back together.

Each time I feel myself being pulled into her orbit, I run screaming in the opposite direction.

But not this time.

Aurelia's the sun, a flaming star, and all I want to do is revolve around her, but I know that if I get too close, I'll burn.

Is that why Seth calls her Sunshine? Did he feel it too? Obviously, he hadn't wasted any time resisting her lure, but Seth is green. Like Icarus he ignored the warnings because he doesn't know how it feels to have your heart torn out of your chest and shredded by the only person you trusted it with.

Or maybe he does.

I know Seth is still there, but he won't let me feel him. He won't talk to me either. Khalil and Thorin said that Seth and Aurelia were alone at the time of the attack. What if he didn't tell them everything? What if she's hiding something?

Aurelia sighs, but the sound isn't quite right. It sounds more like a shudder, like someone shedding a paroxysm of pain or fighting the urge to cry. It's something she has a habit of doing whenever

I'm around. Begrudgingly, I can admit that it's one of the reasons I stay away. I know my presence is only causing her anguish. But then she asked me—no, *dared* me to stop running and for some fucking reason, I didn't want to disappoint.

"You okay?"

"What?" Like a startled doe, her head swings toward me, and her red eyes are glistening and wide, but no tears have fallen. Her light brown skin is flushed, and she looks moments from shattering. She's beautiful. "Yeah, I'm-I'm fine. I think I'm allergic to the pollen."

She walks faster until we're no longer keeping pace with each other, and even though my skin is suddenly pulling tight with the urge to chase after her, I let Aurelia have her space.

"If you say so," I quietly respond as I stop at the edge of the glade and watch her rush inside the cabin. She disappears from sight, and I tell myself to go. She's safe. She's home. There's no reason for me to follow her inside. It's reckless to think she'd welcome my company or that any good could come from staying with her a little while longer.

I return to the lake with Khalil and Thorin.

CHAPTER THIRTEEN

THORIN

"Ugh!" Aurelia shouts. "This is useless. I'm never going to catch anything."

It's just before sunrise, and the three of us—Zeke, Aurelia, and me—are standing in the shallow waters of a wide river, waders on, fishing rod in hand, and net at the ready. "Because you lack patience," I tell her.

"Exactly," my wolf agrees. She then sends me an accusatory look. "I thought you said fishing was fun?"

I sigh. "Only if you have patience."

Aurelia grumbles but doesn't bother arguing. She knows herself and owns up to it, one of the many qualities I admire about her. Instead, her gaze travels over to Zeke, who is standing as far away from us as he can get. "Why do you think he came?" Her tone suggests she's not bothered by it. She's curious.

"To keep an eye on us probably."

"But why is he so far away if he wants to babysit us?"

"Don't know. Could be that he's worried your incessant complaining will scare the trout away."

"Is that your way of telling me to shut up?"

"Is that the way you heard it, wolf?"

Aurelia responds by letting out a roar. She runs forward with her arms up, stomping through the shallow water. She makes a few circles around me for good measure before ending her petty rampage with a beaming smile.

"There you go. I got them riled up for you. Gooooo trout!" She pumps her arm in the air like a cheerleader before sauntering past me.

My hand is moving before I can even think about it, and I put everything I have into the strike, ensuring she feels it even through the Gore-Tex of her waders.

"Ow!" Aurelia yelps before rubbing the sting from her ass.

"Brat."

"Creep," she volleys back.

I watch her go to make sure she makes it to the riverbank safely despite it only being ten feet away, and then I wade over to Zeke since my spot is blown.

"What was that about?" he asks the moment I'm within earshot.

"She wants to be fucked," I answer plainly. "And soon."

"Odd way to go about it."

I feel my smile when I answer, "Not the way we do it."

Zeke doesn't respond, and I recast my line. Within minutes, I have a bite and use my net to secure it before releasing the fat trout from the line. Feeling smug, I look back toward the riverbank to show Aurelia and find it empty.

"What the fuck? Where the fuck did she go?"

"Who?" Zeke asks absently as he secures his own catch.

"The tooth fairy, Zeke. Who else?" I wade back to the bank and toss my trout into the cooler full of ice with the others before peering through the trees. "Aurelia!"

"She left these behind." I didn't even realize Zeke had followed me out of the river. I follow his voice and see him holding up Aurelia's waders. "Maybe nature called."

"Her pack and bow are gone."

Zeke tries to act like he's not interested in where she could have gone or why, but in the end, his curiosity and distrust of Aurelia win him over. "Well, you're a hunter, aren't you? So *hunt*. We can come back for this shit later." He drops the waders, sheds his own, and then grabs his pack.

I do the same, and then we're off, but we don't make it more than a few feet before I stop and swear viciously.

"Problem?"

"Aurelia's hidden her tracks."

Zeke's brows shoot up. "She can do that?"

"I've been teaching her," I say through gritted teeth.

"Yeah, seems like a good idea."

"Can you not be a dick about this for two seconds?"

"Maybe you should ask yourself why you don't like being reminded that she could be playing you."

I grab Zeke's shirt and shove him against the nearest tree, keeping him pinned there with my forearm against his throat. "Because I don't fucking appreciate another man trying to tell me about *my* girl. Make this the last time I warn you, Ezekiel."

"But she's not just yours, is she? She's Khalil's too, and judging by the way she pines for me day and night, I'm guessing I could have her if I wanted. She's mine too, Thorin. I bet that's what's really eating you. I don't even have to want her and she'll crawl for me."

"What the hell is wrong with you?" I roar in his face.

Zeke shoves me off him, and it's equal parts reflex and rage that makes me swing. My fist connects with his jaw, snapping his head to the side and sending spit and blood flying. Zeke recovers quickly and throws one of his own that barely grazes my chin before he tackles me to the ground. He punches my temple at the same time I throw a vicious jab into his ribs. We roll and then he's on the bottom but the fucker bites me and then we're rolling again, striking wherever we can as we roll and roll and roll.

I'm on top when I hear a throat clearing.

The sound stops me mid-punch, and I look up to see Aurelia standing ten feet away with her hands on her hips. "The game was for you both to find me, not fight over me. *You're playing it wrong.*"

Zeke and I shove away from each other and stand. The genuinely ruffled look on Zeke's face at being caught coming undone is a thousand times more satisfying than any punch I could throw.

He scoffs as if the notion is ridiculous. "We weren't fighting over you."

Aurelia gives him one of those slow withering looks that starts from his feet and ends when her gaze meets his. I don't even try to hide my grin. "Looked like it. Sounded like it too."

"What did you hear?"

Her now blank gaze remains on Zeke when she answers, "Enough."

For a moment he actually looks like he wants to apologize, but his stubbornness gets the best of him and he closes his mouth at the last moment and looks away. It's Aurelia's turn to scoff, and when she takes a step forward, she winces. It's the first time I notice she has a skinned knee.

"What happened? Where did you go?"

"Up there." She points to a large tree with a thick trunk. None of the branches are low-hanging and are pretty far apart, meaning it would have taken incredible skill to get up there. It's also the tree I shoved Zeke against before our fight.

"Impressive."

"I know."

"Come here, songbird. Let me look at that knee." I direct her over to one of the fallen logs, and she takes a seat while I crouch in front of her and dig through my bag.

"Exactly how many pet names does one person need?" Zeke grumbles.

"Why do you ask?" Aurelia immediately retorts with a narrowed gaze. "Jealous you missed out on all the good ones or upset that you're not man enough to use yours around your friends?"

"Shrew?"

Aurelia tosses back her head and laughs. "Nice. Very nice. Did you come up with that on your own or did you have help?" She lifts a brow.

Zeke is too stunned to respond when he realizes she means Seth, and I know it's because Khalil and I have always treated his DID with kid gloves. But not Aurelia. That's when I realize that something's shifted between them.

Aurelia is no longer playing nice.

Neither of them are.

It's…interesting.

Mostly I'm just happy as fuck to watch Zeke look like he's been hit in the face with a fucking blender. He's been acting like a real bastard lately, and my patience is wearing thin.

Apparently, I'm not the only one, since Aurelia is baring her claws once again.

I cough to cover up my laugh, but I lose control of it and a snarl directed at me rips from Zeke's throat.

"Don't," he snaps before storming off into the thicker copse of trees.

Aurelia watches him go until he disappears from sight, and then her nose wrinkles like it always does when she's deeply frustrated. "What's his problem? He started it."

"And you finished it," I remind her gently. I'm proud of Aurelia for holding her own, even though it's probably driven this tenuous tolerance they have of each other a few bars lower. "Just… Try not to take it too personally. He can't help but look at you and see Tatum. He thinks he's protecting Khalil and me. *And you*…believe it or not."

Because Zeke isn't just afraid of whatever Aurelia might be plotting. He's also afraid of our reaction if it turns out to be true. Khalil and I don't carry that fear because we know her feelings are as real as ours.

Aurelia sighs, and her shoulders drop as she deflates. "Yeah, I know," she says remorsefully and then in a blink, her claws are back. "But just so you both know… That Tatum excuse is getting really old, don't you think?"

Pulling out my first aid kit, I pop it open and sigh with a nod. "Yeah. I do."

Aurelia is quiet as I clean and bandage her cut, and though I can feel the weight of her thoughts growing, I patiently wait until she's ready to voice them.

"How can you be sure he'll come around? And what if he doesn't? This is where he feels safe, Thorin. I…I can't help but wonder if I've taken that away from him. I've done a lot that I regret, but sometimes, I feel like being here and falling in love with Zeke's friends *and* his alter is the most monstrous thing I've done."

"She finally admits it," I grumble.

"What?" Aurelia sniffs and blinks down at me in confusion, and it's clear she doesn't even realize all of what she confessed.

"I said Zeke fell in love with you once, wolf. He can do it again."

Aurelia huffs a breath. "That was *Seth*. You said they're not the same."

"In a way, they are. To some degree Seth, Zeke, and Bane are one and the same. The alters manifested because Zeke needed a way to cope with what was happening to him without causing further damage, right?"

"Uh…yes?"

"He doesn't just use Seth and Bane to escape further trauma. He also uses them to compartmentalize his emotions. There's a reason Seth doesn't ever really get sad or angry. It's because those aren't emotions he's familiar with."

"Before Seth and I were ambushed in the dell, he thought I was running and he got really upset but his voice… It didn't sound like him."

"Because it was Bane. Seth was losing control because he didn't know how to handle his anger." I don't tell Aurelia that his fierce need to protect her was the only reason Seth was able to overcome those emotions and keep Bane at bay. I don't want to risk giving Aurelia a false sense of security when it comes to Bane. Keeping him from manifesting is like stopping a runaway train. It can only end with derailing.

"What are you trying to say, Thorin?"

"It was Zeke who found you in our cabin. It was Zeke who saw you first. He could have woken either alter if he thought you were a real threat, but he chose Seth. Why?"

"I thought Zeke had to be in mortal danger for Bane to wake up?"

I shake my head. "That's how he loses control of Bane, but he can wake him up at any moment, songbird."

"Oh." She seems to pale a little. "Well, then I don't know why he didn't," she admits in a small voice.

"Yes, you do."

She huffs in frustration. "You're saying Zeke somehow fell in love with me with one look but couldn't handle it, so he used Seth to let himself feel everything he was too afraid to feel?"

"It's possible."

"No offense, Thorin, but that sounds like a load of baloney."

I let out a low laugh. "Just wait. You'll see." I toss the bloodied gauze in a Ziploc bag, clean my hands, and pack up my first aid kit before standing.

"And in the meantime?" She speaks so quietly that I almost don't hear the question. Aurelia's gaze is on her lap and I lift her chin so her expressive, brown eyes are on mine. Right now, they're full of longing, worry, and confusion. And hope. Hope that I'm right.

"In the meantime, you keep giving him hell, wolf." I take her hand and help her stand. "Zeke already can't take his eyes off you. Be yourself and you can be sure he won't be able to take his mind off you either."

"I never pegged you for a matchmaker, Thorin Thayer."

I let my lips brush her temple. "I promised I'd take care of you."

"I don't want to confuse him into being with me, Thorin. Just because Seth likes me doesn't mean Zeke has to."

"I know that. And you won't have to. Zeke will come running all on his own, pretty girl."

"You promise?"

"Damn straight." I kiss her forehead and then tip my head back to glare up at the tree she climbed. "Now tell me how you got up that tree. I didn't teach you that."

"No, this lovely thing called a childhood did."

I grunt. "Smart-ass."

"My parents actually had a tree like this one in our front yard. It was taller than our house and had branches big enough to fit a treehouse. My father started building me one before he died but never finished. He'd been working on that thing for over four years, and I didn't have the heart to tell him I was too old for a treehouse by the time he was almost done."

"Are you rambling, Aurelia?"

She makes a choking sound at being caught. "Yes."

"What's on your mind? Tell me."

"You."

Grinning, I dip my head to run my nose along her neck. *Fuck, she smells good.* "Me?"

"Mm-hmm."

"What are you thinking about?" I purr as she runs her hands across my stomach.

"That you look nice today."

"Only nice?"

"Handsome," she amends.

My hands encircle her waist while my thumbs sweep her lower belly. "How handsome?"

"Hot handsome."

"Stop," I plead playfully. "I'll blush."

"You don't blush," she accuses with a grumble.

"I'll blush for *you*, songbird."

"Why for me?"

"Because you are the best and most terrifying thing that's ever happened to us."

Aurelia grins and winks. "Back at you, Thorny baby."

"No."

Her brown eyes light up with delight at my horrified shudder. "Yes," she insists sadistically.

"You are not calling me *Thorny*."

She snorts. "He says thornily."

"*Wolf*," I growl in warning.

"Let's make a deal," she returns unperturbed. "Take me home right now so you can come for me, and I won't call you Thorny."

A twig snaps and my head rises. I search the direction the sound comes from for Zeke. I taught him better than that so if I'm hearing him, it's because he wants me to. He appears in my line of sight a few seconds later, and I use the thirty feet or so that I have to kiss my girl.

Aurelia gets a little carried away though and tries to whip my damn dick out. Zeke walks up on us while Aurelia is wrist deep in my jeans and I'm half-heartedly fighting her off.

"I'm going to have to take a rain check, baby. We have company."

"So what?" Aurelia returns as she kisses a hot trail up my neck. "He's watched us before."

What the fuck? My eyes travel to Zeke's, silently asking when, but he doesn't answer and ignores us, heading back to the riverbank to retrieve our things.

"See?" Aurelia pleads. "He's gone now, and I've changed my mind. I want you to fuck me right here."

I stare at her warily. "What the fuck's gotten into you?"

There's something wild and desperate in her eyes that isn't fueled by lust. "Clearly not you, Thayer. Are we doing this or not?"

"Not." I force her hand away from my dick.

"I can convince you, you know."

My grin is full-blown as I stare down at her. She's so cute. "Can you? Well, in that case, you're welcome to try."

Her nostrils flare. "I hate you."

"That's not what you said earlier."

"I don't know what you're talking about," she lies. "And even if I did, you haven't told me you love me either."

"Haven't I?"

Her gaze narrows to slits. "Saying it when I'm asleep and can't hear you doesn't count, Thorin."

"I guess we're both cowards then."

"That's all I'm saying, dude."

Aurelia's the first to lose her composure and snorts out a laugh while I chuckle. We're still laughing when Zeke returns with the cooler and our waders.

"Oh, thank fuck," he breathes. Aurelia and I give him a questioning look. "I thought I was going to have to see Thorin's pasty ass again."

I flip him off and then grab Aurelia's hand. "Come on. We're going home."

Aurelia tugs against my hold. "Not yet. I want to check on Meera," she announces.

"Meera?"

Aurelia flicks her gaze toward Zeke, who posed the question, but she's too angry with him to hold it. "My friend. Sort of."

"She's a *wolf*, songbird. A wild animal. She can take care of herself. And her pups."

"Fine. I have my bow. I'll go myself."

She starts to walk away when I catch her neck and use my hold to tilt her head back with my thumb pressed under her chin. "You are trying my patience," I warn calmly.

My little wolf smiles a little. "I know."

CHAPTER FOURTEEN

AURELIA

S he moved it," I announce in disappointment. "She moved her den."

"Of course she did," Zeke responds, sounding a little too pleased with my disappointment. "Didn't you say it was a bear that did this?" He gestures to the destroyed den that Thorin is currently crouched in front of.

"Yeah."

"It was likely a rogue male," Thorin says as he inspects the den. "This is his territory now. The she-wolf will want to take her pups somewhere safer."

Oh. Well, I guess that makes sense. "You can track her, can't you? Where would she go?"

Thorin stands and comes closer until he's standing right in front of me.

Weirdly, Zeke is the one who doesn't seem to want to leave my side. He's been hovering ever since we left the river. He probably thinks I'm leading them into a trap and his proximity to me will lessen the chances of it working.

"Songbird, the last thing we'll want to do is disturb her and force her to move her pups again."

"I understand. She doesn't have to know we're there, and I promise I'll do whatever you say. I won't make noise. I'll stay downwind. I just want to make sure they're okay."

"Why is this so important to you?" Zeke asks in that word-vomit way that tells me he didn't really mean to.

"I told you," I say without meeting his gaze. "She's my friend."

"Khalil and Thorin must be sore company if you're befriending the wildlife. You should know it's one-sided, Aurelia. The she-wolf is a wild animal. She can't be tamed."

"You didn't think so when you pet her."

"I…" He blanches. "*What?*"

"Technically, Seth did. I wasn't there, but Khalil and Thorin told me all about it. To be honest, I still think they're making it up. Care to humor me with a replay?"

Zeke recovers from his shock and sneers at me, but it lacks conviction. "Hoping I lose a hand?"

"Don't be silly, rabbit. I'm not unreasonable. A couple of fingers will do."

Zeke's lips part, and I brace myself for whatever vitriol he feels I've earned this time. Fortunately, Thorin interrupts before he can. "If you two are done flirting, we should get moving."

"We're not flirting," Zeke and I deny at the same time.

"Let's go," he orders again.

Thorin leads the way, and it takes us two hours before we finally track Meera's den to a small cave halfway between Big Bear and Maia. The cave is burrowed into the sidewall of a dried riverbed. The mouth of the den is small, though, making it impossible for a human to enter unless they're on their bellies.

Of course, Thorin won't let me anywhere near it.

He only allows me close enough to spot the pups playing outside of the cave while Meera devours a gray hare soaked in blood.

"So that's Meera," Zeke says as he studies the tawny wolf.

"Yup." I grin.

"She's beautiful."

"Isn't she?" I squeal like a proud mama.

Thorin gives me a sharp look in reprimand, and I wince and lower my voice. "Sorry. Can she see us?" The three of us are lying on our bellies on the much higher elevated side of the riverbed.

"Not at the moment, but she'll hear us if we're not careful. We're downwind, so as long as we stay quiet, we should be fine."

As if fate had other plans, Zeke's radio crackles and then Khalil's deep voice comes through with a boom. "Hello? Hello? Zeke. Zeke! If you're getting this, pick up!"

Across the dried riverbed, Meera raises her head. Her warning growl is faint when it reaches my ears, but it still raises the hair on my nape all the same.

"Shit," Zeke swears before crawling away to keep from giving away our position. I watch over my shoulder as he stands when he gets far enough and unclips the radio attached to the back of his jeans.

I'm reluctant to leave Meera's den behind, but my worry for Khalil wins out when I remember that we left him alone this morning. I cast one last longing look at Meera, who's standing now and staring in our direction but not seeing us. Her hackles are clearly raised, so the best thing I can do for Meera and her pups now is to leave them be.

The guys are right. Meera is an unusual wolf but a wild one all the same. She's a predator who won't hesitate to rip out my throat. I have to either trust that she can take care of herself or…

I gulp.

Let nature take its course.

Up ahead, Zeke presses the receiver button while Thorin and I catch up. "Khalil?"

"Goddamn," Khalil immediately fusses. "Where the fuck y'all at? You were supposed to be back hours ago."

"We went sightseeing, asshole. What do you want?"

The radio is quiet for a few seconds before Khalil finally answers in a more subdued and curious tone. "Is Aurelia okay?"

Zeke rolls his eyes and presses the receiver with a quick glance my way that at the last minute becomes searching as if he's assuring himself of his answer. "She's fine," he offers curtly. He lets the receiver go and then he presses it again. "Thorin and I are fine too. Thanks for asking."

"Look, I ain't ask you about all that," Khalil immediately retorts. "Let me talk to my baby."

Zeke hands me the radio, and I reach out to take it. There's a brief moment when our fingers graze, and it feels as if my entire body has been electrified by that small, accidental touch.

I don't have to question if he felt it too.

Zeke snatches his hand back so quickly someone might think he'd actually been electrocuted. Cursing to himself, he avoids further eye contact as he stomps off. His mood swings are really starting to piss me off.

I press the receiver. "Hello?"

"Hey, Goldilocks. Where are you? Where did you go?"

"To find Meera's new den." I grin again. "Her pups are getting big."

"What is it with you and this wolf? She's a wild animal, Goldilocks."

I huff. "So everyone keeps reminding me." It's not like I'm trying to domesticate her. Jeez.

"You're on your way back now?"

"Yeah."

"Cool. See you back at the cabin, Goldilocks. And hurry up. I miss you."

Zeke looks back at me at the same time I feel my smile widen. "You wouldn't have to miss me if you had come with us like I begged you to."

"Fishing? Nah. That shit is boring."

"Thank you!" I shoot Thorin, who's walking a few feet away, a smug look. Hearing me, but not looking away from his constant scan for threats, he flips me off.

Khalil is saying something else on the radio, but I don't hear a word of it because in my peripheral vision, Zeke has gone deathly still. He was leading the way home, but now he's facing me and his green eyes are full of panic.

A moment later, there's a low growl that comes from my left. Fear melts into my bones, and I wish that I could evaporate too. Better than being torn apart by whatever made that sound.

"Aurelia, don't move," Thorin warns.

"Really? Because I was leaning strongly toward running for my life." Another low growl reaches me from another direction, and my voice trembles when I ask, "Wolves?"

Why is it always wolves? I swear they're drawn to me like flies to shit.

"It's not Meera."

"Does that really matter?" I hiss. All around us twigs snap as the brush is disturbed by the padding of multiple sets of paws. Two more wolves finally come into view and... Fuck, they're huge. Bigger than Meera. A shuddering breath escapes me. "What do we do?" I whisper-yell.

"Try not to look appetizing?" Zeke suggests like he's bored.

"Oooh, I don't like the way that one is looking at meeee," I squeal as I point toward a black wolf. He snarls and snaps at me, and I flinch, yanking my hand back.

I'm vaguely aware of Khalil screaming my name over the radio.

"Aurelia, back toward me slowly, baby. Do *not* run."

I don't immediately do as Thorin orders because terror has me rooted to the spot. My gaze shifts to Zeke, who's farthest away, wanting to see for myself that he's still in one piece.

"No," he immediately scolds, sensing more than seeing my gaze on him. He's staring down a brown wolf with a missing eye. Oddly, I think of Meera's pups, wondering if this wolf or one of the others could be the father. I thought Meera was a lone wolf, but maybe not. "Keep eye contact. Make yourself appear as big as possible."

Thinking of a bear standing on its hind legs, my arms immediately shoot into the air, and I take big stomping steps backward to Thorin.

The punchline: it actually works.

The black wolf that was eyeing me like fresh lamb chops suddenly looks unsure as it whines and looks at one of the others. Zeke breaks his own rule and glances at me, making a strangled sound that sounds suspiciously like choking back a laugh when he catches sight of my ridiculous movements.

Seriously? Who laughs when only seconds away from being torn apart?

I'm reminded of Seth, but there's no room for longing when I'm this close to death. I take another exaggerated step, and then I feel Thorin grab my shirt, tugging me the rest of the way. The drooling, gray wolf that wants Thorin *bad* growls again. He must be hungry because a second later, he looks as if he's about to go for it and leap.

Sensing this too, Thorin curses and releases me as suddenly as he grabbed me.

I assume he's going to do something stupid like try to fight the wolf, but he starts yelling and beating his chest like he's King Kong. Catching on, Zeke and I join him. We jump up and down, clapping, stomping, and screaming at the top of our lungs.

After what feels like forever, the gray wolf howls, and the three of them run off.

"Whew," I exclaim as soon as it feels safe enough to do so. I don't have to mock wiping the sweat from my brow. My entire body is soaked in it. "That was a close one, am I right? It's a good thing I suggested that walk, huh?"

Thorin and Zeke both throw me vicious glares.

"Is this what you wanted, Goldilocks? Is that what you wanted to feel?"

"Yes," I answer Khalil while strangling Thorin's sheets in my fists. Thorin's fucking my ass from below while Khalil pounds my pussy between my thighs. I'm in heaven. "I want it."

I'm trying to be quiet. I'm trying to be good.

Zeke is somewhere in the cabin, and I can't help but mourn how empty my mouth feels.

But Zeke isn't Seth.

The three of us returned to the cabin less than an hour ago. I'd barely gotten through the door before Khalil was on my ass wanting to know what happened. I told him about the wolves. He was angry at me for being so reckless and pissed at Thorin for being so indulgent. The two of them turned on each other while Zeke silently looked on, ready to blame me for it all.

Khalil ended up tearing the clothes from my body so that he could see for himself that I wasn't hurt. But all that had done was remind me that I'm horny. And now naked too. One thing led to another and…

"I think Khalil is ready to come," Thorin whispers in my ear while thrusting so deeply my eyes cross. "Where does it go, songbird?"

I stare at Khalil from under my lashes as I say, "Inside me."

"So tell him," Thorin urges while he uses my body like he uses his fist. "Tell Khalil you want his cum."

"I–I w-want you to come in-inside me."

Khalil makes a rough, cruel sound that sends goose bumps down my flushed skin, and I know he's about to deny me. "Only good girls get my cum inside their pussy. Have you been a good girl, Goldilocks?"

"No. Never." Khalil groans, his pace increasing, and I whine because it's too good. "You're not…making it…easy…to be… quiet."

Thorin pulls my hair in a vicious tug while Khalil wraps a hand around my throat. Their hold is possessive and sends a hot flare shooting from my chest down to my stomach. "*So don't be,*" Khalil purrs against the flushed skin over my sternum.

Not as daring as them, I keep my lips smashed firmly together and true to their nature, Thorin and Khalil see it as a challenge. Khalil captures one of my sensitive nipples between his teeth, serving a bite of pain while Thorin tugs on the other from below, slapping the side of my breast every so often before gripping it possessively.

They work together to make me scream so that their best friend, wherever he's hiding in the cabin, will hear. And Khalil and Thorin will take it as far as they need to—as far as I can handle—in order to stake their claim.

It happens a moment later, when Thorin's and Khalil's rhythm changes and they plunge deep inside me at the same time. The move steals my breath and then returns it with a scream that signals their triumph and leaves me shaken.

Not wanting to come yet, Khalil pulls out and grips the base of his dick before slapping the heavy length against my abused pussy lips. He becomes entranced with the sight as he uses the glistening, angry-looking head to tease my clit. Khalil slips down through my swollen slit and back again. My lashes flutter when he does this a few more times until his next downstroke strays too far and his thick head accidentally meets Thorin's tunneling length and becomes lodged there.

I moan at the sight, and Khalil smirks at me. He frees his dick and shoves inside me again before my desires can twist into new forbidden wants.

It should be impossible for both of them to fit inside me, and I secretly love that they give me no choice but to take it. A huge part of what draws me to them is their unrelenting brutality. It makes my twisted heart feel like I'm not alone in the darkness that sweeps me up when I'm most vulnerable. My mountain men never hesitate to step into it with me.

They use me, push me, and sometimes hurt me, but they're always right there, falling apart with me.

"Fuck, Aurelia." Thorin sounds close and when he takes over the rhythm, Khalil and I have no choice but to follow. It would be easier to stop a team of racing horses.

He makes it impossible to hold in what they do to me.

Cries escape my lips in small bursts that I desperately try to swallow, but Khalil and Thorin aren't having it. They're watching me closely and noting every ounce of resistance from me before adjusting the angle, depth, and speed of their thrusts until those little cries turn into screams.

They *want* me to scream.

They *want* Ezekiel to hear me. They want him to know just how brutally they use me and how much I crave it. I don't *hate* the idea even though I know I'll regret it once I have to face Zeke again.

Right now, my lips are falling open and my screams barrel

through, mixing with their grunts and groans and the sound of our sweat-slicked skin slapping.

When my orgasm hits, it's almost surprising since I didn't expect them to let me come. My pussy clamps down on Khalil without warning and almost immediately, I feel his dick began to jerk inside me. I hear Thorin's mumbled curses and know he must feel it too through the thin wall that separates them.

Keeping his promise, Khalil pulls out with a hiss and gives his thick length a few furious strokes before he groans and his dick begins to spit up. The first spurt of cum lands on my jaw, the second and third on my chest and stomach, and the last on my thigh. Thorin is right behind him, slamming into me one final time before he comes with a grunt that vibrates his chest.

It's so good. I want to cry, but I know I can't.

Losing Seth was a temporary seal on whatever's broken in me, but now the part of me that allows me to cry is fracturing again, and the devastation that it may never heal again bowls over me.

The bead of sweat I feel slowly running down my sternum catches Khalil's eye and he pauses. One of his hands leaves the back of my thigh, and he thumbs the wetness. He studies the drop for a moment before he does something I don't expect.

With a tender look to his face, Khalil brings his wet thumb to my face, and he drags it down one cheek before doing the same to the other. He collects more drops of sweat and repeats the action until the gathered wetness begins rolling down my cheek. I realize with the force of a punch to the gut what he's doing.

Tears.

Khalil is giving me tears.

Involuntarily, I lift my wobbling chin, and Khalil grants my silent request, craning his neck to kiss me tenderly. The kiss lasts long enough for my fake tears to join the tangle of our tongues, and

I taste the salty sweetness. Behind me, Thorin rises to kiss my nape, shoulder, and back. Anywhere he can reach to soothe these cracks.

Khalil ends the kiss a moment later.

"Better, Goldilocks?"

"Yes," I answer shyly. I feel a little ashamed, but I keep it to myself, knowing my mountain men wouldn't welcome me feeling that emotion for any reason. It's even more obvious to me now that they are extremely protective of my feelings. "Thank you."

"You don't ever have to thank me for that."

Just as I feel this overwhelming sense of gratitude welling until it feels like I really might cry, Khalil slaps my breasts hard enough to leave a red handprint and those sharp edges of my mountain men return.

Once again, I realize belatedly that they aren't done with me.

Khalil carefully lifts me up, freeing me from Thorin's softened cock before he throws me down on my tummy next to Thor. I barely have time to lift my head from the rumpled blankets before Khalil is on top of me, shoving my thighs apart with his knee and entering me fully with one stroke.

I'm trapped between his hard body and the mattress while he batters my sore pussy a second time. When I start to wiggle and struggle, Khalil growls and bites my shoulder to make sure I can't escape this second claiming.

I think I black out, but I'm sure that bastard kept going.

I don't mind. I've already confessed I'm into it and promised to let him know the moment that changed. When I come to, Khalil and I are alone. His cock is tucked away, and he's dozing next to me. Thorin walks into the room a second later with a glass of water filled to the rim in hand. I sit up expectantly, knowing it's for me, and he hands me the glass before perching on the edge of the bed where he watches to make sure I drink it all.

Once I'm hydrated, Khalil scoops me up, leaving me to wonder if he was ever really asleep. He brushes his lips across my forehead as he carries me inside the bathroom. I'm silent and contemplating passing out again as he turns on the shower and steps inside before setting me on my feet. Thorin doesn't join us since the shower is too small. Just Khalil and I together is a tight fit with his shoulders alone nearly taking up the entire width.

Sensing that I'm sapped of energy, Khalil makes quick work of cleaning us both up while I stand there uselessly with the back of my head resting against his chest and my eyes struggling to stay open. Khalil doesn't seem to mind even when he remarks to himself that they're spoiling me.

Once we're both clean and out of the shower, Khalil dries me off and grabs the lotion from the counter when I grumble about dry skin. He walks me out of the bathroom after I'm properly moisturized, and we fall into Thorin's bed again.

Thorin wordlessly retreats into the bathroom, and I hear the shower turn on again while Khalil arranges me on top of him just like Thorin usually does since they know how much I detest the hardness of Thorin's mattress. He rubs and massages my butt with his big, capable hands and before long, I'm drifting off to the sound of his strong heartbeat.

When I wake up, Khalil is gone, and it's just Thorin and me in his bed together. I stretch and groan at the ache already settling into my muscles. I don't miss the dull throb between my thighs either.

"Thorin." When he doesn't answer, I reach over and shake his shoulder until his breathing changes, signaling that he's waking.

"Wolf," he finally answers with a tired grumble. He immediately reaches for me, and once I'm within grabbing distance, he pulls me into his side where I rest my cheek on his lower pec.

"We've got to talk about getting you a new mattress," I complain. "I don't think I can take sleeping on a slab of stone for much longer."

"Feels good to me," he slurs in that way that says he's already falling asleep again. A grin nearly breaks free at knowing I wore him out just as much as he'd done me.

"Clearly you've never slept on a cloud before."

Thorin doesn't answer. Feeling restless despite the thorough fucking he and Khalil gave me, I roll over in the safety of Thorin's arms and look out the window. The position of the sun though has me frowning as I reach for Thorin's wrist and glance at his watch.

It's after four.

Shit.

Sheriff Kelly will be expecting me to check in soon. His conditions for me returning to the cabin were clear. I have to radio him at the station every day before the end of his shift or he'll be back here in force to *rescue* me.

For good reason, I haven't told the guys. They'll only see the sheriff's misguided determination to save me as a threat to their ownership of me. I don't want the sheriff harmed. I don't want to tear myself open again to live with that guilt, and I don't want my guys doing so either.

I let go of Thorin's wrist, and his arm falls back to the bed like deadweight. It's all the confirmation I need that Thorin is asleep again before I quietly crawl from the bed and grab my robe. Feeling right at home in the cabin, I don't bother to tie the sash as I leave Thorin's room.

I immediately regret it once I reach the switchback stairs that lead down to the den.

Zeke is coming up the stairs, and he's wearing dark blue basketball shorts, *no* shirt, and headphones. There's an old iPod in his hand, and even though it looks ancient as fuck, I'm actually impressed.

Our eye contact is brief before his gaze drops.

I feel my nipples tighten the moment his green eyes land on the inner curve of my breasts peeking through the robe panels. All too soon his focus is shifting again, over the swell of my belly and then between my thighs. It feels clinical more than appreciative, so I quickly tie my robe to remind myself that he isn't interested and clear my throat.

Zeke's gaze snaps up to meet mine.

"Hoping to jog your memory?"

"Something like that," he mumbles as he starts walking again. He's careful not to touch me as we pass on the stairs. Meanwhile, my body is already recalling our brief touch near Meera's den and wanting more.

"Well, at least I didn't make it weird!" I retort as I reach the landing. When he doesn't respond, I glance over my shoulder and catch him frozen in front of the front door.

He's glaring at my ass like it's personally wronged him in some way. If I were less confident, I'd feel self-conscious, but I know my ass is amazing, so I wiggle it a little and it snaps him out of whatever the hell is going on in that head of his.

Zeke meets my gaze, and his frown deepens at the same time his grip on the door handle tightens. But in a blink, the reaction is a mere memory. Or maybe I imagined it. "If they ask, tell them I've gone running, will you? I should be back in a couple of hours."

"Sure." With a curt nod in thanks, Zeke opens the door and starts to leave. I feel my heart leap inside my chest when I can't stop the words already forming on my tongue. "Wait!" To both of our surprise, he does. "Can I come?"

His green eyes flare. "What?"

"R-running. Um…" My hands are shaking. Why are my hands shaking? "Khalil is teaching me how to defend myself, but he wants me to improve my stamina first. The only problem is that he was a professional athlete and I'm not." Some of the suspicion leaves Zeke's eyes, and he actually looks amused when he snorts. "I'm serious. The man's gone mad. You have to help me."

"Yeah, there's a reason Thorin and I work out alone. Khalil can be intense."

"I think sadist is more accurate."

Zeke's lips twitch, and my eyes are drawn to them, remembering the way they felt when he kissed me. Seth wasn't as practiced, but he learned quickly how to melt my bones from one kiss.

Would Zeke? I'm sure he knows how to kiss, but would it feel the same or earth-shattering in another way?

"Yes," he answers before I can think about the answer too hard. "You can come."

"I only need twenty minutes."

"You have ten," he says just to be a dick. Zeke's gone before I can say something to mess up this tenuous truce of ours, so I hurry downstairs to the basement.

There's a lot of noise coming from behind the closed door of Zeke's room. Khalil must be in there working on the new bed. It was meant for me, but now that Zeke is awake, it's only right he has his room back.

Maybe if he's willing, we can share it.

Not together. Obviously. We can alternate nights, or Zeke can use it whenever I sleep in Khalil's or Thorin's bed, which is often considering the two of them act like it's impossible for them to sleep without me now.

Seth will wake up, and though I don't wish to see Zeke in pain, I know it's inevitable. In fact, it's all Khalil and Thorin tell me when I ask about him. Seth will wake up soon.

Weirdly, they never sound as if they actually believe it, but I can't put my finger on why.

I radio the sheriff before hunting for clean clothes. It takes a while since I've been slacking in my "duties." Only the milkmaid dress is clean, but I obviously can't run in that.

After a full minute of internal back-and-forth, I finally decide to raid Seth/Zeke's clothes in Khalil's closet for some shorts and a T-shirt. I do manage to find a clean sports bra, so I quickly slip on the clothes and go hunting for my new trainers that Khalil got me from town a few weeks ago. It gives me goose bumps how he's always anticipating my needs before I'm even aware of them. When I open the box for the first time, I'm surprised to see a note tucked inside, and now I'm anxious and feeling guilty for not wearing my sneakers sooner if Khalil had left me some kind of love note.

Feeling my heart race with a thousand apologies for being the world's biggest bitch already forming in my head, I quickly pluck the note from inside and set the box aside. But when I unfold the single sheet of paper, I realize it's a letter, and it isn't from Khalil.

It's from Seth.

Sunshine,

If you're reading this, it means I'm sleeping now. With any luck, it's Zeke who's awake.

I'm so sorry for leaving you, Sunshine. You must be so confused and have a lot of questions that those assholes Zeke

calls friends won't answer. I know my Sunshine will get curious.
I want you to know that I'm okay with it. With you and Zeke.

But don't try to win him over by being nice. He won't buy
it, and that isn't you—

I pause reading and look up from the letter as if I'm going to find Seth standing in front of me so I can argue that I'm a fucking delight. Instead, I'm standing alone in the den with only the sound of Khalil hammering away behind the closed bedroom door. My heart seems to match the rhythm of the hammer, and this note is the nail piercing it.

Exhaling shakily, I go back to reading.

Tatum's got him all twisted up and no amount of tugging will
unravel that knot.

All he needs is you. Give him hell, baby.

I'll miss you.

—Seth

P.S. Oh, and if you're ever in trouble, just say CHRYSALIS to
make it stop.

My breath is caught in my chest by the time I finish reading the note.

What the hell, Seth?

I fold the note and tuck it back safely inside the box where I found it before slipping on my sneakers. After, I rush through the front door, five minutes late and half expecting to find Zeke gone.

Instead, I find him in the middle of a side lunge and waiting for me. His gaze is impatient when he looks over at me while continuing to stretch, and then something shifts in his gaze when he notices a moment later that I'm wearing Seth's clothes.

His clothes.

"Sorry. Laundry day." I tug at the hem of the T-shirt self-consciously. Seth loved when I wore his clothes. He practically preened when he caught me in one of his shirts.

But Zeke isn't Seth. I should have asked.

"It's fine," he answers curtly and then avoids my gaze. "You should probably stretch before we hit it."

"Umm…" My mind recalls the many ways Khalil and Thorin took turns twisting, bending, and folding me to their will. My abused muscles are still twinging from it. "I think I'm good."

"Let's go." Zeke takes off before I can ask him where we're running to. I'm left with no choice but to follow, staying a few steps behind him. He keeps the pace easy for the first mile, but the moment I find the courage to move up and run beside him, he starts running faster like he's trying to get away from me. I match his pace, and this cat-and-mouse game goes on for another mile until it feels as if I'm being dragged along by my stubborn pride rather than keeping up.

"He-ey," I croak out. "Can we…can we…take a…break?"

Zeke ignores me and keeps running. My vision becomes spotty while my head swims. There's a stitch in my side that shortens the length of my strides. I could just stop and let him run off, but I don't want a repeat of three weeks ago if I get lost. I know Thorin and Khalil still don't fully trust me and it's that shred of doubt that feeds Zeke's.

Until my men trust me completely, Zeke won't be able to trust me at all. Of course, they don't see it, and I'm too much of a coward to confront them about it.

I guess…I guess I don't fully trust them either.

When the death squad came for me, Thorin's solution was to pack us up and run again, but I can't live like that. Our cabin and these wilds feel like home. A life on the run is just another prison.

Something has to be done. About Isaac and my uncle.

But first, the four of us need to be on the same page. We need to be a team.

We need Zeke.

Spotting a rock small enough to fit inside my palm, I slow down just enough to swipe it from the ground and then I throw it at Zeke's retreating back before he's out of range. "Hey!" I yell as soon as it hits his right shoulder blade. "Asshole, I'm talking to you!"

He stops and turns to face me, his green eyes wide with shock. "Did you just throw a rock at me?"

I nod. "I did."

Zeke looks at me like I might do it again. "Why?"

"I need to rest."

"So rest."

He turns away like he's going to run off and leave me, so I grab a fistful of much smaller rocks this time and start throwing them like I'm playing Down the Clown at an arcade.

"Aaargh!" Zeke whips back around and starts ducking the little round missiles. "What the hell is your problem?"

"You!" I aim for his midsection, and the rock ricochets off his glistening abs. He doesn't even flinch. "You're my fucking problem, asshole." I throw another rock, and he swats it away.

"Oh, I see. We're away from my brothers now, so you finally drop the act."

"On the contrary. No one knows me better than them."

Zeke visibly revolts at the idea. It's like we're divorced and fighting over who gets the kids. His lip curls as his gaze narrows. The expression is the complete opposite of the adoration and obsession

I'm used to seeing even though the face it adorns is the same. "You're so full of shit."

"No. I'm just fed up with yours, Ezekiel."

He looks as if I'd slapped him. "I told you not to call me that."

"Oops."

"You're such a bitch," he says as his gaze sweeps my face and then my body. It feels suspiciously like he's checking me out—like he's seeing me for the first time. And his tone... It was filled with more heat than ice.

I'm stunned enough that I forget to respond.

I don't even notice that he's moving closer until Zeke seizes my wrist and twists it, forcing me to drop the remaining rocks in my palm. He then uses his hold to spin me around until my back is pressed to his sweaty chest, and he wraps an arm around my waist while he pins my arm at my lower back.

I can feel his breath skate along my cheek and his lips by my ear. But even more distracting is the long, hard ridge I can feel pressing into my trapped arm. "Let me make something clear to you, princesa. I am not yours. We are not in a relationship. This is not happening."

He's clearly rejecting me, so why does it feel like he just struck a match and lit my blood on fire? Confused and eager to get out of his hold before I do something embarrassing—like begging him to kiss me—I nod. "Okay."

"I am not Seth." He stalls like he wants the opposite. An excuse to keep me in his arms.

"I know that." A scoff that sounds more like a sob escapes my throat. "Don't you think I know that? How can I confuse you when you look at me like you hate me? Seth never did that."

Zeke spins me around but doesn't let me go far. He grips my upper arms and pulls me right back in until the front of our bodies are melded together and I can see the small brown flecks in his green eyes. "You look at me like I'm *him*," he accuses harshly. "Like you don't even see *me*. It drives me fucking crazy."

"I don't mean to. I just…" *I love him.* "I miss him." Zeke closes his eyes as if my confession pains him, and then he nods and exhales slowly. His breath still smells like the mint from his toothpaste mixed with citrus from the orange juice he drank earlier while listening to Khalil curse me out. On the other hand, I'm still falling apart at the seams. "Do you think—is there any way I can talk to him? Just for a minute?"

"No." My heart drops like a boulder, and Zeke releases me suddenly, moving away as if he's desperate for the distance. Moments ago, I could swear he wanted to kiss me. My lips are still tingling from that brief but suspiciously deliberate contact. "I'm sorry, Aurelia." He backs up another step while keeping his gaze on mine. "It's going to take a lot more than some pebbles thrown at me to force him out."

"No, that's not—"

"We should go."

Zeke starts running again, but I can't bring myself to follow, and he doesn't look back to make sure that I am. He disappears through the trees, and I take a moment to catch my breath.

What the fuck was that?

I think it's safe to say that Zeke has my head in a tailspin. He's hot one moment and ice cold the next.

I can't take it anymore.

This has to stop.

I look in the direction he's running and see him disappear over the hill. The guys must be rubbing off on me more than I thought because the instinct to give chase kicks in and I'm running before I realize it.

Fuck it.

When I reach the top of the hill, I stumble to a halt when I spot him at the base, looking as if he's waiting for me. I'm even more embarrassed that it was clear I was chasing him. By the time I reach him at the bottom of the hill, I'm more than ready for war.

"For the record," I seethe as I come to stand in front of him, "I never asked you to be with me, but it doesn't have to be this way either. We can be friends."

Zeke perks a brow while the rest of his face remains impassive. "No."

"No? What do you mean no? Why the hell not?"

"Because I don't trust a word that comes out of that pretty little mouth, princesa."

"See...*that*. There! Why do you say things like that?"

His green eyes turn challenging, and he takes a step closer. "Like what?"

I refuse to back down, but I can't deny my voice sounds unsure when I answer. "You said my mouth is pretty."

"So what?"

"Soooo... You don't say things like that to someone you *hate*. You say it if it's someone you want to...kiss." Zeke doesn't respond, but the knot in his throat bobs as if he just swallowed a really large pill. For some reason it gives me a false sense of confidence, and I inch forward. "Do you want to kiss me, Ezekiel?"

I expect him to deny it immediately. Instead, he stares at my mouth for a really long time before he rejects me. "No."

"Are you sure?" I inch a little closer, something like hope tightening inside my chest. "Not even one little kiss?" I decide to taunt. "It's just us. The others don't have to know."

"You want me to help you cheat on my brothers?"

I close the last bit of distance between us, and Zeke breaks first, stumbling in retreat. I take a page out of Thorin, Khalil, and Seth's book and I don't let him run. I chase. His back hits the huge tree behind him, and his green eyes flare wide when I boldly invade his space. When I place my hands on his shoulders and mold the front of my body against his, his eyes take on a glassy look. "It's complicated."

"It's really not," he returns dryly. And yet he's still staring at my mouth.

"You've kissed me before."

"Seth kissed you."

I roll my eyes. "Ta-may-toe, ta-mah-to."

Zeke swears. "You enjoy provoking me, don't you?"

"Yes, but only because you make it so easy." I breathe deeply when it doesn't feel like the whole truth and I begin pushing toward it. "And," I add reluctantly, "when I make you angry, it hurts less to know that you're not the man I love anymore. Sometimes, I see you and I forget. And then you see me too and... I remember. At least when you're angry about something I actually did, it feels like I deserve the way you look at me."

"I'm sorry," he says with a pink tinge to his cheeks. "I'll...try to stop. But won't kissing you just confuse you even more?"

"Maybe. Maybe not. We won't know until we try. It could be good for us both."

"And why is that?"

"Because I'm confused and you're curious. You want to know what made Seth and your brothers fall so hard for me. Well, here's your chance."

"I'm pretty sure it wasn't that set of lips that made them fall, princesa."

"You could kiss those too," I blurt and then I have to swallow my surprise and keep up the pretense that I'm in control of this dangerous game we're playing. "But we probably shouldn't go that fast. Just to be safe."

"You think?"

"Kiss me," I demand again.

"No."

"Because you're scared."

"Because you're dangerous, Aurelia."

"So? Rumor has it you like courting danger. Maybe it's why no matter how hard you try, you can't stop flirting with me, Ezekiel."

"Is that your version of what's been happening between us?"

"No. It's the truth."

"I don't want to kiss you, Aurelia."

"I won't offer again, Ezekiel." I use his full name purposely and watch his nostrils flare as he bites back the command that I never do it again. And still he doesn't take his eyes off my lips. A moment later, this tormented look enters his eyes as if the demons in his mind are divided on what he should do and waging an all-out war. "It's okay," I say softly, taking pity on him and deciding to end this game. "You don't have to."

I start to push away when he reaches out suddenly, and I feel his palms burning their brand around my biceps. "Wait. Just… wait." He sucks in a sharp breath, and a certain resolve settles over his features.

This time it's my turn to panic when I realize he might do it.

Zeke might actually kiss me.

Suddenly, it's my demons that are screaming obscenities at me for courting danger.

My heart is thundering when his head finally dips and he leans forward. My belly swoops with want, and I can't quite catch my breath. When his hold tightens and he pulls me closer, I realize I'm not breathless. I'm hyperventilating.

"No," I say to my surprise and his.

Zeke stops immediately with a question in his eyes and a confused furrow in his brows.

We're frozen in place, our lips a hair from meeting while I search pretty desperately for the reason I stopped him after damn near begging him to kiss me.

"No?" he echoes, his voice thick with need but his eyes full of resentment for it.

It hits me then—why this feels wrong.

"Zeke… I can't imagine what you went through in that place, and I'm sorry for it." I gently place a hand over his heart and keep my gaze pinned there. I'm not surprised to find his heart racing, but the rhythm is unsteady, as if the war in his head is also being waged in his heart. "You have no idea how sorry I am that you're hurting." Inhaling, I drop my hand but cowardly keep my gaze on his chest as I take a reluctant step back. His hold shifts from my arms to my waist so I don't go far, but the absence of his hard body pressed against mine is enough to strengthen my resolve. "I wish to God that I could take away your pain, but I won't be your punching bag. I won't pay for what Tatum did. It doesn't matter what you feel for me if it isn't intentional. I'm not a side effect or an experiment. I'm a woman who deserves to be loved." Finally, I let my blurry gaze meet his, only to find it blank. The resentment is gone, but so is everything else. "You can kiss me when you mean it."

I go to pull away when his hands tighten on my waist, and I gasp as something dark, possessive, and very much intentional swims across his features—until he doesn't look like Zeke anymore. He looks like a nightmare and a dream wrapped up into one. It raises the hairs on my arms. The chilling sense that I'm in danger skates down my spine, but when I try to pull away again, he growls and I feel his fingers bite into my spine.

"Z-zeke?"

His gaze narrows at the name, making the harsh planes of his visage that much more frightening.

A terrified whimper tears from my throat.

The sound snaps him out of it, and I watch without breathing as Zeke visibly sheds the violent reaction.

It shouldn't be possible the way his eyes seem to brighten from seafoam on a stormy night to their usual spring green, but the more his expression relaxes and returns to normal, the more his eyes do too.

"Fair enough," he says as if he didn't just scare the shit out of me. His tone is casual but cool, leaving me to wonder if I just imagined the whole fucking thing or if Zeke is wholly unaware of what the fuck just happened. Clearing his throat, he avoids my gaze as he drops his hands from my waist and steps around me. "Come on. We should get back."

CHAPTER FIFTEEN

KHALIL

I do one last coat of wood polish over the newly carved headboard before I drop the oily cloth in the bucket with the other supplies and take a step back to admire my handiwork. On the large headboard is a scene depicting a meadow. A bird with its beak open in mid-song sits on a tree branch in bloom while a she-wolf lounges underneath surrounded by flowers and her three pups dancing around her as she stares at the blazing sun. On the opposite end of the headboard is another tree with a thick trunk and a large bear with its back to it mid-scratch while another slumbers on one of the branches and a third sniffs a flower.

In the middle of the scene, like she's the center of this alternate universe, is a faceless girl in a dress with a riotous set of curls.

The rest of the bed was easy to construct, but this part had taken me weeks. I've never attempted anything as intricate. My own headboard was simple compared to this one.

"All done?" Thorin asks from across the room where he's applying the top coat on the freshly painted wall that Seth and Bane destroyed. Zeke dragged in the trunk where we kept extra weapons and was currently kneeling in front of it as he neatly folded her clothes and placed them inside.

It isn't much, but it was all we could give her.

Zeke unsurprisingly hadn't cared much about losing his bedroom to Aurelia, but Thorin and I knew better than to call him out on the reason why.

Sounds drift down the stairs from the first floor, telling me that Aurelia is finally awake. After she came back from her run with Zeke a couple of days ago, she's been spending the night in her loft and lost in her head during the day. I know she hasn't been sleeping either because I could hear her up there pacing when she was supposed to be sleeping.

Something had spooked her, and for whatever reason she and Zeke had been hush-hush about it.

"The mattress should have been delivered by now," I announce as I head for the door. The plastic protecting the floor rustles beneath my feet as I maneuver around all the equipment. "I'm going to take the truck into town and pick it up."

"Take Aurelia with you, will you?" Thorin suggests while meeting my gaze. "She's been itching to go back, and we're running out of excuses for why she can't."

Sticking to the script already written, I smirk and reply, "Was going to do that anyway."

"Cool. Zeke and I will finish up here and clear out the room to get it ready for your return. That cool with you, Zeke?"

It was a performance meant for him so that Thorin and I could divide and conquer and get to the bottom of whatever happened between Aurelia and him on their run. Thorin would talk to Zeke without Aurelia's presence to deter him while I probed Aurelia without Zeke around.

It's been three weeks since Zeke woke up, and we're still running interference. Admittedly, we'd underestimated Zeke's stubbornness because it was clear he was interested in Aurelia but his fear of her won't let him fully realize that attraction.

Zeke, who already looked ready to bolt the moment he heard Aurelia upstairs, gritted his teeth and nodded. It's been like this for two days.

While Aurelia has been lost in her head, Zeke has been avoiding us all.

I leave the room and head upstairs where Aurelia is barefoot in the kitchen singing and dancing to no music while wearing only one of my muscle tees. It's the liveliest I've seen her since I left her in Zeke's brief care, and I've spent two days wrangling back my possessive urge to fuck him up for upsetting her.

On the other hand, I've also had to quell the desire to spank her thoroughly for regressing him.

Hence, the reason we were separating them. At least for a few hours.

She doesn't hear or see me as I approach her from behind. She has the can of coffee beans in hand, and it looks as if she's getting ready to start a pot.

I move in behind her and wrap my arms around her waist, enjoying her gasp of surprise when she feels my morning wood digging into her spine.

"How is it that you've never danced for me?" I whisper in her ear.

"Khalil," she greets with a smile. "Good morning to you too."

I don't respond as I curve my hand around her thigh in a possessive grip. "Answer me."

"I-I didn't know you wanted me to dance for you."

Slowly, I trail my hand up toward her pussy. I can already feel the heat coming from it, so I'm not surprised to find her wet when I finally tease her lips. They're no longer as smooth as they were when she first arrived, and I realize quickly it's the reason for all of her squirming.

"No, don't. I need to shave," she whines.

Snorting, I ignore her protests and push two fingers inside her. "And I promise you, Goldilocks. I don't give a shit. There's no pussy on this planet more perfect than yours." She doesn't reply, but I can tell she's still uneasy, so I use my free hand to shove my shirt that she's wearing up her body until it's bunched under her chin. She's naked underneath, causing her nipples to harden to pinpoints from the cool air meeting her flushed skin. "And these tits," I continue as I palm one. "I love your fucking tits. Beautiful."

"What else?" she urges, enjoying the praise but not truly needing it. Aurelia knows she's the shit.

"This ass of yours keeps my head on a swivel. Some days I just want to take a bite out of it."

"That's not quite how I imagined it going, Khalil Poverly."

"Oh, you want me to eat your ass, Goldilocks?"

"I wouldn't say no."

"Maybe later," I say as if it's not a certainty. There was no time for that now, and with that reminder I reluctantly freed my fingers from her pussy and slapped her ass, making her yelp. "Come on. We gotta go."

She pulls her shirt down and turns to face me with a frown. "Go? Go where?"

"To town. Unless you changed your mind," I add, knowing she hasn't.

Her smile makes her brown eyes brighten. "Really? I was beginning to think you guys were keeping me cooped up here on purpose."

We were. "Of course not. You better hurry though. It's supposed to rain later."

Aurelia squeals and runs out of the kitchen to get dressed. I take over making a pot of coffee, and by the time she returns, I already have a thermos filled up for her. She accepts it gratefully, and I grab my own before we head out.

"Oooh! There's a spot." Aurelia points to the third empty parking space she's spotted since we drove into town. The depot where the mattress is being held is on the outer limits of town, so I ignored the last two spots she's pointed out. Even though it's not where we're going, I can't bring myself to deny her unspoken request a third time, so I pull in. It's clear my baby is eager to sightsee, and who am I to not turn that frown upside down?

Aurelia is practically bouncing in her seat by the time I shut off the engine.

She reaches for the door, and I stop her. I can feel her confusion when I step out and her gaze following me as I round the hood and open her door.

"Come on, baby." I hold out my hand, and she blushes as I help her down. Thorin insisted on having the truck lifted when we bought it a few years back, so it's a long way down.

Once she's out, I lock the truck, and she grabs my hand and pulls me onto the sidewalk. Aurelia starts walking with no clear destination in mind, and I let her guide us while I scope out the faces of the people we pass, watching for anyone who stares in her direction too long.

Aurelia isn't wearing her disguise like she did the first time we brought her into town.

There's really no need for that now that the sheriff knows who she is, but it still makes me nervous. There's always a chance someone will recognize her and blow our spot up.

Aurelia is still talking excitedly about where to go first when we pass the ice cream parlor. I squeeze her hand, but she doesn't notice because she's too busy contemplating which store to go to first, so I stop walking, but I don't let her go, and it finally gets her attention when she's met with resistance.

"I—What?"

"What about here?" I suggest with a nod to the shop.

She turns and reads the pale blue and pink lettering on the window. "Ice cream? As in…sugar? But you hate junk food. Something to do with your deeply unhappy childhood."

"I didn't have a deeply unhappy childhood."

Aurelia's brows snap down. "Then there's no excuse for torturing yourself like this, Khalil Poverly."

Grinning, I pull her back toward the door, and she eagerly follows. "Prepare yourself, Goldilocks. You won't believe the flavors they have."

The store is cold when we walk in, but Aurelia doesn't seem to notice as she looks around in awe. You'd think she'd stepped through a portal into another world. She doesn't notice either when I let her hand fall from mine and come to a standstill as I fight off the guilt that suddenly hits me like a train. It's not the first time it's happened, but it takes a little longer this time to overcome.

Sam and Molly, the couple that owns this joint, hadn't changed a thing since I'd last been inside. The ceiling is still cracked. The paint is still peeling. The floor is still its usual dingy black-and-white tile, and the catchy pop music plays over a crackly speaker. And the velvet barrel-backed chairs are still tearing at the seams and in danger of losing all of their foam.

Through Aurelia's eyes, it is a wonderland.

There are a few people inside sitting at the tables or standing along the walls, but thankfully most of them pay us no mind as they enjoy their sundaes and milkshakes.

However, the mood toward us has shifted—if only a little. A

few years ago, the townspeople gawked whenever Thorin, Zeke, and I would come into town since we were a rare sight with an even more mysterious history. Left with no choice but to fill in those blanks themselves, we became some cheap urban legend. Over time those stares became less frequent and lengthy, but there were still some.

They whisper when I pass, and for the first time, I don't grit my teeth or glare them into looking away. I take in all their stares and curious whispers because it means they aren't giving her a second glance. My presence *is* the perfect disguise.

I'd managed to move and force an indulgent smile by the time Aurelia realized I wasn't responding to her many questions and comments. She was standing in front of the specials board contemplating her many choices when her head popped up and she looked around in search of me.

Smoothly, I reappeared by her side and reclaimed her hand. "I'm right here, baby. What was that?"

"Oh. I said I don't know which flavor to get. They all sound so good and gross at the same time." She wrinkled her nose. "How is that possible?"

I smirked at her. "Why don't we get them all so you can try them?"

"Really?"

The teenage cashier with a large septum piercing and more freckles than not wore a bored expression when we stepped up to the counter, and she barely suppressed an eye roll when Aurelia and I ordered all nine of the specials. Sam and Molly had dozens of flavors that were constantly changing, but Aurelia and I were determined to make a sizable dent in their menu.

The shop was busy today since it was a warm, sunny day and a Friday. I even spotted a few kids who had clearly decided to skip school. The cashier handed one of the servers our ticket, and he hurried away to get started on our big order.

"Thanks," Aurelia said.

"Sure."

Placing a hand on Aurelia's lower back, I start to move her out of the way when the cashier's gaze snags on Aurelia's face and the recognition that flashes in her eyes puts me on edge.

"Hey. Has anyone ever told you that you look like that singer?"

Aurelia stops, her face as alarmed as I'm feeling. "W-what singer?"

"I don't know. Anastasia, I think."

"Oh. Yeah," Aurelia plays it off with a laugh. "Yeah, sometimes. Are you a big fan of hers?"

"Not really. I think she died or something." Clearly bored with us now that she believes Aurelia isn't a mega celebrity, the cashier sighs and turns away to restock the cones.

My gaze is stuck to Aurelia as we walk away while worry churns in my gut at how she might feel at seemingly being so easily forgotten. Her expression is confused, and she's pensive for a few seconds before she snorts and then lets out the most obnoxious sound I've ever heard from her. She quickly claps a hand over her mouth to smother the rest of her laugh, and I reach out to wrangle her hand away from her face.

Aurelia grins up at me and giggles. "It's not the first time that's happened," she whispers when we're far enough away from the cashier. "But I have to say it's the first time it's felt that good."

"Congratulations. You're a nobody like the rest of us. How does it feel, pleb?"

"Honestly? Like for the first time, I can truly do anything, and no one will give a shit. It's great."

Her smile is not only infectious, it lights up her face and

emphasizes her beauty and I'm not talking about the allure that's easily recognizable to anyone who sees her.

It's the beauty within that captivates me. The one you have to trudge through darkness and thorns, bitter words, and sneers to see. But if you know where to look, it's right there in the quick little breaths she takes when she's excited, the way her brown eyes brighten, or the way her smile takes over her face. She's a vision that nearly sends me to my knees.

When I peek over at the server, he's barely gotten through our third dish so I quickly pull Aurelia over into the dark hallway between the dining room and the employee area and I kiss her while she clings to me for the air I'm denying her.

When I finally release her, she's panting for breath with a look in her eyes as if she wants to ask me what she's done to deserve a kiss like that when really it's me who feels as if I passed some sort of test.

"Order ninety-two!" the server calls out.

"That's us," Aurelia pants.

I kiss her one more time, albeit briefly, and then I pull her over to the counter and retrieve the large tray with our order. Aurelia leads the way to an empty table tucked into a back corner by the window. It's been freshly wiped, so I set the tray down and we take our seats.

Aurelia has her eye on a sundae with scoops of cookies and cream, bubblegum, and strawberry ice cream. It's studded with Oreos, sprinkled with gummy bears, drizzled in caramel, and topped with a cherry. I go for the other sundae with the least number of toppings—vanilla bean ice cream, caramel drizzle, peanut butter cups, and pretzels.

By the time we're done, neither of us have finished a single dish, but we've sampled them all.

"I don't think I can eat another bite," Aurelia groans after one sip of a blue shake with a Cookie Monster theme.

"You ready to go?"

She peeks at me from under her lashes. "Only if you're carrying me."

I snort and throw a few bills on the table for the tip. "Let's go, greedy girl."

Aurelia groans when I help her out of her chair, and then we leave the parlor and step out into the sun. We walk for a little bit, just enjoying the warmth after the freezing cold of Sam and Molly's. Unlike before, Aurelia is utterly disinterested in the shops we pass until we reach a florist. I let her pull me inside while she grumbles how our cabin is in desperate need of a feminine touch.

The bell above the door dings as we enter the empty shop.

"Welcome to Buds of Joy," the shop owner calls out from the storage room. "I'll be out in just a minute." Aurelia and I look around for a few minutes before she joins us. "Hi. Thanks for coming in. I'm Til—Oh, hi, Khalil."

"Tilda, hey."

Our familiarity doesn't go unnoticed by Aurelia, but since Hearth is a small town and everyone knows everyone, there's nothing more than polite interest in her gaze as she observes quietly.

"I have to say I'm surprised to see you in my shop after you boys told me you had no need for flowers." Finally, she notices Aurelia. "Who's this you got with you?" Her gaze bounces between Aurelia and me as I debate which answer to give her—our cover story that she's my cousin or the truth.

"I'm his girlfriend," Aurelia recklessly answers for us both, whether purposefully or without thinking, I can't say, and I definitely can't question her in front of Tilda. "Aurora."

So half-truths then.

"Oh my word. Aren't you just the prettiest thing? What are

you doing with him? You do know he's got the manners of a boar, don't you?"

"Well, you know," Aurelia says, being perfectly charming like she's not worse than me. "They're not all first-round picks."

Tilda tosses back her head and laughs like it's the funniest thing.

"You know, I don't think I've seen you around before. What brings you to Hearth, Aurora?"

"Well, I kind of got lost and stumbled by accidentally. I made the mistake of asking this brute for directions, and that was all she wrote. I had no choice but to stick around."

"Oh my gosh! That is so delightful." While Tilda giggles like she's just heard the beginning of the cutest Hallmark love story, I cut my gaze at Aurelia. Tilda doesn't recognize the sarcastic curve of Aurelia's smile, but I do.

Aurelia glances at me with a smug look in her eye once Tilda walks away and I mouth, *behave*.

Aurelia shrugs and makes a face like it's not up to her.

Thirty minutes later, I'm walking out with an armful of four different bouquets while Aurelia and Tilda chat like old friends. They're a few steps behind me while I walk to the truck, and the flowers are blocking ninety percent of my vision, which explains why I don't notice the woman glaring daggers at me until it's too late.

"Khalil?"

"Fuck," I grumble as I try to duck farther behind the bouquets in vain.

"Seriously? Khalil Poverly, I know that's you."

I lower the flowers just enough to spot Karla, Tilda's daughter, standing ten feet away. I can tell by the scornful look in her eyes that she isn't going to keep walking.

Shit is about to hit the fucking fan.

My girl is territorial as fuck, and Karla never could catch the hint after throwing herself in my path every time we'd come into town. Aurelia won't hesitate to stake her claim, and Karla will react like a jealous ex—even though she isn't. I've never even touched her. Neither woman will back down, and here I am uselessly waiting for the first missile to fire with an armful of flowers.

"What's up, Karla? How have you been?" I ask even though I don't give a shit. Last I heard, she was fucking around with a married man in the next town over and bragging to anyone who'd listen that he was going to leave his wife and kids for her.

"I don't know, Khalil. You tell me."

"You want me to tell you how you've been?" It was obvious that Karla had a script in her head of how our conversation would go once she ran into me, but she hadn't counted on my interest in playing my part being nil.

"You don't have to be rude."

"Well, being nice doesn't seem to land with you, so…" I shrug.

"What have I done to make you hate me?"

You won't leave me alone. "Karla, I barely know you," I point out instead. "It's complicated."

"It's really not though," Aurelia dryly states from beside me. I didn't even hear her reach us. Aurelia's presence draws Karla's stunned gaze, but before she can ask the question in her eyes, Aurelia beats her to it. "Who are you?" she demands rudely, but not entirely hostile. No, that wouldn't be Aurelia at all, to feel threatened when she knows she owns me entirely.

"Oh." Karla releases a nervous giggle. "I'm Karla. Khalil and I are old friends. I'm sort of his best girl friend."

"That's funny. I could have sworn I was his girlfriend." Aurelia glances up at me before turning and smirking at Karla. "I'll have to talk to him about that."

"No, sweetie. I meant his friend who's a girl. See? His girl friend."

"No, *sweetie*. I heard your ass the first time."

Karla's fake smile falters for the first time. "You…you look really familiar. Have we met?"

"I doubt it," Aurelia answers coolly.

Tilda, sensing the sudden tension while being fully aware of her daughter's attraction to me, takes Karla's arm and steers her away. I send her a grateful look as they pass and then I guide Aurelia to the truck without a word. When I look back, I see that Karla is frowning and watching us walk away, but her stare is directed at Aurelia, clearly still trying to place her.

Aurelia's mean ass sees this and smiles and waves at Karla, who turns away and disappears inside her mom's shop.

Shaking my head, I unlock the truck and carefully place the flowers in the back seat. Once I'm sure they're secure, I turn to get Aurelia situated only to startle when I find her standing directly behind me while staring in the direction Karla went with a contemplative furrow in her brow. "You think she recognized me?"

"I doubt it." When Aurelia's frown only deepens, I realize being recognized isn't the only thing that troubles her. "Talk to me," I beg.

Leaving Aurelia to fill in her own blanks is never a good thing. "Have you fucked her?"

"No. Never," I answer honestly.

"But you could have."

"Is that a problem?" I ask, genuinely confused.

"I don't know. I thought…I thought when you guys took me, it was because you were desperate and had no options. And I don't even know why I thought that. I mean look at you." She gestures at me. I don't take my gaze away from her. "I thought—" She stops before she can voice her deepest insecurities.

And if it hadn't been for Karla, I never would have known that this was in the back of Aurelia's mind, feeding whatever doubts that lingered.

"You thought any ol' pussy would do," I finish for her. Aurelia doesn't even look surprised that I'd read her mind. "Well, now you know. And I'm glad we can clear this up. It was more than wanting to fuck you that made us desperate to keep you. Your soul called out to us, Goldilocks."

"I was literally dying, unconscious, and covered in filth."

"Exactly. That should tell you everything."

"That men are disgusting?"

"That's two strikes, Goldilocks."

"Strikes?" she squeals. "For *what*?"

"Earn a third and you'll find out when we get home," I tease.

Aurelia and I make a few more stops to pick up supplies and whatever other useless things Aurelia swore up and down she desperately needed before we finally make it to the depot where the mattress I ordered a month ago is stored.

"Are you sure you don't need any help with that?" she asks for the second time as she trails me to the truck. "It looks really heavy."

With a great heave and a grunt, I toss the queen-size mattress onto the bed of the truck while she stares on in astonishment. I'd already loaded the box spring, which was much lighter and easier to carry. I turn to face Aurelia once the mattress is in position to be tied down. "You were saying?"

"Wow, you're really strong," she says as if she's only just realizing it for the first time. "Show-off."

Grinning, I grab the cords from the lockbox and hop onto the bed of the truck to get to work tying it down for the journey up the mountain. Aurelia leans against the side of the truck and doesn't offer her help again once she sees how much trouble it's giving me. She tunes out my cursing while singing softly to herself. I'd be amused at her change of heart if I wasn't ready to set the fucking mattress on fire and demand she sleep in my bed only for the rest of her days.

I'm wrangling the final cord into submission when I hear her curse and see her tense out of the corner of my eye.

"Khalil? Incoming," Aurelia warns under her breath.

I immediately stand to my full height and see the sheriff approaching. There's tension around his shoulders and mouth, so I know he's in a foul mood before he even speaks.

"Aurelia. Khalil," the sheriff greets tersely. He's made no secret that he's unhappy with us after we betrayed his trust. Still, he hasn't arrested us even though his sense of duty is probably telling him that he should. "I was just about to head your way."

I glance at Aurelia who's nibbling her lips at an alarming rate. "Is something wrong?"

"We need to talk. Meet me at the station in ten minutes." The sheriff walks off without another word.

"Any clue what that's about?"

Aurelia has her look of pure bewilderment perfected. "How would I know?"

"Right. Come on."

Once I'm sure the mattress won't fall off, Aurelia and I hop in the truck and ride back to Main Street where the station house is. When we walk in, one of the deputies immediately shows us to the empty sheriff's office and tells us to have a seat.

The sheriff walks in a couple minutes later carrying a file that he throws onto his cluttered desk and a steaming cup of coffee that he hands to Aurelia, who smiles gratefully.

I don't miss the slight, but the man overestimates how much I give a damn. "All right, Sheriff. What's this about?"

"I think the four of you should know that Aurelia's uncle paid me a visit."

"My uncle was here?" Aurelia's question comes out in a terrified squeak. "In Hearth?"

"Yes."

"When?" I demand.

The sheriff exhales a harsh breath, and I know I won't like the answer. "A few days ago."

"And you're just telling us now?"

"I didn't have to tell you at all. You've already lied to me once. I haven't forgotten that."

"Okay. Let's focus on the actual problem at hand here," Aurelia says before I can tell the sheriff to kiss my ass. "What did my uncle want?"

"What do you think? He wanted to know what happened to the men he hired. You forget. They disappeared under *my* jurisdiction and care, which makes me responsible unless I hand in a culprit, which would be you four."

"What did you tell him?"

"Nothing. It's an open investigation. He did, however, seem more than a little curious about you three."

"Such as?"

"Who you are, where you came from, your involvement in the search."

"That's not public record."

"No, it's not," the sheriff agrees grimly.

Marston George has been doing his research and digging deep, no doubt using Aurelia's checkbook to get the information.

"So where is he now? I assume he's left town."

"You assume wrong. He's at the ranch." The sheriff shifts his gaze to Aurelia, who's become pensive again. "Your ranch if I'm not mistaken."

The one Aurelia never made it to.

It's not far from Hearth. The house is big and comfortable and probably comes with all the amenities and luxuries our cabin doesn't have, with a nice clear view of the mountains as a backdrop. She probably would have loved it there.

The idea of her uncle using it after what he did—and still plans to do—fills me with the urgent need to ride over there alone and burn the house down with him inside. The sound of his screams would no doubt rock me to sleep every night like a sweet lullaby while I held his niece safely in my arms, knowing she'll never have cause to fear him ever again.

"Apparently, he wants to sell it now that it's of no use."

"Take me to him."

I'm snapped out of my violent fantasy by Aurelia's insane request that I immediately deny. "Absolutely not. You're not going anywhere near him."

"That's not up to you, Khalil. He's my uncle. It's me he wants dead. He's going to find out I'm alive sooner or later. Why not let it be on my terms?"

"Because it's dangerous. Think about what he gains by killing you, Goldilocks. He'll try anything."

"You won't let him hurt me," she says quietly, appealing to my protective side.

It almost works, but she forgets one thing. "You're damn straight because you're not going. You'll have to try harder than flattery to convince me to risk you."

Aurelia's lips part to tell me once again that it's not my decision just for it to once again fall on deaf ears.

"I'll take her," the sheriff interrupts with a sigh, as if he's volunteering to end our bickering.

"Thanks, but we'll pass."

The sheriff gives me a hard look. "As the young lady has already pointed out, Mr. Poverly, it's not up to you or me. I'm not any happier about it than you, but if what you both claimed is true, Ms. George is not your prisoner, and the ranch is legally her property, which means she can damn well go where she likes. Personally, I'd feel better if I were there as a deterrent to any unsavory acts given your claims about your uncle's intentions."

"So you believe me?" Aurelia asks with a high note of hope.

The sheriff's expression shutters. "I'm not saying that either, but it doesn't matter what I believe. I've failed you once, and I won't do it again." Knowing when I'm cornered, I grit my teeth and say nothing. To do otherwise would only poke more holes in that bullshit story Aurelia gave him. "I'm glad we're all in agreement," the sheriff says with a grunt before snatching his hat from his desk and plopping it down over his thinning hair. "Shall we go?"

CHAPTER SIXTEEN

AURELIA

Khalil hasn't spoken a word to me since we left the sheriff's office. I'm pretty sure it's by design, choosing instead to silently fume the entire drive as we tailed the sheriff to the ranch. But there's also a distracted pinch to his brow that tells me this isn't about control.

He's using the limited time we have until we reach the ranch to come up with a plan for how to keep me safe.

He also wants to throttle me, but he'll have to get in line.

As soon as we left the station, Khalil had radioed up to the cabin to warn Thorin and Zeke where we were going. There was violence in Thorin's tone when he signed off, and I still felt the tight grip of his fury twenty minutes later.

My nerves are shot by the time we reach the short gate blocking access to the paved driveway. The gate and the brown picket fence it's attached to are both easily climbable, so I figure it was built by the previous owners more for the aesthetic than for security.

It would have been the first change my uncle would have ordered if I'd ever arrived—higher walls and armed guards because he doesn't understand how to keep a low profile. After a couple of months in hiding, he probably would have leaked the information himself to a few of his most loyal paps just to spark intrigue and keep me relevant.

The rustic house, which is bigger than I imagined, sits about a thousand feet away with rolling hills behind it and the Cold Peaks looming even farther away in the distance.

We wait for a few minutes while the sheriff speaks to someone over the call box. A few seconds later, the gate slowly parts with a mechanical whir and we're driving through. My arm shoots out to grab Khalil's hand that's dangling over the cupholder, and he gives mine a squeeze in return that says he's here.

He's got me.

I didn't expect him to comfort me since he's clearly pissed at me for putting myself in this position, but I'm even more surprised that I doubted him. The first thing I fell in love with about Khalil is his unerring loyalty.

As we get closer to the house, more of the characteristics that were obscure when we first arrived become distinct.

What if my plane had never crashed, and I'd arrived here three months ago?

Once my resentment and anger at being exiled eventually faded, I would have found peace in the solitude. I might have even come to enjoy the view. I can almost imagine myself relaxing on the wraparound porch with my bare feet propped on the railing as I sip from a steaming cup of coffee and admire the beauty of the snowcapped mountains that belong in a painting.

Never once guessing that my destiny lay within those peaks.

After a few months away, once the world began to crave Aurelia George—flaws and all—my uncle would have shattered my peace and whisked me back home to give the people what they wanted. And I would have gone back never having known *them*. My mountain men.

But no, that's not right either. Because if my uncle had his way, I never would have made it home at all. Rather than wait for the world to change their hearts, his plan all along had been to send the death squad after me and preserve what was left of my image and my legacy while he could.

I wonder how they would have done it.

Finnegan said they were supposed to make it look like an accident. As we inch toward the house, my gaze catches on the paddock not far away and the horses grazing inside it.

Crushed by a temperamental mare perhaps?

One thing was for certain, this house—as alluring as it may be—wasn't my home.

It was my grave. My final resting place.

We've only been gone a few hours, but even now, my heart longed for the cabin and all of its simplicity.

Khalil and the sheriff park their trucks, but I don't move and Khalil doesn't kill the engine. I just stare straight ahead while Khalil waits silently, ready to drive us away if I give him even the smallest sign that I'm not ready to face my uncle.

After a few minutes, I sigh and the small sound from me is enough to break Khalil's silence.

"We doing this, Goldilocks?" His glare is fixed on the house through the windshield as if he can see my uncle through the stone walls.

"Yes. I have to do this."

He's careful not to react and nods instead. "Okay."

Khalil reaches under his seat and pulls out a handgun. He checks the clip before reaching behind him and shoving it in his waistband. He looks at me once he pulls his shirt over it and gives me a crooked smile once he finds me watching him. "Just in case."

"We're not killing my uncle, Khalil. At least not today."

"No promises," he says before he opens his doors and steps out.

I don't wait for Khalil to come around and open my door because if I don't get out of the truck now I never will, so I quickly unbuckle my belt and practically fly from the seat.

The sheriff steps out of his truck too, and none of us say a word as we make our way to the front door. The luxury car parked outside is obviously a rental, but it has my uncle written all over it. He always has to put on a show wherever we go. The reminder that I was funding his lifestyle and all of these luxuries, and that I have done so half my life, fuels me up the stairs and onto the porch.

Khalil keeps his rigid body in front of mine, keeping me from view and harm like a shield that will never bend, break, or fold. My stomach turns knowing my uncle won't miss it and will do everything in his power to test and batter my defenses.

The three of us reach the door, and the sheriff knocks. Almost immediately, I hear footsteps approaching on the other side. I can't see thanks to the immovable wall of flesh and muscle in front of me, but judging by the voice, it's a woman who answers the door. She lets us inside after the sheriff asks for my uncle, and then we're left alone in the foyer while the woman I assume is a housekeeper disappears into the house to fetch my uncle.

I take the time to look around.

There's a formal dining room immediately to my left with a crystal chandelier above the long table that only makes me think of the antler one hanging above the table at home. The one Khalil had carved with his bare, capable hands. I huddle a little closer to his strong back and breathe in his cardamom scent with strong notes of mint.

The ceilings become higher the farther we travel inside the house until we reach the cavernous living room. I immediately drift over to the huge windows when I spot the mountains framed by the glass like a painting in a frame.

Unwilling to leave my side for even a moment, Khalil shadows me over to the window and stands close behind me, lending me his heat and his strength as he places his hands on my shoulders. I close my eyes and lean against him as he massages the tension in my muscles.

Just as I start to relax and center myself, my uncle's voice penetrates the fog and I'm tense again.

"Ah, Sheriff," Uncle Mars greets without an ounce of concern for why the sheriff called on him out of the blue. It's the voice of a man who's used to having his will enforced. Already, the crushing weight of his presence is heavy in the air, making it hard to breathe. "I wasn't expecting you. How can I help?"

"Yes, well, we had an unexpected development regarding your niece that I thought you might want to know."

Khalil's hands tighten on my shoulders. Neither of us move from the window, but I doubt my uncle has missed our presence. Khalil is blocking me from view, but the massive man would be hard to miss by anyone, including someone as egocentric as Marston George.

"Is that right?" my uncle asks in a tone that doesn't sound like someone concerned. Even in death, I'm still causing him problems. I don't realize I'm smiling until I catch my fiendish grin in the reflection of the window. "Well, what have you found? Has her body been recovered?"

The sheriff stammers and stumbles for a response.

Meanwhile, I grab that powerful feeling of being a thorn in my uncle's side by the reins and decide to harness it by stepping out from the protective shield of Khalil's body.

Uncle Mar's golden-brown skin becomes white as a sheet when

he sees me. We share the same complexion and are often mistaken for being biracial by people who don't understand that Black folks come in fifty-'leven shades. There have been many occasions—like forcing me to dye my hair blond—that my uncle has used our proximity to whiteness to get ahead, and his colorist views are just one of the many reasons I have to fight back the sneer that wants to take over my faux-calm expression.

While I'm fighting to not react at all, he blinks as if he can't believe his eyes.

I'm sure I look like a stranger to him, but I've never felt more like me. My natural hair is longer, unkempt, and splitting at the ends. The gold in my curls that's become my trademark has become dull and is receding by the day, giving way to the dark brown that I inherited from my mother.

I'm not dressed in one of those ridiculous costumes that he insists makes millions of girls across the globe want to be me while at the same time appearing desirable to men yet unapproachable.

Whatever that means.

My face is also clear of makeup, but it was never something he allowed me to overindulge in once our PR team caught wind of my natural beauty being praised in the media.

I don't look like the superstar he created.

Instead, it's just me. Daughter to Jamila and Logan George. Wolf. Songbird. The sun in Seth's world. Goldilocks. Princess. Survivor.

"You look like you've seen a ghost, Uncle Mars." Fitting since I'm supposed to be dead.

"Aurelia?"

"In the flesh. Surprised?"

"I don't understand," he says after struggling to recover. The shock is fake. The horror that I'm alive and dared to show myself to him is very much real. "How is this possible?"

"Well, there was a tree. My guess is it broke my fall from the fireball that was once my plane and by the grace of God or the devil's amusement, I didn't die from the freezing cold or get torn apart by wolves like Cassie."

"What an ordeal you must have had," he dryly replies with a strained smile. "Thankfully, all of that is behind you now. You're safe. You're alive." More pointedly, he adds, with his gaze flickering toward the silent, fuming man next to me, "You must be eager to get home."

"Eh," I say with a shrug. Khalil grumbles unhappily when I move away to slowly circle the room, giving myself a tour. The living room looks straight out of a home catalog. There's no personal touch to be found anywhere. "Not really."

"E-excuse me?"

"I said I'm not ready to go, but you can. As you can see, I'm perfectly fine and enjoying this little corner of the world, so not to worry. I'm sure you have a lot to do back home."

"Is this a joke?"

"What part sounded funny to you?" I stop to pick up a statuette of a slender deer with large antlers. While we were in town earlier, Khalil had been approached by a few people who were eager to have him carve custom pieces like this statuette for them. I was even more surprised to learn that he sold his for a fraction of the price of whatever designer company the decorator had purchased it from.

"Aurelia, you can't possibly think that I'll allow you to stay here. Your place is with me back in the States."

"You didn't seem to think that when you sent me here."

"That was for your own good," Uncle Mars volleys back.

"I think a plane crash and all the people who died horrible deaths *except* for me would beg to differ."

"You can't blame yourself for that." He waves dismissively.

"Then who should I blame, Uncle? You?"

"It's no one's fault. It was a rogue blizzard. An act of God."

"Well, that *act of God* came with a warning that you ignored, and it got nine people *killed*."

"Eight."

I freeze, and out of my peripheral I could swear Khalil does the same. "Run that back?"

"The crash only killed eight. You weren't the only survivor, Aurelia."

It feels as if I've been punched in the gut. Sensing the change, Khalil rushes over to me, and I grab his arms to steady myself. I don't even care that my uncle is witnessing me fall apart or that I'm accepting comfort from a strange man.

"W-who?" I finally ask even though my tormented heart has already whispered his name to me.

"Tyler Westbrook," he offers immediately. "Your bodyguard."

"No. I...I saw him. The avalanche... It pushed him over the cliff."

Thorin and Seth's whispered conversation during one of my brief bouts of consciousness after they saved me from the storm came rushing back.

"She kept calling me Tyler."

"You mean the kid we found a week ago?"

And then later, when the four of us were lounging in Khalil's bed just needing to be close after Thorin tried to give Seth a haircut and Seth tried to disembowel him with the scissors. Khalil had been acting like a jealous boyfriend wanting to know if I'd slept with my bodyguard.

I told him that the answer didn't matter because he was dead, and none of them corrected me. They let me believe the worst so they could have me all to themselves.

"No." I shake my head. "That's impossible."

Was it? the voice in my head asked. Was it truly impossible that Tyler survived the avalanche, or did I simply not want to believe that my mountain men had lied to me?

"He survived," my uncle insists. "Tyler's *alive*. He was found by search and rescue and brought home."

My gaze flies to Khalil, whose jaw twitches when he reads the accusation in my eyes.

You told me he was dead.

I know. Later, his eyes seem to plead.

But what possible explanation could he have for intentionally causing me pain?

"Westbrook was in a coma for a few weeks, but he's already made a swift recovery," Uncle Mars continues. "I'm sure knowing you made it too will make up for the loss of his leg."

My uncle coldly delivers that last bit of news like the dagger to the heart it's intended to be.

Bile riles in my throat when I fail to push away the image of Tyler waking up in the hospital, confused, scared, and missing a limb.

All my fault.

"Come with me." My uncle's tone is gentle when he holds out his hand. "I can take you to him. I know how close you two were."

It's a lie. If my uncle had the smallest inkling how much Tyler had meant to me as my only friend, he wouldn't have hesitated to fire him and have him blackballed from the industry to ensure we were never in the same room again.

"I…I can't." I realize how that sounds when the sheriff shifts in agitation and starts eyeing Khalil like he's imagining him in handcuffs. "I-I mean I want to stay. My place is here."

The microscopic shift in my uncle's demeanor would be undetectable to the untrained eye. Unfortunately, I've had a lot of practice recognizing and navigating my uncle's temper. I know the moment his mask starts to slip when he realizes his plot to use Tyler to manipulate me is failing. "What about Tyler? Don't you want to see him?"

"Yes, but not if it means going back with you."

"Why the hell not?"

I barely suppress the urge to flinch and keep my voice light like I'm just a girl who's lost in the throes and machinations of love and new beginnings. It can't be helped. "Because I like it here. I want to stay."

"No. That is not an option."

Seeing that we're getting nowhere, I turn and face the gruff older man who looks like he'd rather be anywhere else. "Sheriff, would you mind waiting outside?"

The sheriff's gaze bounces between Khalil, my uncle, and me. "Would that be wise?"

My uncle visibly bristles when it becomes clear that no one in this room trusts him alone with me. "My niece is perfectly safe in my care. If anything, I should have your badge for your blatant incompetence in finding her and bringing her home. She's been missing for months, and here she is standing in front of me without a scratch on her and no explanation. It's clear she's no longer sound of mind, and I'm still deciding who to hold responsible," he says with a pointed glare at Khalil.

Khalil merely cracks his neck before adjusting his stance and crossing his arms. The move makes the huge muscles in his arms bulge, effectively warning off anyone stupid enough to consider trying him.

Ignoring my uncle's tirade, I turn to the sheriff, who suddenly looks unsure. "I'll be fine."

"If you insist. I'll be right on the porch," he warns before nodding, tipping his hat, and leaving.

When my gaze travels to Khalil, he immediately catches on and growls before I can make the request. "Don't even think about it, Goldilocks."

Foolishly, I wanted the chance to face my uncle alone and prove he had no real power over me, but I can tell that Khalil won't give a damn.

"Fine. You can stay," I utter under my breath. "But promise me that no matter what you hear, you will not interfere. I have to deal with him on my own. In my own way."

A few emotions play across Khalil's face as he internally battles with that part of himself that sees me as being strong and capable and the other part that wants to defend me no matter what.

One false move and he won't hesitate to snap my uncle in half. Actually, as amusing as that would be to watch, it's not worth the risk with the sheriff right outside. On the other hand, Khalil doesn't look like he gives a damn about that either. It's hard to be upset with him knowing he'd do anything to keep me safe, but it's not a get-out-jail-free card.

I'll scream and curse and cry at his betrayal later. Better to do it when Thorin and Zeke are around to receive my ire as well. I won't have to rinse and repeat.

As soon as the sheriff is gone, my uncle gestures toward Khalil—the only other threat in the room that's keeping him from saying and doing whatever he wants with me. "Who are you?" he demands even though the narrowing of his gaze tells me he already knows.

"He's the man who saved my life. One of them anyway."

"And you've been with him? This whole time?"

"Pretty much."

"So what do you want?" my uncle asks Khalil. "Money?"

Khalil growls and bares his teeth.

I clear my throat. "I wouldn't do that again if I were you."

"Do what?" my uncle snaps.

"Insult him. He's not here for money. He's here for me."

"Aurelia, you're an incredibly wealthy woman. Don't be so naive. This is why you need me. This is why you cannot stay here and continue pretending you're dead. It's going to be hard enough explaining your disappearance without some internet personality with a few followers calling it a hoax. How many gullible people do you think it will take for the rumor to spread like wildfire and become popular opinion?" Before I can respond and tell him just how little I care, he plows on, his voice turning desperate and pleading. "Right now, the world is mourning you. For fuck's sake, you've practically been given sainthood! But if it gets out that you're not only *alive* but allowing everyone to believe you're dead so you can shack up with this…this…*Neanderthal*, we'll end up right back where we started. Worse even!"

Classic Uncle Mars. Only ever concerned about the optics. I'm so glad I've decided not to live like that anymore. The best part of being dead is no fucks to give. "I hear you, Uncle Mars, but I don't care, and it's not up to you. I'm not the same girl you sent up here to lick her wounds. You can't control me anymore."

"Is that what you think I was doing? I raised you. I protected you. Goddamn it, I *made* you!"

"No. You *used* me."

"I made you a *star*."

"And fattened your pockets while you were at it, so I'd say we're even. I don't owe you a thing."

"Like hell you don't. You think a strong voice and a pretty face is what got you where you are? I could have made a thousand of you. It's time to grow up and realize you're nothing special. Everything you have is because of *me*!"

My uncle hits his chest, and I hate myself for flinching.

Khalil—my Neanderthal—must take it as a threat because he steps forward, pushing me behind the protective shelter of his body.

"What the hell are you doing?" Uncle Mars stumbles in retreat when Khalil keeps going, backing him down without a word. "Move out of the way. I'm speaking with my niece."

"And if you want to keep speaking to her in my presence, I suggest you lower your voice with the motherfucking quickness."

"You don't have any authority here! This is between my niece and me!"

All Khalil said to that was "Lower."

"You don't—"

Khalil's hand moved with lightning speed, wrapping around my uncle's neck and lifting him off the ground. "*Lower.*"

It's all I can do not to laugh when my uncle flails his dangling feet and claws at Khalil's hand. "You don't…have any authority… here," my uncle chokes past lips that are already turning blue.

Satisfied, Khalil sets him on his feet and removes his hand. Nearly half a foot taller, he looks down at my uncle while the man who's ruled me with an iron fist coughs and drags in air.

"Good. Keep it right there and not a decibel higher and I won't have to fuck you up." Khalil pats my uncle on the cheek hard enough to look more like a slap and then he returns to my side like a dutiful boyfriend. When our gazes meet, he shrugs. "I tried it your way, but then he threatened you. End of story."

It was hardly a threat, but I know better than to argue. Especially when I'm fighting a grin after seeing him make my uncle his bitch. Khalil is already wound tight and a hair trigger away from exploding. It reminds me of the day we met and how I could feel all the energy packed away inside of him just waiting for an outlet.

He hasn't been this way since we first fucked, but that violent energy is quickly returning now.

My uncle glares at us both while rubbing his neck. I make a show of examining my nails like I didn't see a thing and try not to cringe at how bad I need a manicure.

"You were saying, Uncle?"

Uncle Mars takes one last gasping breath and says, "I think you should leave."

"Oh, now he wants us to leave," I whisper to Khalil. My boyfriend's only response is to smirk and run his knuckles down my arm. "Out of curiosity, whose money bought this house?" When my uncle simply glares back, I smile.

So mine then.

"I'm guessing my name is on the deed as well?"

More silence.

"I'm surprised you even bothered since your plan was to have me killed. It would have been one less asset to transfer once you proved my death and took everything."

The bitter expression clears from my uncle's face, and his next words come as no surprise. "I don't know what you're talking about, Aurelia. You're my niece. My blood. Of course I'd never harm you."

"So you didn't hire Finnegan and his men, who tried to kill me?"

"Of course I did. I thought you were dead. You can't imagine how hard it's been thinking you were out there alone and without a proper burial. I promised your father I would take care of you, and *that* is *exactly* what I have *always* done." He waves away the obvious hole in his story. "Obviously, Finnegan and his men got a little overzealous in getting the job done. I certainly didn't permit him to take you against your will or harm you."

Yeah, and pigs fly.

"I've never known you to be overly sentimental or religious," I say.

"What is your point, Aurelia?"

My gaze narrows. "I think you know, Uncle."

"This is ridiculous. I don't know what these men have been filling your head with, but I will not stand here and be vilified after all I've done for you." Even after all of that, he was still careful not to raise his voice just as Khalil had warned him.

"They haven't been filling my head with anything." As for the rest of me... "I came to the conclusion that you were a monster all on my own."

"Ungrateful as ever. I can see some things haven't changed."

"And some things never will," I confirm. A little catty and a little bratty, but at least I'm free.

My uncle's phone starts to ring and since he never misses a call if he can help it, it doesn't surprise me when he snatches the phone from his pocket. "I have to take this call, and since you insist on staying, when I get back, I want to know the exact nature of your relationship with this man."

"I look forward to enlightening you."

Actually, I'm already wishing I'd listened to Khalil and had gone back to the cabin. My uncle would have left in another day or two, and I wouldn't be battling nausea from being in the same room with him again. Now that Uncle Mars saw for himself that I am alive, I know he isn't going anywhere. My uncle isn't the kind to be defeated so easily. One way or another, he isn't going to return to the States empty-handed.

The moment my uncle disappears inside a room across the hall,

I blindly take Khalil's hand, and he lets me lead him into the same hall. There's another room next to the one my uncle disappeared in, and it's empty, so we quickly duck inside.

The room turns out to be an office with a view of a pond. Inside of it, there are large geese swimming peacefully.

"Why are we in here?" he asks, breaking his silence once more.

I could feel his quiet fury during the entire exchange with my uncle, but more than that I feel grateful that he respected my wishes and trusted me to handle it on my own.

For the most part.

I will never *ever* forget the sight of Khalil yoking my uncle up for as long as I live.

I let go of Khalil's hand and walk over to the weathered gray executive desk, wondering at its sturdiness as I trail a finger across the polished surface. Turning around, I lean against the desk to face Khalil with a smile.

It drops a moment later when I remember Tyler. "You lied to me."

Khalil, who is busy looking around the small room with a disinterested eye, stops to regard me. "Yes."

"How could you?"

"Is it truly the worst thing I've done to you, Goldilocks?"

I feel my hackles raise along with a little natural resentment at him for reminding me of our twisted beginning. "Are you saying that makes it okay?"

"No," he answers calmly before eyeing me closely. "I'm just wondering how important it is to you that I didn't tell you the man you may or may not have been fucking is still alive. Let me know what's up."

"Don't you dare turn this around on me. Who I fucked before you is *none* of your goddamn business. Tyler is the only reason I lived long enough to be standing here having this stupid argument. I deserved to know he lived, and even if I didn't care, the point is that you were purposely deceitful. It doesn't matter what you lied about. You still lied."

"Okay." Khalil nods and then comes to stand in front of me before kissing my neck. "I won't do it again."

"You—" Not expecting Khalil to yield so quickly, my mind had already formulated an argument before my ears caught up. "Oh." Still feeling the need to be combative and realizing he never actually apologized, I make the reckless decision to push further. "Now say you're sorry for lying about Tyler."

Khalil bites into my shoulder hard enough to make me gasp and dig my fingers into his shoulders. My panties become that much wetter. "I would, but I just promised I wouldn't lie to you again."

I hit his chest. "Stop provoking me."

"Impossible, Goldilocks. You're fine as fuck when you're angry."

I squirm against his hold, suddenly feeling like my clothes are too restrictive. "Sexy enough for you to finish what you started this morning?"

Khalil lifts his head to kiss me on the lips. "Let me guess," he says between firm presses of his lips. "You mean right now."

"You have something better to do?"

"Depends. Does this have to do with your uncle being in the next room and wanting to piss him off?"

"No, but we'll call that a bonus."

Khalil lifts me onto the desk, and I'm eager to spread my legs to give him access. "I suppose it would be fruitless to tell you that you shouldn't antagonize him like this." He works the button on my shorts free.

"He's the one who should be worried. I'm going to destroy him, Khalil. He has to pay."

"And he will," Khalil promises as he wrestles my shorts over my hips and ass. "But it won't be today. We need a plan that doesn't land all of us dead or in prison."

"Promise me," I plead once my shirt is over my head and discarded on the desk. "Promise me we'll end him."

"He's a dead man walking."

"Good," I growl, feeling my nipples harden. "Now fuck me. Make me scream."

Khalil seizes my chin so that I can't look away when he peers into my soul. "Is he the only reason why?"

"Other than the obvious, which is that I think you're sexy, addicting, and irresistible? Not a minute goes by that I don't want you inside me." Khalil's grip loosens as he chuckles. I ignore my own amusement and let my expression remain serious as I stare up at him. "I'm serious."

"Oh, I know you are."

"He doesn't think you're worthy of me," I blurt, feeling my acrimony double at how my uncle treated Khalil.

Khalil has the opposite reaction, snorting like he doesn't give a shit as he removes his gun from his waistband and sets it on the desk next to me. "So?"

"So I want to show him how you won me over. I want him to know just how worthy I think you are."

"I'm at your service, Goldilocks."

Khalil kneels in front of the desk and folds me in half by pushing my thighs into my chest and keeping his hands locked behind my knees. He prefers to eat me out this way because there's less chance of me squirming to get away and interrupting his meal when it gets too intense. I can already feel my arousal seeping free from the heat of his stare.

The goal was never to be silent and secretive, but from the first swipe of Khalil's tongue, I know that it would have been impossible anyway. I resist the urge to let my head fall back because half of the enjoyment is watching him savor my pussy. I don't try to quiet the moan that slips from my lips when Khalil performs that little trick with his tongue that I like.

"Oh, Khalil, fuuuuck."

I'm just getting into it when Khalil lifts his mouth with a loud smack.

His handsome face is twisted with desire when he stands suddenly and yanks me off the desk. I'm nothing more than a rag doll for him to fuck and use when he spins me around and bends me over the hard surface. I hear the jingling of his belt and then his jeans hit the ground around his ankles. Another moment and I feel his impossibly thick dick pressing inside of me.

I claw at the desk as he forces me to take it all. When it feels like he can't go any farther even though he's only halfway, he lifts my leg onto the desk, opening me up some more before sliding in the rest of the way until his pelvis rests against my ass.

We both let out a long moan because it feels like coming home.

"I would let the world burn for a shot of this pussy," he grumbles against the back of my head. "You don't even fucking know."

The smile I was wearing from his words falls when he begins to move without warning. At first, his pace is easy though not gentle, but then slowly it becomes more and more desperate until his pounding rhythm has me grappling for purchase.

In the clear reflection of the window, I spot Khalil with his head thrown back, eyes closed, and his teeth sinking into his lip as he rides me without mercy. It's perfect, too much, and not enough at the same time. I reach back and place a hand against his abs to try to slow his pace and ease my delirium, but he slaps it away.

"You wanted this dick," he reminds me as his thrusts become short and brutal.

"Yes, I want it. I want it!"

"Then fucking take it." Khalil wraps my long braid around his wrist and uses it to force my head from the desk just as a scream rips from my throat. The desk isn't bolted to the floor, so it skids across the hardwood from the force of Khalil's thrusts while the empty desk drawers open and slam closed.

Khalil isn't as mean as Thorin when he fucks, but he usually dangles just this side of traumatizing, which makes it even harder not to come crawling back for more each time.

It's impossible for anyone, much less my uncle, not to hear us. I can almost imagine the sheriff hearing us from outside and rushing away to hide in his truck, but since I don't want to imagine it, I shove away all thoughts of anyone outside this room.

Anyone but Khalil and me.

"I'm going to come, Aurelia, and I want you to swallow it. I want you to taste my cum on your tongue all the way back to the cabin to remind you where you belong. Do you hear me?"

"Yes."

Khalil pulls out of me and takes a step back, giving me only enough room to fall to my knees in front of him. His dick is glistening with my juices, and I don't hesitate to wrap my lips around him. I don't shy away from the intensity of his dark gaze as he watches me swallow him. And when I reach the limit of what I can take, Khalil forces me to take more.

My abused pussy is gushing and dripping his juices and mine onto the floor, and it doesn't escape his notice.

"Touch your pussy. Rub that clit. That's it. You want to come, Goldilocks?" I nod with a mouth full of dick. "Not yet. Put your fingers inside your pussy."

I do so, loving the way my walls grip me immediately.

I always love when Khalil fucks me because my body never forgets him after. It just demands more.

When Khalil gets close and finally gives me the green light, it doesn't take much at all for me to tumble over.

Khalil isn't far behind. Pausing from choking me with his dick, he suddenly pulls back just enough before he comes with a grunt, and I feel the first hot splash on my tongue. When he's done, he frees his dick while holding my gaze.

"Show me." I obediently hold out my tongue that's still a little blue from the Cookie Monster milkshake. Khalil's nut is wadded perfectly on top like a filthy ice cream sundae. "Good girl. Now drink it."

Closing my mouth, I let his cum slide down my tongue.

Khalil fixes his jeans before grabbing my arms. Unlike his roughness from before, he helps me stand and then places a gentle kiss on my forehead when I wobble a little. "You okay?"

"Yes, that was perfect."

He kisses me again and then helps me dress before backing me into the desk that's now shoved against the window where he trapped it. "You know I'm not done with you yet, right?"

"I know."

"Come on. Let's go home. We're not staying. I'm done playing with my food."

The house is silent when Khalil and I slip from the office. The door next to the room we played in is wide open, and I see that it's another office.

Our clothing is rumpled and the dull throb between my legs won't allow me to forget what I did.

My uncle certainly never will.

"So what do you think?" I whisper when I spot the fury on my uncle's face as we near him standing in the foyer. "You think he knows the nature of our relationship now?"

"I think he's been duly informed, baby."

As we pass my uncle, I try to think of something to say, but my uncle beats me to it. "I'd say it was nice to meet you, but we both know why that isn't true." Uncle Mars glowers.

"Oh, and don't sell the house," I call back as we reach the front door. "I kind of like it."

I don't say goodbye to my uncle as Khalil and I leave, and he doesn't say a word either.

CHAPTER SEVENTEEN

KHALIL

"Hold still," I order gently as I move the razor through the shaving cream with a gentle hand. "I don't want to nick you."

A naked Aurelia giggles and twitches on the chair I pulled from the dining table as if my touch is ticklish to her. She looks like a queen and the chair her throne. She has one foot planted on the floor and the other rests on the lip of the tub while I kneel between her legs. Her breathing quickens and her eyes glow as they rake my arms, chest, and shoulders for the thousandth time. She never can hide how much she enjoys seeing one of us on our knees for her. But not nearly as much as we enjoy it.

"That would be a shame."

"Yes, it fucking would." Aurelia was fucking stunning. Every complicated inch of her. She had the face and body of an angel with the fiery temperament of a hellion. And I was too fucking gone for her to ever turn back. "If you cause me to mar this pretty pussy or shed one drop of your blood, you'll have me to deal with."

"Sorry." She giggles again. "I just never had anyone…shave me…before."

Pleasure and possessiveness spear through my chest as I dip the razor in the warm water filling the tub before shaving away another strip of the fine hairs growing from her mons pubis. It takes an incredible amount of will to bite back the urge to demand that she never allow anyone other than me near her perfect pussy.

She was in a relationship with two other men—my best friends—after all.

"Back home, I'd get laser treatments, so I guess it's not all that different, but it *feels* different, you know?" Quietly, she adds, "More intimate."

"It definitely feels intimate," I agree since it really seems like she needs me to.

It's just the two of us in the cabin. Thorin and Zeke were gone when Aurelia and I returned from her ranch. While she got to work unpacking the bags, I unloaded the mattress and box spring from the truck and got it set up in Aurelia's new bed. When I returned upstairs, I caught her escaping to Thorin's bathroom with the shaving kit she'd picked up from town in hand.

The air in the bathroom is still damp from the shower we'd taken together before I ordered her into the chair.

I swish the blades through the warm, soapy water once more and shave away the last of the hair on the fleshy mound. There isn't a lot even though it's been months since her last treatment, so it only takes a few more stripes before I'm done with that part.

I tap her thigh. "Lift your leg."

Aurelia hesitates, and I raise both brows, silently reminding her that I've seen and put her in more exposing positions. She sits back in the chair and tilts her pelvis as she lifts her leg, which allows me to reach her vulva. I carefully shave away the hairs on her puffy lips followed by her perineum.

Once I'm done, I towel away the rest of the shaving cream, grab the jar on the floor next to me, and scoop some into my palm before massaging it into her newly shaved skin. I can't resist leaning over to kiss her glistening pussy.

I'm not done though, so I clean the razor before lifting her foot into my lap and spreading more shaving cream over her leg.

"Ooh, my legs too?" Aurelia says excitedly while wiggling her pretty little toes.

Focused on my task, I nod without looking up. "I meant what I said. I don't mind your pussy having a little hair, but the ones on your legs have got to go, Goldilocks. You be scratching the hell out of me while I'm asleep."

"Stop!" she squeals while shoving my shoulder with her other foot. "I do not."

"You do. Sometimes, I wake up in the middle of the night and I got to check because I don't know if I'm in bed with you or Thorin."

Aurelia's cheeks turn pink with shame, and then she's laughing so hard she almost falls off the chair. I smirk when she stops suddenly to check my seriousness. "You do not."

"I do."

"Oh my God." Embarrassed, Aurelia covers her face with her hands and shakes her head with a groan.

I gently pry her fingers away. "I'm just playing, baby."

Wearing a little smile, she kicks me. "Shut up. You were not."

"Nah, I really wasn't, but I love you anyway."

"I—" All the breath seems to leave Aurelia at once. "I love you too, Khalil."

"I know." I can't fake surprise even a little.

She'd taken so fucking long telling me that I figured I might as well tell her first. It wasn't planned, but it felt right. I'd never said those words to a girl before. I always imagined immediately regretting it the day I finally did, but instead, I feel nothing out of the ordinary—as if loving Aurelia to the depths of my soul and having her love me back was just an irrefutable fact and not some great epiphany. My heart had known all along, even if my head sometimes doubted I was worthy.

I take my time shaving her legs because I've got nothing better to do than make sure my girl is good. I take so long and such tender care that Aurelia starts to tease me about enjoying it too much, but I don't care. Aurelia's body is my temple, and I'd pray to it every minute of the day if I could.

Once I run a hand over her smooth calf and shin, I'm finally satisfied, so I let out the water and clean the tub while Aurelia remains motionless—likely fighting to stave off the dizzying feeling of how fast our relationship is moving.

At least, it feels that way for me.

Never in my life had I imagined ever shaving a girl's pussy. Fuck it, finger it, suck it, and pass it on to the next player once I'm through, yes. Most definitely. I never found myself wanting to care for it as if it were an extension of me.

I meant what I said earlier—I didn't care if she was bare or had a full bush. Her pussy as well as her heart belonged to me, and I'd care for both in any way she needed me to.

After I was done cleaning the tub and putting away her shaving kit, I stand and gather Aurelia to her feet before kneeling to work some fresh panties over her legs. I stand and pull a T-shirt over her head. One of mine, I think. She practically falls into my arms after that, and I wrap them around her waist. Her eyes still have that glazed look in them, and her smile is lazy, as if she's high on drugs. It's how she always looks when she feels cherished.

"What do you say, Goldilocks?"

"Mm-hmm… It's your turn?"

I snort out a laugh and let her go as I step over to the sink to wash my hands. "Appreciate it, but I think I'll pass, baby girl. Ain't nobody shaving my damn balls."

"No." She snorts out a laugh. "Not that. I meant the hair on your head, silly." She wrinkles her nose at my braids, so I glance at the mirror and run my hand over them, silently admitting that they were getting a little tired. Seeing the look on my face, Aurelia grabs my hand and leads me out of Thorin's bathroom.

She directs me to one of the dining chairs and tells me to sit before returning to Thorin's bathroom and making a pit stop in the one downstairs in order to grab everything she needs. When she returns, she begins undoing the six cornrows in my hair. At first, she works in silence, and even though I can't see her face, I know something's heavy on her mind, so I sit and wait patiently for her to tell me what it is.

It's not until my hair is detangled and I'm sitting at the kitchen sink, facing away from the running water, that she does.

"Can I ask you something?" she says as she squirts some shampoo into my hair.

I sigh, feeling my shoulders ease from the weight of her worries now that she's unburdening herself to me. "Is it about your uncle?"

"No, but we should talk about that too when Thorin and—" She stops herself when she realizes she was about to say Zeke's name. "When Thorin is back," she amends.

I reach up and grab her wrist while I twist in the chair to meet her sad eyes. "Whatever it is, Zeke will want to help too. He cares more than you think."

Aurelia sighs and goes back to lathering my hair. "Actually, it's Zeke I wanted to talk to you about."

I don't react other than to readjust in my seat. "Go on."

It's another minute before she finally asks her question. "You said Bane only awakens if Zeke is in danger. Is that the only way?"

"No. Bane has a trigger word. You say it, and all hell breaks loose."

I wait for her to ask me what it is, but she doesn't. Either she already knows it—which is possible considering Seth's reckless obsession to give her anything she wants—or she knows I won't tell her.

Against my will, my eyes drift closed when I feel her fingers massaging my scalp. "But are you *sure* those are the only reasons?"

I feel my frown but my eyes remain closed under the workings of her magical fingers. "DID is a proven disorder, but it isn't an exact science. Much of what Zeke's alters can or will do is bound to whatever the main identity needs in order to cope, so… Yes, I guess it's possible that Bane can choose for himself when to step in, but he never has. Only when Zeke feels threatened." Aurelia's fingers pause, and I feel the hair on my arms rise. "Why?"

Rather than answer my question, she asks one of her own. "Would Zeke be aware if he does?"

"Not really. He said it's just like falling asleep. One moment he's there and the next he's not. And he never remembers anything when he wakes up. Not unless he goes looking for the memories himself, but he never does for two reasons. One, they're not easy to retrieve—like any of the memories we have before the age of five, except these are only moments, days, weeks old."

"And the second?"

"He doesn't want to know what Seth and Bane did while his subconscious was locked inside the cage of his own mind."

Aurelia finishes washing my hair in silence. Once it's conditioned, she towels it damp and then we move over to the table where she sprays some of her heat protectant on my hair and then grabs the blow dryer. She begins working to dry my hair completely, and we don't speak again until she shuts it off. "Have *you* ever seen him split?"

"A few times." They weren't pleasant memories, and like Zeke, I'm not wild about reaching for them.

"Can you always tell?" she prods as she parts my hair with the tail of the fine-tooth comb. "What are the signs I should look for?"

"The slight variation in his voice and demeanor are the biggest tells, but by then it's already too late. The alter has fully taken over. I'm guessing that's not what you're asking."

"No."

"It's almost like a reset button," I explain. "Once triggered, he stops moving and reacting to stimuli because his mind is shutting down for a reboot. It all takes place within a few seconds, so if you're not aware of what's happening, it's really easy to dismiss."

"You make him sound like a robot."

"In some ways, he is. He has to be. Zeke went through every emotion while trapped in that fucking cult, and you better believe his brother used them all against him, so—"

"So he's in constant pain."

"Zeke doesn't always trust what he feels, and when he does, he's afraid of how it will be used against him. Sometimes, the best thing he can do is shut it all off."

"But he doesn't come back when he does."

Not caring about my hair when I'm assaulted with the sadness in my girl's voice, I pull her around and into my lap. "He always comes back, Goldilocks. Just not right away."

"It's not that I don't want to see Seth again. I do. I *love* him. It's just that…I feel like shit wanting that when I know it means hurting Zeke." She groans and hides her face again. "I thought loving multiple men who all know about each other was complicated."

I smile a little. "But it has nothing on being in love with a man with multiple identities." I rub Aurelia's back while she takes deep breaths. "Do you have feelings for Zeke, baby? Is that it?"

With her face still hidden, she shakes her head. A moment later, her shoulders tremble and she nods.

"It's okay to love them both."

Aurelia finally drops her hands. "But impossible to be with them both, right? Think about it. How does that even work?"

"I think this is something you need to talk to Zeke about." Before she can protest, I add, "When you're ready." Her lips snap closed. "Right now, I want you to tell me the real reason you're asking me about him." I make sure to push some firmness into my tone to make it clear I'm not letting her slide without an answer.

"When Zeke and I were on our run, something happened," she finally tells me. "Something that's happened before, but it felt different this time."

"What happened, baby?"

"I, uh…I sort of goaded Zeke into admitting he wanted to kiss me, and then he almost did and I panicked, so I stopped him."

"Seems…" I almost say mean, but then I think better of it and choose another word. "Wise. Why would you do that?"

"I don't know," she whines. "Because I wanted him to kiss me and then I didn't?"

"What changed?"

"I guess I wasn't ready either. I just hated not knowing. Some days, he barely tolerates me, and others he watches me like he… wants…me."

There's no question of that, but it's not for me to speak on another man's heart and dick, so I decide to move on to more pressing matters. "You said this happened before?"

"Not that part. When Zeke almost kissed me and I denied him, he wasn't himself."

My chest is tight and my voice is strained when I ask, "What did he do? Did he hurt you?"

"No, he…changed."

"Changed…" I echoed.

"He wasn't Zeke. His voice and demeanor changed just like you said. Khalil, it was just like that day the death squad tried to take me when—"

"Bane woke up," I interrupt through gritted teeth. "Are you sure?"

"Positive."

"And he didn't hurt you? Are you sure?"

"Zeke woke up before he could, just like Seth did. It was so quick I almost didn't even notice. All I had was this feeling of being hunted. To be honest, I thought Zeke switching would be more dramatic than that."

"It rarely is," I say. "Zeke doesn't normally fight it, but lately he has to. Seth too. It's obvious they're terrified of Bane waking up."

But from the sound of it, Zeke hadn't fought it at all. Or maybe Bane just wanted out that badly. Aurelia had dangled forbidden fruit in front of him only to take it away. I knew firsthand how swiftly and viciously the need to claim her took hold. It was that same compulsion that slithered itself around my neck when I first saw her lying broken and bleeding in my bed. It wouldn't let me go, wouldn't let me breathe, until I claimed her.

"Khalil?"

"Yeah," I say, snapping out of my trance to see the alarmed look on Aurelia's face. "What's up?"

"You're hard. Why are you hard?"

"Don't worry about that," I say while pushing my crotch into her like a sleaze. "I'll give it to you later. Now focus. You said this time was different. What changed?"

"Well, the first time it happened it was because Seth was pissed. I mean *really* angry at me. This time it was because…because…"

"Zeke wanted to kiss you."

Aurelia makes a sound of frustration and stands to pace in front of me. "You said Bane only wakes up if Zeke feels threatened, and now I'm worried that I pushed Zeke too far. I didn't mean to make him uncomfortable. I just thought…the way he looks at me sometimes…I swear he… I just thought I'd go for it, you know? Shoot my shot. Test the waters. I'm told some guys like it when girls make the first move. Now I feel like a thirst bucket and a creep, and I don't want to face him, but it's kind of hard when you live together in a cabin the size of a shoebox. No offense. It's a really lovely shoebox, and I think it's sexy as hell that you guys built it with your bare hands, but the three of you are just so *huge* with your giant muscles and overwhelming personalities. You all take up a lot of space, and a girl can only hide so much, you know?"

"Aurelia."

"Huh?"

"Focus."

"I'm *trying*."

"First of all, you're not a creep." Aurelia snorts derisively as she returns to braiding my hair. "If Zeke tried to kiss you, it means he wanted to. He stopped because it's what *you* wanted."

"So then why did Bane feel like he had to rescue him from me?"

I'm silent for a really long time because I don't have the answer. Something about Aurelia triggers Bane in a way we haven't seen before. I didn't have a ready answer. I only have theories to offer, and each is more frightening than the last.

"Maybe he didn't," I finally offer. "Maybe it was something else that made him step in. Something about you."

"I'm sorry. I don't follow. Bane is supposed to be the really scary one. The alter whose button you press if you want everything to go *BOOM*, right?"

"Look, one thing is clear, and that's the fact that we're all influencing each other in major ways, and we're going through some changes that we may not be ready to understand."

"And in the meantime?"

"I think it's better if you're not alone with Zeke anymore. Just until we figure out what is making Bane act out of the ordinary."

"I think that's going to be a bit of a problem."

"Because we live in a shoebox?" I arch a brow. The cabin isn't small by any means, but it's easy to forget that Aurelia is a billionaire. Our cabin could probably fit in her living room.

"You all could try shrinking your egos a little. That should save some room for me."

I grin and get comfortable in my seat. "Not a chance."

"Worth a shot," she grumbles.

Two hours later, Aurelia is finishing the last of the plaits when the sound of footsteps on the front porch reaches our ears. Thorin and Zeke must be home. When Aurelia goes to greet them, I stop her and make her stay while I check to verify that it's actually them. Her uncle not only knows that Aurelia is alive, he now knows exactly where to find her. It's not a coincidence that he's been checking up on us.

I leave the dining room and breathe a sigh of relief when the front door opens and I see my brothers walk in. They're wearing hunting gear, so I figure Thorin must have taken Zeke out to blow off some steam.

"Catch anything good?"

"Not really. You?"

"Just a whole lot of trouble," I respond.

"Can I come out now?" Aurelia calls out needlessly.

Thorin raises a brow, but he doesn't look surprised that I made Aurelia wait out of sight. He would have done the same thing.

"Come on," I grant.

Aurelia inches out, and I roll my eyes at her antics since mocking our need to protect her is her favorite brand of sarcasm. "Hi." She awkwardly waves a hand.

Zeke nods at her before flopping down on one of the armchairs. Usually, he prefers to hide somewhere alone and brood, but this time he stays with his gaze trained on Aurelia.

He watches me, I hear Aurelia saying.

Thorin crooks a finger at her, and Aurelia nervously shuffles over. She knows she's in trouble.

"You went to see your uncle?"

"That's what normal people do when their family is visiting from out of town."

"I'm sure you can make the exception for family that's already tried to kill you once."

"Semantics."

"Aurelia, my hand is twitching."

"I don't see what the big deal is. My uncle isn't stupid. He's here for a reason, but we've got the upper hand."

"Do we?" Zeke challenges.

Aurelia spins around to face him, and he tries to hide his surprise. "I mean, I guess?"

"So what is the plan now that we have the upper hand, wolf? I'm dying to know how going to see him is keeping you safe and alive."

"I'm still working on it."

"I'm pretending to be shocked, but I'm having a really hard time at it. You were reckless."

"I'm sorry?"

Thorin smiles sharply. "Even if you meant it, it wouldn't be good enough, songbird."

"I'm really sorry?"

Even though I can feel his exasperation, the look Thorin gives her is utterly devoid of emotion. It does its job and makes Aurelia squirm. Her brown eyes turn pleading, but it has no effect on Thorin whose mind is already made up.

Aurelia needs to be punished.

"You will be. After a few days of not being able to sit comfortably." Thorin produces a long and thin but sturdy enough looking branch, and Aurelia's eyes widen as she backs away. "You're going to be spanked, and you're going to take your punishment like a good girl. Do you understand?"

"That depends. Do I get a turn stripping *you* bare and bending you over to be spanked? I know about Tyler, you *pieces of shit*. I know he's alive, and you kept that from me." Only Zeke reacts to the news, but he's probably just wondering who the hell is Tyler.

"You also must know the reasons we didn't tell you," Thorin admits unfazed. "You're ours and *we don't share*, so what now? Are you breaking up with us to go back to him?"

"What?" Aurelia is visibly startled by the question. "No, of course not. What does that have to do with anything? Tyler was my *bodyguard*, not my boyfriend."

"Yeah, and I'm not wild about him having anything to do with your body. Protecting it, fucking it, touching it—it makes no difference to me. He's treading where he doesn't belong. Unless Tyler being alive changes things for you, there's absolutely zero point in knowing his fate. You'll never see him again."

Aurelia's lip curls. "Yeah, you made sure of that, didn't you?"

"Yes, and I'd do it again."

"You're an asshole," she hisses at Thorin. The two of them always fight the hardest because Thorin *is* an asshole and Aurelia doesn't back down.

"And you're deflecting. I'm done talking about Tyler Westbrook. Take off your fucking panties."

"What if I say no?"

"Unless you use your safe word, that means nothing to me, wolf." We wait for her to use it and safe out, but she doesn't. "Good girl. Now take off your panties."

Aurelia looks like she wants to argue, but one look from Thorin and she thinks better of it before reaching under the T-shirt she's wearing. She hesitates long enough to meet each of our gazes before realizing that none of us is coming to her rescue. Not even Zeke is as detached as he needs to be. With no way out, Aurelia finally curls her fingers around the waistband and pushes the cheap green lace down her thighs.

The shirt falls back into place with the hem resting just past the bottom curve of her ass, so I step forward and relieve her of the shirt entirely, until she's standing naked in the middle of the circle we make.

"Get on the table," I whisper in her ear.

"You're a jerk," she whispers back, and I smile.

I go to take a seat on the sofa while Aurelia tiptoes closer to the table, closer to where Zeke is sitting. When she tries to bypass him, I lift my leg, resting my foot on the coffee table so that she can't pass, and I smirk when Aurelia shoots me a look of betrayal.

Thorin is already blocking the other side, so Aurelia realizes with a tormented whimper that she has no choice but to stand between Zeke's spread legs.

She doesn't meet his gaze as she moves into position, and Zeke doesn't move from what is inarguably the best seat in the house.

Once she's standing between the armchair and the table, Aurelia inhales another grounding breath before she slowly lowers her upper half.

Meanwhile, Zeke stops breathing at all.

Remembering what Aurelia revealed to me about her encounter with Bane a few days ago, I tear my gaze away from Aurelia to watch him carefully.

My gaze is drawn back to Aurelia once her hands are braced on the table and she stops.

I clear my throat.

Aurelia sucks her teeth and lifts the rest of her body onto the table, until she's in position with her head down, ass up, and pussy spread for our perusal. I reach out and arrange her hair to fall over her shoulder so that it's not in the way.

Zeke takes his time admiring her body. His gaze is fixed on the roundness of her ass and the dimpled imperfections on the back of her thighs that make her all the more perfect. Finally, his gaze drops to the puffy pink lips peeking out from between her thick thighs. His green eyes burn brighter as he traces the soft petals that are no doubt glistening with Aurelia's dew.

"Zeke," Thorin says while holding out the switch without looking away from Aurelia. "You're up."

Both Zeke and Aurelia stiffen, but neither of them move or say a word in refusal. Aurelia exhales a harsh breath like she's shedding the need to run while Zeke curls his fingers into the arm as if he needs to anchor himself to it.

None of us move or speak as we wait for Zeke to decide if he wants to be a part of this or not. And not just the spanking but everything that it will entail.

Slowly, Zeke reaches out and accepts the branch from Thorin. Even slower still, he runs his fingers over the length, checking for anything that might damage her permanently. No doubt Thorin would have already ensured he found the smoothest branch for this task, but neither of us blame Zeke for double-checking.

Aurelia is precious to us all.

Satisfied with Thorin's choice, Zeke rises from his seat. Either hearing him or feeling Zeke closing in, Aurelia mutters something unintelligible.

Thorin steps forward and whispers something in his ear that I can't hear, but whatever he says helps to chase away the doubt and uncertainty plaguing Zeke's expression.

"Aurelia?" Thorin calls out.

"Yes?"

"This is going to sting," he warns her. "Under no circumstance will you reach back to try to grab the branch. You'll only hurt yourself further, and that will hurt us." Nod if you understand. Aurelia's lips part to speak, so he quickly adds, "Oh, and you will not make a sound unless it's your safe words leaving those pretty lips."

Aurelia mutters a curse, nods, and then falls silent.

Zeke doesn't deliver the first strike immediately, choosing instead to run the branch over her back, down her spine, and across her ass until he reaches her thighs.

The stretch of skin where her ass and thighs meet is where he decides to strike first.

Aurelia, forgetting Thorin's rule, yelps in surprise.

The second strike comes faster than the first in retaliation, and Aurelia does a better job of smothering the sound. The three of us purr our approval. The praise causes Aurelia to unconsciously arch her back and stick out her ass even farther.

Zeke accepts the unspoken invitation. Witnessing Aurelia so eager to please unleashes a part of him that has been dormant all these years. Thin, red welts appear everywhere that Zeke strikes until Aurelia's ass and thighs become a beautiful tapestry of pain and pleasure.

Her wet thighs do not go unnoticed by any of us.

Two strikes turn into five. Five into ten until the twentieth strike breaks Aurelia's silence, and what a sweet, broken sound it is.

Dropping the switch as if it were on fire, Zeke's chest heaves as he fights to catch his breath. Aurelia is dry-sobbing on the table while the three of us are rooted to our spots. We don't trust ourselves to touch her this soon when we're riding the edges of our control.

Zeke is the first of us to break. Cursing, he turns and runs from the cabin. Thorin chases after him. I stay with Aurelia.

Gently lifting Aurelia from the table, I carry her downstairs to my bedroom, where I lay her on her stomach before leaving and quickly returning with a glass of water, a jar of Vaseline, and a cool cloth.

I set the glass and jar on the nightstand before sitting on the edge of the bed and rolling her over carefully. She winces when the skin of her ass touches the bed and the hand that's been dabbing her face with the cool cloth flutters to her side. I'm surprised to find there are actual tears, since she's usually a master at holding them back. No doubt another survival tactic forced on her by her uncle.

I can't wait until the day I can carve every inch of skin from Marston George's bones.

I drop the cloth when I realize it's a lost cause. No matter how many tears I wipe away, more keep coming. The moment I give up, Aurelia angrily swipes at her cheek and then stares at her wet fingers in disbelief before her astonished and broken gaze meets mine. "Why is it that Zeke is the only one who seems to know how to make me cry?" she whispers. "Is it a good thing or a bad thing?"

"I suppose it depends on the reason. Turn over."

Aurelia rolls onto her stomach while I grab the jar of Vaseline. I focus on gently spreading the jelly over the red welts that crisscross her inflamed skin. "How are you feeling?"

"Like my boyfriends are psychos and I'm even crazier for loving them this much?"

I grunt and move on to the welts on her thighs. When I'm done, I set the jar aside and move to sit against the headboard. Aurelia practically crawls into my lap, and I'm quick to arrange her so that she's not hurting herself any more than we already have.

I hold Aurelia until she falls asleep and then I lay her back on my bed, carefully arranging her so that she doesn't feel the sting on her ass before I climb from the bed and leave the room.

When I step outside of the cabin, Thorin is walking back into the clearing alone.

"He okay?" I ask once he's within earshot.

"Sporting a giant boner that he didn't want Aurelia to see, but otherwise fine," Thorin answers tightly. His jaw is twitching, which means he knows something I don't.

"All right. So where is he?"

Thorin shrugs and steps onto the porch. "Said he's going to walk it off."

I nod and take a seat on the steps. As soon as I do, I'm reminded of the promise I made Seth that I would protect Aurelia at all costs, even if it means choosing her first. Feeling myself torn in two directions, with one slightly more persistent than the other, I hadn't really understood the gravity of what I was promising until now.

"I don't remember him being this stubborn," I blurt. "Do you?"

Thorin blows out a breath and shakes his head. "Not really. No."

"Do you think we were wrong?"

"Well, he's handling her being here a lot better than we thought, so it's possible, but my gut tells me no. We just need to let him do this his way. In his own time."

"That might be easier said than done."

Thorin turns to face me at the gravity in my tone. "What did you learn?"

"Bane. He showed himself to Aurelia again. During her run with Zeke."

Thorin is already shaking his head. "Not possible. She wouldn't be alive."

"And yet she came back without a scratch on her, which means we're either dealing with a new alter altogether or Bane is evolving."

"How?" Thorin barks. "There's no stimuli for that."

"Isn't there?"

The color leaks from Thorin's skin. "Aurelia." We're both quiet for a while before he speaks again. "But why? You think he—"

"Wants her? Maybe." Thorin swears. "There's something else," he adds, and the look in his eyes makes my heart drop like an anvil into my stomach. "Zeke told me there was a gap in his memory during their run. He said it couldn't have been more than a few seconds, but all he remembers is that Aurelia was fine one moment and then it felt like she was terrified of him the next."

"Definitely Bane."

"The bright side, if you're looking for it, is that if our theory tracks, we may not have to worry about him hurting her, but I'm not willing to take that risk."

"And if Bane is evolving, it doesn't mean we're safe. Somehow, I doubt that an alter who's already tried to kill us multiple times will be down for sharing a girlfriend."

"No."

"So we monitor Zeke even closer than we are and don't let them be alone together."

"Agreed."

"There's only one problem," I say with a wince. "After what happened tonight, it's only a matter of time before one of them breaks. I'm not so sure we'll be able to pry them apart after that."

"So what are you suggesting we do? Cockblock after we just spent weeks pushing them to fuck?"

"You got a better idea?"

Thorin swears again.

CHAPTER EIGHTEEN

EZEKIEL

My dick is hard.

And I wish I could say it's easy to ignore, considering this has been a chronic condition of mine since I saw Aurelia naked and haven't been able to scrub the image from my brain, but I can't. I've known since our run when she dared me to kiss her that I would give anything—*do* anything—to sink my cock inside Aurelia George.

And now…she knows it too.

It's been a few days since I let Khalil, Thorin, and even Aurelia goad me into stripping her ass raw with her pussy dripping all over our coffee table. Since then, as penance for our depravity, the mountain has sent us constant thunderstorms which, at this altitude, are particularly deadly.

It means we've been trapped inside this cabin under the stifling weight of our need for *days*.

And if I don't get out of here soon, I fear I'm going to pin Aurelia against the bookshelves she's currently perusing, ruck that pretty little white dress with tiny purple flowers up, and fuck her senseless while the books fall down around us until she's as lost in this fog of lust as I am.

And Aurelia is nothing if not vengeful.

Ever since the spanking, she's been giving us all the cold shoulder, but is it just to see us squirm for daring to flex our dominance, or is it because, if not for Thorin and Khalil's meddling that exposed me, she wouldn't be feeling so rejected right now?

Either way, she's barely spoken to us in days.

Whenever our eyes meet or we wander too close, I tug against the natural pull leading me to her, and the frost surrounding her grows.

Meanwhile, none of Khalil's and Thorin's attempts to thaw her cold shoulder have worked. Khalil, who is staunchly against junk food of any kind, even risked the lightning, mudslides, and fallen trees to drive into town and procure all of her favorite snacks. Five grocery bags of them. But the mountain of sugar, saturated fat, and sodium remained untouched on the kitchen island. Even the Oreos that Aurelia had been craving rather crabbily for over a week.

Only I seem to know what it is that she really wants though.

I'm currently lying on the couch and staring at the ceiling, trying to figure out how to tell her that I want her, when Khalil steps into the room carrying her pack and bow.

"Goldilocks."

"Yes, Khalil?"

She speaks, and my heart skips a beat.

When Khalil doesn't respond, Aurelia sighs at the unspoken command and lifts her head from the romance book she's pretending to read as an excuse to ignore our presence. I know because I've barely taken my eyes off her since she plucked one from the shelf before sprawling out on the rug that used to be Bruce.

Every so often her gaze became distant while reading, and she took too long to turn the page, or she turned the page too quickly, only to frown when she realized she had no idea what was happening.

Today, I have a particular fixation on the way her bronzed shoulders glisten in her white off-the-shoulder dress. A gift from Thorin that was conveniently given to her before I screwed everything up by showing my desire for her. Before, I had at least had plausible deniability, even after I almost kissed her, since Aurelia hadn't believed I truly wanted to. But now…now I'm screwed. If not for Thorin's impeccable timing, I wouldn't be rewarded with the bottom curve of Aurelia's ass peeking out from the hem.

Did I mention she's glowing? She's always glowing. I see why Seth calls her Sunshine.

"It looks like the storm is finally clearing up. We thought you might want to get out of the cabin today. Get some fresh air."

"Pass." Aurelia returns her attention to the romance she's reading, turns the page, frowns, and then turns it back.

"Khalil, you tried it your way. Now we do it mine," Thorin says as he joins us in the living room with a change of clothes for Aurelia. "We're all getting out of this fucking cabin for some fresh fucking air, and since it's not fucking safe for you to stay here alone, you're fucking coming with us. On your own two feet or hog-tied and fucking carried. Your fucking choice," Thorin barks.

Aurelia huffs and slams the worn paperback closed. I've read it. It's not bad, so I can understand her irritation at being drawn away from it, though I doubt that's the only reason she's glaring daggers at Thorin. As if there is an invisible leash tethering me to her, I stand when she does, and it draws her gaze over her shoulder. The moment our eyes meet, her chin wobbles from the rejection she thinks she knows is coming, and she turns away again. "Fine."

Khalil walks over to the kitchen island and starts shoving a few of the snacks he got for her into her pack before moving to the sink and filling her canteen with water. Thorin hands Aurelia the yellow bathing suit he's holding, and for the first time, Aurelia notices we're all in swimming trunks.

"Where are we going?"

"It's a surprise."

Aurelia's frown deepens, and then she attempts to sidestep Thorin to enter his bedroom. He quickly blocks her path.

"What the hell, Thor? I thought you wanted me to change?"

"Change here."

"*Why?*"

"I don't trust you not to lock yourself in the bathroom again."

"Sure. That's why." Aurelia turns away and tosses over her shoulder, "Pervert."

She misses Thorin's eye roll as she pulls her dress over her head and drops it on the floor. I suck in a breath at the sight of her naked body, so I notice too late that Aurelia's watching me with a glint in her eyes that spells trouble.

I guess I'm up to receive her ire.

She saunters over to me, bathing suit in hand and completely secure in her nakedness, and I decide in that moment to match her energy. I stay where the fuck I am even though she's expecting me to run. They all are. Thorin and Khalil are already tense from the explosion they see coming a mile away. When Aurelia stands in front of me—so close our bare toes nearly touch—I inch a little closer and watch the way her pulse quickens.

"Something you want to say to me?"

She visibly swallows past the nerves that are warning her I won't be the easy adversary she mistook me for. "Bathing suits are complicated," she says despite the simple one-piece that Thorin procured for her. "Will you help me?"

My gaze flicks to Thorin and Khalil who are both scowling

at their girlfriend. And me, like I'm poaching on their territory. Technically, she's not mine, so it does sort of feel as if I'm stepping over some line.

And just like that, I'm hard again.

Fuck it. If there's any hope of Aurelia telling me what happened between her and Seth that fateful day, then maybe it starts here. By earning her trust. Still, I feel the need to warn her.

"You're playing with fire, princess."

"What can I say, Ezekiel? Maybe I like the burn."

I take the bathing suit from Aurelia and crouch, which puts her pretty pussy level with my face. I want to kiss it so bad that my hold on the suit tightens and I come dangerously close to ripping the material in half. Instead, I stretch the neck wide so that she can step inside. Aurelia braces her hands on my shoulders, and I feel her fingers flex curiously at the bunched muscles there before she sticks one foot through the hole followed by the other, bringing her even closer to my mouth.

Her scent is a goddamn drug.

I lick my lips and then quickly wrestle the snug material up her curvy body until I'm standing again. Aurelia works her arms through the straps and then adjusts the square-neck bodice over her breasts.

"Thank you."

I nod and walk away without a word because I don't trust what will come out if I do.

I go into the kitchen to fill my own canteen, and when I return, Aurelia is wearing denim overalls over her bathing suit and her tan hiking boots with purple laces. She has her pack on and is studiously ignoring whatever Khalil is whispering to her as he hands Aurelia her bow and quiver.

When she doesn't respond, he sighs and takes her hand. Aurelia doesn't snatch her hand back, but that could easily be explained by the tight grip Khalil has on her hand. I frown at it and feel my teeth clench with the effort to feign indifference before Khalil glances my way and nearly catches me. "You ready?"

I nod and grab my pack and the crossbow from where they're waiting by the stairs. "Yeah."

"Wait," Aurelia says when we all take a step toward the door. "I have to do something before we go." She wrangles her hand free from Khalil's and then disappears downstairs.

The three of us exchange a look, but I'm the only one who knows what she's really doing—radioing the sheriff. I can feel Thorin and Khalil's impatience and confusion but none of us say a word when she returns. Khalil just reclaims her hand and we leave.

The four of us hike down to the valley where the ATVs are stored inside a cave at the base of Big Bear. The Ski-Doos we use during the winter months are already stored away until the weather turns. The mouth of the cave is carefully hidden under dense foliage just in case some campers get curious. Khalil gets to work uncovering the entrance while Thorin and I duck inside to pull out the ATVs.

"Wow," Aurelia says as we line up the ATVs. I look up from sticking the key in the ignition to see her staring at the vast expanse of open terrain. The ground is damp and muddy from the storms but otherwise barren and not worth the awe in Aurelia's brown eyes. In the winter, it's a frozen tundra that never seems to end, especially if you're unlucky enough to be caught out there during a storm. "I haven't been back here since Thorin lost that race."

"What race?" I ask before I can remember that I'm not supposed to care. Resisting Aurelia is an exhausting and futile endeavor. And I'm losing.

"Mario Kart," she answers with a smile that tells me the memory is a fond one.

I stare at her because I can't look away. "Who won?"

"I did." She's beaming proudly until Thorin speaks and her smile drops.

"Because she cheated." Thorin rolls his eyes as he walks over to his ATV. "Seth and Khalil helped her."

Aurelia wrinkles her nose and cuts her gaze his way. "Are you saying you want a rematch, loser?"

Thorin throws a leg over the seat and drops down. "Bring it, swindler."

Aurelia looks around and realizes that we're one ATV short at the same time I realize mine is the only one that can seat two. We always make sure we have at least one off-road vehicle that can carry a passenger just in case we come across a lost or injured hiker. It happens at least once or twice every year. Patrolling the Cold Peaks is how we usually spend our days once the temperature rises, but admittedly the reason goes beyond passing time or being a Good Samaritan.

It's to ensure we are truly alone and not being hunted by the demons I left behind.

"You're with me," I say after the awkward silence goes on long enough.

"We can switch—"

"She's with me," I repeat firmly, cutting off Khalil's offer. I hold out my hand to Aurelia, and I forget how to breathe as I wait to see if she'll accept it. Aurelia is visibly surprised and suspicious. She probably thinks it's a trap or a test, and I do nothing to assure her because it's both.

I don't know what it is about this girl, but I can't help dancing the fine edge between wanting her close to me and pushing her away. Maybe I'm just hoping she'll get tired of my shit and make me choose once and for all. Or maybe I'm just racing toward an agonizing inevitability—Aurelia realizing she doesn't belong here with us. Whatever the reason, it's that look in her eyes when she catches on that sets my blood on fire.

She puts her hand in mine, and hers is both soft and callused in places from training with the bow and working in her garden. Sometimes I sit on the porch with the excuse of getting some air, just so I can listen to her sing while she works the soil.

Without taking my eyes from her, I close my hand around her smaller one and pull her over to me. Aurelia stumbles a little and I catch her by her waist before pulling her the rest of the way until she's between my legs. I blindly reach for the spare helmet and then turn on the mic inside before handing it to her. Aurelia puts it on while I grab mine and do the same.

"You want to drive?" I ask over the speaker.

She shakes her head and then hops on behind me. There's another awkward moment while she debates where to put her hands until I reach behind me and draw her arms around my waist. Her palms feel hot through my shirt, but I block out the sensation when Thorin starts speaking.

"The rules are the same as last time. First one to the end of the valley wins. First one to throw something at me, dies."

"I think you mean last one to the finish line is a rotten egg!" Aurelia yells through the mic. I'm still cringing from having my eardrums nearly blown when she slaps my shoulder repeatedly. "Go, go, go!"

So I press on the throttle and I go.

Thorin is swearing profusely as he uses the cool water from the stream he's crouched in front of to wash the egg from his hair. Aurelia is attempting to help him, but her uncontrollable bouts of laughter are making it difficult. Khalil, having anticipated a rematch, had snagged a few eggs from the cabin before we left, and after Thorin crossed the finish line last again, the three of us ambushed him before he could even dismount and smashed the unbroken eggs over his head.

What I *hadn't* expected was for the prank to trigger one of Seth's memories.

Realizing what was happening, I quickly walked away from the others under the guise of taking a piss while the memory played in my head like a clip from a home video.

In the remembrance, Seth is sitting at the kitchen table watching Aurelia use Khalil and Thorin's thick skulls to crack two eggs open. Apparently, they'd just gotten into a pissing match over her, though the reason why rests on the fuzzy edges of the memory. Seth is clutching his stomach and laughing like a wild hyena. At the same time, I can feel his rising respect for Aurelia at such a bold and rebellious move when her survival still rested on them *wanting* to keep her around. Khalil and Thorin are frozen in shock with egg dripping down their faces and hair when Aurelia's eyes meet mine between them and the memory abruptly ends.

I snap out of it with a gasp and lean my head forward against the nearest tree as I try to catch my breath. The moment my heart is no longer racing, I close my eyes and try desperately to pull the memory back. No matter how hard I dig, that door remains firmly closed to me, and I'm left wondering if the recall was a simple side effect of waking up or Seth *feeding* the memory to me, guiding me where he wanted me to go.

To Aurelia.

Every part of me hopes for the latter because it means Seth isn't gone after all.

For whatever reason, he's staying just out of reach, obscure and lost in shadow along with the memories he *doesn't* want me to see.

"You all right?"

I jerk my head up from where my sweaty forehead is resting against my hand to see Khalil standing next to me. I didn't even hear him approach because the wilds long ago honed each of us into the perfect predator.

I nod. "Yeah."

"You want to talk about it?"

I shake my head. "No."

Khalil nods and then reaches into the pocket of his trunks and pulls out a blunt and lighter. I turn and lean against the tree while he lights the end. "Here."

I take the blunt, and the two of us smoke in silence until I hear Aurelia's excited chattering and Thorin's quiet responses. I'm not naive enough to think this means she's no longer upset with us. I think she's just happy to be out of that stifling cabin. We all are.

"What are you guys doing?" she asks cheerfully when she reaches us. I just handed Khalil the blunt, which he hid from her gaze.

"Nothing." Khalil smirks, and Aurelia gives us both an unamused look.

"Really?" she asks dryly. "Because I smell weed."

"You smoke?" Khalil asks her curiously.

Aurelia wrinkles her nose. "No."

"Then no, you don't." She rolls her eyes and then looks around as if she's searching for something. "What's wrong?" Khalil asks when he notices.

"I'll be back. Nature calls."

She's already walking off when I hear myself say, "Stay where we can see you." Catching onto to what I've done, what I let slip, my gaze drops to the ground like a coward when I feel three sets of eyes land on me.

Aurelia's the first to break the tension by saluting sarcastically.

"Yes, sir." She spins on her heel and walks off, and only then do I let my gaze rise to watch her go.

"You'll get used to it," Thorin says the moment she's out of earshot.

"What?" I ask without looking away from Aurelia's back.

"That incontrollable need to guard what's yours."

"And her mouth?" I ask without denying Thorin's claim. "Will I get used to that too?"

He shrugs and accepts the blunt from Khalil. "Either man up and admit she makes you hard or learn to hide your boners better, brother."

I don't bother looking down to confirm that I am in fact hard as hell. I have been ever since I made Aurelia wrap her arms around me on the ATV and felt her breasts pressed against my back. And it hasn't gone down in the minutes since we climbed off—not after I won the rematch and she threw her arms around my neck to kiss my cheek in gratitude.

"I don't think either of you want me doing anything about it," I say after giving Thorin's words some thought.

"Why not?" Thorin asks before placing the blunt between his lips.

"Because if she were mine, she'd only be mine. I sure as shit wouldn't share." Pushing away from the tree, I walk in the opposite direction of where Aurelia went, feeling my brothers' gazes on me as I go.

CHAPTER NINETEEN

AURELIA

The hike to my guys' latest attempt to get past my iron walls seems to go on forever. I assumed we were returning to the hot springs, but when we bypassed Maia during the race for the furthest edges of the valley, I realized belatedly that I had inexplicably returned to where it all began.

Little Bear.

Honestly, I never thought I'd see it again. I'm not sure what emotions I expected to feel now that I'm back, but I realize a little alarmingly that it doesn't seem as scary as it once did.

Tyler and I had stood on a cliff once that gave a view of the entire wilds, along with the other peaks, and I remember feeling terrified of being lost in all of it.

"Are we near the crash?" I ask.

Thorin shakes his head and points in the direction I believe is east. "The fuselage is about a day's hike that way. The tail was found near the pass between Maia and Little Bear." Thorin looks over his shoulder to meet my gaze. "It was at the bottom of the river."

I guess that explains why Tyler and I never found it and why we nearly died countless times searching in vain.

We hike for another hour before Khalil leads us into what

appears to be a cave on the outside but is actually a tunnel. Inside, there's a shallow stream of water cutting through the middle and leaving only narrow, slightly elevated paths on either side. It only takes us a couple of minutes to reach the other end of the tunnel. A blue bird flies by when we step out, but it's the sound of rushing water filling my ears that causes a prickle of excitement to spear through me.

The sound gets louder the farther away from the tunnel we travel. Wherever they're taking me, I hope we get there soon because my feet are killing me.

"Are you ready for this?" Zeke whispers in my ear when we seemingly reach the end of the path we're traveling. I barely resist the urge to jump out of my skin at his sudden and unexpected proximity. His body is a furnace, making the sun a laughingstock.

Thorin doesn't wait for a response and pulls back the dense foliage overhanging the path. I gasp when the calm turquoise pool at the bottom of a waterfall at least a hundred feet wide and fifty feet high comes into view. Water cascades over the many ledges in the bedrock of the steep cliff, adding to the striking visual the scene makes.

"Holy fuck, that's beautiful," I say as I gape at the hidden oasis my guys brought me to. "Wait… Why didn't Tyler and I come across this when we were looking for the tail?"

"Because we're on the opposite side of the mountain."

"Really? How the hell did we get here so fast then?"

"Because we know where we're going, including the shortcut that shaves half a day," Zeke answers smugly.

I stare at his profile since I'm pretty sure that was a dig at my former bodyguard, but I choose to ignore it because I didn't want to risk the headache pondering all the reasons why Zeke would be jealous of Tyler. It's not like he wants me. Or at the very least, he doesn't *want* to want me.

Feeling my temples throb, I let go of the train of thought.

Eager to dip inside the gorgeous pool, I look around for a way down, but I don't see a clear path. "How do we get down there?"

"This way." Thorin takes my elbow and leads me off the path and into the trees until we come across another rocky path on the side of the cliff. When we reach the bottom, I drop my pack and bow and quickly unclip the straps of my overalls before shimmying out of the denim.

I only stop long enough to apply sunscreen to my chest, legs, and arms.

"I'm not one to photograph every moment of my life, but right now, I'm really wishing I had a camera," I say as I look around.

"No need. We'll bring you back here as often as you need to keep the memory alive, songbird."

I not sure about *often* since the trek to get here was brutal, but I appreciate the offer.

I tiptoe to the edge of the water where I stop to eye it warily. "There aren't snakes in there, are there? This really seems like the kind of place where snakes go to snack on tourists."

"Probably," Thorin answers. "Although, I doubt any of them are venomous."

"Um…"

Seeing my hesitation, Thorin scoops me up and starts walking into the water. "Come on, songbird. I won't let you get eaten."

"From your lips to God's ears."

"I'm pretty sure God tuned us out a long time ago, songbird."

I snort but then flinch when the water gets deeper and laps against my skin. I decide a moment later that I'm being ridiculous. The guys wouldn't have brought me here if there was even the smallest chance of me getting hurt, so when Thorin lets me go, I don't panic.

"Thank you for bringing me here," I coo as I turn to face him in the waist-deep water and slide my hands up and down his remarkable chest. "The only thing that can make this day better is an inflatable and a couple of cocktails."

He smiles. "Can't help you there." Thorin swims away and then disappears under the water. He reappears a minute later near the falls.

I startle a little when Khalil and Zeke race past me, and I follow in their wake, stopping only after a few feet to tread water and watch to see who wins. I realize only after Zeke passes Thorin first and Khalil slaps the water that they were using Thorin as the finish line.

Zeke and Thorin race next, and I stay where I am, knowing that they are racing to reach me first.

About thirty feet from me, they both dive beneath the water and out of sight, and I hold my breath until Zeke bursts out of the water first, directly in front of me. It looks like he's getting ready to say something when his eyes widen and he's yanked under again.

There's a lot of splashing, grunts, and growls while he and Khalil wrestle for dominance.

Rolling my eyes, I swim over to the rocky outcropping on the side and climb onto the rocks, surprised to find the surface smooth. I sit on the edge and wring my hair out, glad that I at least braided the front last night. Still, I'm not looking forward to wrestling with it later when I wash it, but that's future me's problem.

After a few minutes, Thorin swims over while Khalil and Zeke leave the pool.

I watch—but more like drool—as he plants his hands on the rock and hauls himself out of the water.

"Are you hungry?" he asks once he's standing and dripping water next to me.

"Starving."

Thorin holds out his hand and pulls me to my feet. We climb down the rocks and skirt the edges of the pool until we reach our packs and the fire Khalil is building. It's too warm for one, so I assume they're planning to catch our lunch.

Too hungry to wait, I open my pack and peruse the snacks Khalil packed for me.

I do a little happy dance when I spot the Oreos tucked inside. Snatching the pack open, I pluck one from the tray and look around. "Where is Zeke?" I ask when I realize we're one short. I feel like a thirst bucket, but I'm also feeling too good to care. Thorin wordlessly points, and my heart drops when I spot a figure walking along the exposed rock in the middle like a median dividing opposing lanes of traffic in a street. "What's he doing?"

"Jumping."

"What?" The Oreos tumble from my lap when I stand abruptly. "He can't! What if he hits the side? What if it's too high?"

"He won't, and it's not."

"You don't know that. Get him down from there!"

Thorin looks up at the cliff. "Sorry, wolf. No can do."

I spin around just in time to see Zeke sprinting toward the edge. At the last moment, he leaps in a wide arc that just barely clears the sharp ledges jutting out of the falls and waiting to break his body in half and splatter him in a crimson display of carnage. I watch with my heart in my throat as he speeds toward the pool like a bullet and then tucks his arms and legs at the last moment before plunging beneath the surface.

He made it.

It does nothing to calm the angry beast howling inside of me as Zeke swims for the shore, so I storm to the edge of the water to give him a piece of my mind.

"Easy," Thorin says as he drops what he's doing and follows. I ignore him.

Zeke walks out of the water with a grin that drops when I plant my hands on his chest and shove him back. "Are you crazy?"

"What's your problem, princesa?"

"Don't you princess me. What the hell was that?"

"What?" He grins again, making his dimples appear as water drips from his dark hair. "You didn't enjoy that?"

"What do you think, you gigantic ass? Does it look like I enjoyed watching you scare me to death?"

Zeke laughs, and as much as I enjoy the sound, I want to punch him for not taking my worry seriously. "That's too bad because I'm about to do it again."

"Oh, no the fuck you're not."

Zeke gives Thorin and Khalil a dry look over my shoulder and turns away to head back up the path that takes him to the top of the cliff. I find myself following, cursing him out the whole way. "Zeke, I'm serious. Don't you dare."

"Why do you care?" he tosses back without any venom. He sounds like he's genuinely curious.

"Why *don't* you care?" I retort. "That was incredibly reckless. And stupid."

"It was fun."

"Not for me!"

Zeke gives me a blank look, but his tone is even more devoid of emotion. "Unlike Seth, my world doesn't revolve around you, princess."

"Well, maybe it should since I'm the only with any sense around here."

I'm so racked with worry I don't even catch on to the ruse until it's too late. It doesn't even occur to me that Zeke is leading me up the cliff to get me alone until we're standing at the top and he quickly takes my hand.

"I've been wondering all day how I was going to get you away from them."

Okay, now I'm confused. "Why would you need to get me away?"

Zeke huffs in frustration. "Because my brothers are overbearing, meddling bastards, and it's impossible to talk to you or even get near you without them hovering."

"I don't want you to jump," I plead when I realize he's standing near the cliff again. "Please?"

"Tell me what happened that day, and I won't."

"I told you already. *Nothing* happened. Why won't you let it go?"

"Because nothing has made sense since I woke up, and it all leads back to you."

"Well, if you feel that way, then jump. See if I care." I go to storm back down the path when Zeke snatches my hand and yanks me back. I stumble into him, and Zeke pinches my chin between his thumb and forefinger to pull me even closer.

"Is it me you're really afraid for, or is it Seth, princesa?"

"Why does it even matter when you clearly don't care about yourself?"

"I care."

"Yeah, it really seems like it," I toss back sarcastically.

"I won't jump," he promises.

"What are you telling me for?" I say as I cut my gaze away. "I don't care."

Out of the corner of my eye, I can see Zeke smiling at me, and his teasing makes me irrationally angry. "Is this the real reason why you pulled me up here?" I ask. "To interrogate me more and make me feel even more awful than I already do?"

It's a long time before Zeke answers, and I almost believe he won't. "No, princesa. I never want to make you feel awful."

"Could have fooled me," I grumble.

Zeke takes my face in his hands and tilts my head back. "It's not the reason," he repeats firmly.

"Then why? If not that, why bring me up here? Why get me alone?"

"To do this." Zeke presses his lips against mine, and the roaring in my ears rivals that of the waterfall. I must make some sound of distress because he stops just as abruptly. "I'm sorry."

"You kissed me."

"Yeah, princess. I did."

My hand reaches up and curls around his nape. I feel his dark hair brushing my fingers, and I can't help stretching them toward the strands. "We're kissing now?"

Forehead pressed to mine, Zeke nods with eyes closed. "If that's okay with you."

"It's been okay since I mistook you for Seth and you shoved me into the snow."

Zeke winces at the reminder. "I'm sorry about that." Eyes low as if drugged, he kisses me again before I can tell him it's okay. That I understand why.

When it feels like my knees are going to give out, I shove him hard enough that he stumbles over a rock and lands on his ass.

We're both fighting to catch our breath as Zeke stares up at me with a frown, waiting for me to explain why I stopped him or demand for him to kiss me again. I do neither, choosing instead to fall to my knees and climb on top of him. "Don't be," I finally say.

Zeke reaches for my hips and settles me over him at the same time I lean down to pick up where we left off. Lips fused and limbs tangled, we kiss above the roaring waterfall. It amazes me how differently Zeke and Seth kiss even though they share the same lips and feel the same. Seth kisses me like he might never get the chance again, while Zeke kisses me lazily like it's the only thing he was made for.

And then he shocks the shit out of me when he asks, "Can I touch you, princess?"

I nod, and Zeke kisses me one last time as if he can't resist before rolling me onto my back. He then curves the front of his body along my side rather than climbing on top of me and trapping me under his weight like I'm craving for him to do.

I don't realize I'm shaking like a virgin—even though I've been fucked and sucked and turned inside out by all three of them— until Zeke slowly runs his palm down the inside of my thigh and back up again. By his third pass, my trembling stops and on his fourth, he grabs the seat of my bathing suit that's damp from more than just the pool water and shoves it aside.

The mist and breeze from the falls immediately work to cool the hot flesh between my thighs until Zeke places his palm there and I'm burning for him all over again.

"Now it feels like we're both playing with fire," he grumbles as he teases my pussy. "You're so fucking sweet, aren't you, princess?" Feeling like I need him close, I whine as I reach for him, but then his eyes suddenly flash and his voice deepens as he rumbles, "*Mine*."

"I think you're getting a little ahead of yourself." Zeke doesn't answer though because he turns his head away and takes a few deep breaths as if shaking off some dark influence. I pause. "Are you okay?"

After a few more seconds, he finally answers while sounding like he shoved his head underwater and he just barely kept from drowning. "Yeah," he chokes out roughly. "I think we should stop. I don't want to hurt you."

My heart kicks painfully against my chest as I feel my panic rise. *No, we're so close.*

I lift my head enough to kiss him, and he doesn't hesitate to kiss me back, accepting my gift of the air he seems to be fighting for. When I end the kiss, I pull back enough to see his green eyes. "Does it feel like I'm worried, Zeke?"

Curling my hand around his between my legs, I push on his fingers resting against my hole, and Zeke groans and shudders before curling and pushing them deep inside me.

"Fucking hell," he swears as his shoulders tremble once more. "You're so—" He stops as though he's at a loss for words. My clit throbs like it has a pulse against his palm, and I squirm for the friction I definitely need. Zeke's green eyes become sharper, more focused when he sees me trying to race to the finish. "If we're not allowed to stop, you're not allowed to come yet, princess."

I watch with quickening breaths as he plunges them deep one last time before freeing his fingers and bringing them to his mouth. Somehow, I still don't believe that the man who's been scowling, taunting me, and wishing I would disappear is going to actually taste me.

And then he does.

I don't breathe as he slips his fingers between his lips.

With his gaze locked on mine, Zeke sucks them clean and then promptly pushes them back inside, driving them deep and drawing those sounds from me again that make his pupils dilate and nostrils flare. I'm on the verge of pulling him on top of me and begging him to fuck me when he finally turns those torturous fingers to my swollen clit.

"Zeke…"

"Just let it happen, princesa. I'm here."

He circles my nub, and I come with a cry that he quickly muffles with a kiss. "Shhh. We have to be quiet, princess," he pleads against my lips. "Thorin and Khalil can't hear."

Zeke continues kissing me even after my body's settled and I'm quiet. It goes on and on with the two of us only stopping long enough to catch our breath before we're drawn back together like polarized magnets. Weeks of longing and lingering looks have left us hypnotized and powerless to resist now that we've given in.

That is until I feel something tickle my cheek.

It's easy to ignore with Zeke's fingers still stuffed deep inside my pussy like he's opening it to draw out another orgasm, but when that light fluttering feeling returns, I frown and lift my hand to slap it away.

Zeke grabs my wrist and I open my eyes to see that his are full of wonder. "Wait."

Okay, now I'm freaking out. "What is it? What is it?"

He exhales in awe and disbelief. "It's a butterfly."

"No, really. What is it?"

Zeke lets go of my wrist and presses the back of his fingers to my face below my cheek. The ticklish feeling leaves me a moment later, and then he pulls his hand back to show me a blue butterfly with black spots balanced on his bruised and scarred knuckles.

"What the—" The butterfly flaps its wings and flies away. Zeke and I follow its flight path to a swarm of them flying under a copse of trees not far away. "Oh, wow."

"They must have just hatched." He kisses me one last time and then frees his hand from between my legs and fixes my suit before rolling away.

Zeke makes a pained sound, and I tear my gaze away from the butterflies just in time to see him adjusting his erection inside his swimming trunks. Guilt and desire mix together, creating a swirling vortex of need until I can't stop the words from tumbling out. "I can help with that."

Zeke stiffens and then he sits up like he's already regretting what we've done.

But he's not pulling away, and I realize belatedly that he's not remorseful. He's terrified. And he doesn't want me to see. It raises more questions than it answers, but there's no time for that like now.

"That's okay," I say in an easy tone as I sit up. "I've got better things to do anyway. Like reading about sex instead of having sex."

Zeke turns his head, and I can see the terror fading in the wake of his amusement. "And how are you enjoying the titillating romance of Damien and Willow?"

Surprise flows through me. "You've read it?"

"Once or twice."

"And?" I press when he doesn't say more.

"Honestly, I didn't care for the hero."

"What?" I squeal. I can't control my snort and giggle as I move to sit closer to him. "Are you serious?"

"Yeah. I did *not* like that guy. Instead of just telling the girl he supposedly likes how he feels, he kept being a dick to her. I spent the entire book wishing he'd just walk into traffic and leave that poor girl alone."

"It's a good thing he didn't, because that would be tragic. Damien is bae."

"Wait, you mean you liked him?" Zeke raises his brows, and I feel my cheeks warm.

"I mean, yeah, kind of. I guess I empathized with him? I don't know. Even when he was being an unreasonable asshole, I still wanted to hug him. Actually, I thought—" *No, that would be crazy to admit.*

"What?" Zeke urges while tipping his head closer to mine.

I inhale deeply, and Zeke licks his lips as if he can still taste me. I can definitely still taste him. "I thought he reminded me a little of you."

Zeke jerks his head back and chokes out, "What?"

All I can do is shrug when words fail me. I can't believe I just admitted to thinking about him while reading a romance novel. Silently, I pray he finds it as awkward as I do and changes the subject, but no such luck.

I've already looked away like a coward, staring as Thorin and Khalil take turns diving from the outcropping of rocks near the falls and into the water. Khalil is currently doing his best to drown Thorin after he beat him at whatever competition they're having now.

"Am I a dick to you?" Zeke practically whispers.

I continue staring at the beautiful, sparkling water below that reminds me of Zeke's green eyes. "Sometimes, yeah."

"And you don't...hate me?"

I shake my head. "No."

"Why?" he challenges gently. "Because you feel sorry for me?"

I turn my head to face him and meet his stare dead-on. "Because I know what it's like to be betrayed and how hard it is to trust again after. Because I know what it's like to be used and abused by someone you share blood with. Because I know what it's like to love deeply and have it all fall apart. I don't feel sorry for you, Zeke. I just feel you."

"You've been in love before? With the bodyguard?"

I snort. "No. Not with Tyler." I smile like I'm sharing a naughty secret. "It's a recent development, but already it feels like I've gone ten rounds in the ring."

"You're still upset," he says like it only just occurred to him.

"Of course I am. You can't seem to decide if you want me or hate me, and I haven't forgotten you all lied to me about Tyler. Well, not *you*," I correct with a grumble. "The other you." *Seth.*

"You know you really should let that go," he says gently to not come across as dismissive. "Your feelings are valid, princess. They just won't change anything. When it comes to other men, Thorin and Khalil are not going to apologize for wanting to hoard you for themselves."

"And what about you? You don't want me all to yourself?"

"I don't think I should answer that," he says. "I wouldn't want to send you anymore mixed signals."

"Will you answer something else for me then?"

"Sure."

"Why do you call me princess? Is it because you think I'm spoiled?"

Zeke chuckles derisively, but it feels aimed at himself. "It's what I told myself at first so that I didn't have to face the truth, but no. I don't think you're spoiled."

"It's okay if you did. I am a little." Zeke laughs, and I join him until it dies off shortly after. "So why?" I ask when my curiosity won't allow me to let it go.

Zeke's olive-toned cheeks turn a startling shade of red, and he barks out a nervous laugh. "Because every time I'm near you, I can't help but feel like you should be wearing a crown and I should be kneeling at your feet." He stares at his palms as if his head is asking him what the hell he's doing admitting all of this to me.

My head however has left the chat, and my heart is doing backflips in my chest. "You want to kneel for me?" I whisper.

"All the time." Feeling like there's more he wants to say, I wrap my arms around myself and stare at our feet dangling over the sixty-foot drop. "I don't want to be a Damien," he finally confesses. "I don't want to wait until it's too late to tell you that I want you."

I swallow past the emotions that threaten to choke me. "I'm sensing a but in there somewhere."

"But… I don't know how to want you without this voice inside my head warning me that none of it is real. That it's all going to come crashing down on me."

"Bane?" I gasp, and it feels like a blind reach in the dark for a way to understand him.

Zeke's eyes are sad when he shakes his head. "A different kind of voice. The kind you and I both have."

This time the sadness I sense is my own. It isn't paranoia, resentment, or a broken heart telling Zeke that I'll betray him. It's intuition.

But no, that's not quite right either. Zeke's concern has never been for himself. This terror that kept him from loving or even accepting me is also for his brothers.

Tears threaten to spring free. "Oh, Zeke."

"I wouldn't blame you if you did. And I don't think they would either." He jerks his chin toward the bottom of the cliff where Khalil and Thorin are, and we watch them trade matching violent grins as they circle one another in the water. "If you're going to hurt us, do it gently, princess," Zeke begs. "If there's any part of you that isn't sure, if you're just biding your time, tell me now." Zeke's green eyes grow darker when they swing my way, and it feels like a warm vise around my neck. "Because I'm losing, Aurelia. I don't want to listen to that voice anymore." I stop breathing when Zeke gently takes my hand and places it on his searing chest where his heart is pounding fast underneath. "I'd rather follow this if it means falling into you."

"Zeke…"

"Tell me now," he pleads again. "Once I'm cured of this fear keeping me from you, I won't be able to turn away. No matter where you go or what you decide later, I'll follow you to the ends of the earth, princess. I'll live only for you." Quietly, he adds, "Even if you don't want me to."

I don't know what to say to that, and since I have the feeling Zeke isn't expecting a response to his—what even was that? A promise? A threat? A proclamation of love? Somehow, it feels like all of the above, and my stupid heart is eating it up.

Am I seriously going to let Ezekiel Cura win me over that easily? *Yes.*

We sit on the cliff above the waterfall in comfortable silence, watching the sun set and only speaking to make fun of Thorin when he keeps tripping over the same rock.

"It's getting dark," Zeke says when my stomach growls loudly. It's only then I remember that I never got to eat.

We both head down just as Khalil returns from taking a leak.

"I don't know if I can walk back," I say as I wiggle my aching toes. "I'm pooped."

"Good. Because we're not going back tonight," Khalil says as he reaches inside the extra pack he brought and pulls out a tent. "We're camping here."

After dinner, the four of us find ourselves back in the water under the full moon, but this time we decide to skip the swimsuits after the guys goaded me into a striptease. The three of them are sipping on the warm beers they stowed away in their packs. I had a sip of Zeke's, who surprisingly had been the first to tip his toward my lips when I mentioned wanting to try it. It was gross, so the guys grimacing after every sip is definitely warranted.

"I think we should kill my uncle," I blurt as I stand in the water near the rocks. The waterfall behind me almost drowns out the words, but when the relaxed expressions of my mountain men morph into tight jaws and tense lips, I don't have to question if they heard every word.

"And if he's already left Hearth?" Thorin asks.

"Then we follow him back to the States. Kill him there."

Khalil and Thorin glower at me. I can't see Zeke's face, but I feel and hear him push through the water to stand a little closer behind me. "You know we can't do that," Khalil says bitingly.

"We have to. My uncle will never stop, which means I can never stop. Next time, he won't send more men. He'll get more creative than that. My death was always meant to look like a tragic accident, and I'm not wild about all the ways he can make that happen. We need to go on the offensive."

"It's not safe for us to return home. Isaac could still be looking for Zeke."

"So we kill Isaac first." I shrug.

Khalil gives me a weird look before shaking his head and staring at the water. "Weed makes you bloodthirsty," he grumbles. I bet he's regretting talking me into trying it now. It took me an hour to stop giggling and another two before I was no longer convinced the woodland animals were rising up against me.

"I've actually been thinking about this since the death squad showed up on our doorstep," I correct. "So that's the plan then? We kill Zeke's brother and then my uncle? Any more family members we should put on the chopping block?"

Thorin flashes a condescending smile. "If it were that easy to kill Isaac, we would have done it by now."

"It's been ten years. Do you even know if he's still alive? A man like that has to have enemies. Also, karma. *Also*, what he's doing to people is incredibly illegal. Who's to say he's not in prison by now?"

"He's not," Khalil confirms. When I give him an inquisitive look, he matches Thorin's condescending look. "You really think we'd let ourselves stay in one place for so long without keeping tabs on him?"

"How?"

"A friend from back home. Someone Isaac would have no reason to connect us to."

"So call him. Get the four-one-one so we can one-eight-seven his ass."

"It doesn't work like that. Quentin will only send us a message if we have a problem. No message, no problem. It's safer this way."

It's quiet for a while, and then I let my intrusive thoughts win. "What if Quentin's dead?"

Khalil gives me a blank look. "Then someone he trusts will let us know."

"Right, okay, sure. I still think murder is the only way." Thorin, Khalil, and Zeke visibly clench their teeth, and I spot at least one twitchy palm.

"Aurelia may be right," Zeke says, weighing in for the first time. "We're too exposed here now."

"There is another solution. We can leave," Thorin says with his dominating gaze locked on mine. It's all I can do not to squirm and agree to whatever he says. "Disappear again."

"Like…forever?"

"I wouldn't mind somewhere warm and tropical this time," Thorin says as he tips his warm beer to his lips and takes a swig. "Aruba, maybe."

"But like…forever?"

The three of them stare at me, but Khalil is the first one to break the stony silence. "You agreed to this, Aurelia."

"No. I agreed to a life with you. I'm just trying to offer an alternate reality of what that looks like. You have more reason to go back than any of us. Don't you *want* to see your family again?" It was a redundant question because I'd glimpsed Khalil's sadness when he thought no one was looking. Of the three, he had given up the most, leaving his old life behind—a rising career, a chance at marriage and kids with someone not in love with his best friends, and his family.

"Of course I do," he snaps back. "But I'm not willing to risk any of you to make it happen."

"It doesn't have to be your burden alone. If we could just be on the same page for once, we could do this together. *Share* the risk *together*. We wouldn't have to spend the rest of our lives looking over our shoulders. We could be free."

"And is this what you need?" Zeke asks. I turn in the water to face him, and for a moment my focus is locked on the troubled pinch between his brows. "To be happy…with us?"

"No," I answer easily, and the furrow clears. "Killing my uncle and your brother will just be the cherry on top. I think it's what we *all* need to finally feel safe, and I don't think we should have to choose between one or the other. We can and should have both."

"Okay," Thorin says and I'm turning again with my wide eyes shifting between the three of them.

"Really?"

"Yeah," Khalil says and then downs the rest of his beer and tosses it onto the shore. I frown at that and make a mental note to make him pick it up later. This place is too beautiful for him to litter. "If that's what you want, then fuck it. We'll kill them all for you, baby."

I only just remember not to smile like a loon at that and choose to appear responsibly grim about taking a human life instead.

CHAPTER TWENTY

KHALIL

U gh, my feet hurt," Aurelia whines for the second time in ten minutes. We're finally heading back to the cabin after spending a couple of days camping by the falls, rather than leaving the next morning as planned.

I stop walking and wait for her to pass me before I scoop her spoiled ass up since I know it's what she wants. We're not far from the ATVs anyway, and I'm tired of damn near breaking my neck to make sure she's still behind me every time she rolls an ankle or falls a little too quiet for my liking.

"Aww, thank you, my big, strong man. That's why you're my fave." She pats my cheek.

Thorin damn near trips over his feet and I smirk at the instant jealousy flooding his blue eyes when he turns around. "Wait, what? Why is he your fave?"

Aurelia hoods her eyes and raises her nose like the princess Zeke proclaims her to be. "Because both of you pretended not to hear me. That's why."

Thorin looks at me in complete confusion. "Hear *what*?"

I could explain to Aurelia that he really hadn't heard her complaints because he was deep in thought figuring out how to deliver her uncle's head to her on a platter, but I'm not willing to give up my spot as number one, so I leave his ass out to dry. "No clue."

I walk past him and Zeke who's quietly chuckling at Aurelia's antics. A month ago, he would have been convinced that Aurelia pitting us against one another was a sign of her being up to no good. Now, he finds it amusing, his green eyes twinkling like she's the most adorable thing ever.

Just what the actual fuck were they doing at the top of that waterfall?

We reach the ATVs and ride back to the foothills of Big Bear, where we store them inside the cave before making the slightly grueling trek up to our lonely cliff. One of the reasons we chose it was for how hard it was to find and difficult to reach if you did happen to spot it. Aurelia must have been truly desperate the day she found our cabin.

We breathe a collective sigh of relief once we reach the haven of our clearing and see that it remains unmolested.

"Home sweet home," Zeke says as he holds open the front door of the cabin for us.

Aurelia smiles up at him as she passes, and when he grins back and immediately goes to follow her like he's possessed, I grab him by the collar and yank him back out onto the porch. Thorin sees and drops his arm over Aurelia's shoulder, steering her toward his bedroom before she can see.

The front door slams closed, and they disappear from view while Zeke rips away from my hold. "What the fuck, Khal? What the hell is your problem?"

I shove him into the door, and he grunts from the impact. "Is there something you want to tell me, Ezekiel?"

"Yeah." He shoves me back and shoulder checks me as he walks past me. "Don't call me that."

I don't point out that he doesn't seem to mind when Aurelia does. He's stopped correcting her, but apparently, she's the exception. Instead, I spin around and grab his nape before he can leave the porch, and then I force the front of his body against the pillar cornering the stairs and railing.

"You can't be around her," I warn while he grunts and growls to get away. "Not while we don't know what's happening with your alters. Seth and Bane are even more unpredictable now. I mean it, Zeke. It's not safe."

"That's not your call."

My fingers loosen from the unbridled possession in his tone. "Oh, so you want her now? Just like that?"

Zeke manages to twist enough to throw an elbow into my face that I see coming a mile away and still narrowly miss. "All you need to know is that I'm not going to hurt her."

Unconvinced, I shake my head. "You can't promise that. Something's changed. You almost died, and Bane couldn't care less. Aurelia almost kissed you, and he charged to the surface before you even knew what was happening. The only thing we *do* know is that Aurelia is affecting Bane, and until we know why or what it means, stay *the fuck* away from her."

I feel Zeke's dark energy follow me into the cabin, but he doesn't come inside. I watch through the windows as he retreats into the woods, and it's a few hours before he returns.

Just in time for dinner.

Unhooking my tool belt, I give Zeke's old room one last surveying glance and then leave, following the smell of pasta, tomato sauce, and freshly baked bread up the stairs.

Zeke walks into the cabin sweaty and disheveled just as I reach the landing. He lets the front door slam behind him and then walks past me on the stairs without so much as a glance.

I'm tempted to follow him and talk some sense into him without my own jealousy and anger riding my every word, but I know it won't do any good.

When I reach the kitchen, Thorin is spooning a huge heap of spaghetti onto the last plate. My mouth waters when I see steam curling from the thick, meaty sauce.

Aurelia is getting really fucking good.

Pride spears my chest just like this morning during training when she made me lose my footing and very nearly put me on my ass. I know how tenacious Aurelia can be. I've seen it when we're training. Even when her mouth is complaining, her eyes and ears are soaking up everything, feeding her need to master any task put before her. I also know her secret. Though she's usually so full of confidence, I know that Aurelia still doubts whether she can survive without her uncle controlling every aspect of her life. That insecurity only doubled after seeing him at the ranch, but one glance at the subdued pleasure in her expression as she admires her handiwork tells me she's coming around again.

That's right. My baby can do any-fucking-thing and I dare anyone to tell her differently.

She's standing at the island across from Thorin when I wrap my arms around her waist. Aurelia immediately melts into me with a sigh, and I kiss her neck. "I hope you're hungry."

"I'm starving. Thank you." I kiss her neck again and then pull away to help Thorin carry the plates over to the table. He made four even though Zeke still won't eat. As always, he'll wait until Aurelia has climbed into bed with one of us for the night and then make himself a sandwich or something. During meals, the broody bastard usually sits quietly at the far end of the table to watch the rest of us interact. Still, Aurelia always makes sure he has something to eat despite the sting of rejection that always comes from her efforts.

Once the plates are in their correct settings, I grab the leftover food and set it on the table in the middle for easy-to-reach seconds. Aurelia pauses at that since we never have before. It took us a while to get past the awful taste and fear of food poisoning to even finish our plates despite our size and voracious appetites, so until now, a second helping was out of the question.

I wink at her when she gapes at me and then I lick my lips with a different kind of hunger when she blushes so prettily. The three of us sit, and then I hear the shower turn off downstairs, and minutes later, footsteps on the stairs.

Zeke and I lock gazes when he walks into the dining room wearing only basketball shorts and socks. Water from his shower still clings to his bare chest while his black hair looks ruffled, sticking out in every direction as if he'd quickly toweled it dry.

"I hope you like spaghetti," Aurelia says as he joins us at the table.

He doesn't sit. Instead, he stares at his plate, *not* touching it at the end of the table. In what can only be described as a fuck you to Thorin and me, Zeke lifts his plate and moves into Seth's old seat across from Aurelia. She's in the middle of pouring a glass of water for herself when he sits down. She keeps pouring, her gaze locked on Zeke while I watch the water get dangerously close to the rim with no signs of her stopping. Thorin reaches out at the last moment and relieves her of the pitcher before the ice water can spill over the top.

He sets the pitcher down with a thud, and it finally snaps her out of it. Aurelia's questioning gaze becomes embarrassed, dropping to her own plate as she shifts and fidgets in her seat like she's suddenly nervous.

"Looks good," Zeke compliments, and her wide-eyed gaze flies back to his. "I love spaghetti."

He *hates* spaghetti. I barely suppress the urge to roll my eyes. Even if he liked the dish, Zeke won't eat her food. He never does, so what the fuck is he playing at? One glance at Thorin and the annoyed look on his face at the lie, and I know he's thinking the same thing. We're not left wondering for long.

I've got one eye on my plate in front of me and the other watching Zeke so the moment he reaches for the fork sitting next to his plate, my entire focus shifts that way—as does Thorin's and Aurelia's. We all watch in shock as he stabs the huge mound of spaghetti and slowly twirls it around the prongs, his gaze pointed with intent across the table at Aurelia.

One glance at the girl sitting next to me and I see she's no longer breathing. Her lips are parted just the tiniest bit as she watches Zeke twirl that fucking spaghetti.

Finally, he raises the fork, his lips parting halfway, and then he cleans the fork with one bite. He chews, slowly…thoughtfully. It feels like it goes on forever before he finally swallows.

"Mmm," Zeke hums rather dramatically. "It tastes good too, princess. Really fucking good."

A rush of breath escapes Aurelia. "I…" She seems at a loss for words for a moment. "Th-thank you."

He winks, and out of the corner of my eye, I see Thorin roll his eyes. "You're welcome."

The rest of dinner passes uneventfully with the four of us mostly eating in silence. After dinner, Aurelia grabs the ice cream from the deep freezer and fills up four bowls before passing them around.

"You going to fuck that spoon next, Zeke, or can the rest of us eat in peace?"

Aurelia throws Thorin a confused frown, but he's too busy glaring at Zeke to notice.

Zeke laughs but says nothing. He digs into his ice cream, and the rest of us do the same. After dinner, Thorin and I do the dishes, both of us quiet so we can listen to Aurelia and Zeke playing cards in the living room.

"Want to clue me in on what the fuck is going on? What exactly did you say to him?" Thorin whispers as he stacks the dried plate with the others.

I blow out a breath as I scrub a glass cup too hard until it shatters in my hand. Cursing, I drop the broken pieces inside the sink and hold my hand under the running water while Thorin grabs a first aid kit from under the sink. "Keeping them apart isn't going to be as simple as we thought," I answer as Thorin takes my hand and inspects the wounds. "He likes her."

"Since when?"

"Since always," I answer with a grunt. "Wanting her was never the problem. Trusting her was."

Thorin's brows furrow skeptically. "Zeke trusts her now?"

"Not yet," I say with a shake of my head. Zeke won't come around that easily. "But I think he's warming up to the idea."

"Great," Thorin spits out like a curse as he wraps clean gauze around my shredded palm.

I shrug, feeling defeated and relieved at the same time. "We have no one to blame but ourselves. We kept pushing them together to make life easier for all of us. We can't be upset with them now that it's finally working."

"He's being reckless," Thorin maintains like I hadn't spoken. "We didn't know then that Bane could apparently pop up whenever the fuck he wants, and what he seems to want is Aurelia. Seth and

Zeke were able to stop him before any damage was done, but what if they can't next time?"

"We keep training her. Tomorrow, you need to teach her how to use the tranquilizer gun."

Thorin spits out another string of vicious curses that I take as agreement.

"What are you two girls whispering about?" a soft but dry voice interrupts.

Thorin pauses mid-*fuck* and the two of us turn toward the kitchen entrance where Aurelia is standing with Zeke hovering close behind her. She takes one look at my bandaged hand, and the suspicious expression fades as she rushes over and takes my hand.

"What happened?"

"It's nothing. Broke a glass." The worried pinch between her brows doesn't ease until I lift her joined hands and kiss the back of hers. "Come on, Goldilocks. I want to show you something."

I pull her out of the kitchen, and I can feel Thorin and Zeke following as I lead our girl down the stairs and into the basement. The outward trepidation she used to feel when coming down here is long gone, but I know she still feels it sometimes, inside where she hides it from us. The knowledge that I can never fully erase that feeling or redo that first night claws at the inside of my chest with sharp, vicious talons until nothing is left but tattered shreds that I hide behind an easy expression once we reach the bottom of the stairs and Aurelia glances up at me.

The room has been habitable for days now, but I couldn't stop working to make it perfect.

She doesn't *need* a bed. She has mine and Thorin's to share. But I know firsthand after living in a one-room hut with my best friends for years how important it is to have a space for yourself. The loft offers little comfort or privacy if she needs space from us, and even though the idea of being separated from her fills me with dread, she should have that.

The four of us pause in front of the door, but no one speaks as they all wait for me to open it. I grapple for the right words to say until it becomes awkward, and then I expel a breath and rub the back of my neck before meeting her soft gaze. "I hope you like it," I say simply but earnestly.

I grab and turn the handle and push open the door before I can lose my nerve.

Stepping back, I allow Aurelia to step inside the room first so that I can give myself a few extra seconds before I have to see her face. She's quiet as she looks around, completely unaware or uncaring of the three of us crowding in behind her. I take the moment to look around and try to see it through her eyes.

There's the bed pushed sideways against the far wall with the headboard facing the window to give her ample floor space since she likes to dance at random moments during the day or night, and I like to watch her. The canopy mounted to the ceiling above the bed is a sheer, light material with small fairy lights woven through it. There's a small nightstand with a drawer and a shelf that already houses her favorite books shoved under the window. At the foot of the bed is a secondhand vanity table I found for a bargain and repainted. Her makeup and toiletry bags are already resting on top. Mounted on the wall above the bed are a couple of floating shelves with the scented candles she'd picked up as well as more of the books she favors that wouldn't fit inside the nightstand.

The entire room is a soft blue—from the walls to the ceiling, bedding, canopy, round rug, and smaller furniture pieces. I chose the color after learning that it is actually her favorite and not gold, as her uncle decided it should be for her image. I chose a soft tone because, while the world might have forced Aurelia to expose her harder, thornier side, I know she is gentle and vulnerable at heart, and only with those who matter.

It's all secondhand with the exception of the bed, mattress, and sheets. All those trips for supplies I volunteered to make had been to secretly procure all of this.

For her.

I watch as she stops in the center of the room and silently notices it all, taking in every detail. After a full minute, Aurelia finally drifts over to the bed, and I watch her bend to get a better view of the headboard. She gently—almost reverently—runs her fingers over the carvings, but I still can't see her face to get a clue at what she's thinking.

Aurelia's shoulders tremble, and then she makes a sound for the first time. It sounds like shock and pain.

Shit, did she get a splinter? I was so careful making sure all the wood had been smoothed after I was done carving.

Shit. Fuck. Shit.

"Are you okay?" I ask as I step forward, my hands already reaching for her arms. "It's okay if you don't like it. Maybe we can—"

Aurelia allows me to turn her, and her brown eyes aren't only wide and brimming with unshed tears, her cheeks, jaw, and lips are soaked with all the ones she's already shed. "I love it." Surging onto the tips of her toes, she throws her arms around my neck and kisses me while I squeeze and pull her closer. "Thank you, thank you, thank you," she chants cheerfully between kisses.

Something settles inside me, and I allow myself to smile. "You're welcome, Goldilocks."

"Hey, what the fuck?" Thorin sputters. "I know Khal did all the work, but we helped. Where's our gratitude?"

Aurelia giggles, and I reluctantly release her when she pulls away to hug and kiss Thorin. When she gets to Zeke, he offers her a closed-lip smile that doesn't match the burning look in his eyes, and she rises onto the tips of her toes to kiss his cheek. "Thank you for giving up your bedroom for me."

"You're welcome, princess."

CHAPTER TWENTY-ONE

EZEKIEL

I crest the steep hill at a jog, focused on the path in front of me and putting one foot in front of the other when Aurelia, who is running alongside me, drops to the ground suddenly. I stop and turn in time to see her roll over onto her back. "Go on…" Her breath is a rattle as she draws in as much of the warm summer air as she can. "Go on without me. Save yourself."

Rolling my eyes at her dramatics, I walk over to her and cross my arms as I stare down at her. She's staring up at the canopy, but her eyes slide my way when my shadow casts over her. "So close. You almost made it to the finish line this time."

Aurelia groans and rolls her head away from me, exposing the lovely slope of her neck. "You're just as bad as he is."

He being Khalil. "He's also waiting for you to continue your training."

She makes a sound that's a cross between a cough and a burp. "Why? So that I can protect myself?" She doesn't say it mockingly, but it does feel like she's reaching for a reason why she's letting us push her so hard.

"So that you can kill your uncle," I remind her.

"Ah, yes. That."

My gaze snags on the handheld tranq gun strapped to her hip. Carrying it with her always was Thor and Khal's only condition on letting her run alone with me. I offer my hand, and when she accepts it, I pull her to her feet. "Changed your mind?"

"Not a chance."

Tipping my chin back the way we came, I meet her gaze that seems more focused now. "Then let's get going."

Aurelia groans but then starts running. Neither of us speak again until we reach our stopping point. The lake.

"I still don't think all of this is necessary," Aurelia complains.

It's been our routine for weeks now. Aurelia and I run every morning at the crack of dawn, and then we meet Khalil by the lake for some hand-to-hand combat before she goes to Thorin for weapons training.

"What?" I ask with a raised brow.

"The training. The fighting. It's not my uncle's way. He'll never meet me head-on. He'll try to stab me in the back instead. I have to beat him at his own game."

"Do you?"

"What do you mean?"

"You've been living by his rules for half your life. Maybe it's time you start writing your own. *Make* him meet you head-on."

"You really think I can make my uncle do anything?"

"I think you have a better shot at that than being deceitful, princess. I don't know how I didn't see it before, but it's not in your nature. You're much too open and honest. Sometimes to a fault."

"Should I be insulted or…"

"Do you feel insulted, princesa?"

"What I feel is torn. I don't know if I like it when you call me princess or princesa more." Before I can figure out a response to that, she glances over at Khalil, who crooks a finger at her with a rigid look in his eyes that says he won't be taking it easy on her this session. Neither will Thorin later, but for different reasons. Last night, the two of them got into it again over opposing ideas about how to deal with her uncle. Thorin went all alphahole and Aurelia called him out on his shit.

Aurelia sighs and looks up at me as if hoping I'll save her.

"Good luck," I mumble before I walk away, ripping my shirt over my head as I start for the water. I stop at the edge and drop my shorts before tossing them a safe distance away. The water is cool despite it being the middle of July, and it feels like heaven against my sweat-slicked skin as I wade in.

When I'm deep enough, I begin swimming laps until my thoughts are no longer muddled and I can focus.

We're going back.

And going back means Isaac will find me that much sooner. I don't know how to feel about it yet. A part of me wants it to be over so I can finally start living—for Aurelia, for my brothers... for me. The other, quieter part is whispering that it can't be done. Isaac can't be defeated. Even now my muscles are threatening to lock up at the thought of him, but I force my arms and legs to keep moving through the water as I sort out my own secret plan to keep my family safe.

We've already decided that getting into Isaac's compound a second time won't be possible. My brother is nothing if not a perfectionist. Any flaws that Khalil and Thorin already exposed getting me out will have already been compensated for twice over.

The only viable solution is drawing Isaac out.

And straight to me.

Of course, Khalil, Thorin, and even Aurelia rejected that plan, which means I'm alone in this. Maybe it's the way it should be. The way it was always meant to be. Khalil and Thorin might be able to hide me from Isaac, but they haven't been able to shield me from the memories. Those are never far away.

I'm swimming toward the shore when Khalil shoves Aurelia against a tree and traps her there by her throat. Aurelia escapes his hold quicker than she did yesterday, and Khalil's visible surprise costs him when she slams the heel of her palm into his nose unnecessarily.

I hear his shout of pain as he stumbles backward while clutching his nose. "Goddamn it, Aurelia." His tone is more growl than anything, but Aurelia is far from intimidated. She crosses her arms and leans most of her weight on one leg as I leave the lake.

"I told you that I'm hungry. You said I can eat when I manage to make you bleed." A tiny smirk—all she dares with Khalil glaring at her—plays at the corner of her lips. "Mission accomplished."

Khalil doesn't say a word. He just repositions his fingers over his broken nose and then snaps it back into place before walking the few feet to the shoreline to wash away the blood. He walks past me again and then snatches Aurelia's bag that he brought with him from the ground. Inside is a plastic-wrapped sandwich filled mostly with meat that he tosses to her.

Instead of eating it, her gaze finds mine. "Are you okay?"

Her question draws Khalil's attention, and since he knows me better than anyone and Aurelia is beginning to, I turn my back on them both as I answer. "I will be."

CHAPTER TWENTY-TWO

AURELIA

I have no one to blame but myself when Khalil knocks me to the ground for the third time. It's our sparring session, and I'm distracted. It's getting hotter every day with the sun in my eyes becoming more obnoxious by the minute, but that's not what's bothering me.

"*Ow*," I say accusingly toward the sometimes-gentle giant—when he's not training me to become a killing machine. Khalil really takes these sparring lessons seriously, and the bruises I usually walk away with are starting to overlap but none more than my confidence so I wear them with pride.

"You're not focusing," he snaps when I send him a knowing glare.

The reason for my distraction is currently watching us spar from the porch a few feet away.

Zeke and I have gone right back to where we were pre-waterfall—before he had his fingers in my pussy and his tongue in my mouth. Before he told me how he feels.

Guiltily, I guess I still find myself comparing him to Seth sometimes, which only adds to my confusion. Seth was steadfast in his feelings for me, never wavering once. Zeke runs hot and cold and leaves me feeling less secure.

I'd sworn at least a million times in the weeks since the falls that I was done with him, but the moment he looks my way I'm stuck in place wondering if today will be the day he tells me again how he wants to kneel for me like I'm his princess and he's my knight.

But he never does.

It's like he gave me a taste of what could be before snatching it all away.

In Zeke's defense, he did warn me that he wasn't ready, and silly me, I still hoped for more.

"On the contrary," I say as I struggle to rise and dust myself off. "I haven't stopped fantasizing about seriously maiming you since you forced me out here to practice."

"And yet you still haven't been able to land a single punch." I swing on him, and he easily blocks it. "Just as I thought. Pathetic."

"This is abuse. You're mean."

"I'm not your boyfriend right now. I'm your trainer. Now try to hit me."

I swing on command, once again forgetting to keep my guard up, and Khalil decks me with his gloved hand right between the eyes. The blow is hard enough to send me sprawling out into the grass.

We do this for ten more minutes before I threaten to send my other boyfriend to beat him up. Khalil tosses back his head and laughs as if it is the funniest thing in the world.

"Thoooooorin!" I shout.

It only takes a few seconds before Thorin appears at the door. His gaze is alert even though his rumpled clothing makes it obvious that I woke him from a nap. "What's up?"

"Oh, nothing. Khalil just told me that he can easily beat you with his eyes closed and one hand tied behind his back."

A few feet away, I hear a quiet snort, but I'm not brave enough to look Zeke's way. He clearly has no qualms about looking because I haven't stopped feeling his eyes on me since Khalil dragged me out here and Zeke followed without a word.

"Really?" Khalil scoffs. "You're going to sic Thorin on me? That won't work. I taught him everything he knows."

"Maybe not everything," Thorin denies with a roll of his shoulders to show off his power. "I've picked up a few things on my own."

When Khalil narrows his gaze like he wants him to prove it, I grin like I'd just won a prize.

Men are *so* easy.

"Get him," I command with a finger pointed at a glowering Khalil. "*Show no mercy.*"

Thorin hesitates, but we both see the moment he capitulates to my demand. He removes his shirt, and Khalil rolls his eyes before he removes his gloves. I think that maybe he's refusing until they both square off with narrowed gazes and a calculating look in their eyes that says they know this will be no easy match.

Flouncing over to the porch where Zeke is lazily lounging on the steps as if he doesn't have a care in the word, I keep my distance—as much as the stairs will allow—and pop a squat a couple of steps below him.

It's not until the first punch is thrown by Thorin, which Khalil narrowly dodges, that Zeke speaks. "You're good. You know that?"

I peer over my shoulder with an innocent expression perfected by years of pretending I was someone I wasn't in order to sell out stadiums. "I don't know what you mean."

Zeke nods toward Thorin and Khalil. "You got them to fight so you can get out of training."

"Maybe." I shrug. "Can't prove it."

He chuckles and then leans forward, bringing his face closer to mine. "I don't have to, princess." Reaching out, he fingers a curl. "Or maybe I don't want to."

Feeling like he'd reached a flaming hand inside my chest and used it to squeeze my heart, I turn my head away, forcing him to let go of my hair. "You didn't eat this morning."

"I ate."

"But not what I made."

"You know why I can't, Aurelia."

I scoff. "No... I don't know why."

I can feel his gaze burning into the side of my face, but I don't take the bait. Instead, I watch Khalil throw a vicious jab into Thorin's side before throwing him off of him.

"It feels...intimate."

"And we're not intimate? Are you serious? You finger banged me over a waterfall and then spit a lot of game that I was stupid enough to fall for. You've been inside me. And yes, I know it wasn't *you* you, but it was *your* dick. You saw me naked. You spanked me with a switch. You..."

"I what?" he challenges when I fall silent.

"Seth ate my ass," I confess just to be a bitch. Zeke's eyes flare and then they lower like he's wishing it had been him. Seeing this, I shake my head and chuckle dryly. "You're also full of shit."

"Am I? Or maybe you just can't handle the fact that I don't want you, so you twist the truth however you need to."

"It sounds to me like that's all you. And for the record, I don't want you either."

"So if I offered to nibble on your sweet little pussy while you watched your boyfriends fight over you, you'd say no?"

My pussy clenches at the vision while I outwardly scoff at the notion. "Obviously."

"Obviously," he repeats softly.

"You're teasing me."

"You teased me first," he says, referring to that first time we ran together.

"That's not the same. I actually wanted you to kiss me," I blurt before I can think better of it. My eyes squeeze closed, but no matter how much I pray, the ground will not open up and swallow me whole.

It feels like forever before Zeke finally replies. "My offer was as real as yours, princesa."

My jaw drops, but when I turn to face him, he's gone. The front door slams closed behind him.

I'm torn between following him and staying when Khalil flips Thorin over his shoulder in a spectacular move of power. When Thorin lands on his back and doesn't immediately regain his feet—in fact, he doesn't move at all—I shove away from the steps and run over to him.

Thorin finally groans and sits up when I'm two steps away. Khalil, the victor of the match, holds out a hand to help him stand, which Thorin accepts.

I push away the concern once they're both standing and facing me. "Oh, wow. I am so turned on right now."

"That's too bad because your punishment for baiting us into fighting is no orgasms for twenty-four hours."

Something in the corner of my eye catches my attention so I don't react immediately to Khalil's decree. Instead, my gaze follows the movement at the far edge of the clearing. "What the hell?" I mutter when I make out fur. "What is that?"

"Nice try, wolf."

"No, seriously. There's something there." I point to where I just saw movement a second ago.

Khalil and Thorin follow my finger and wait, but nothing happens. "I don't see anything."

"I swear to you I saw something moving a moment ago. I think it's an animal."

Thorin pushes me behind him while staring in that direction.

"Possibly. We are in the wilds." Despite Khalil's dismissive tone, he walks over to the shed and grabs the shotgun. When I arch a brow at him, he shrugs. "Just in case."

"Look! There!" I whisper-shout when I see movement again. "You guys see that, right?"

"Yeah." Thorin tilts his head and squints. "It looks like—"

"A wolf," I finish for him and then I whine, "Oh my God. Not again."

"It's not fully grown," Khalil says. "It looks like it's just a pup. Maybe it's lost."

"Or not," Thorin says in a dark tone when a much larger wolf appears from the trees. I instantly recognize the tawny fur.

"Meera?"

I start forward, and Khalil grabs my arm with a warning look. "Don't you dare."

"Is that blood?" I say when I realize her fur is matted and darker than usual in some spots. "I think she's hurt!"

"And still capable of seriously injuring or even killing you. If she is hurt, it just means she's that much more dangerous."

I watch helplessly as Meera drops the black pup she's carrying inside one of the brown whiskey barrels I was saving for the strawberries I was going to try to grow later. She picks up the smaller gray one and drops it inside as well before bounding off into the trees.

The three of us move to the steps on the porch to sit and wait, but after half an hour, Meera still doesn't return.

"We need to find her," I decide after I've grown anxious.

"It disturbs me how much we have to keep reminding you that Meera isn't a pet, Goldilocks. She's a wild animal."

I hear the front door creak open behind me and glance back to see Zeke walking through with a glass of milk in one hand and a grilled cheese that I certainly didn't make him in hand. I barely suppress the urge to roll my eyes and turn back to watch the tree line where Meera disappeared.

"What's going on?" Zeke asks around a mouthful.

"It's the she-wolf," Thorin says tightly. "She just dropped her pups off on our doorstep and left."

"What?"

"We think she's injured and needed a safe place to hide them."

"Well, that doesn't make any fucking sense, does it? Wolves *avoid* humans. They don't use us for daycare."

"I keep telling you guys. Meera *isn't like* any other wolf. She's smarter," I say proudly.

Beside me, Thorin stares at me like I've lost my mind and then looks over my shoulder at Ezekiel, who's standing over me. In fact, he's so close, I can feel his jeans brushing against my shoulder anytime I move. "Zeke, do me a favor. Go get Aurelia's bow and my gun."

None of us move until Zeke returns minutes later with his arms loaded with weapons. He hands Thorin his hunting rifle and then gives me the bow and my hip quiver full of arrows while keeping the crossbow for himself.

Once we're all strapped, we make our way over to the edge of the clearing where the pups are. They don't make a sound—probably to keep from being detected by predators—and if I hadn't seen Meera leave them, I would have been in for a deadly surprise later. The four of us keep our footsteps just as silent with our gazes scanning the tree line for the same reason.

Some of my worry abates once we're all close enough to see them huddled together at the bottom of the barrel. The pups, realizing they've been had, tuck their tails and growl.

"There's only two," I announce despondently. "She had three. Where's the other one?"

When none of the guys respond, I glance at each of them, noting flaring nostrils, twitching jaws, and the flat lines of their mouths. They also avoid my gaze as if they already know what must have happened and don't wish to share it with me.

Oh no.

Breathing through the pain that slashes at me like a barbed whip, I step forward and kneel two feet from the crate, ignoring the panicked hiss of one my guys behind me.

The gray pup proves to be the more curious of the two, stretching onto his hind legs. His head pops free of the barrel—which is only a foot or so high and two feet in diameter—while his front paws come to rest on the wooden lip. The pup audibly sniffs the air for our scent. Another head, no bigger than my palm with a tawny patch of fur on top of its black snout, pops out of the barrel next to his brother. The black pup takes one look at us and releases a few more warning growls just to be sure.

I decide to name them Romulus and Remy.

Mostly because I've been diving into my mythologies lately after reading every gardening book my mountain men have in their collection, and they're the first names that pop into my head. It's almost fitting actually, if you ignore the tragic end.

I don't even realize I'm reaching out a hand toward Romulus until Zeke gently scolds, "Whatever you do, don't touch them. We don't want Meera scenting you all over them and perceiving you as a threat to her pups."

"Yeah, okay. Good point." I pull my hand back just in time to miss the angry snap of the black pup's teeth. I might be willing to lose a few fingers to scratch that adorable patch that makes him look meaner and cuter at the same time, but it's not worth dying over.

Meera had come a long way with her pups in tow. She'd obviously been forced to change dens again, which means she's probably feeling very defensive and ornery right about now.

What if it were other humans this time instead of a bear? Finally understanding how dangerous it is for the pups to get used to me and lose their natural fear of us, I back off and they go back to trying to chew their way free of the wooden barrel.

Not a minute later, their weight topples the barrel and they tumble free.

"You two stay here with the pups," Thorin says once they're free. "Khalil and I will try and track Meera."

"You'll help her," I ask, "if she's in danger?"

I feel all three of their gazes, but I hold only Thorin's, who bites back whatever he wants to say and nods instead. "I will."

"Promise me," I urge despite my voice catching.

"I promise, songbird. I'll help her."

"Thank you."

Thorin walks away, and Khalil runs a hand down my spine as he passes and follows Thorin to the trees. Worry churns in my stomach when the forest swallows them and I can no longer see their large shadows.

"What's taking them so long?" I ask twenty minutes after Thorin and Khalil leave to track Meera. I'm more than a little anxious.

"Tracking." It's all Zeke says from his seat in the grass next to me. His legs are propped up, and he's resting his forearms on his knees as he stares at Rom and Remy. The wolf pups sniff the ground around the barrel and nip at each other, but they mostly keep their distance. Every so often, he has to toss a rock to lure their interest elsewhere when they venture too close to us.

"But do you think something happened?"

"We would have heard shots if it had."

I'm getting really sick of his short answers. "I'm going," I decide.

Zeke exhales but doesn't try to stop me. Instead, he jumps to his feet, startling me and the growling pups, and then he holds out a callused hand to help me up. I stare at it incredulously for a few seconds before I slip my hand in his. Our gazes meet and his thumb moves across the back of my hand, and I might call it a caress if I didn't know better. Within a blink of an eye, the moment is gone and then he's hauling me to my feet. "Let's go."

He doesn't let my hand go as we follow the bloody tracks Meera left behind and head for the trees.

God, there's so much blood.

I take one last worried look back at the puppies who aren't playing anymore. They're both still as they watch us go with their ears raised.

"You think they'll be okay all alone?"

"They're not old enough to hunt yet, so Meera must leave them hidden in their den for hours while she does," he says while squeezing my hand. "They'll be fine."

I choose to believe him—to have faith—because Rom and Remy need their mother, and right now Meera needs *us*.

We lose the blood trail and neither of us are good enough trackers to find and follow Thorin and Khalil's tracks, so for twenty minutes, Zeke and I walk in circles until a shot rings out and the echo sends the birds nesting in the trees above us into flight.

Zeke and I take off in the direction the sound came from, and less than a quarter mile later, we finally find them.

Thorin is kneeling over something I can't see with Khalil standing by his side. I purposely step on a twig, and it puts them both on alert as Khalil whirls around and Thorin shoots to his feet doing the same with his gun already taking aim.

"You two okay?" Zeke asks.

"We told you two to stay with the pups," Thorin snaps.

"We heard a shot," I tell him. "What happened?"

"Bear," Khalil answers, making my stomach twist itself into knots. "Thorin fired a shot to scare him off."

"So what is that?" I point to whatever they're doing a great deal to hide from me. "What did you find? Is it Meera?"

Thorin's jaw ticks before he glances at Khalil. The two of them silently communicate before they finally move out of the way, and I feel my eyes well when I see the small, lifeless form lying on the ground.

The wolf's blue eyes are still open while its white fur is covered in crimson.

Meera's missing pup.

Oh God. "A b-b-bear did this?"

"No. It just stumbled upon a fresh kill and easy meal."

"Then what—"

"Wolves," Thorin answers before I can finish voicing the question.

"Wolves? Why would wolves kill Meera's pups?"

None of my guys respond, not even to remind me that this was the wilds and a natural part of it. The air is thick with grief, and I realize it's not just mine. They're not as unaffected as they pretend to be.

After a while, the weight of my sorrow surges, and it sends me to my knees before the slaughtered pup. My lips tremble and my shoulders shake and pretty soon there are actual tears.

It's a foreign feeling that I chase away with a resolving breath.

"Aurelia," Khalil warns when I reach out to run my fingers

through the pup's fur. His blood is still warm, telling me this happened recently. I stare at it for a long time and then I'm on my feet, searching the forest floor.

"What are you up to, songbird? What do you need?"

Ignoring all of them, I continue my search until I finally find a big enough branch, one that's as big as my arm, and I return to the pup. "We need to bury him," I answer distractedly as I start to dig. I know the guys carry portable shovels, but none of us have our packs, so the branch will have to do.

I'm so devoted to my task that I don't even notice the three of them finding sticks of their own and joining me. I stop when they start to dig and I blink in astonishment as I watch them stab the end of their branches into the soft ground.

"You…you don't have to help me. I know you think it's stupid."

"It's important to you, so it's important to us," Zeke says. His gaze only meets mine briefly before he returns to the task.

After ten minutes, my arms are burning and I'm quickly losing steam. "How deep do you think—"

I'm interrupted again, but this time it's by the rustling of the foliage behind me and the pitter-patter of little paws. My heart drops as I stand and spin around to see Remy and Rom scampering out of the bushes. "Shit," I say with a gasp and wide eyes. "They followed us."

The scrape of multiple sticks stops immediately as the pups approach.

They don't seem to be paying us any mind with their noses low to the ground and their tails wagging.

Remy reaches my ankles first and I brace for an offensive nip, but all I feel is his fur as he passes me with Rom next to him.

I look down to see them sniff and nudge their brother who doesn't respond.

Rom whines and barks a few distressed sounds while Remy sits back, tilts his nose up to the canopy and howls. Rom joins him a moment later. They're still so very young so it isn't a fully formed, coordinated sound, but it's impossible not to feel their loss. Their pain.

When they're howled out, Rom and Remy lie down next to their brother with their little heads on their paws and their solemn gazes peering up at me.

Seeing no other course since I can't exactly console them, I go back to digging their brother's grave. Only Zeke helps me. Khalil and Thorin decide to watch the pups closely for any sign that they might attack me.

Their vigilance puts me at ease, and Zeke and I are able to complete digging the hole deep enough that there's no chance of another predator coming along and digging the pup back up.

"Um…how do we do this?" I ask when I stand and dust my hands off. Rom and Remy still haven't moved away from their brother. Their brother who still doesn't have a name. One comes to me easily enough, but mostly because I try to convince myself it doesn't matter. "I don't want to lose a hand putting Roman to rest."

"You named them?" Khalil groans and pinches his nose. "Why am I not surprised that you named them already?"

"So what are their names?" Zeke points to the pups who are now growling at Khalil as if they understood him.

"That cutie," I say pointing to the gray pup, "is Remy. It's short for Remus. And that adorable lump of fur is Rom. Short for Romulus."

"As in the brothers from mythology who were abandoned as infants on the shore of a river and nurtured by a she-wolf until a shepherd and his wife found and raised them?"

"Yup. Fitting, right?"

"Sure, but doesn't the story end with Romulus killing Remus?" Khalil asks.

I roll my eyes skyward. "I didn't say it was *perfect*."

Rom yawns, stretches his body, and stands before lifting his leg and peeing. The stream arches toward Khalil's foot, who curses and quickly steps out of the way before any can get on him.

The rest of us smother our laughs to avoid startling the pups while Khalil throws Rommy a dirty look.

"Damn, he even has your manners, Khal." Thorin tilts his head to the side and studies the black pup. "He kind of looks like you too."

Khalil flips him off and then leans down, quickly grabbing Rom by the scruff. Zeke repeats his action, grabbing Remy the same way and lifting him off the ground. With the coast clear, Thorin lifts Roman from the ground and gently lays him inside the grave.

Thorin and I make quick work of pushing the pile of upturned dirt back inside the hole. Once we're done and the grave is covered, I sit there for a few seconds and stare at the mound of dirt. I feel like I should say something, but I don't know what. I never had a pet before, so I have no clue what to do when one dies.

Not that wild wolves should ever be considered pets.

After a few moments of floundering, my lips part and the first song that pops into my head spills free. Khalil, Thorin, and Zeke are all quiet around me as I sing "Over the Rainbow." It's times like these when I wish I could be as hardened as them. I wish it didn't matter so much, but how could it not when death has become a constant companion?

"That was beautiful," Thorin says when the last note is sung.

"Thanks."

Zeke and Khalil set the pups back on the ground. Khalil narrowly misses losing a thumb, but Zeke isn't as quick. Remy clamps his jaw down on his forearm, and Zeke has a hell of time shaking him off.

The moment Zeke is free, Khalil runs the pups off, and I rush over to Zeke. Blood is already running from the punctures in his olive skin. Thorin curses and removes his shirt, tearing the bottom hem away to make a bandage for Zeke's arm. "We need to get back to the cabin *now*."

"What about Meera?"

"Aurelia!" Thorin roars so loudly I jump. The rage in his eyes makes me want to run in the opposite direction. "Enough. This is serious. We don't know what those pups have, and the wound could get infected."

Shame courses through me, and if I could slap myself without looking like a nutjob, I would. "I'm sorry. You're right. I don't know what I was thinking. Of course. Let's go home."

I start forward to lead the way, but Zeke stops me with a hand on my stomach and pulls me back until I'm by his side again. "I'm fine. The bite can wait."

"We need to clean the wound before infection sets in," Thorin argues.

"She can clean me up later. Right now, she wants to find her wolf, so that's what we're going to do."

She can clean me up later. Those words repeat in my head as Thorin and Zeke engage in a pissing contest. Khalil turns out to be the tiebreaker. He pulls me out of the band of Zeke's arm, leaving Thorin and Zeke no choice but to follow.

"We can't just leave them," I tell Khalil when I remember the pups.

"They followed you once," he says.

Sure enough, when I look over my shoulder, the pups are weaving in and out of trees as they trail us from a distance.

"This way," Thorin says after we walk for less than a minute.

He and Khalil must have been following Meera's trails—or the wolves that killed Roman—when we stumbled upon the pup.

"There are multiple tracks here," Thorin says when we reach some downfall and a creek running downhill. "Meera's," he says, pointing out her distinct tracks. She's wounded, so they're off unlike the multiple sets we find. "There was a fight here." Thorin swears. "Meera was outnumbered."

My heart doesn't speed up or slow down.

It breaks.

I completely forget the pups are stalking us until they sniff the ground and whine before suddenly taking off in the direction of the creek.

"What the—"

"Fuck. We need to follow them." Zeke takes off after the pups, giving us no time to ask why. The rest of us follow, forming an arrow of desperation with the pups making up the head followed by Zeke, me, Khalil, and Thorin bringing up the rear.

Finally, we come across four trails that form an intersection, and lying in the center of that crossroads is—

"Meera!"

I run past Zeke, dodging his hands when he stops instead of pressing forward. I ignore their shouts for me to stop. The pups have already reached their mother. They're climbing all over her and tugging at her ears and tail, begging her to rise and ease their fears.

But she doesn't.

The she-wolf continues lying on the ground, and her breaths are so shallow that I'm not sure she's breathing at all.

As soon as I reach Meera, Zeke snatches me back. "Careful, Aurelia. This just happened. There's a chance that the wolves that did this to her are still in the area."

"We have to help her."

"She's dying."

"We have to help her!" I scream. When none of them move to aid the she-wolf, I turn my teary gaze to Thorin. "You promised me."

Thorin curses and then reaches for his belt. He quickly unbuckles it and then snatches it from the loops in his jeans before kneeling in front of Meera. The pups' ears flatten, and they growl but don't attack. Neither does Meera, who I realize is conscious but weak. Her eyes are glued to Thorin, and worry still churns my stomach at the thought of him getting hurt because of me. My vision is blurry as I watch him wrap the belt tightly around Meera's snout, creating a makeshift muzzle, but I pay the unshed tears no mind. Instead, I kneel when she growls, and for the first time, I allow my fingers to run through Meera's tawny fur. A warm feeling spreads through me when Meera stops growling.

I hear Khalil and Zeke also removing their belts and quickly securing them around her forearms and hind legs.

"That should be enough to get her to the truck," Khalil says before he carefully scoops Meera up. The wolf whines and then goes deathly still in his arms.

Thorin and Zeke grab Remy and Rom by their scruffs, and then we're off.

I realize, after we've taken two steps and I hear footsteps all around us, that their arms are full and we're really fucking exposed.

Meera, the pups, and my mountain men—I'm their only line of defense.

"Aurelia," Thorin warns when he spots the same thing I do. A large wolf stalking us from the brush up ahead. The wolves that attacked Meera have returned to finish the job. "Take Remy."

"That's okay," I say as I draw an arrow from my quiver, load it, and take aim. "I got this."

My gaze snags on Rom. His ears, which were previously flat with displeasure over being carried are now twitching in awareness. A moment later, Remy's ears do the same, and he whines as he stares off into the bushes.

Khalil shifts his hold on Meera. "Goldilocks, I really think—"

A wolf we didn't see stalking Khalil lunges from the bushes. There's no hope for Khalil to react in time, so heart in throat, I don't think. I spin toward the sound and let the arrow loose the moment I see my target. It only takes a single breath, but it feels like a lifetime before the arrowhead spears the wolf in its hind leg and sends it flying back into the bushes.

"Shit," Khalil chokes out when he sees how close he came to death. "Guys, I think she's got this."

"We need to hurry this the fuck up," Zeke says. He hands Rom off to Thorin and then removes the crossbow from his shoulder.

Anticipating a second attack, I quickly load another arrow, and Zeke does the same while falling behind to take up the rear. I continue to lead the way five paces ahead.

We nearly make it to the clearing when the wolves try their luck again.

One goes for Khalil again, and I'm not quick enough to stop the large, gray wolf from tackling him. Meera tumbles out of his hold and the pups yip and whine, but I don't look to see if the she-wolf stirs. My focus is trained on the snapping teeth and foaming mouth of the wolf currently trying to rip out Khalil's throat. His own teeth are gritted from the effort of holding the wolf back. My confidence wavers as I redirect my aim to the struggling forms ten feet away.

What if I hit Khalil?

Or worse. What if I hit Khalil and it leaves an opening for the wolf to finish the job? All it would take is the smallest opening, and Khalil would be lost to me. Lost to us all.

Sweat forms on my brow, and my arm quivers from the strain of keeping the arrow drawn, but still I don't fire.

"One of you better take the fucking shot," Thorin warns quietly. "Now." He's a better shot than all of us, but his hands are full with Meera's pups, who are doing their best to wriggle free and go to their mother.

It's only then I realize that Zeke hasn't fired either, but I don't dare look away from the battle to see that pinch in his brow that tells me he's worried about the same thing.

A moment later, Khalil roars in pain. Blood blooms through his shirt near his shoulder where the wolf's claws shredded his skin to gain purchase.

My uncertainty fades as if it had never been, and Zeke and I fire at the same time, sending two arrows into the wolf's side. It falls to the side with a yelp and Khalil shoves it off him with a groan before clutching his shoulder. Zeke steps forward to help him to his feet.

Nearby, a wolf howls and several more—too many to count—follow in a bone-chilling chorus.

"This isn't over," Thorin warns. His hands are free now to yank the rifle off his shoulder and quickly chamber a round. "The first two were tests of our strength. Get ready."

I hear him flick the safety off his hunting rifle while my frantic gaze follows the sounds of the pups' cries to a tree with a small burrow halfway up the trunk. Rom and Remy are huddled inside, safely out of reach. Meera is lying at the base of the tree, her shallow breaths coming too far apart to settle the knot in my gut.

We're not far from the cabin. If it were winter, we would probably even see smoke curling from the chimney above the trees. We could make a run for it, but that would mean leaving Meera and her pups behind to be slaughtered.

Obviously, that's not an option.

"Are you okay to shoot?" Thorin asks and I tear my gaze away from Meera and the pups to see him inspecting Khalil's shoulder while Zeke keeps an eye out for more wolves.

"I'm fine." Khalil's jaw is clenched as he yanks the shotgun off his shoulder.

All around us I see the occasional flash of fur and hear paws hitting the ground, leaves rustling, and low growls as the remaining wolves surround us. The guys try to form a circle around me, but I push through Zeke and Khalil and load an arrow just in time for the wolves to finally show themselves. They push through the cover of the denser foliage to the small clearing where the four of us chose to stand our ground.

I realize with the force of a boulder falling into the pit of my stomach that they're not like Meera. They don't have the intelligent look I could swear I've glimpsed in her eyes. They look truly wild and, a few of them, alarmingly rabid.

My gaze flicks to the open wound on Khalil's shoulder. He wasn't bitten thankfully, but if even a drop of saliva had gotten into the wound during their struggle…

I take in a resolving breath to keep from spilling my guts and giving the wolves the weak link they are currently searching for.

"I count seven," I whisper.

"Eight," Thorin corrects.

"Nine," Zeke says hoarsely.

We don't stand a fucking chance. There are too many.

"Keep eye contact," Thorin warns, "and whatever you do, do *not* fucking run."

Thankfully, I've been living with predators for months now, so I already knew running would only trigger the wolves' instinct to chase.

"Anyone got a plan?" Zeke asks.

"Yeah," Khalil bites back sarcastically. "Don't miss."

A moment later, my ears are ringing from the thunderous crack that suddenly rends the air from too close behind me. The burnt and acrid scent of smokeless gunpowder follows, mixing with the petrichor of last night's rain.

The wolves are attacking.

Thorin fires another shot just as Zeke takes the offensive and looses another green arrow at a black wolf that darts by. There's no time to wonder if the arrow hits its target because a wolf with tawny fur like Meera's bursts over a fallen log and leaps for Zeke, whose focus is on the growth where the black wolf disappeared.

Swallowing the scream rising from the depths of my soul, I spin, breaking rank and leaving myself exposed. There's no time to hesitate or second-guess. I let my arrow loose and then I'm frozen, watching it cut through air misted with blood, rain, and fear until it pierces the wolf's eye midair.

Holy fucking shit.

I'm about to ask if anyone saw that when Khalil screams my name, and I'm reminded in the most horrifying way that this is a battle for my life—*our* lives—and not target practice.

There's a brown wolf with patches of gray fur sprinting straight for me, and I know there's no time for me to react. No time to draw another arrow and load it before it's on me. I'm most surprised by how easily my fate slides over me.

It never sat right with me that I was the one to survive and make a life for myself after the plane crash when so many others died. It was only a matter of time before the hand of karma pointed its finger at me once more.

The wolf lunges, and I close my eyes. A moment later, I'm knocked back and pinned to the ground by an impossible weight that knocks all the breath out of my lungs.

The fucking wolf is heavier than I thought.

Not wanting to see my death coming, I keep my eyes screwed shut and wait for claws and teeth to shred me apart. Someone screams in pain, but I realize belatedly that it isn't me.

"Shit! Zeke!"

Hearing Thorin's panicked shout, my eyes fly open at the startling realization that it's Zeke on top of me, fending off the wolf that already has its teeth sunk into his forearm.

It only takes me half a second to realize how it happened. Zeke threw himself between the wolf and me. There wouldn't have been enough time for him to hesitate or consider if I was worth it. For him, it was an easy decision that spoke to truths I couldn't think about right now.

Zeke is in trouble, and the reminder of what will happen if I don't do something is more terrifying than the wolves. Thorin and Khalil are still shooting, busy keeping the other wolves off our asses because if they swarm us, we're done.

Do something! I scream internally.

In my peripheral vision, I spot the black wolf stalking us from the brush, its yellow gaze pinned on Zeke. Thorin and Khalil don't see it, and from the sounds of the vicious swearing and commands coming from them behind me, stealing their focus away would mean certain death for us all.

There's a knife tucked into my hip quiver, but it's pinned under me and I can't risk jostling Zeke to go for it. My gaze is searching the ground for a weapon when I eye the crossbow that Zeke dropped. It already has an arrow loaded. I splay and stretch my fingers toward it, but the weapon is just out of reach. The black wolf stalks a little closer to the edge of the brush and I strain once more to reach for the shoulder sling.

The very tip of my fingers finally curl around the black strap, and I yank it toward me. The black wolf's claws dig into the dirt, readying to go in for the kill. Twenty feet away, it darts into the open just as I raise the crossbow and pull the trigger. The sear rotates, and my arm vibrates from the force of the bolt releasing. Heart in throat, I don't breathe as I watch the arrow cleave the air toward the wolf…and sail right past it.

Shit.

With the wolf closing in fast and no chance of stopping the inevitable, my mouth opens with a bloodcurdling scream that cuts short when a massive form with grizzled fur suddenly appears. Before the wolf can react, the bear snaps its jaws around the wolf's hind leg.

The wolf yelps in pain, its yellow eyes shifting from that of predator to prey, and then it whines as the bear drags it back before snatching it off the ground.

A bear.

A fucking *grizzly* bear.

I'd seen one before of course but never this close—not even when I saved Meera's pups from becoming a snack. Uselessly, I wonder if it's the same one. Too much happened that day to trust my powers of recollection.

The brown wolf that still has a hold on Zeke lets go and races toward the bigger threat. It lunges onto the grizzly's back, and the bear roars when the wolf sinks its teeth into it.

Zeke rolls away and immediately reaches for me at the same time I reach for him.

"Did it get you?" he asks in a panic while his hands roam all over my body. "Talk to me, princess. Are you hurt?"

"No. But *you are.*" Anguish like I've never felt before causes my hands to tremble. "Let me see," I demand while reaching for his bleeding arm. "Let me see, let me see."

Before Zeke can brush off my concern, I feel strong hands under my arms. "No time for that," Khalil says as he hauls me to my feet. "We've got to go." He's breathing hard and covered in sweat and blood. Guilt tears at me immediately, and it doesn't escape Khalil's notice when he turns me around to face him. "No time for that either, Goldilocks. Move your ass."

The bear roars again and shakes its body violently until the wolf that took a chunk out of Zeke is dislodged. The bear immediately swipes its massive paw, sending the wolf crashing into a tree. It doesn't get back up, and three other wolves pounce on the bear in a coordinated attack that sends a chill down my spine.

We definitely never stood a chance.

Thorin swears, obviously realizing the same. "Shit, shit, shit! We need to run."

I whirl on him with wide eyes. "But you said not to!"

"The bear is defending its territory, which means it thinks *we're* food. Running while it and the wolves are distracted is the only smart option here."

Leaving no space for argument, Thorin quickly scoops up Meera, since Khalil's shoulder is damaged, while Zeke and I pluck the pups from the tree. Rom and Remy must realize we're their best chance of survival because they don't fight or try to take a bite out of us as we literally run for our lives.

Out of the frying pan and into the fire…

It's a few heart-pounding moments before the sound of battle behind us fades and there's only the pounding of my heart and our heavy, labored breaths.

The cabin finally comes into view, and we make our way into the clearing.

I stop only long enough to deposit Remy into the whiskey barrel. Zeke does the same with Rom before lifting the barrel. The weight causes him to clench his teeth, but he only waves me off when I try to take the pups.

The four of us hurry over to the truck parked on the side of the cabin now that all the snow has melted and the pass is clear. It's still treacherous to traverse unless you're an experienced driver, so the guys still limit their visits to town, coming back with as many supplies as possible each trip.

Thorin carefully lays Meera on the bed of their truck while I open the back door for Zeke to place the pups inside. I try to follow them in, but he shuts it down immediately and grabs my arm. Sensing that they're all pretty fed up with me, I don't fight him as he leads me around the truck, but I also don't expect for him to push me against the door and rest his forehead against mine.

He inhales deeply, and his entire body seems to shudder from the effort of holding back whatever he's feeling inside. "Are you sure you're not hurt?"

"I'm sure. You saved me."

Zeke brings his face closer, and I'm not sure if his lips brush mine purposely or by accident, but it sends a wave of something desperate through me. I want the waterfall again. "You saved me first."

My heart is racing, and it has nothing to do with what we just survived. "We'll call it a new cabin rule then: we have each other's backs no matter what."

His lips skim mine again, and this time, I'm sure it's not an accident. Something fiery explodes in my belly, and I surge forward for more, but Zeke pins me to the truck again with a possessive hand around my throat that feels like a hot brand. My pussy immediately wants more of his dominance.

"There are cabin rules?" he asks with a purr that says he knows I'm losing control while he's got a firm grip on his. But he has tells too. For one, he's breathing with short, quick breaths, and his pupils are trying to swallow all the green.

"Six of them to be exact. All of them for me. To keep me here. To use me."

"Jesus." He lets our lips touch briefly again like a reward for telling him. "Do I want to know?"

"Probably not."

Zeke swears and then uses his hold on my throat to tug me away from the truck. We almost died, and here I am wanting to beg him to fuck me. He opens the door and then ushers me into the front passenger seat. I jump a little when he slams the door shut, but mostly because it feels as if every single one of my buttons have been pushed.

Rom and Remy whine behind me, reminding me that their mother and only chance of survival isn't out of the woods yet.

Thorin's voice is faint, but I hear him ask Zeke if he's good to drive. There's a second layer to the question that has me turning in my seat. Through the back window, I can see the three of them standing together at the back of the truck.

Zeke almost died today. We all came close to death, but for Zeke it carries a different meaning. A bigger risk. If Bane had woken up, none of us would be standing here right now.

So... Why didn't he?

I'm still turning over the many scary reasons when the driver's side door is yanked open and Zeke hops in. I'm cautious enough to stay silent as he turns the ignition. A moment later, either Khalil or Thorin pounds on the back window, and Zeke immediately takes off down the only drivable pass.

CHAPTER TWENTY-THREE

THORIN

I need to say something," Aurelia quietly confesses as she faces the observation window overlooking the small enclosure. It's the most timid I've ever heard her. The word *timid* and *Aurelia* have no business being in the same sentence. She's fierce, and I never want to see her as anything but.

Still, I know the reason for her caution.

The three of us have been silently fuming ever since we arrived at the wolf conservation center that Ezekiel raced the entire way to reach. There was no time to stop and get patched up and vaccinated by a human doctor, so we settled for the emergency vet the sanctuary used. She was already waiting for us after Zeke radioed Sheriff Kelly to inform him that we were bringing a wild wolf through Hearth.

The sheriff met us on the edge of town with a couple of deputies and escorted us the rest of the way. It's been hours since the vet and her team wheeled Meera off to surgery. The pups were also taken for evaluation and were now sleeping off the harrowing day on the other side of that window.

Zeke, Khalil, and I continue our stony silence as we wait for

Aurelia to speak whatever's on her mind. It's an area she normally excels in, but words escape her now.

To be clear, we aren't as pissed at her as we are at ourselves.

We knew better than to get involved with the she-wolf, but this hold Aurelia has on us makes it impossible to deny her.

I'd call it a spell, but spells can be broken.

There is no getting over our girl.

Aurelia spins suddenly, and her flinch when she meets each of our gazes has me reeling back my anger. I don't have to look to know Zeke and Khalil are doing the same. "I'm sorry about today. Obviously, it wasn't my intention for any of you to get hurt. I—" Seemingly giving up her train of thought, Aurelia's shoulders slump. "It won't happen again."

Doubting that, I hum.

"None of us are looking for you to change who you are," Khalil states. I remain silent since he's better at bringing Aurelia to heel with the least resistance. I only step in when she's feeling particularly bellicose and needs a firmer hand. "We wouldn't be in love with you if you were anyone else." Zeke shifts uncomfortably at the mention of love, but he doesn't deny Khalil's statement. "We just ask that you be smarter. Listen to us when we tell you something is too dangerous. The three of us have been out here a lot longer than you, and there's a reason we've survived. We've made and learned from all the mistakes you're making right now."

"I know," she says with her eyes on the ground.

"Do you?" I challenge.

Aurelia's eyes rise to meet mine, and I lift a brow, silently daring her to spew whatever smart remark I see brewing in her eyes. Her gaze shifts to Zeke's bandaged arm and hand and then Khalil's injured shoulder. The dressing is hidden under the wolf conservation T-shirt one of the keepers tossed him after the vet patched him up. Both had to get shots around their wounds to treat for possible rabies exposure. Aurelia and I were the only ones not seriously injured through sheer dumb luck.

The fight winks out of her eyes, and she nods.

"Good." I stretch my tired muscles and check my watch, silently urging the vet to hurry the hell up. Aurelia refused to leave without learning Meera's fate, and after everything we nearly lost getting her here, none of us were keen on leaving without knowing if the she-wolf made it.

"The one thing I can't wrap my head around is why?" Aurelia asks when enough time passes that it's clear we're no longer interested in scolding her.

"Why what?"

"Why would those wolves attack her? Is it… Did they want to mate her?"

I shake my head and stretch again. Aurelia cringes when my bones audibly crack and I smirk. "Wolves are not like lions. A roaming male, or in this case *males*, won't typically kill pups to force the female into estrus."

"Then why?"

I think about it for a minute. "Could be that she moved into their territory and they were simply running her off or she failed to integrate. The problem is that depending on the pack size and scarcity of prey, the natural radius of what the wolves consider theirs could be larger than all of the Cold Peaks put together. To put it plainly, there's an overabundance of predators in the area, so these rivalries happen a lot more often than you'd think. If it's the same wolves we encountered near Meera's den, I'd wager either their resources are low—which is likely considering they tried their luck with us—or…" The horrified look in Aurelia's eyes make me stop and swear.

"Or?" she presses after schooling her expression. "Go on."

"Or Meera isn't submitting, and the alpha is trying to enforce his dominance," I say, returning to my original theory of integration.

"By killing her babies," Aurelia surmises aloud. I nod, and a distressed sound escapes her as she presses a hand to her stomach and turns away. Khalil is the one to react first, standing to go over and pull her into his arms. Aurelia takes a few deep, calming breaths and then lifts her head. "How do I do it? How do I turn my back on them? How do I be more like you?"

"You think about what's most important," Khalil tells her. If going even an inch out of our way puts Aurelia at risk, we'd never do it. "Us or them?"

"You," she answers without hesitation. "Always you. I really am sorry. I don't know why Meera feels so important to me, but she's not more important than all of you. I won't put you in danger again."

I catch Khalil's hand skating down her back in a soothing motion. "We know that, Goldilocks."

"So what do we do now? I can't just leave them here."

"Can't or won't?" Zeke challenges.

Aurelia's gaze snaps to him and hardens a moment later when she realizes Zeke isn't sipping from the fountain of Aurelia. "What's your problem, Cura?"

"My problem is that you're good. A little too good." Zeke gives a lazy stretch like they're discussing the weather and he doesn't have a care in the world, but his muscles are still coiled tight when he goes still once more. "You're very careful with your words, aren't you? Who taught you how to lie so prettily? Your uncle? You promise not to let your obsession with Meera put us in any more danger, but you said nothing of yourself. What were you planning to do? Sneak behind our backs while you turn her into a pet? Continue to put yourself at risk while we're tucked away safely in our home?"

My gaze narrows when Aurelia moves away from Khalil just as his hand stills.

Holy shit. Zeke's right. She was planning to do exactly that, and I was too busy trusting her to notice. Aurelia's remorse is real but so is her kinship with Meera, and she's nothing if not stubborn to the bone.

"I don't have to explain myself to you."

Zeke shoots to his feet and is across the room before Aurelia can turn her back and dismiss him like she planned. "Say that again. I dare you."

"Why? You heard me the first time," she returns coldly.

"You want to bet, *princess*?" He backs her down, and Aurelia retreats a couple of steps until her back hits the window. Her eyes are wide with more shock than terror since it's Zeke cornering her, but Zeke doesn't seem to care as he invades her space. He's so close that for a moment I could swear he's going to kiss her. I can tell Aurelia is thinking the same because her breathing quickens. "What's the matter? Where's all the fire from a second ago?"

"Fuck you," she whispers without any real venom.

"You're such a fucking brat," he returns lowly.

Khalil's brows raise at the heated exchange that makes me feel like a voyeur, and then he turns his head to look at me, making it clear he's not touching that with a ten-foot pole.

I roll my eyes skyward. Zeke and Aurelia's hot-and-cold bullshit is beginning to wear on my fucking patience. "Enough, children."

It's as if they're the only two people in the room. Both ignore me and refuse to back down.

"I'm going to help Meera with or without your help," Aurelia makes the mistake of saying.

"And how are you going to do that chained and gagged to a bed, hmm?" Before anyone can react, Zeke snatches her up and throws her over his shoulder. He ignores her fists pounding on his back as he starts for the door. "We're leaving," he barks without looking my or Khalil's way.

Shrugging, I stand and Khalil moves to follow.

The door to the observation room swings open before Zeke reaches it, and the head keeper steps in with a grin that drops when he notices the look on our faces and Aurelia's wriggling body.

Zeke slaps her on the ass hard enough that she goes still immediately.

"Uh…hello. Ahh…sorry for the wait. We're a little understaffed today. I just came to tell you the good news and thank you."

Aurelia's head pops up, and she starts wriggling anxiously again, so Zeke puts her gently on her feet in front of him. It doesn't escape my notice that Aurelia doesn't try to move away from the hand Zeke places on her hip to keep her there.

"She's okay?" Aurelia asks hopefully.

"Yes, yes. She's fine. It was touch and go since she lost a lot of blood, but Axa pulled through."

"Axa?"

"Oh, yes." The keeper's eyes brighten. "That's the good news. We wanted to thank you for returning Axa home. A few months ago, one of our fences collapsed from a nasty bout of torrential rain, and a few of our wolves escaped. We were able to recapture all but one. Axa proved to be pretty elusive thanks to her failed tracker. After a few weeks of extensive searching, we'd lost all hope of ever finding her alive. She was born in captivity, you see, so the odds of her surviving in the wilds were slim to none. Not only did she survive, but she delivered two healthy pups."

"Three," Aurelia corrects a little petulantly at learning Meera had belonged to someone else all along. I know firsthand how possessive Aurelia can get. "She had three pups. And we call her Meera."

"Ah. I see. Yes. Well, Meera's pack will be happy to see her again," the keeper says good-naturedly. "That's what's most important."

"Can I see her?"

"She's heavily sedated at the moment, so I don't see why not. If you'll follow me."

Aurelia turns to look at us, and I'm the one to nod. "Go ahead. We'll be right here," I assure her.

She steps out with the keeper and the door closes, leaving the three of us alone.

"Huh…" Khalil says while scratching his chin and staring off at nothing. It's only been a few minutes since Aurelia left.

"What?"

"I guess that explains why Meera hid her pups near our cabin when her natural fear of humans should have kept her far away. And why she let Seth pet her."

Khalil had a point. The she-wolf wasn't afraid of humans because she'd been cared for by them all her life.

Aurelia had been right after all. Meera was smarter than the average wild wolf because she wasn't wild or average. Knowing how long she survived on her own while lost in a place she no longer belonged from the moment of her birth made her all the more impressive.

Much like a girl we all know and love.

Aurelia spends an hour with Meera before she returns to the room. The four of us stop by the pharmacy to refill Zeke's meds and re-up our antibiotics, bandages, and ointment before heading home. We're on guard from the moment we step out, knowing there's not only an aggressive pack in the area but a territorial bear as well. It's nothing we aren't used to, but with Aurelia to keep safe, it puts us on teeth-grinding edge.

"I'll clean the weapons and then get started on dinner," Aurelia offers the moment the door is shut and locked behind us. She quickly collects them from us and then disappears downstairs into the basement before any of us can turn her down.

It's going to take more than weapons maintenance to get her out of the hot water she landed herself in yet again, but we're all too exhausted to tell her so.

"Dibs on the shower," Zeke says to Khalil before he disappears downstairs too.

I tear off my shirt and head into my own room where my jeans follow my discarded shirt on the floor. Despite the fatigue creeping into my bones, I linger in the shower, enjoying the hot water coursing over my sore muscles. When I can barely stand, I turn off the water, wrap a towel around my waist and stare at myself in the mirror. Not for the first time, I contemplate cutting my hair before leaving the bathroom and dropping my towel. I step into a pair of boxers and then sweats before walking over to the bed and collapsing face down.

I'm asleep before I can work up the strength to pull the covers over me.

My eyes fly open hours later when the bed dips. The room is too dark to see, and the only sound is the rain and thunder outside, but I know it's her.

"Everything okay?" I murmur as I reach out with my eyes closed and wrap my arms around her. She lets me pull her close before she answers.

"Yes. I just wanted to check on you. You didn't wake up for dinner."

I smile as I dip my head and bury my face in her neck. "You were worried about me?" I feel her nod, so I lift my head to nip her jaw. "Are you attempting to finesse me, little girl?"

"No," she lies with a grumble.

I hum and then inhale. "You smell like Khalil."

"He bent me over the kitchen table and fucked me after dinner."

"Yeah?" My eyes open and I roll Aurelia onto her back. She immediately spreads her thighs to make room for me, and I kiss her lips as I settle between them. "Greedy girl. You want more?"

Aurelia moans and arches her back. The flannel she hastily threw on after Khalil was done with her parts and a hard nipple slips free. Bracing one hand on the mattress to keep my weight off her, I run my hand softly down the front of her body. Her skin is warm and slightly damp, telling me that Khalil worked her over good. I'm not surprised that I didn't hear a peep. Exhaustion still clings to my bones, but I ignore my body's demand for sleep for something much more tempting.

Curving my hand around her ribs, I let my thumb sweep her taut nipple.

Aurelia groans in frustration at my slow pace, and I dip my head under the guise of worshipping her to grin against her sternum. I feel her fingers slide into my loose hair as I kiss the soft curve of her breast. My own fingers trace the dips and curves of her body until I reach her hip, and then I slip my hand between our bodies and find her wet heat.

"Did he let you come?" I ask when I feel how wet she is. She nods, and I press two fingers inside her, feeling her walls grip me immediately like she's on the verge of coming again. It must be why a moment later, she squirms and groans again.

"I didn't come here to be teased. Get your dick in me now, Thorin."

Kissing her hard, I warn against her lips. "Don't tell me what to do."

Aurelia responds by gripping the waistband of my boxers and shoving them down. "I said fuck me *now*."

"And *I* said…" Fisting a handful of her riotous curls, she yelps when I yank her upper half off the bed and then drag her forward until she's kneeling on all fours with that gorgeous ass of hers facing the headboard. Her mouth is already parted from the pain and shock of my rough treatment, so I shove my hard cock between her lips until she's gagging on the length and clawing at the sheets. "…don't tell me what to do. I tell you. Now *suck*."

Aurelia moans and then her tongue begins lashing at the underside of my dick. It's all she can do with me stuffed so far down her throat so I pull back until only the flared head of my dick remains between her lips, and I watch through lowered lids as she suckles at the tip.

When she tries to take more, I press forward slowly until her lips are stretched wide and I'm lodged in her throat. I rest there for a moment to enjoy the sound of her gagging and the feel of her digging her nails into my thighs before pulling out to the tip again.

"Get ready, baby. I'm going to fuck your mouth and then you're going to sit on it. Understand?"

When Aurelia nods, I grip her hair with both hands to hold her steady and then I proceed to work my dick in and out of those gorgeous, pouty lips that cause me so much strife. I'm not gentle. I know it's not what she came to me for. She wanted to be used, so I use her. I choke her with my cock and drink up her muffled cries until the sight of her round ass wobbling with every thrust steals my focus.

I'd never been an ass man until Aurelia George. There was just something about hers that I couldn't resist. Naturally, she's lost a little weight since being out here, but those delectable curves of hers remain delightfully stubborn. Slipping free of her mouth, I drag Aurelia to the foot of the bed and arrange her the way I need.

"I thought you wanted me to ride you," she whines as I put her on her tummy and force her legs together.

"In a minute," I mumble as I straddle her thighs and grip my dick. I'm still coated in her saliva, so I tug on it a couple of times until some of my pre-cum spills free and then I slip right in between the cheeks of her ass. I nearly blow my load right then and there. "Shit."

"You and Khalil are more alike than you know," she remarks with humor as I saw in and out of her ass.

I press my hand against the back of her head and force her face into the bed. "Don't say his name," I growl.

She mumbles something into the blanket as I continue to dry fuck her, and when I feel my balls drawing up tight, I pull away only to press forward again and force my way into her pussy.

Aurelia lifts her head and moans at the sensation of the impossible fit, and my groan joins hers in a duet of pleasure as I keep digging deep until my hips meet her ass.

"Fuuuuuck, baby, fuuuck." Stars burst behind my eyes as I bury my face in her curls. "How the hell can you feel this fucking good, huh?"

"Thorin," she whimpers when I thrust a little too hard. "You're so deep."

"Shhh…" I wrap my arm around her front under her breast to hold her in place while I fuck my fill.

My wolf gets off on being used, and I get off on using her.

Already, I can feel her coming on my dick, and the force of it makes my knees quake while the sound of her cries makes my toes curl.

When she's finally spent, I fuck Aurelia into the mattress so thoroughly, the bed begins to squeak and groan from the abuse, but I keep going because God help me, I can't stop. Finally, I feel that familiar tingle in my spine that tells me I don't have much longer between her sweet thighs, so I rise onto my knees and bring her with me.

The clap of our sweat-soaked bodies echoes around the room, mixing with her cries and my groans while being drowned out by the thunder outside.

It's the reason I don't hear the knock on the door until it's too late. The bedroom door is already opening by the time I'm aware of his presence, but it would be easier to stop a team of racehorses than stop me from chasing my nut.

"Yo, Thor. You awake? I'm looking for Aurelia. Have you seen—"

Zeke's question is cut short at the sight of Aurelia's shoulders and face pressed into the bed as I keep her there with a hand around her neck. I can't speak as I spill my cum inside her pussy, but my gaze travels to the doorway where Zeke is standing. The room is dark, but lightning flashes at that moment, showing his genuine shock at walking in on us.

"Shit, uh…shit." His gaze is still glued to Aurelia when he shakes his head to free himself from the trance. "Sorry. I—sorry."

"Zeke," I call out when he turns to go. Despite his initial reaction to flee, he obeys my unspoken command without turning around. "Aurelia, can you hear me?" She has a habit of passing out after being fucked hard and coming harder. I thought she'd get used to it after a while, but no such luck. Khalil, on the other hand, is *thrilled*. Twisted fucker. With her cheek still pressed to the mattress, Aurelia nods and I run my hand up her spine. "Open your eyes, songbird. Zeke has something he wants to ask you."

"I can come back," he offers hoarsely. He still hasn't turned around.

"Close the door," I order.

Zeke swears and closes the door before resting his forehead against the fractured wood. It happened one night recently after I fucked my wolf too hard against it. Aurelia opens her eyes and searches for Zeke in the dark. As if he can feel her gaze, he turns the moment it lands on him.

"Yes, Ezekiel?" Her voice is a hiccup since I'm still fucking her despite already coming, and I swallow my growl at hearing her say another man's name while I'm inside her.

He speaks, but thunder rolls in at that moment, drowning out his words.

"Come closer, Zeke."

Zeke inches forward like he's drawn by an invisible force he's powerless to resist. When he reaches the bed, I pull out of Aurelia and draw her into my arms as we collapse on the mattress together. I draw Aurelia's leg over my hip before my gaze returns to Zeke, who is staring at the gap between Aurelia's legs where my and Khalil's cum is seeping out.

I see the desire to add his own and watch his lips part as I run a hand over Aurelia's ass before dipping my fingers between her thighs and plugging her pussy with them. I keep them there as I kiss the top of her head.

"That's better," I say with a rumble. "You were saying?"

Zeke's gaze rises, but it's a little wild and unfocused, and his nostrils are flaring like he's trying to scent the room. Or scent Aurelia. "We need...we need to talk about Seth."

"No." But my instant refusal still comes too late because Aurelia is already stirring at the sound of the alter's name.

"Seth?" Aurelia echoes groggily as she sits up and turns around to face Zeke. His gaze drops to her breasts, and he makes a rough sound when he sees her peaked nipples that Aurelia doesn't hear because she's frantic now. "Did you say Seth? Why? Is something wrong?"

Zeke doesn't answer though because he's forcing his gaze away from the tempting swells of her breasts. His green eyes search for mine past Aurelia and I beg him silently not to do this.

It's been a long day.

We nearly died.

I don't want Aurelia sad and distressed.

I'm too fucking exhausted to deal with this right now.

He can take his fucking pick for why this isn't the right time to talk about Seth. Zeke wants to tell her that something is wrong in the hopes that she might have some answers for why. I want to know too because I'm fucking worried about him, but I also know that what Seth wanted above all was for Aurelia to be protected no matter what.

Do I think she's hiding something? Probably.

Do I think she did something to Seth? Fuck no.

There has to be another explanation, and trying to force it out of her won't work. She has to trust us enough to come to us. We have to be patient.

Not to mention Seth will *fucking kill us all* for upsetting his Sunshine and I'm not looking forward to him trying to set me on fire again. Or was that Khalil?

I'm still not sure who he was aiming the flamethrower at that day since Khalil and I were standing pretty close.

Zeke must come to the same conclusion because he shoves his fingers through his dark hair and blows out a quaking breath that has me sitting up. "No. Nothing's wrong."

He's already backing away from the bed and fleeing before I

can examine him more closely, so I snatch up my discarded sweats and quickly tug them on. Something's up with Zeke, and I have a feeling it has nothing to do with Seth. The alter might have been what brought him in here, but it's not what sent him fleeing.

"Stay here," I order Aurelia, who's frowning at the empty doorway like she wants to run after Zeke. She must have seen the same thing I had. Cursing, I quickly leave the bed and the room, but I don't have to wonder where Zeke has gone.

The front door is wide open, and rain is blowing in from the strong wind.

There's only time enough for me to pull on a pair of boots before I throw myself out into the storm behind my best friend.

CHAPTER TWENTY-FOUR

EZEKIEL

My ears are ringing, and my heart is thundering in my chest like it's trying to break free of the chaos.

Something is *wrong*.

I burst through the cabin's front door, and by the time I reach the bottom step, rain has already soaked through my clothes. The downpour feels like needles stabbing my scalding-hot skin over and over. An unhinged laugh bursts from my lips, and then a sound more animal than man answers back.

I sprint away from the cabin as fast as I can until I stumble at the edge of the glade. Inexplicably, my limbs grow heavy like lead while my thoughts become increasingly muddled as if bidding me to sleep.

Except I don't feel the least bit tired.

Understanding of what's happening dawns and I bark, "Fuck!"

Freeing the knife from my pocket, I don't hesitate before slicing my palm open. The skin splits, and blood splatters the ground before being immediately washed away by the rain. The pain of the wound does the trick and chases away the drugged feeling until I'm alert again.

Keep going, keep going, keep going. Panic lances through my chest when I realize that I can't tell which one of them is trying to break free. It feels like Seth and Bane are battling for control, but of what? Of me? Or each other?

This isn't how it normally feels when one of my alters takes over. The split happens so quickly that I'm not even aware of it until hours, days, or weeks later when I wake up to the aftermath. No, this is something different.

The agony and confusion are enough to slow my pace until I remember Aurelia and how close she still is—how dangerously within reach.

I have to keep going. I have to keep her safe.

Clenching my teeth, I push my legs faster, harder, but no matter how much distance I put between the cabin and me, it never feels like enough.

And then I trip over a fucking rock.

I land in the mud with a curse and go rolling down a hill that sends me over a rocky ledge and down into a riverbed that's usually dry but floods quickly during heavy rain—like now. To be anywhere near it is a death knell. My body twinges from the impact of hitting the rocks in the water, which isn't nearly deep enough yet to soften the blow. A growl builds in my chest, and it burns to force it down.

Terror has tears spilling from my eyes as I laugh maniacally at my pain. Rage like I've never felt before bids me to punch a hole through my chest and tear out my own heart. I haven't felt a loss of control of my own body this deep since the table.

Somehow, I pull myself to my feet, but the moment I do my head explodes, and the blinding pain sends me right back to my knees, clutching my head with a scream.

"Stop! Pleeeeease! Stooooooop!"

My pleas go ignored, and the war inside my mind continues.

I'm left screaming in the rain and the mud, and just as I begin to fear that I'll be trapped like this forever, the chaos that Seth wrought vanishes in an instant with a brutal and violent finality. I feel the cold hollow of his absence only briefly before the phantom and acrid taste of ash and blood building in the back of my throat leaves me gagging.

Bane. It's only him now.

One by one, the mental chains I use to keep him constrained in the abyss of my splintered mind snap like twigs. Suddenly, my shirt feels too abrasive against my skin, and I tear it off with a growl. I realize too late what it was all for.

Seth wasn't fighting to get out. He was fighting to keep Bane *in*.

"Zeke!" The echo of Thorin's call reaches my ears, followed by swift footsteps drawing him closer.

"No." *No, no, no, no!*

If Thorin's already caught up with me, there hasn't been time to grab the tranquilizer. Thorin won't kill me, which means he left the cabin without any protection. I open my mouth to scream, to warn him to stay away, but my throat constricts like there's a hand around it, squeezing and keeping me silent.

No matter how hard I try, I can't get the words out, and it dawns on me then why this time is different. Usually when I switch alters, I go willingly, the transfer of control so smooth that I'm barely even aware of it. Splitting is my mind's way of protecting itself, to keep from fracturing further. This loss of bodily autonomy is a punishment from my mind for resisting its defenses—for rebelling in order to protect someone other than myself.

Seth, I silently plead. *Please. Help me.*

But Seth doesn't answer because he isn't there. He lost the battle, and now there's only me standing in between Bane and Aurelia. Remembering the knife I carry, I tug it free and place the serrated edge already stained with my blood to the throbbing pulse in my neck.

My death will crush her. I know that now. But if my blood on the ground is the only way to keep her safe so be it. My fingers tighten around the handle, and I feel the muscles in my arm coiling to strike, to slice, and to slay when I hear a vicious curse behind me.

"Zeke? *What the fuck*, man?" I feel the commanding hand of my best friend on my shoulder, and my body stills at the perceived threat. "Give me the goddamn knife."

All I can do is choke out a sound, something that sounds like *run* before the darkness creeping at the edge of my vision snaps forward, spilling over everything that I am until I am nothing.

CHAPTER TWENTY-FIVE

AURELIA

Thorin told me to stay, and in an effort to obey him for as long as I possibly can, I shower in his bathroom and get ready for bed. When I emerge to find that he still hasn't returned, I go in search of Khalil downstairs.

I find him in the bathroom lining up his beard with clippers in his hand and a towel around his waist. Beads of water from his recent shower still cling to his brown skin and the muscles he's honed over the years. Usually, the sight would be enough to distract me, but not this time. I can't get that frenzied look in Zeke's eyes out of my head.

Khalil's gaze meets mine in the mirror when I step inside the bathroom.

"It's Thorin's night," he says, referring to the turns I take sleeping in their beds so that they don't get jealous and kill each other.

"Thorin isn't here. He ran after Zeke and told me to stay."

The clippers shut off abruptly, and Khalil turns around with a frown. "What are you talking about?"

"Zeke. He said he wanted to talk about Seth, but then he ran out of the cabin before he could, and Thorin went after him."

Khalil swears and then brushes past me to leave the bathroom. I follow him into his room where he drops his towel and then disappears inside his closet. When he emerges, he's wearing dark cargo pants and a rain jacket. The hood is already pulled over his head as he passes me again to go into the den where the weapons locker is. They don't keep it locked anymore, so he wrenches it open without delay and reaches inside.

My heart punches against my chest when he pulls out the tranquilizer rifle and handgun and quickly loads them both with a dart.

Oh God. Oh no.

Zeke. *Thorin*.

"I'm coming," I say as I rush forward to get my compound bow.

Khalil slams the locker closed with a fierce scowl that warns me not to push.

"So is all the training just bullshit then? When it really comes down to it, you'll treat me like I'm fucking helpless?"

"No. I want you to stay here just in case Zeke or Thorin come back. My guess is neither of them have their radios." He grabs a handheld off the charger from the small table next to the locker. "I will. If something pops off, we can let each other know and regroup. Can you do that for me, baby?"

"Sure," I grumble reluctantly, still feeling like I'd be more useful by his side protecting him.

"Good girl." Khalil kisses my forehead and then hands me the smaller dart gun and a radio. He grabs another radio, and then we check to make sure we're on the same frequency before I follow him up the basement stairs.

My stomach turns, and it feels like I can't breathe as I follow him over to the door.

Khalil opens the door and twists to block me from the onslaught of the storm that is only getting worse. It matches the one inside my heart telling me that something was very fucking wrong. "Stay here, and I swear to fucking God, Aurelia. Do not leave this cabin. I'll be back as soon as I can."

He's gone before I can plead with him one more time to let me come. The wind slams the front door shut behind him, and I jump. Alone, I pace for a little while, then I blindly grab the first book my fingers touch before I go up to my loft. I'm much too restless to sleep, and I don't see that changing even once they're all back. Like Khalil said, it's my night with Thorin, and even when exhausted, he's too light a sleeper to slumber peacefully if I'm awake, so the loft it is.

Ignoring the book in my lap, I watch the door, but I can't see shit beyond the loft except for the spots in the cabin where the pale light of the moon stretches through the open windows.

Outside, the thunderstorm continues to rage on, growing in strength and temperament. The wind howls, rain falls in sheets, thunder rolls, and lightning flashes. Usually, I'm unfazed by it all, but my boyfriends and their best friend are out there. I sit with my back to the cool pane of the window behind me and try to convince myself that they're okay. They've survived worse, and they've survived it without me.

I tell myself it will be easier if I sleep, that when I wake up, they'll be back and safe in their beds and all will be well. But midnight comes and goes, and another hour ticks by with no sign of sleep or them.

If Khalil were here, I'd wake him up and he'd fuck me right to sleep without a word. But he's not here, and I'm done waiting.

I tried calling him on the radio a few times, but the heavy rain must be blocking the signal because he doesn't answer. I crawl toward the edge of the loft and the ladder Khalil built for me, and I slowly descend until my bare feet are planted in the soft fur of the rug that was once Bruce—the bear that mauled Thorin years ago.

I run down to the basement and get dressed, but I don't really have any gear that will protect me from the rain, so I pull on some shorts and my all-weather boots before finding Zeke's poncho and pulling that on. Once I'm dressed, I sling my bow over my shoulder and then grab my quiver, arrows, the dart gun, and a flashlight.

I leave the fucking radio since it's useless in this storm.

I throw open the door but stop on the threshold as I take in the endless darkness that awaits me beyond. The trees sway and taunt like a haunting silhouette, and all I can think is that my guys are somewhere in there, so I step out into the storm and I don't look back.

My body grows heavy, and my lashes become weighed down from the torrential rain, making it hard to see as I jog across the clearing. When I reach the tree line and the worn path the guys usually take, I stop and turn on the flashlight to study the ground as I try to remember everything Thorin taught me about tracking. I haven't had much practice, but luckily because of the rain, I don't need it.

The clear impressions of three sets of large boot prints are my breadcrumb trail, so I follow the story they tell. Deeper inside the forest, I find a body impression where it looks like someone fell. Beyond that, I come across crushed grass and follow it to the elevated bank of a rising river. I use my flashlight to search the churning water just in case.

It's blessedly empty.

"Zeke...Khalil...Thorin!" I start to turn away when I spot something black and familiar clinging to the sidewall on the other side of the riverbed.

It's Zeke's graphic T-shirt of Bound—his favorite band—caught between some rocks just above the water.

I don't think twice before jumping over the slippery slope and down into the river. It's a struggle to cross against the natural flow of the water, but eventually, I reach the other side and when I pan the flashlight over the rocks, I don't just see Zeke's shirt.

I see blood. Oh God. So much blood. It's splattered on the side of the rocks hidden from the rain and rising water like a fucking crime scene. My throat burns with bile as I search for more clues with only the small beam of light to guide me in the dark.

Someone didn't just get hurt. There was a struggle here. I can see blood in a small puddle turning the rain pooling there into a light pink.

"Khalil!" I shout. "Thorin! Zeeeeke!" Nothing but the howling wind answers me back, so I continue down the riverbed, my boots splashing in the swiftly rising water. "Khalil…Thorin…Zeke!"

The water surpasses my shins, slowing me down and erasing the breadcrumbs, so I climb out of the riverbed, but it's not easy to do because the bank is a few feet above my head and the wet ground is too slippery to get a good hold. I manage to use some of the embedded rock to pull myself up until I'm lying on the ground panting and shivering. Eventually, I have enough strength to crawl to the trunk of a tree at the edge of the bank and rest there.

Get up. Keep going. They need you.

I pull myself up and continue following the riverbed, but I don't make it more than a few feet before it feels like I'm being hunted. Call it a sixth sense from nearly dying earlier, but I don't question it as I reach for my bow and draw an arrow from my quiver.

Those wolves could still be in the area, and so could the bear.

And I ran out of the cabin and into a storm in the dead of night like a fool in love.

I force myself to keep going, to put one foot in front of the other, my eyes and ears on alert as I call their names over and over. Thorin, Khalil, and Zeke.

No one answers me.

The water in the channel below me is rising higher and higher as the rain continues to pour. It rushes alongside me as I come to a crossroads and consider which direction to go. Lightning flashes then, and I see a lone figure walking toward me from the trail that leads back to the cabin.

It has to be one of the guys but an ominous feeling crawls down my spine because I don't recognize the gait. I know all of their walks pretty well by now—even Zeke's.

Thorin walks like he never stops hunting—silent, deadly, and focused.

Khalil walks with a confident strut that says he's used to being watched, coveted, and admired.

Seth walks with a perpetual bounce in his step and trouble in his wake.

Zeke walks like he's alone…trapped under a cloud of turmoil.

The tall figure moving through the dark has a stride I don't recognize. He walks like he's trying to blend with the night and become one with shadow. He walks like he's darkness incarnate, looking for something to consume. How do I know? The instant fear coiling around my heart and begging me to stay away.

Instinct from living with predators tells me not to run the other way.

As if testing my resolve, thunder claps and I jump. I continue to eye the figure that walks through the downpour as if he doesn't notice the storm.

"Hello?" I shout.

"Aurelia!"

I'm startled by the voice that answers because it doesn't come from in front of me where the lone figure is still walking toward me.

It comes from behind.

Spinning around, I gasp when I see Khalil with one arm thrown around an injured Thorin as he holds him up. Disturbingly, I note that they're on the *other side* of the river. Thorin clearly needs help, and so does Khalil judging by the way he's struggling to keep Thorin upright, but there's no way I can get to them. There's no way they can get to *me* either.

A twig snaps, and I'm suddenly reminded that I'm not alone. But if Thorin and Khalil are over there, then that must mean…

I spin around just as his face comes into view.

"Zeke?" He doesn't answer, and something about the anesthetized look in his eyes—as if his soul had been wiped of feeling—makes me uneasy, but I'm still relieved to see him. I can already feel some of my worry melting away now that I can see he's…*mostly* okay. His dark hair is plastered to his forehead and curling around his ears. He's shirtless, and I can see bruises from earlier as well as fresh red ones forming. What the hell? Had he gone ten rounds with a brick wall since leaving the cabin? "Are you okay? What happened? Where did you go?"

I reach out a hand toward him despite the malevolence rolling off him in waves and to my surprise, he reaches back.

Our fingers are stretching toward one another, lightning flashes, and my stomach pitches for some reason. The tips of our fingers just barely meet when Khalil screams again. "*Aureliaaaaaa!*"

The desperate cry is dosed with panic unlike anything I've ever heard from him before, so full of fear that it easily rises above the rain and roaring river.

Startled by that unbridled scream, I drop my hand before Zeke can seize it and turn away in search of whatever caused it. When I don't see anything except for Khalil and Thorin standing unharmed at the very edge of the opposite bank, my confusion spikes. "Are you okay?" I shout.

Khalil screams his answer, but thunder rolls and drowns it out.

"I can't hear you!" I shout as I walk away from Zeke, who still hasn't spoken a word to me, and toward the river. Khalil yells again…something about Zeke. My side of the river is a little higher than they are so it's even harder for his voice to carry. I decide to take a shot in the dark. "Yes, it's Zeke! I found him!"

"That's not Zeke!" I hear echo across the storm this time.

Glancing over my shoulder, I'm greeted by the familiar green of Zeke's eyes, the toasty olive-toned skin, and the tattoo of a skeleton hand clutching a moon between its fingers on his right bicep. It's pretty fucking definitive. "Um…" I turn back to face Khalil. "I'm pretty sure it is!"

Lightning flashes, highlighting the stark terror on Khalil and Thorin's faces even from here. It's the latter who yells this time. "For fuck's sake, Aurelia! It's—" Thunder booms and I flinch. The sky calms and the thunder is a distant roar just in time for me to hear, "Shoot him!"

Shoot him? I turn again, intending to search the shadows in the trees surrounding us for the target, but I damn near jump out of my skin when I'm met with Zeke standing right in front of me, much closer than before. A little too close with that chilling emptiness that makes him seem so cold and distant. It's so unlike Zeke even when he was *actually* trying to keep his distance.

This time it's not so easy for me to dismiss. This isn't just him upset about whatever drove him from the cabin in the middle of a storm.

This is…this is…

Heat blooms in my face as if I'd been slapped with the answer.

Goose bumps pepper my skin and I shake my head in terrified denial as I back toward the slippery edge that feels far less dangerous than the taciturn man in front of me.

"Zeke?" I squeak, hoping I'm wrong.

"Mine."

"Oh God. Oh fuck." My vision blurs, and I slap my hands over my mouth as if my silence can save me. If Bane is awake, then... nothing can.

My breath is a hitch of terror in my throat as I stumble to put more space between us while cataloging everything I noticed before but ignored because I began to think the alter standing before me was an urban myth.

No, he was very much real.

There was no trace of Zeke or Seth anywhere in the harsh cut of his cheekbones, from how hard he must be clenching his teeth or the flat line of his mouth. "B-Bane?"

"Mine."

My body trembles uncontrollably, and it has nothing to do with the wet clothes clinging to my skin while the wind batters my body. The eyes of the terrifying alter pinned impassively on me are *cold.* The frost is enough to root me to the ground while my fight-or-flight response plays tug-of-war with my common sense. I want to reach for the dart gun resting in its holster, but his eyes are tracking me too closely, so I ignore my twitching fingers.

Play it smart. Keep him talking.

Solid plan, Aurelia. Maybe he'll forget *to murder you.*

Every step I take to put myself safely out of reach, Bane takes one equal to two of mine to keep me close. He follows without speaking, without doing anything other than hunting me. I'm the entirety of his focus as he tracks me to the water's edge.

The sound of the river becomes louder, drowning out the sound of my heart pounding in my ears. I'm running out of ground, but Bane gives me no time to think, making me choose between drowning or…him.

"What do you want?" I decide to ask while my fingers creep toward the tranq gun. Distract him, and he won't anticipate my next move. Khalil, Thorin, and Zeth all claimed that he was nonverbal, but he clearly has no problems terrifying the shit out of me.

"Mine."

"Yes, you said that." My fingers meet the cold steel of the dart gun, and a rough sound bursts from Bane in warning. Lifting my chin, I curl my fingers around it anyway and force my voice to remain steady. I'm done baring my neck to assholes. "What happened to Zeke? Why are you awake?"

It can't be for anything good. Did something or someone attack Zeke? Harm him?

"Mine."

"Oh, for fuck's sake. *What's* yours?"

Bane cocks his head, his stormy visage making Zeke's normally pale green eyes seem even more muted. "Au-re-li-a."

Oh fuck. He thinks I'm *his*? His to *what*? His to kill?

I don't stand a chance against the shudder that agitates my muscles, and there's absolutely nothing I can do about the dread creeping down my spine like taunting little fingers that say it's only a matter of time.

Bane was the one who killed Tatum, the girl Zeke had been in love with, and he'd done it with his bare hands and without hesitation. Zeke certainly didn't love me. He barely tolerated me. There was very little stopping Bane from snapping my neck too.

And the reality of him is so much more terrifying than the stories.

As if he can hear my thoughts, Bane slowly reaches out a hand toward my neck, and I try to force my limbs to unlock, but I'm a statue as he claims a golden curl plastered against my neck and for the first time, something alive flickers in Bane's eyes as he rubs the strand reverently.

"Touch her and I swear to God, I'll end you!"

I'm too terrified to tell Thorin that he's already touching me. Thorin's shout draws Bane's attention away from my hair. His brows slam downward as he looks over my head, and his bare chest expands with a deep inhale, and then something rough and angry rumbles from within before he moves as if he's going to step around me.

And go where? Into the river? It's suicide. The water is chest high now, and the current is too rough to swim.

"Wait. Stop." Bane keeps going while I stumble after him. His focus is directed across the river, on Khalil and Thorin, with deadly intent, and he's one step from walking off the ledge when I do the dumbest thing ever.

I grab his arm.

Bane is nothing more than a blur of movement as he reacts.

He spins while I pull the tranq gun free of its holster. I watch in absolute horror as Bane knocks it from my hand, and I don't see where it goes because his hand is around my throat in a vise grip.

"No," he roughly commands. *No?* No what? "Stay."

"You can't—" His fingers tighten in warning, cutting off the rest of my sentence. Panic flares in my chest and my stomach, because for fuck's sake, this is *Bane*, but just as swiftly I cut off the emotion and focus. *You know what to do.*

Dropping my chin to protect my airway, I lift both arms and bring my hands together to form one fist before I bring it down as hard as I can into the sensitive joint of his elbow. The blow doesn't break his hold completely, but it loosens it enough for me to twist away and out of reach.

Bane is still scowling, but he doesn't try to reclaim me.

When I sneak a glance across the river to assure myself they're unharmed even though I stopped Bane, I see Thorin leaning against a tree in pain and Khalil searching for a way across.

There's another loud crack a moment later, and I assume it's more thunder until I hear Thorin's shout. "Aurelia! Look out!"

I see him pointing to something above my head, but there's no time to think or question before I'm yanked toward the ledge and out of the way. I'm knocked into Bane, and I don't have time to dread those lethal hands on my body again because a tree comes crashing down right where I was standing.

Thorin shouts my name and an order to stay put, but I only get a glimpse of the tree's long trunk hovering over the churning water now before Bane and I begin to slide.

Too late I realize we're right at the edge.

My heart drops like a deadweight in my stomach when the mud separates and sends us both careening over the side of the slippery slope. I hear someone scream as we fall through the air, and I'm certain it's me before I plunge into the cold water. I'm tumbled, swept, and pushed downriver as water fills my ravaged lungs, and I wait for death to claim me.

CHAPTER TWENTY-SIX

KHALIL

I watch with my heart in my throat as lightning strikes a tree near Aurelia and Bane, splitting it in half. Thorin shouts a warning, but Bane is already tugging a wide-eyed Aurelia out of the way. It's a decision I'm going to have to dissect later since it doesn't fit everything we know about him.

Nothing about Bane has been normal since Aurelia arrived at our cabin.

He didn't wake up earlier when Zeke was in danger, so why now?

I'm pulled from my train of thought when Thorin shouts to Aurelia that we're coming. It's only then that I notice the tree that nearly crushed Aurelia creating a makeshift bridge between our side and theirs.

Before I can come up with a safe way for Thorin and me to cross it without falling into the water, Aurelia and Bane both fall into the river.

They're gone in an instant.

Aurelia's terrified scream is cut off as they both disappear underwater.

It's a few terror-stricken moments before Bane resurfaces, and then Aurelia. She's too busy struggling to keep her head above water to notice him fighting against the current to reach her. I'm not even sure which she would prefer—the knife's edge that comes with Bane or drowning. The turbulent current carries them downriver until they disappear from sight around a bend.

I burst into action.

"You have to go after her," Thorin says when I return and pull him to his feet. Bastard weighs a fucking ton. "Leave me here. Go."

I won't lie. My heart is torn, but the decision is an easy one. Thorin tries to make it for me by shoving me away, but I tighten my hold and drag him along toward the tree's crown. "I'm not leaving you."

Thorin is injured, bleeding, and can barely stand. I'm not leaving him out here to fend for himself. As if on cue, a wolf howls in the distance. Luckily, it doesn't sound too close, but that could change. It makes my fucking point, reminding Thorin where we are. He doesn't say shit else to me as I struggle to get us over the branches.

The sooner I get him to the cabin, the sooner I can search for Aurelia and Bane and get them both back home.

But if he hurt her…

"Can you cross?" I ask Thorin curtly.

"I'll manage," he answers with a twitching jaw.

Dude still hasn't stopped blaming himself. Bane caught him unaware, lodging a serrated knife in his thigh and then in his shoulder before Thorin even knew he was awake. Even injured, Thorin still managed to fight him off before lightning struck too close and gave Thorin an opening to get away.

Bane's only advantage was that he didn't react to pain. He was adamantine. Zeke's unbreakable armor. Aurelia only managed to escape his hold earlier because he *allowed* her to. Something else to dissect later once everyone was safe.

And to think, once upon a time, my greatest fear was living a boring, mundane life. Right now, I'd be willing to beg on my knees for seventy-two hours drama free.

I allow Thorin to cross first so that I can monitor his slow progress across the tree.

It's a risk we wouldn't normally take, but the time it will save us from having to find a way around makes it worth it. I don't breathe until Thorin is on solid ground again, and I'm not far behind. The trek back to the cabin takes twice as long with Thorin pushing his body to ignore his injuries, but we make it.

We burst through the front door and hurry to the dining room. Thor grunts when I set him down on one of the chairs at the kitchen table, and then he snatches up the bottle of tequila left out on the table from dinner and uncorks it with his teeth. I watch him take a healthy swig, glare at me, and then drink some more.

"Maybe we should radio the sheriff to send a medevac."

"Yeah, you should do that if you want me to deck you." Thorin slams the bottle on the table with a snarl. "Bane didn't do *that* much damage," he denies with a scowl. "He just got a cheap shot."

I smirk at Thorin's obviously bruised ego. "Yeah, okay. He fucked you up."

But my smile falls a moment later when I remember that the man who easily put Thorin on his ass is out there right now with Aurelia.

Aurelia is out there right now with *Bane*.

Swearing, I walk away from Thorin and begin frantically searching all the drawers in the kitchen until I find a map folded inside. I walk back to the table and snap it open before spreading the map out all over the table.

"This is the river," I say, pointing to the blue line on the map. I trace my finger along the winding river until I find the spot I'm looking for, and then I tap it. "I think this is where they fell in." I study the map a little longer and then feel my blood go cold as I swear. "Fuck."

"What?" Thorin leans forward.

I don't respond right away. My finger is still following the line across the length of the map. "The goddamn river goes on for miles. Who knows how far the current carried them? They could be any-fucking-where."

We glare at the map for a few minutes as we try to figure out where to look for them.

"This would be a good place to start." Thorin points to a spot on the map. The foothills near the ridge between Maia and Big Bear where the river joins another along the southeast base of the second largest peak. "This is the best spot for catching trout. The water is calmer there, and I've taken Aurelia a few times. She'll know the area. If she's alive and she's trying to get back to us—"

"She's alive," I say.

Thorin doesn't miss a beat. "Then this is where she'll go," he says, tracing the route that he always takes back home.

"Cool." Trusting his judgment without a fucking doubt, I grab the map and fold it, but I stop short of stuffing it inside my pocket that's soaked through.

I consider stopping long enough to change clothes, but one look through the window at the rain and the deluge outside, and I nix the idea. And there's no fucking way I'm waiting until the rain stops to get my baby back either.

"I'm coming with you," Thorin says, and it's all I can do not to roll my eyes.

"You're injured and useless," I point out as I shove away from the table to gather the supplies I'll need. "You'll only slow me down."

Thorin snorts but doesn't argue since he knows I'm right. "I love you too, man."

I locate my pack and start shoving things inside, including a fresh first aid kit. I have no idea the state I'll find either of them in, but I'm praying I don't need it. Speaking of which, I ignore the need to run out into the storm after my girl and best friend and I help stitch Thorin back together and then ignore his grumbling as I help him into bed before shoving a bottle of painkillers and a radio in his hand.

"Call me if you need me," I order as I turn for the door.

"I won't," Thorin says with a grunt. "Don't come back without them."

Glad that we're on the same page, I nod at that as I leave the room, grab my pack, and throw myself back out into the storm.

CHAPTER TWENTY-SEVEN

BANE

The river exacts a heavy toll.

Ezekiel's body is no match for the fury of the mountain and the deluge it sent to keep me from her. This is Thanatos's doing, but Death can't have her. Zeke is safe with her. He wasn't safe with Tatum.

For that reason, she is mine.

Each time I reach for her though, she cries out and flinches away as much as the current will allow her.

She's afraid, and I am powerless in the face of that fear. No doubt the friends' of Zeke's doing. Someday soon, I'll succeed in killing them. I'm more determined now than ever since they have what's ours, and by ours, I mean the horde.

Even Seth, who I thought was smarter than to believe they were his friends.

Aurelia and I continue to fight against the current that tries to take us under, but instead of growing calmer, the river seems to stretch wider and become more winding. I'm eyeing the shore, wondering how to get us both over when she won't let me near her when we round another bend in the river and the water becomes choppy.

And at the center of these rougher waters is a large boulder parting the river like a force. Aurelia sees it a moment later, and her eyes widen as she screams again, knowing she'll never get out of the way in time.

And I can do nothing to save her.

The whitecaps froth and spew like a rabid elemental as the water slaps against us and pushes us both toward our doom. The boulder looms ever closer, but Aurelia doesn't give up the fight. She reaches for the exposed broken branches of a downed tree, but her fingers barely graze the wood as she sails past it. I come much closer to it but ignore the offered salvation as I keep my focus locked on her progress down the river.

She's got her eye on me too, tracking me and making sure I don't get too close.

She forgets about the boulder, and there isn't enough time to warn her. Aurelia is slammed against the hard surface of the rock, and her body immediately slumps in the water before she's swept away again.

My turn is coming, but at the last minute, the current shifts and carries me just far enough to the side that I miss it. My gaze is already locked on an unconscious Aurelia again. Just as I think there's no hope of catching up to her, Aurelia gets caught between some rocks, and I throw out my hand just in time to grip her shirt and pull her along.

We're swept away again down the river.

I'm unable to determine at the moment what to do about the unconscious girl in my arms, who wants nothing to do with me, but one problem at a time.

I still have to get us both out of the river.

CHAPTER TWENTY-EIGHT

AURELIA

I wake up inside a cave.

It's a struggle to open my eyes, but when I do, I'm met with darkness. I'm so deep inside the cave that the rock walls surrounding me are barely visible. The only sound to greet me is the heavy rainfall outside that tells me it's still storming.

How long was I out? It's impossible to tell from the back of the deep cave where I'm lying on a slab on my side. Long enough for my clothes to become damp and for my mouth to feel dry and sticky from thirst. I can still feel the sweat, fresh water, and fear clinging to my skin while my hair is a dry, frizzled, and tangled mass.

I clutch my head with a groan as I sit up, and then I wince and hiss when I feel the wound and dried, sticky blood caked at the back of my head.

What happened?

The last thing I remember is the river. The storm caused a flash flood, and Bane and I fell in.

Bane.

He was awake.

My muscles immediately coil with apprehension as I look around the cave, but I see no sign of the alter.

"Hello?" My voice is carried away on an echo, but no one answers back. "Bane?" I try again. "Are you there?" When nothing but the sound of the storm answers back, I finally accept that I'm alone. I can't decide if that's a good thing or bad, and I won't know until I get a good assessment of just how fucked I am, so I rise from the slab.

I'm immediately bowled over by nausea.

My bow and quiver are resting on the slab, but my arrows are missing, likely lost to the river. I grab them both and sling the bow over my shoulder before uselessly clipping the quiver to my hip.

Leaning over, I place my hand on the damp cave wall and I use it to hold me up as I inch toward the faint light coming from the entrance. I see moss growing on the ground as I get closer to the front, and the moment I feel strong enough, I let go of the wall and quicken my steps toward the mouth of the cave.

It's rockier toward the front, with stones ranging from small pebbles to large boulders. I roll an ankle as I step on one of the smoother ones, and only then do I realize I'm not wearing shoes. I hadn't even noticed the feel of the ground or the mud between my toes because everywhere else on my body hurts like hell, so why not my feet too?

I consider going back into the cave to search for them, but a voice in my head warns me to leave them, that I only have a small window of time to escape the cave, so I keep going. There are vines hanging from the top of the cave's entrance, partially blocking my view like a privacy window. I burst through them and brace myself to be immediately drenched in the rainfall all over again, but there's nothing. The sky is gray from the storm with no sign of the sun or even the moon anywhere, but the air is impossibly dry. How? It's impossible to tell what time of day it is. Suddenly, I'm regretting not stopping to grab my watch—and choosing to leave behind the radio.

That was stupid.

The cave, as it turns out, is built into the side of a steep cliff that immediately gives me vertigo when I look down at the mist and fog blocking my view for miles. It's only a few steps from the mouth of the cave to the edge of the cliff, and with the wind blowing hard enough to bend and blow down a tree, it feels incredibly risky to leave the cave.

But I have no choice, so I don't turn back.

Instead, I look around in search of landmarks to try to figure out where I am. The storm makes it hard to see anything, but when lightning strikes and some of the clouds part at that exact moment and I see everything previously hidden from me, my chest tightens painfully.

This high up, I should be able to see each of the mountain peaks in the distance, but there's nothing. Nothing but more trees— though not nearly as dense as the foliage I'm used to seeing—and a stretch of desert that tugs at something from my memory.

Like I do onstage to recall the steps of my routine just before a performance, I close my eyes as I draw forth the image of the map.

There's Little Bear where my plane crashed at the northernmost edge of the range.

Maia has the sheerest drop and the most foliage. It's also where the hot springs are.

Big Bear has the widest mass and tallest peak. An insurmountable and unpredictable bitch of a mountain that I'm eager to get back to.

The Cold Peaks mountain range forms a rugged arc with the wide mass of Maia encompassing most of the curve and Little Bear and Big Bear forming the endpoints. The valley and all the wilds within that curve are my way home, but instead, I'm staring back at an unfamiliar sight. A dry wasteland where even the storm won't reach.

Damn it. I'm on the leeward side of the mountain. I'm in the shadow of the storm. Or at least partially. It's why the air is dry even when the storm is so close and why there are small signs of vegetation even without precipitation. The cave must bestride both faces of the mountain.

It means life points the way home.

And if I had to guess, I'd say it was Maia that I woke up on.

Suddenly, Thorin's insistence on making me study the map of the Cold Peaks for an hour each day doesn't seem so unnecessarily cruel now. Without those sessions, I'd be completely fucked with no chance of mapping a way home. There's still a chance of me getting lost though, since Thorin and I never got to the part of his plan where he'd drop me off somewhere random and force me to find my way home.

It won't be easy barefoot and without my pack, but left with no choice, I start down the rocky slope that Bane must have carried me up. The thing I've learned about traversing mountains and untamed landforms is that you often have to go around to go through and up to go down, which is no less true in this case. By the time I reach the foothills, my feet are scraped raw and blistered from being ravaged by the ground. I'm leaving bloody footprints in my wake, and I'm limping by the time I reach the foothills.

I don't know how I expect to make it all the way back to the cabin, but I know I have to try. I can't wait for them to rescue me. Khalil and Thorin will check Maia, but they won't think to look for us on *this* side of the mountain. It could be days before they are desperate enough to consider it.

Unable to take another step, I lean against the boulder at the base of the rocky path and tell myself I'll only need a few minutes. After ten, I still haven't moved. All that lies before me is more desert. Without the high vantage point the cave provided, I'm quickly disoriented. I have no idea which way to fucking go.

I'm contemplating hiking back up to the cave to reset when I lean back to stretch my sore muscles and my fingers brush something damp and soft like a sponge. Standing, I limp around the boulder I was using like a chair, and my heart speeds up a little when I find a patch of moss growing on the opposite side.

There was some of it in the cave, but I'd been too focused on leaving to consider what it meant.

Moss means moisture.

Moisture means I'm not going to fucking die.

There's more of it on the rocks ahead, the moss growing thicker until it covers most of the surface on the rocks and mountain face. I follow that life-saving green with my gaze to a gap in the wall that would have been easy to miss without the moss pointing to it like an arrow. The passage is narrow, only wide enough for one person to fit through at a time, but already I can see moisture clinging to the walls.

Ignoring the pain in the soles of my feet, I jog toward the gap. It's a tight squeeze, and I wonder how Bane carried me through it. It had to be him since Zeke, and even Seth, would have had the self-preservation to go back to the cabin.

It takes me a few minutes to reach the other end of the passage, and when I do, I'm met with the most beautiful sight.

Foliage.

Some of the trees are downturned from the storm, and I can see rain clouds in the distance. I'm limping along the soggy earth that is like a balm to my abused feet, and after a while my dried skin and hair becomes damp from the mist cooling the air.

Despite feeling closer to home, my steps become slower and slower, but I force myself to keep going. I keep pushing toward the storm that marks my way home. I know I'm getting close when the sky grows darker, and the mist becomes a steady drizzle.

The ground is becoming dangerously slick, and I have my arms up to keep my balance as I hurry down the slope. The muscles in my calves are twinging from the abuse, but I ignore them too as that voice in my head returns telling me to *go, go, go*.

The rain is coming down in sheets now, but I can't stop, not even when my body begs me to risk taking some of the rainwater in my palm and drink. I'm pushing my body too far. It's been hours since I had anything to eat or drink, I'm wounded, and I might have a concussion from whatever knocked me out.

Brightly colored spots begin to shield my vision, and my tongue feels like sandpaper.

A wave of dizziness overcomes me, and the world begins to shift. I'm falling before I even realize I've lost control, and the last thing I see before I lose consciousness is a blurred figure walking through the storm toward me.

I'm back in the cave again, and it's still storming.

It feels like déjà vu when I sit up, but this time, I'm not alone. I can't see him, but I can feel his dark influence like a band around my neck telling me to stay. I don't move from the slab—mostly because my feet are throbbing like they've been scraped with a cheese grater and slapped on a hot grill. The cave is cold, and I think about starting a fire when my thoughts should be on how to escape. When I shiver for the fourth time, I give in and start a fire. I have a hell of a time finding dry kindling and a stick and flint to start it with though.

Once the first of the flames burst to life, I stay crouched and wrap my arms around myself as I look around the now-lit cave to ensure myself I'm alone.

I'm not.

There's a thump of panic against my chest when I spot a shadow larger than the others hovering near the back of the cave. I keep my gaze on it and wait for him to step out into the light, but he doesn't. He continues to hover there as if I'm the one needing hiding from.

"I know you're there," I call out hoarsely. My throat feels raw from thirst. "Show yourself."

Finally, the shadow moves and parts from the others against the corner of the cave where the faint light of the fire doesn't quite reach, but I don't need it to know it's him.

Bane.

There's no question of that now, and I feel foolish for not recognizing that he wasn't Zeke or Seth earlier. Except he looks at me like they do—like I'm already his.

I almost forget to be afraid because the weight of his stare feels so very familiar, but from Bane, the feeling is more like a freefall than an anchor.

Zeke's vengeful alter. His sword.

I used to think that was what Seth was until I saw for myself how eager he is to share his heart and affection and to be loved and accepted in return. He's dangerous, but only makes me feel like I'm wrapped in a warm blanket and protected.

But that isn't Bane. I have no idea what he dreams of or what he wants. And I realize it's the unknown that makes him so terrifying. I hop up when he gets too close and back away despite my ravaged feet.

"Juuu-sss-ttt stay right there. D-d-don't come any closer." I hold up a hand that ends up pressed against his scalding-hot chest when he ignores me.

"Mine."

"No. No. I'm not y-yours. I won't let you hurt me."

"Hurt you," he repeats as if tasting the idea on his tongue. He frowns a moment later like he finds it distasteful. "No."

A bolt of confusion spears through me, and then my mind shifts when I realize… "You can speak." He spoke to me in the dell when he woke briefly, but I was so freaked out about what almost happened that I didn't pay much notice to what shouldn't have happened.

Bane pauses and then he answers as if he's reluctant to admit it. "Yes."

"How? Thorin and Khalil said you couldn't."

Hearing their names draws forth that malevolence again that makes the green in his eyes seem like they're bleeding obsidian. I make a terrified sound, and that darkness retreats as if he's calling it back.

Okay, note to self. Don't bring Khalil and Thorin up in front of Bane. Ever.

"Zeke speaks. I speak, Au-re-li-a." He says it matter-of-factly like it should have been obvious. I guess it never occurred to Thorin and Khalil that Bane didn't speak to them simply because he didn't want to. He speaks to me though, and the light, warm feeling it causes in my stomach makes me think I need my head examined.

Seth is naive in a lot of ways, but I wasn't prepared for Bane's regression.

How much pain? How much pain did Isaac have to cause for Zeke to go to these lengths just to cope and feel safe? It haunts me when I wonder about it for too long. What about Bane—besides the obvious murderous rage—makes Zeke feel safe when Seth can't?

It breaks my heart.

Right now, it's just frustrating because I'm lost in the wilds *again*, and this time, it's with someone who may or may not want to kill me. Other than scare the shit out of me, he hasn't tried yet, but rather than put me at ease, it fills me with anxiety. It's knowing the knife in your back is coming but having no clue when.

"But you only speak to me. Why?" I'm almost afraid to know the answer.

"Mine."

I whine my frustration and rub my brows to stave off the impending migraine. "Not this again."

"Au-re-li-a."

"Yes, Bane. That's my name, not *Mine*, so use it," I snap before I can decide whether it's wise. Bane stares at me and then walks away and the last thing I expect to do is follow him. I should be running from him in terror, not stalking him across the cave. As crazy as it sounds, it really doesn't seem like he'll hurt me. Or maybe I'm just a gullible fool. "Where are we? Where did you take me?"

"Safe."

I don't feel very safe, but he's only partially to blame. "We need to get back to the cabin. We need to go home."

Bane looks around the cave and then back at me. "Home."

I'm racking my mind for how to get him to understand that this isn't home when I catch on to his meaning and my stomach swoops suddenly. "No." A hysterical laugh escapes me. "I am *not* staying here. You need to take me back right now."

Bane ignores me as he walks over to the fire and crouches to warm his hands. His hair and clothes are still wet—mine are too—which means I wasn't out for very long this time.

"Bane," I say softly, trying a different tactic. "Please."

"We stay."

"I can't stay. *We* can't stay. We need food. We need shelter. We—"

Bane rises to his feet, and I try not to let it get to me how easily he towers over me. How did I never notice before how tall Zeke is?

Bane makes him look taller. Bigger. It's obviously just my perception of him but logic isn't helping me right now. He's glowering at me now, and I wonder if this is it, if he's finally going to live up to his name. "Safe *here*."

I sigh in defeat. What else can I do? I refuse to leave without him, and I obviously can't make him go. I need one of the others to reason with, and until Seth or Zeke wake up, we have no choice but to stay. It shouldn't be long, right? Khalil and Thorin said that Bane never sticks around for long.

"Well, I'm thirsty," I announce. "And if we're going to stay, we need to find food and water."

Bane scowls at me for a long moment and then he walks away. At the mouth of the cave, he turns his head enough to address me. "Stay."

"I can help—"

"Stay," he repeats with a growl before he leaves the cave.

It feels like forever before he returns with the snapped necks of two bunnies and a large leaf full of fresh spring water carefully balanced in his hands. He makes several trips for more water, and when he returns the final time, I'm not prepared for him to kneel in front of the slab where I'm sitting and wait anxiously, taking my foot gently in his hand. Carefully, he turns my foot, upending my sole, and pours some of the cool water in the leaf over the wounds.

"You are…hurt," he says as he trails his thumb down the side of my sole that isn't damaged.

"Yes."

Bane lets go of my foot and grabs the other, pouring the cool water over it and washing the debris away. "Never again."

"I don't have any control over that."

"*No more*," he barks with enough gravel in his tone that it scrapes the part of me that desperately wants to obey. To be a good girl.

"Fine," I whisper gently just to appease him. "I won't get hurt again."

I don't want Bane upset, and not just for my sake. Zeke and his alters have already been through so much. I wouldn't forgive myself if I ever caused them more pain.

Bane takes the leaves that he used to carry the water and creates a makeshift wrapping for my feet. I'm shocked and impressed, but I don't let either emotion show because my confusion still reigns supreme.

Never one to keep my thoughts to myself, I ask the question that's not a question. "They said *you'd* hurt me," I grumble.

Bane's jaw ticks and his green eyes flash with irritation. "They were wrong."

Sleep doesn't come easy.

After we eat, Bane disappears from the cave again, and even though I'm exhausted, I won't let myself close my eyes until he returns. Call me crazy, but there's something comforting about his presence. He says he doesn't want to hurt me, and I'm not sure yet if I believe him, but he did save my life.

Is he still terrifying? Holy fuck, yes. But I can't help but think that those jerks got it wrong. At least partly. Bane did try to kill Khalil and Thor many times, but he's obviously more complicated than that. Besides, who wouldn't want to kill Khalil and Thorin? I'm also guilty of trying and failing. In fact, I would like to right now for the image they planted of Bane in my head and let fester.

When Bane returns, I start to fidget, and I don't know why until he keeps his distance and I feel my body, which has already taken so much abuse in the last twenty-four hours, relax. He sits with his back against the cave wall. He's facing me while guarding the entrance at the same time. Why? To keep me in or to keep others out? Bane needs sleep as much as I do, but I don't want to sleep either. I'm too worried about tomorrow. What will happen, what I'll do…

"Will you talk to me?" I ask just to get out of my head. Only silence answers back, but Bane's gaze remains steady. "Is Zeke okay?" I sit up when he doesn't answer and draw my knees to my chest. "Bane, I can't stay here. You know that right? I have to go back."

A frustrated sound comes from him then that almost makes me spring to my feet.

I blow out a shaky breath and tell myself to get a grip. If he were going to hurt me, he would have.

"No offense," I say with frustration lining my tone. "I really appreciate you saving my life, but I really need Zeke back now."

I don't wait for a response that never comes. Instead, I lie down on the hard slab once more and turn my back to him. When sleep comes for me, I don't fight it.

There will be plenty of battles tomorrow.

CHAPTER TWENTY-NINE

AURELIA

Morning comes too soon.

I'm lured awake by the flap of a bird's wings, and when I open my eyes, I see one flying around inside the cave. It chirps emphatically and then swoops low over the slab before circling the back of the cave and then flying over to one of the stalagmites and perching on top with another chirp. I'm still watching it and listening to the storm outside when I feel the hair on my nape rise. This time I don't question my instinct. I leap from the slab and whirl around in one move.

Bane is crouching on his haunches in the shadows, and the only part of him that moves is his eyes as he tracks my retreat. His forearms are resting on his strong thighs as if he's been keeping vigil like that all night.

"Bane, *what the fuck*?"

"Mine awake." Rising to his full height, he runs and leaps from the slab, landing right in front of me. I stumble back, fall, and land on my ass. Bane crouches again and then prowls forward on his hands until his body covers mine while I'm left trembling on the rocky cave floor. "Mine safe."

"I would really like to t-talk to Zeke or Seth now."

Bane makes a rough sound that sounds like frustration. "Mine scared."

"Yes, Bane. You scare me."

His frown deepens, but he looks tortured more than angry. "Safe with Bane."

Realizing I'm getting nowhere with him, I suck in a resolving breath meant to give me courage and then I place my hand on his cheek. "I don't feel very safe right now," I say as I caress the rough stubble gathering there. "And that's not your fault. It's mine. I shouldn't have left the cabin. I know that now, so can you help me out? Please?"

Bane tilts his head closer, and I force myself not to make a sound even though he can probably hear my heart pounding. For an insane moment I wonder if he's going to kiss me, but then he stops just short of his split lip touching mine and then he inhales and a rumbling sound vibrates from his chest. "Not safe...at cabin. We stay."

I don't even realize my hand is moving until I feel the soft, damp strands of his dark hair slipping through my fingers. It's shorter now that Zeke is awake. Bane practically purrs when I dig the pads of my fingers into his scalp, but I pause when I feel something warm and more viscous than simple rain. When I pull back my hand, I see red coating my fingers and I gasp. Bane surprisingly lets me sit up, and even more surprisingly, lets me touch him as I practically crawl into his lap to inspect his head for the wound.

It's impossible to forget that it's Bane though, so when I feel his hands circle my waist, I suck in a fearful breath and force myself to keep going. I let him explore me while I search his hair. He seems particularly fascinated with my belly button as he pushes a thumb inside. I finally find the source of the blood near the back of his skull, but I can't see more than that, so I stand and limp over to the mouth of the cave. My feet are fucked. I don't think about it as I let the rain soak the hem of my shirt.

"Ah!" I yelp when I turn back to find Bane standing over me like a shadow. "Bane," I say, exhaling his name wearily with a hand over my heart. "What are you doing?"

He's frowning now, and oddly, it scares me less than the stillness. "Mine can't leave."

"I'm not leaving you." I punctuate my promise by tentatively claiming his hand and walking him back over to the slab. "I need you to sit down," I say, and to my surprise, he lowers himself onto the slab without taking his gaze from me. My teeth dig into my bottom lip as I move between his legs, and then I stretch a corner of my long loose shirt toward the cut on his head, dabbing away at the blood until I can see the wound.

Thankfully, the cut is small and isn't serious.

But it is one more reason we need to get back to the cabin. We're both injured, lost, and unarmed. Although, it just occurred to me that I might be the only one lost.

"Bane?" He doesn't respond, but I know he's listening. "Do you know where we are?" I let go of my now-bloodied shirt but keep my hand on his shoulder. His muscles are relaxed, telling me he's not coiled to strike when I least expect it. I just wish I could convince my anxious mind of that.

"Safe."

"Yes. But *where* is safe?"

"*Cave*."

"Bane," I force through gritted teeth.

"Mine?"

"Yes," I say with a defeated sigh. "Yours." At least until I figure out how to get back to Khalil and Thorin and wake Zeke up. God, Thorin… I hope he's okay. "If we're going to stay here," I say to

Bane, who is watching me like he knows my thoughts betray him, "we need to find food. We need to hunt."

I glance at the mouth of the cave and see that the rain has slowed, so I kneel in front of Bane who doesn't move and pull up his mud-stained pant leg before retrieving the hunting knife sheathed inside his boot and stand again. I'm not so good with knives yet, but I'm sure it's on Thorin's survival syllabus. Would he be proud of me now? It's been a day since the river and I'm still alive, though much of that is thanks to Bane. Knife in hand, I ignore the pain from the bottoms of my bare feet as I walk over the damp rock and soil toward the cave entrance.

I don't hear Bane follow, but I know he does.

What he doesn't do is stop me when I step outside and into the rain. He just follows silently like a protective shadow while I make my way down the path. I don't look back because I'm a coward.

The air outside is damp, unlike the cave, but not as much as it would have been if we were on the windward side of Maia. Just like before, I find the gap in the mountain face and squeeze through it until I'm standing inside the dense forest, being soaked. I stop to wait for Bane who has a harder time than I do since he's larger and his shoulders are broader. His bare chest and back are wedged between the walls as he scoots sideways. When he's finally free, the skin on his chest is scraped, the olive tones blooming red but Bane doesn't seem to notice or give me the chance to fuss over him as he walks past me, taking the lead.

"If we're safe here, why hasn't Zeke woken up yet?" I ask Bane just because his silence makes me nervous. It's impossible to tell what he's thinking, and I want to know more than I want my next breath.

"I sleep, Mine leave."

Fuck. So much for staying calm and waiting him out. Bane

already knows that once he goes, I'll take Zeke and head straight back to the cabin.

He's cunning. I hadn't expected that. Mostly because the others only ever warned me about how dangerous he is. They've never seen this side of him, but all it makes me wonder is, why me? What makes me different? Why doesn't he want to kill me?

"Do you still want to hurt Khalil and Thorin?"

"Yes."

Thorin once told me that Seth and Bane are how Zeke sorts and deals with his emotions. What if... My stomach sinks and I run forward to cut off Bane, grabbing his arms like a bitch with a death wish. "Does Zeke want to hurt Khalil and Thor?"

Bane's eyes remain woefully blank, but he gives his emotions away in the flexing of his arm muscles trapped beneath my palm and the slight growl in his voice when he answers, "*Everyone.*"

Zeke wants to hurt everyone.

"Then why haven't you killed me yet?" I challenge.

Bane's expression darkens before he moves me out of the way and keeps going. I don't follow, and he doesn't look back. The rain has slowed to a drizzle, but I hardly notice it as I watch the drops fall into a puddle near my feet. I can see my reflection inside and I don't realize I'm falling to my knees to get a closer look until I feel the cold mud sinking between my fingers. The first thing I notice isn't the sticks and leaves stuck in my hair or the scrapes and bruises.

It's the absence of fear in my eyes.

Of course, the image isn't a perfect reflection, so it might just be all in my head, but I still remember vividly what it felt like after the plane crash when I was lost out here the first time. I could barely eat whatever Tyler managed to find, could barely sleep, and feared death every second that Tyler pushed us to survive.

Right now, I'm just deeply annoyed that my boyfriend's alternate identity dragged me off to some cave like we're cosplaying in some raunchy horror. I need to figure him the fuck out, and I can't do it kneeling in a goddamn puddle, so I rise.

Bane isn't lurking like I expected when I look around, so I start off in the direction he disappeared, looking for sticks that I can use to make a snare as I go, but I don't find him. I do find a deer though, and it's browsing for food like I am. The doe's head is bent as it sniffs at an acorn. I reach for an arrow out of instinct only to remember that they were lost to the river.

All I have is Zeke's knife, but I'd have to get close…

I keep my steps light. The wet ground helps to keep them silent. My position isn't great since I'm in the doe's direct line of sight. I'm also upwind, but the petrichor is heavy in the air, creating a scent mask. Still, if the doe lifts her head, I'm fucked.

I'm carefully reaching for Zeke's knife when I see a shadow move beyond the deer. My gaze flicks toward it to make sure it isn't another predator creeping up on my kill, and I see Bane, still shirtless with his dark hair plastered to his head. He's stalking the doe too, but unlike me, his focus is intent on his prey while I can't help but watch him and wonder…

What the *hell* is he doing?

I have Zeke's knife. Bane has no weapon.

I'm so busy watching him that I forget to watch my footing and I step on an acorn. The doe lifts her head and she sees me. Thankfully, she doesn't bolt immediately. The elongated ovals of her ears twitch as she watches me and wonders if I'm dangerous enough to fear, if she's seen me before, and if I'm a hunter. I don't move and try my best to look like none of those things while Bane closes in like a quiet storm, but Bambi's mom isn't fooled.

Her right foreleg raises, and I tighten my grip on the handle of Zeke's hunting knife.

Come on. Come on, Bane.

The doe leaps at the same time Bane does. My heart feels like it's lodged in my throat, and my stomach feels twisted into a pretzel as I watch them collide.

Ohhhh…my fucking God.

Bane actually wrestles it to the ground with the stealth and power of a jaguar hunting a gazelle.

Except he's just a man.

He's not superhuman, or *other*, and he's certainly not a goddamn animal. He's real. As real as Zeke. As caring as Seth. Has anyone ever known this Bane?

The doe bleats and kicks as it fights to get free, and I wince when some of them land. After the third kick to Bane's shoulder, a distressed whimper tears from my lips and I move in with the knife. Bane has the doe pinned but is struggling to hold on to it. I'm worried that he'll get seriously injured if he holds on for much longer, so I hurry to close the gap when Bane wraps his arms around the doe's neck. The muscles in his bicep and forearms bulge just before I hear a sickening crunch, and I realize he's snapped the doe's neck.

Bane stands and meets my gaze. "Food."

"*That* was your plan?" I yell. "You could have gotten yourself killed!"

"*Food*," he repeats with a glare. And then softly, "Food for Mine."

Like the tide, I feel my anger being carried away—or rolled away as if Bane had just kicked it down a grassy knoll where the sun always shines. It's impossible to stay mad at him. I run my gaze over Bane's chest. Other than a few blooming bruises nothing seems out of place like a dislocated shoulder or a broken arm or rib. But Bane doesn't seem to feel pain, so how can I really be sure without Seth or Zeke to tell me? It just reminds me that I need to stop letting my curiosity get in the way of finding a way to wake Zeke.

"Thank you," I finally say before turning to the doe.

Transporting it will only increase the risk of spoiling the meat, so I quickly get to work field dressing the dead doe with Zeke's hunting knife. Bane disappears again, but this time I feel him close by, warning me not to run.

Fortunately, I've played this game already, so I know instinctively that he's testing me.

"You might as well come out now," I call out once I'm done gutting and partially skinning the doe. "I'm not going to run." My muscles are aching, and I'm sweaty, spent, and even more ravenous than before. The river and trying to escape the cave must have taken more of my energy than I thought. I don't have the fight in me for another test.

Bane reappears just as I wobble to my feet.

A wave of dizziness overcomes me just as I do, but I shake it off and meet his fruitless gaze—except it's not hollow or empty or unfeeling at all. There's something deeper with Bane that I know I can never fully explore because it's too dangerous. For Thorin, Khalil, and anyone else who crosses his path. I know because while Zeke's pain might dull over time, it will always remain. Bane will always be the kill switch that Zeke keeps tucked away just in case. To take that away from him...

I distract myself by starting a fire and gathering some sticks for a spit, and then I ask Bane to show me where the water is so I can wash off the blood and fur sticking to my hands and wrists like glue.

The stream isn't far away, and I'm pleasantly surprised to find that it's deep enough to submerge at least part of my body in. For now, I settle for cleaning my hands as thoroughly as I can, and then we head back to the campfire. The venison is tough as hell to eat since we don't have a few days to wait for it tenderize, and I don't even want to think about all the foodborne illnesses we're exposing ourselves to, but we have no choice but to risk it.

Once Bane and I are done torturing ourselves with the badly cooked meat, we hang around the campfire for a few hours until the sun sets. Bane watched silently from across the fire with his corded arms resting on bent knees as I spent the day spewing curse after curse while trying and failing to whittle arrows out of sticks and branches. Eventually, I gave up and settled for three semi-decent stakes.

It's dusk when we put out the fire and return to the stream where I strip off my clothes and bathe away the blood, sweat, and dirt from our harrowing journey.

Bane doesn't join me though and ignores my many attempts to convince him. He just stands sentry on the shore watching me with a focused possession in his gaze that should terrify me.

Mine.

That's what he's thinking, and I can't help but think it too.

Mine.

Biting into my bottom lip, I hold his gaze as I slowly leave the wide stream and reach out with fingers curled uncertainly until I seize the button on his pants and undo them. "You need to bathe, Bane," I argue even though he doesn't resist me. "We're filthy."

The last is said on a breathless whisper that makes it sound like I mean something else. I swallow past the knot in my throat and work Bane's pants down over his narrow hips. Zeke apparently had forgone underwear when he dressed, so his dark pubic hair comes into view first and then the hardening length that pops free as I work the pants down his thighs.

There are more purplish bruises on his thighs and legs, and I get the bright idea to press on one, but Bane doesn't react. He doesn't flinch or even growl at me as he's prone to do when I annoy him.

No pain then.

Kneeling when I reach the barrier of his boots, I undo the laces before working them off with Bane's silent help. He steps out of his pants, but before I can stand, he roughly grabs my hair and forces my head back so that I meet his gaze. From this vantage point, his jawline looks impossibly sculpted with a lock of his hair falling over his forehead. The moon hovers behind him now and makes his green eyes glow. His dick is fully hard now—angry veins and purplish tip jutting out over my face like a prize and a trap. Because I know what he wants.

And I…I want it too. I want to claim all of them. Zeke, Seth, and Bane.

But if I'm right and I'm triggering Bane, then giving in would be a colossal mistake because Khalil and Thorin are also mine and I can't risk them.

"Let me go, Bane."

I feel his fingers flex like he's going to do the opposite, but then he releases me. I don't trust my legs when I stand, but somehow, I manage it and then I lead Bane by his hand to the stream. The cool water greets our ankles first and then our knees and lastly our thighs.

It feels like heaven.

I get Bane to kneel in the water, and then I get to work washing his hair. It takes a lot of massaging and patience to really feel like I'm making a difference without the help of shampoo, but once his hair feels less sweat-slicked and oily, I wash his shoulders, his chest, and abs.

"All done." I offer Bane a smile, and his eyes drop to my lips. He still doesn't speak to me, but that's okay. There's more than one way to communicate. "We should head back," I suggest.

I start to leave the stream when I hear Bane stand. I assume he means to follow until my throat is suddenly seized and I'm hauled back against him. His erection is now lodged between us, and it hacks away at my self-control, especially when he starts to mimic the path my hands took. My breath quickens when his free palm skates over my shoulder and down my arm. Goose bumps follow in his wake, and I tip my head back and moan. I don't ask myself how or why he knows how to break down my defenses. I just enjoy this moment for as long as I can let it last. Just before Bane reaches my wrist, he skips it entirely to explore my hip and then my lower belly.

My skin tingles whenever he touches me and I want more. I want him to touch me all night. Forever. But I can't. I can't, I can't, I can't.

"Mine," Bane says as if he read my thoughts and rejects them.

"I'm yours when I say I am," I grumble with my eyes closed.

Bane responds by sliding his hand down from my belly and cupping my pussy. He presses his cool lips to my temple just as I feel his middle finger searching for my hole and groans, "Mine."

"That too," I echo. "Yours when I say."

"Mine…when I say," he echoes incoherently.

Bane finds my entrance, and I gap my legs open a little wider when he presses against it in silent demand. My pussy yields to him and I do too by doing the unthinkable. I turn my head and lift onto my toes to reach his lips. Bane lowers his head to meet me halfway, and I can feel the last of my walls crumbling the second our lips meet. His tongue sweeps inside my mouth, and my eagerness to feel him inside of me grows.

I hear a moan that I think comes from me, and a chuff in the distance answers back, followed by the soft thump of paws hitting the damn ground. I turn my head with a gasp to see a fucking bear about a hundred feet away approaching the stream.

It's probably just thirsty and not hunting for food, but I'm not willing to take that chance.

I twist in Bane's hold and say to him, "We've got to go."

We quickly grab our clothes but don't bother putting them on as we leave the stream before the bear notices us. Another squall arrives, and the rain begins again before we make it back to the cave. Bane and I are trapped under the storms for two more days.

As soon as the rain stops on the third day, I make my second attempt to escape the cave while Bane is away relieving himself. And for the second time, Bane finds and drags me back to the cave. He actually has my hair in a vise grip as he drags me screaming back inside, and the idea of what this must look like is almost as upsetting as the fact that it's actually happening.

He's gone full fucking caveman.

The only thing missing is his club and a loincloth.

As soon as he releases me, I jump to my feet with an agility that would make Khalil beat his chest with pride, and then I jump on Bane, digging my claws into his face as I try my best to gouge out his eyes. "Don't you *dare* do that to me again!" I screech. "I'm going back!"

The initial shock of my weight throws off his balance, and his back collides with the cave wall, but he quickly recovers and plucks me from the front of his body by my nape before dropping me to the ground.

I'm breathing hard, and he's barely winded.

"Told you. Cabin not safe. Mine stay."

"And I told *you* that if Thorin and Khalil are in danger, I *have* to go back. I have to warn them. It's bad enough you won't tell me why."

"Trust."

"Trust is *earned*." Bane makes a sound of frustration and tries to walk away, but I catch his arm and he lets me stop him. "Please," I say in a softer tone. "At least let me talk to Zeke. I need to know he's okay." I place a palm on his cheek when he still doesn't respond. "It doesn't have to be forever. We'll see each other again."

If Bane is right about the cabin being unsafe, it's more than just a promise. It's inevitable.

"Stay," he finally says, "and I'll go…Au-re-li-a."

"Okay," I agree, even though I want to ask him why he believes the cabin is unsafe. Bane didn't say Khalil or Thorin. He said the cabin. What does he know? What does *Zeke* know? "I'll stay in the cave."

Bane lowers himself until he's sitting on his heels with his knees digging into the ground. I lower myself too until I'm kneeling in front of him. I don't know if I'm supposed to do something, but it feels important that I be as close as possible. His palms are resting on his strong thighs, and he's staring at me like he knows I'm lying but is choosing to trust me anyway.

And that makes me feel guilty as shit.

"Bane, wait," I say, intending to come clean and tell him that I have no intention of staying in this cave, but it's too late.

Bane doesn't react to my request. His head drops, and then he doesn't move at all for several seconds. And then… He twitches. When his head rises, his eyes open slowly and then he blinks.

Slow.

Catlike.

I watch as his green eyes look around, taking in the cave and then down at his hand. Somehow, instinctively, I know he's checking for blood. There's some caked in his nails along with dirt, but they are otherwise clean.

"Zeke?"

His eyes snap to me, and he actually looks shocked to see me. And then worried. He looks back down at his hands, turning them this way and that to recheck them, and then his gaze returns to me as he frantically looks me over for wounds.

"I'm okay," I assure him. Grabbing his hand, I place it over my heart to show that it's still beating fiercely. For him. For all of them. "I'm okay. Please talk to me, Zeke."

He makes a pained sound, and then finally, he speaks. "Sunshine."

"Oh my God! *Seth*?" I grab at his shoulder, his face, and his hair. Anywhere I can get my hands on him.

"Hey."

"*Hey?* Is that really all you have to say? I thought you were—" I shake my head, unable to even speak the words. "I'm glad you're okay."

Seth sucks in a ragged breath that has me clutching him tighter. "I'm so sorry, Sunshine. I tried to stop Bane from waking up. I never wanted him to hurt you. I failed you."

"You could never fail me, Seth. *You came back to me.* I missed you so fucking much."

"You don't have to say that, Sunshine. I know you don't mean it." He turns his head away from me and leaves me gaping at his handsome profile.

"Seth, look at me. I didn't mean what I said. Please believe me. I would have said anything to keep you safe, and that's the only thing true that happened in that dell. You are everything to me, and the last place I want to be is away from you. It's been killing me to think that I might never get the chance to tell you how much I love you. That I will always love you. And I will never stop loving you. I will never leave you. I know sometimes that you'll have to leave me, but I will always be here waiting for you to come back to me. Please say you believe me."

"I believe you, Sunshine. And I'm glad to hear it. It would have made growing old together really fucking awkward if you didn't want to be with me." A laugh bursts out of me. It's such a Seth thing to say. The perfect mix of romantic and unhinged. I kiss him then because it's been too long, and he groans like he feels the same. "So you and Zeke, huh?"

I hit his chest. "Don't tell me you're jealous. You said you were fine with it."

Seth hums. "Yes, well, you just remember, I'm a lot more fucking fun than he is."

"He's not so bad." When Seth scowls at me like a jealous boyfriend, it takes an effort to be a good girlfriend and hide my amusement from him. I'm just so fucking happy to see him.

Seth's smile breaks free like he read my mind, and then he hops to his feet with a *whoop*. He holds out a hand to help me up, and with my palm still in his, Seth lifts my hand and twirls me around, and I'm laughing again as I let him. He lets me go and then dances away while singing "My Girl" by the Temptations.

He hops onto the slab like it's his stage, and when he hops back off, Seth shoves his fingers through his hair to get it out of his face. His forehead and cheekbones are on display again, making him look more like Seth.

He's back.

He's really fucking back.

"I'm surprised you forgave me so easily. To be honest, I thought I'd have to grovel a little more."

Seth hooks a finger in one of my belt loops and pulls me onto his lap as he takes a seat on the slab. I fight off a shiver when he runs his nose along my collarbone where my shirt is torn. "I'm crazy about you, Sunshine. You never have to grovel to get me on my knees. I don't want you to either. I'm yours. My heart is yours. You can break it a thousand times and I'll just piece it back together for you to do it again."

"I have no intention of breaking you, Seth."

"You probably have a lot of questions," I say when I catch him looking around again.

"Actually, I only have one. Why are we in a cave? Don't get me wrong. It's a nice cave, except for the fact that it's a cave. It doesn't really seem like you."

I tell Seth about Meera and her pups, Bane waking up hours later like a delayed fuse, the storm, and waking up here. I tell him about my encounter with Bane, which seems to disturb him even more, and then Bane's warning not to go back to the cabin.

"Did he say why?" Seth asks once I'm done.

"Only that I wasn't safe there."

"Hmm."

"Any idea why?"

"No." Seth sighs as he slides his hands into his pockets. "None. I've kind of been preoccupied keeping the son of a bitch from getting out." He eyes me then. "Are you sure he didn't hurt you?"

"I'm sure. Bane is, um…not what I expected."

"Oh yeah? How was he?"

"Well, for one, he kept saying I was his, and then he saved my life. More than once. I really don't think he wants to hurt me."

"Bane is dangerous, Aurelia. If he's fixated on you, it's just one more reason to be afraid."

"Maybe, but… I don't know." Just then, my stomach growls, so Seth and I search the cave for my boots, which Bane hid behind some rocks, and then we leave the cave to hunt for food.

I show him the narrow passage I found, and we squeeze through.

"The storm's breaking," he says as we search for whatever stream Bane had gotten our water from. "We'll head back first thing in the morning. I'm sure Thorin and Khalil are losing their minds."

"I feel like *I'm* losing my mind."

"Join the club," Seth retorts.

"So what's the plan? We don't even know where we are."

"Bane wouldn't have been able to carry you far after being in the river, so my guess is we're on Maia. We'll just have to keep heading south. Eventually, we should run into something familiar."

The stream isn't far away from the cave, and the moment I see the clear water, Seth and I drink our fill and then we tear off our clothes to bathe away the day. We even find some mint leaves growing by the edge of the stream and trout upstream hiding out near some log jams.

When we return to the cave, Seth pulls me close while we lie on the hard slab, and once again I have trouble falling asleep, but for a different reason.

"Sleep, Sunshine. You'll need your strength tomorrow."

"Promise me you'll still be here when I wake up."

"I promise. I'm not going anywhere until you're safe."

But if Bane is right about the cabin, who knows when that will be? I'm asleep before I can let the impending doom torture me further.

CHAPTER THIRTY

SETH

I lie awake while Sunshine sleeps soundly in my arms where she belongs. Brushing off the alarming fact that Bane thinks the cabin isn't safe wasn't easy. Without any real answers to offer, I didn't want to worry Aurelia, but now I can't stop thinking about it. I don't know if it's Bane's lingering influence, but I almost want to follow his lead and keep her here just to be sure.

I'm so lost to my thoughts that I don't even notice Sunshine stirring until I hear her sleepy grumble. "Seth, you're crushing me."

"Fuck. Sorry." I loosen my hold around her waist, and her head immediately pops up. I'm thankful for the lack of light because I feel her trying to study me in the dark. There's a fire, but it's small, so the warm, golden light mostly mingles with the shadows rather than casting them out completely.

"What's wrong?"

"I can't stop thinking about how beautiful you are."

"Flatterer. Now what were you really thinking about?"

"Bane's warning."

"Oh… And what have you come up with?"

I blow out a breath that's part frustration and part amusement as I drop my head down on the slab. "Absolutely nothing."

"Seems to me like you need a distraction."

"What kind of distraction?" I ask absently.

"A thorough one."

My head pops up again when Aurelia crawls down my body. I want to be gallant and tell her she needs to save her strength, but she makes quick work of unbuttoning my pants, and the moment she licks her palm and reaches a small hand inside to pull my dick free, I know I won't. My breathing quickens as she strokes it to full hardness, and then I watch her kiss the flared tip and feel my dick jerk eagerly in her palm.

"Fuck," I swear roughly. "You want to suck my dick, baby girl?" Aurelia nods, and then with her eyes on me, she opens her mouth, and I slip right in. My head falls back and I groan, but just as quickly, I'm lifting my head again to watch her try to take all of me. Her cheeks puff out as I slip farther into her mouth until I'm touching her throat. "Such a good girl, tasting that dick."

I feel her tongue working me while her head bobs in my lap. Spittle and pre-cum leak down the sides of my shaft, but I'm stuck watching the way her long lashes fan her cheek and the way the firelight makes her golden hair burn like embers in the dark.

My attention shifts when I notice Aurelia sneaking a hand between us and down the front of her shorts. Her arousal is a wet sound in the dark, and there's a wild desperation in her eyes while she greedily sucks me off.

It's painful to do, but I stop myself just short of coming down her throat. I use a fistful of her curls to force her head away when she makes a sound of protest, and I free my dick from that sweet vise of a mouth of hers.

"What's this?" I say as I watch her hand moving fast and unpracticed over her clit. "Has Zeke not been taking care of you, Sunshine?"

"We haven't…um…we haven't had sex yet. I don't want to rush him."

I force my expression to remain neutral rather than roll my eyes. Zeke is more stubborn than I gave him credit for. "That's okay, sweet girl. He might just need a little nudging. That's all." Aurelia's brows dip and I can see her questioning my meaning, so I quickly wrestle her clothes off her until she's naked and shivering in the dark. "Come on, Sunshine," I plead as I shove my jeans down my legs. "Sit on it, baby. Take what you need."

Aurelia whines and then throws her leg over my waist while I hold her hips to keep her steady. My fingers are digging possessively into the soft globes of her ass, and I can't resist smacking it a few times, each slap harder than the last until her moans turn into sharp cries. The moment she's in position, I tease my thick crown between the lips of her pussy before I lodge it against the small seam I want to possess, and then I lower her over my dick. My toes curl the moment I feel her tight, warm pussy embrace me so snugly. It feels like coming home.

"Jesus fucking Christ, Aurelia. *Fuck*."

"Oh, Seth," she moans as she works her hips. The sound of our skin slapping echoes around the cave. "You feel so good inside. Fuck me, baby. Please."

"Just try and stop me." I tighten my hold on her and snap my hips up to meet her halfway, and she cries out while her nails curl into my chest. I want to beg her to make me bleed for her, but then the light from the fire catches her bouncing breasts and I'm rendered mute as I watch the way it dances across her dark, puckered nipples.

I lunge for her like I'm possessed and wrap my lips around a nipple, sucking hungrily while she rides me with abandon. My mouth releases her only long enough to give her nipple the same attention, and I don't let go even when she shoves my back down on the slab to get the angle right to tease her distended clit.

I tighten my hold on her to keep her still. "I'm afraid you can't come yet, Sunshine. I need you to say it for me."

Aurelia whines at being denied an orgasm and then I feel her body tremble uncontrollably from the lost orgasm while she glares down at me. "Say what?"

I began to work her hips over me again, slowly getting her back to that point. Her lids lower, and her mind shifts to that single-minded purpose once more as she follows my slow, leisurely rhythm. "Do you remember that word I taught you?"

Her body stiffens, so I force my dick a little deeper to lure her mind back into that cloud of lust. "The one that wakes Bane?" she questions with a little moan.

"It doesn't just do that." Aurelia tightens around me at the thought of Bane, and I feel my balls tighten. *Not yet. Not yet, not yet, dammit.* But I'm as lost to the pleasure as she is.

"Say it," I command gruffly from the effort of holding back my cum. "Say it, and I'll let you come, baby." I loosen my hold, and like a greedy little cum slut, Aurelia takes the bait and starts bouncing again. Her face slackens with pleasure as she leans forward with her hands on my chest and uses me. "Say it, baby." I grunt, feeling her pussy pulsing around my cock and her ass softly slapping against my thighs. "You're almost there. Say it."

I see the moment she lets go of her fear, and I quickly reach for the door inside Zeke's mind while her lips form the forbidden word.

"Chrysalis."

CHAPTER THIRTY-ONE

AURELIA

I'm going to come."

Eyes firmly shut, I'm so lost to the pleasure that I don't even notice when Seth stops moving, his hands falling from my body as I eagerly tunnel his dick in and out of my pussy. Wanting to feel him deeper, I sit and take hold of my breasts as I bounce and bounce and bounce, covering his slick dick in more of my juices. A moment later, those hands return to my ass like they were drawn by a magnet, but the hold becomes tighter until I'm unable to move and I feel my orgasm drifting away once more.

"Seth, pleaseeee. I was almost there," I whine.

"Princess?"

My eyes fly open, and I stare down in horror as I realize too late that it's no longer Seth that I'm fucking.

It's Zeke who's awake.

"Oh my God!" I immediately move to get off him, but he won't let me go, tightening his grip even more and confusing me. His eyes are blown wide too as he takes in my nakedness. His gaze lingers on my breasts before he dismisses my lack of clothing to look around.

"What's happening? Where are we? Are you hurt?" His gaze returns to me at last. When I just gape down at him because I'm too freaked out to speak, he sits up, and I stifle my groan at feeling him move inside of me. I still don't speak and instead cover my face with my hands from sheer embarrassment. But Zeke won't let me move or hide in peace. He lets go of my waist and forces my hands from my face. "Talk to me, Aurelia. What's wrong? Did he hurt you? Did I—"

Catching on to where his mind must be leading him without any direction to fill in the blanks, I say, "No. Zeke, no. He didn't hurt me, and neither did you. I'm okay. Okay?"

"How? How is this possible? Bane—"

I shake my head. "I don't know. He just didn't."

"And Seth?"

My temper flares as I feel the need to defend the misunderstood alter. "Seth would *never* hurt me."

Zeke doesn't look convinced, but he nods anyway. His hand starts caressing me as if in apology and wanting to soothe the anger from me, but just as suddenly, his hand stops moving and he gapes at me.

"Aurelia… I'm inside you."

"It concerns me that you're only now noticing."

"I noticed. I just… I don't understand. How did we get here?"

Something tells me he isn't talking about the cave. "Bane woke Seth up instead of you, and we um…we got a little carried away."

"I see."

"I am so sorry, Zeke. This isn't right. I wasn't thinking." I wiggle again, and Zeke's eyes flash with warning, as if ordering me not to try to move away again.

"Don't be sorry. Did you come?"

I scowl at him. "Is that really important right now?" I snap. "God, you must feel so violated." Since Zeke won't let me get off of him, I wrap my arms around myself and look away.

Zeke leans back and braces his shoulders against the wall before throwing his arm on top of his head. He looks much too relaxed for someone who woke up not knowing where he is and with a girl on top of him. "I'm feeling a lot of things, princess. Violated isn't one of them. Now answer the question." His fingers dig into my ass. "Did you come?"

"No, okay? No, I didn't come."

"Well, we can't have that." He rolls me onto my back and immediately shoves himself balls deep in one smooth move. "Tell me you want this, princess."

"Zeke…" I lay a hand on his chest.

It's not the response he demanded, but he doesn't stop fucking me either. Instead, he reaches behind him and grabs my ankle before pinning my leg away from my body to open me up more for his thrust. "I'm going to make this pussy mine, princess. Tell me you want it or say your safe word."

"I want it, Zeke. I want it, I want it, I want it!"

He groans and starts moving inside me faster. I can feel his balls slapping against my ass and our sweaty skin creating a scandalous echo around the cavern. "God, you're so fucking wet. Seth got you all nice and warm for me, didn't he, baby?" I nod emphatically when the ability to speak proves elusive. "Such a good fucking girl, getting all nice and wet for us. Come here."

I yelp when he pauses fucking me to drag me roughly by my ankle across the smooth slab. He slams back inside of me as soon as I reach the center, and then he presses my thighs against my chest, giving him full control.

I'm powerless as he drives into me over and over again. All I can do is moan nonsensical things and beg for mercy that I don't want, and that falls on deaf ears as he tosses back his head and uses me like I used Seth.

I can't look away from the strong column of his neck and the distended veins that make him look dangerous. I'm so transfixed that I don't even notice the change in his pace or his hips slowing until he's completely still inside of me.

Slowly, his head lowers a moment later, and a smile that is as beautiful as it is unhinged takes over his features. "It's good to see you're having fun, Sunshine."

Confusion over the switch gives way to anger. "Seth, you creep!" I slap his face hard, and he laughs. "I can't believe you did that."

"Yeah, well, it wo—"

He stops midsentence and his eyes flare before he goes still again. I see the shift this time, and my heart speeds up as I wait to see which alter takes over.

Please don't be Bane. Please don't be Bane.

I'm all too aware of still being trapped underneath the hard body as I wait to see which alter takes over.

"Princess," Zeke says while panting. "Fuck. What happened?"

"Seth," I answer dryly. "Listen, I don't care which one of you gets me off just so long as one of you gets the job done."

Zeke chuckles and then flips me onto my stomach and yanks my ass into the air. "As you wish, princess."

He slams back into me, and all I can do is brace my hands against the hard slab as Zeke does his best to fuck me into it. Seth doesn't interrupt us this time, and I come screaming into the slab. Zeke comes with a hoarse shout and three hard shoves, and I reach between my legs to fondle his balls, wanting every drop of his cum for myself.

For a few moments there's only the sound of our heavy breathing and the crackling fire, and then I feel him lean down to whisper in my ear. "See you later, princess."

"What?" My eyes fly open, and I peer over my shoulder in time to see his close and his body go lax. It's ten heart-wrenching seconds before his eyes open slowly again. "Seth?"

He kisses my shoulder, and I exhale my relief. "I'm here, Sunshine."

CHAPTER THIRTY-TWO

SETH

We leave the cave just before daybreak, but the sun is beginning to set now, and we're only about halfway to the cabin if I had to guess. I don't know these mountains as well as Zeke and the others, so for the first couple of hours we go around in circles trying to find our way. Wanting more time with Aurelia and wanting to see her home safe myself, I'm too stubborn to wake Zeke, and Aurelia doesn't seem to care about making it easier on herself either.

"Oh, fuck, Seth. Right there," Aurelia moans. "I'm gonna come."

The biggest delay comes from this though. The constant fucking. Aurelia and I haven't been able to keep our hands off each other, stopping every other hour to fold to a need that can never be sated.

We'd found the river she and Bane fell into two days ago and we'd been following it for a while before we stopped for water, which led to this—Aurelia with her shirt shoved over her tits, shorts around her ankles, and her ass bent over a tree stump while I fuck her pussy like we're the only two people in the world.

"Come for me, Sunshine. I want to fucking feel it."

Aurelia obeys my command and comes with a cry so sharp and loud it sends the birds in the canopy above us into flight. I empty myself inside of her and then I pull out and fix my pants before leaving her spent and boneless over the tree stump. I walk toward the river, pulling the scrap of her shirt that we'd torn from the bottom to use from my pocket as I go.

After dipping it in the river, I return to Aurelia, where I clean my cum and her juices from her pussy before re-pocketing the cloth and pulling her up to kiss her forehead. "I love you," I whisper with a rumble as I pull her against my chest.

"Ditto, Seth. Have I told you lately that you're my favorite?"

I chuckle, knowing it's the orgasm talking. Her favorite is always changing, which only serves to make us dote on her more. "Only the last three or four times I made you come."

"You're so good at it. For a virgin."

Aurelia yelps when I pinch her ass. "Keep talking," I growl as I sink my teeth into her bottom lip. "I'll bend you back over that stump and prove to you again just how *not* a virgin I am, Sunshine."

"Really? Because I was thinking that sturdy-looking tree over there was feeling pretty left out."

"We can't," I regretfully groan as I rest my forehead against hers. "We have to get going, and I know you're getting sore, Aurelia. You've been walking funny for the last few miles."

"Fine."

We leave the river, and two hours later, Aurelia gets her wish when we stop for dinner and I somehow end up fucking her against a tree.

"I'm serious this time," I say with a glare as I yank my jeans back over my hips. "No more. We're losing light, and I don't even know where the hell we're at," I growl.

My frustration is with myself because I can't say no to her, and what's more, I don't want to. I could really use Thorin right about now. He's good at putting his foot down when Khalil's gentle steering doesn't work.

Aurelia rolls her eyes at me as she ties up her hair. "Actually, I think we should make camp," she suggests once we're both dressed again.

"Oh, you do, do you?"

She shrugs. "It's getting late. Neither of us know where we're going, and I'd rather not stumble around in the dark. I have a bow and no arrows, and you have no weapon at all. It's safer if we stay."

I scrub a hand down my face. "Fine, but no sex. I mean it."

Aurelia builds a fire while I hunt for food. After I manage to catch a snake, we cook and eat it over the fire as darkness falls.

"How did you do it?" she asks later while we rest against the tree we had sex against earlier.

"Do what?"

"In the cave, you woke Zeke instead of Bane, and then you took over again while we were…you know. How did you do it? Zeke wasn't in pain or in trouble." And then she pauses as horror enters her gaze. "Was he?"

"No, baby. He wasn't. Things have changed. *We've* changed. The rules from before don't apply anymore, and I think you're largely the reason why."

She winces while still looking unsure. "Is that…good?"

"Yes and no. I can wake up without Zeke being in pain, but it also means Bane can too. Zeke doesn't have control over him anymore. Neither of us do."

"But Bane doesn't want to hurt me?"

"Not *you*, no."

As in, he's still a danger to Khalil and Thorin and anyone else within reach when he wakes up.

"Shit," Aurelia swears as she sits up. "This is worse. So much worse." And then she turns on me with new hope alight in her eyes. "Can the trigger work both ways? If it wakes him up, can it put him back to sleep?"

I feel dread seeping into my veins as I slowly shake my head. "I don't know, Sunshine. It's never worked before. We've tried it."

"But it's like you said. The rules have changed."

"The only way to know for sure is to try it, and I seriously doubt that's wise. By keeping Bane away from you, I gave the trigger new purpose. I gave Bane a new purpose. As long as it's you pressing the trigger, we can open any door we like, but that's it."

"Khalil and Thorin think I'm affecting Bane. Zeke wasn't in any danger when Bane woke up, nor was he any of the other times. He was reacting to *me* and something *I* did. What if this thing between Zeke and me is putting them in danger?"

"Sunshine, I think that ship has sailed. What's done is done."

"What does that mean?"

"It means Zeke won't be so easy to shake now that he's been inside you. Sex is no small thing for him. He would have warned you before he went that far with you. Trying to stay away from him might do the very thing you're trying to prevent. Bane and I are his alters. We give Zeke what he needs…what he wants. And what he's decided he wants…is you. Denying him won't end pretty. For anyone."

"Maybe we should have stayed at the cave."

"Yeah, but—" A twig snaps in the distance. Aurelia gasps and looks in the direction the sound came from. We aren't armed, so her fear is palpable. I can feel it seeping into my bones and infecting my blood as if it were my own—until I'm filled with a single-minded purpose, and that's to keep her *safe*. It's the last thing I remember before it all goes black.

CHAPTER THIRTY-THREE

KHALIL

I follow the glow of a fire in the distance, trying to keep quiet in case it's someone else and not them. I've been searching for two days, barely eating or sleeping and only stopping long enough to consult the map and all the areas I've already crossed off and to radio Thorin to check on him.

He's getting impatient, and so am I. I don't know how much more I can reason with him that he's in no shape to help me look.

And then there was the sheriff. He's been coming down on our heads since Aurelia missed their daily check-ins. Apparently, they had some kind of secret deal. A condition that allowed her to come back with us and keep her hidden from her uncle until the sheriff decided if he believed Aurelia's story or not. We told him what happened with the storm and that Zeke is missing too. It's the only thing that's kept him from coming up here to arrest us both, but I've been keeping him up to speed on my progress.

Or rather lack thereof.

I'm creeping along trying to remain undetected when I hear a scream.

Forgetting all about caution, I sprint toward the sound and come across a small but empty campfire. Resting against the tree is

Aurelia's bow, but she's nowhere to be found. I kneel and study the footprints on the ground that indicate a struggle, the rock with a snake's peeled skin and bloody entrails, and a knife.

Hearing another scream, I stand and kick dirt onto the fire, grab the knife, and Aurelia's bow and take off in that direction. I hop a log, following the female voice, which becomes more distinct the closer I get.

"Let me go! Do you hear me, you crazy bastard? Let me go, dammit! I'm not going back to that cave!"

I burst through some dense foliage and onto a trail that leads away from the cabin, and I immediately spot Zeke walking down it with Aurelia thrown over his shoulder. At least I assume it's Zeke since he's not hurting her. Aurelia's pounding her fists on his back and screaming bloody murder, but he seems to be oblivious to it all as her protests fall on deaf ears.

"Aurelia! Zeke!"

Zeke doesn't stop walking, but Aurelia's head pops up from where it's hanging upside down, and her eyes widen when she sees me. "Oh my God. Khalil! Help me!"

"What the hell are you guys doing?"

Before she can answer, Zeke turns around, and from the look in his eyes I know it's not Zeke at all.

It's Bane.

"You."

"Fuck." Dropping everything, I pull the tranq from its holster just as he removes Aurelia from his shoulder like she's a sack of flour and tosses her into some bushes. She volleys a string of curses at him as she disappears from view, and then it's just him and me.

He sprints toward me, and I aim the dart gun, letting that shit off before he can get more than a few steps. It pierces his shoulder, but unlike the movies, I know it won't take effect immediately.

I'm going to have to fight this crazy bastard.

Bane slams into me, and I hit the ground with a grunt, and stars spark in my vision. I recover quickly enough to throw up my arms and avoid the slam of his fists. When I get my opening, I toss his ass off me and regain my feet before shoving my boot into his ribs.

Unfortunately, pain and Bane aren't acquaintances.

It does nothing but piss him off.

He lunges for me with a roar that sends a fucking chill down my spine and my head snaps to the left and blood spews out of my mouth. I follow up with a blow of my own that bounces right off him.

How do you beat someone who is impervious to pain?

The answer is: you can't.

I'm just buying time and staying alive until the effects of the tranq can kick in.

I won't lie. The fighter in me loves it. Bane is the perfect opponent, and if he weren't always trying to kill me, I'd make him my sparring partner.

Pain explodes through my shoulder a moment later, when Bane drives me into a tree and dislocates it with a vicious punch that knocks the wind out of me. It's enough of an opening for Bane to take the knife he left behind and press the blade to my throat. I feel it nick my skin, and then he leans close and growls, "She's mine."

Out of the corner of my eye, I see Aurelia pop free of the bushes. She's got leaves and branches stuck in her disheveled hair and a look in her eyes that would give the devil nightmares. I see too late that she's clutching a large branch in her hand as she storms toward us with her eyes on Bane.

"Aurelia, don't you dare," I command with my heart sinking into my stomach. "Stay back!"

Ignoring me, she lifts the branch with a warrior's scream and brings it down on Bane's back. He goes down, and neither of us breathe as we wait for him to stand again.

When a full minute passes and he doesn't, she drops the branch while I'm left gaping at them both.

"Sorry," she says, not sounding sorry at all. "I couldn't wait for the tranq."

"You want to tell me what the fuck that was about? Where was he taking you?"

Aurelia tells me how she doesn't remember anything after passing out in the river and then waking up in a cave on the leeward side of Maia. She tells me Bane's warning about the cabin not being safe and then she drops the bomb that Seth woke up. I don't think I hear much after that because of my relief that Zeke's alter is okay after all. Aurelia tells me that they were heading back to the cabin but stopped for the night when Bane woke up again for no reason at all.

Apparently, he does that now.

"Shit, okay. Well, the tranq won't last the night, and that was the only one I had. We need to get him back to the cabin before he wakes up."

"But your shoulder…can you carry him that far like this?"

"It's not that far, and we don't have a choice. If it's as you say and Bane can wake up at will, then we can't risk it. You'll have to pop my shoulder back into place."

Aurelia shakes her head while backing away. "No. No way. I can't do that. I don't know how."

"You have to, baby. Please. For me?"

Aurelia chews on her lip, inhales, and then nods. "Okay. Tell me what to do."

I run it down for her and then lie on my back and force myself to relax. Aurelia gently takes my arm and extends it but pauses with worry in her eyes that she might hurt me further.

"It's okay, Goldilocks. You can do it."

Nodding, she moves my arm the way I showed her, and I shout a curse when I feel the joint slide back into place. When enough of the pain fades, I rotate the injured arm to test it out and then exhale my relief.

"Thanks, baby." She looks like she wants to pass out, so I make her sit while I quickly examine her. There's no time to be thorough. "Are you hurt?"

"No."

I walk over to my discarded pack and bring it back over to her before reaching inside and removing my full canteen. "Here, drink."

"I'm not thirsty."

"Drink it anyway," I command.

"Is it too much to ask to have just one boyfriend who isn't overbearing and bossy?"

"It is now, since you're stuck with us, and we don't share."

"Except with each other," she says with a devious smirk.

"Sometimes not even then." She rolls her eyes and drinks while I tend to some of her cuts and bruises. Once I'm sure she's fit for the journey, I help her to her feet and press my forehead against hers. "I was beginning to worry I wouldn't find you," I admit. Something about Aurelia always makes me feel like it's okay to be open with her.

"Really?" she says as she slides a hand over my cheek and then rises onto her toes to kiss me deep and slow. "Because I never doubted you would." A moment later, she pulls back enough for me to see her face and the worry in her eyes. "How's Thorin?"

"Alive. Eager to see you. Hopefully getting the rest he needs."

Aurelia snorts. "No chance of that. He's probably pissy he had to be left behind."

"Then by all means, let's get you back to him." I kiss her again and then grab Bane, hoisting him over my uninjured shoulder while Aurelia grabs the rest of our things. "Let's go."

CHAPTER THIRTY-FOUR

THORIN

There's nothing sweeter than the scent of my songbird filling my nostrils again. Khalil, Bane, and Aurelia returned an hour ago. Aurelia spent the majority of that time soaking away her aches and bruises in my tub. Now the three of us are gathered at the foot of Khalil's bed with Aurelia tucked under my arm and dressed only in her bathrobe with her hair still wet.

"What do we now?" she asks as we stare at Zeke's body restrained to the headboard. "How much longer before he wakes up?"

"Hard to say since you knocked him out before the tranq could take effect, but it usually wears off within a few hours."

"He was going to kill you," she reminds Khalil. "He was going to cut your throat right in front of me. What was I supposed to do?"

He looks annoyed while I lift a brow at him over Aurelia's head. I seem to remember him mocking me endlessly, but it looks like Bane got the best of him too.

"I'm not blaming you, Goldilocks. You did the right thing. Uh...thank you for that by the way." It only just occurred to him to thank her for saving his life because we're so used to doing it for each other that we don't even bother bringing it up after the fact.

"You're welcome."

"Nothing we can do now," I say, going back to her earlier question before pulling her from the room. "Are you hungry?" She lost her arrows in the river, which would have made hunting hard. There are shadows underneath her eyes that only a good night's sleep and a well-balanced diet can fix.

"A little," she answers as she lets me steer her upstairs and far away from Bane.

I bring her up to the table and sit her down before walking over to the stove, grabbing some wood, and throwing it inside to get it fired up. I then grab the kettle and fill it with water before setting it on the stove. I get started on fixing her something to eat. I don't want her to wait long, so I grab the fixings for a sandwich and throw together a hearty one with some baby carrots on the side before setting it in front of her on the table.

"Are you sure you're okay?" I ask after she takes the first bite.

"I should be asking you that," she answers around a mouthful. "You're the one who got hurt, not me."

"Had to be a rough couple of days."

"I've survived worse, remember? At least there wasn't snow."

"I see your point." I'm content to watch her eat for a while until the kettle begins to whistle and I hop up to make her tea.

Khalil comes up the stairs, and he pulls her chair out from under the table and lifts her up before taking her place and sitting her in his lap. "Looks good," he says.

She places the sandwich to his lips, offering him some, and he takes a healthy bite of it with his gaze locked on her.

"That's for her," I snap. "She needs to eat."

Khalil sits back with a grin. "Then make me one."

I cross my arms and kick his leg under the table hard enough to make him scowl. "Make it yourself."

When Aurelia wordlessly offers Khalil another bite and he takes it, I roll my eyes and shove away from the table to make the fucker a sandwich so he can leave hers alone.

Aurelia sips her tea while Khalil devours his sandwich in a few bites.

I get up from the table and go into my room before returning with the radio. I hand it to Aurelia, and she looks up at me questioningly. "You need to radio the sheriff and tell him you're okay. He radioed, looking for you the morning after you disappeared. He's been on our case ever since."

"Shit." Aurelia grabs the radio but then pauses. "You know, don't you?"

"Yup," Khalil answers.

"And you're not mad?"

"You saved our asses when you had every reason to let us burn. Resenting you for having a safe way out would only make us deeply unworthy of you," I say. "So no. We're not mad."

Aurelia exhales like she's shedding a heavy burden and then calls the sheriff. After a brief but tense conversation, she ends the call and leans back against Khalil before closing her eyes.

"Time for bed," I say as I stand.

Her eyes pop open, and she sits up. "What about Bane?"

"There's nothing we can do now, and he's not going anywhere. You need the rest."

The three of us head down to the basement, but Aurelia takes us all by surprise when she hooks a left at the bottom of the stairs and goes into Khalil's room instead of hers.

"What's up, Goldilocks?" Khalil asks with a frown as we follow her inside.

"I'm sleeping in here."

"The fuck you are," he snaps.

"Someone has to watch over him, and he won't hurt me."

"You don't know that."

"Actually, I do. He saved my life. Twice."

"That doesn't mean he isn't a danger to you."

"Then stay and keep an eye on us. I don't care what you do, but I'm not leaving. It could be Zeke who wakes up. How do you think he'll feel if he wakes up in these cuffs? The least we can do is make sure he doesn't wake up alone. It's worth the risk."

When we don't respond, Aurelia climbs onto the bed and curls herself against Zeke's side. Blindly, she pats the bed behind her, and when Khalil and I lock gazes, since there's only room for one of us, I tip my chin toward the bed. He's been out there searching for them nonstop. He needs the rest as much as they do. Meanwhile, I feel like I've had enough to last a lifetime, so I head to the chair in the corner and take a seat to keep watch while they sleep.

It isn't long before Aurelia and Khalil are sleeping right along with Zeke.

The sun is creeping into the sky when I'm jarred awake by the rattle of a chain.

Memories from last night come flooding back, and I sit up in the chair with a jolt to see a body sitting up in the bed. The room is still dark, so the furniture is cast in shadows, but it's clear who it is.

"Zeke?" The head turns slowly, eerily toward the sound of my voice, and I sigh. "Bane."

I stand, and he yanks against the chain. The wooden headboard groans, and the sound jars Khalil awake, his rough movements waking Aurelia next.

"What's going on? What's happening?" She rubs at her eyes and then notices Bane. "Oh God. It's you." She then turns to me with wide eyes. "What do we do?"

"I vote we knock him out again." Khalil cracks his neck and stands like he's getting ready to do just that.

"No! Don't. Just…wait," Aurelia pleads. She turns to Bane when she sees us do as she asks, and my body coils tight when she lays her hand on his arms. "Bane?" His gaze won't leave me though, so he continues to struggle against his bonds. "Bane, please. It's me. It's Aurelia."

Hearing her name seems to do the trick, and his gaze slides slowly, cautiously away from me and down to her at his side. "Mine."

"Yes…yours," she agrees placatingly.

I feel my nostrils flare and my muscles flex while Khalil sneers. We hate that fucker, and the feeling is more than mutual.

"Thank you for helping me, but I'm safe now. I need Zeke or Seth. You need to wake them up. Can you do that?"

"*Cave*," he snaps at her with his face too close to hers for my comfort. *All of him* is too close to her for my liking.

"I know, I know. I didn't stay in the cave." Khalil and I swear viciously under our breaths when she swings into his lap without warning. Bane goes still, sitting back against the headboard with his own body tight as if he doesn't trust himself with her.

It's enough for me to walk forward to remove her from his lap, but his gaze shifts to mine when he sees me approaching, and the look in his eyes raises the hair on my body while the unspoken threat echoes around the room.

"Thorin, stay back. I've got this." Aurelia returns her attention to Bane. "They won't hurt me, but they think you will, so I need you to play nice."

Bane's glower darkens even more. "No."

Khalil and I startle at hearing Bane speak. Aurelia said he had in the dell, but hearing it makes it all the more real. Bane can *speak*.

Why the hell hasn't he ever tried talking to us instead of trying to kill us?

"All right then," Aurelia presses on while I silently lose my shit. It's like dedicating your life pursuing a theory just to discover that everything you knew was wrong. We weren't even close to understanding Bane. "Can you wake up one of the others like you did in the cave?"

"No. Mine is not safe."

"Bane, listen to me. I am safe. I'm home. Give me back Zeke or Seth," Aurelia demands firmly this time.

"No."

"Why the hell not?" Aurelia snaps. My muscles coil in preparation to strike and get her out of the way just in case Bane makes a move.

"Cabin is not safe." Before Aurelia can continue this redundant endless loop, he adds, "I-saac."

Khalil and I stiffen and exchange a look while Aurelia sighs. "Isaac isn't here, Bane. It's just us."

"He's coming. Mine not safe."

Bane doesn't speak again after that. He just keeps careful vigilance, growling and struggling against the cuffs whenever Aurelia tries to leave his lap. Half an hour passes like this before Aurelia spins around in Bane's lap, putting her back to his chest as she addresses Khalil and me. "I have an idea, but I need your help."

"What is it?" Khalil asks.

"Leave the room."

"You could have kept that idea to yourself," Khalil replies while crossing his arms. "No."

"Bane is clearly guarding me. I think he feels threatened with you both in the room. He won't believe that I'm safe until you leave. I'm not asking you to leave the cabin. Just step outside the door where he can't see you. I've reasoned with him before. I can do it again without your hovering."

"Fine," I say as I rub my throbbing temples. "We'll be right outside the door, but no farther."

"Good. Before you go, there's one more thing I need."

"What?"

"The keys to the handcuffs." Before I can tell her no, Aurelia holds out her hand and wiggles her fingers. "I promise not to use it until I'm sure he's gone."

Cursing, Khalil shoves his hand into his pocket and removes the key. He places it into her palm with a warning look to keep her promise.

Khalil and I leave and close the door behind us. A moment later, we can hear her talking to him and his short replies. This goes on for two hours with Khalil and me pacing a hole in the floor before we hear footsteps on the other side of the door. When it opens, Aurelia is standing there alone.

My gaze flies over her to the bed to see that the cuffs are hanging there open, and the body on the bed is relaxed as he leans back with a disarming grin and his hands behind his head.

"What's up, bitches?"

CHAPTER THIRTY-FIVE

SETH

I'm staring out the window, watching the turned leaves fall from their trees as we drive through Hearth. I've got one foot on the dash of the truck and my girl tucked under my arm humming happily as she sips her gourmet coffee. Whatever that is. Ever since the temperature dropped and the trees started losing their leaves, Aurelia has been going on and on about wanting something called pumpkin spice. Today, Khalil finally lost it and snatched the keys to the truck before dragging us all from the cabin. After stopping by the coffee shop to get her an extra-large pumpkin spice chai latte, we all piled back into the truck to head to the wolf conservation center.

Apparently, that wolf Aurelia is obsessed with was born and bred in captivity but somehow escaped and ended up lost in the wild for months. Like Sunshine. Aurelia then had this insane plan to save the she-wolf and her pups from the bad, bad wilds and almost got everyone killed in the process.

So that's cool.

I'm not prepared for the keepers at the center to roll out the welcome wagon when we arrive. They usher us in while talking a mile a minute about Meera and the pups' progress. I tune them all out as I follow along, making sure not to let my troubled thoughts show whenever Sunshine sends me curious glances over her shoulder.

She holds out her hand, and I take it, kissing the back of it before dropping my arm over her shoulder and letting her pull me along.

We're pretty much given a backstage pass when one of the keepers leads us through a gate with a sign marked *Danger Ahead. Authorized Personnel Only.*

Hands in my hoodie, I enter last and look around. The first thing I notice is that there are wolves *everywhere*, and that there are no more fences between us and them, but they pay us no mind as we enter and stand around.

The keepers are still talking a mile a minute about the care that went into reintegrating Meera and her pups into the pack. It was a slow process, but the pack seems to have accepted them all with no issues.

After a few minutes of keeping a safe distance, a wolf with gray fur stands and walks closer.

"Uh, don't be alarmed," the keeper says, even though none of us are. We live in the wilds, for fuck's sake. We can't take a walk without running across a predator or two. This is nothing. "Sometimes they get a little curious with newcomers, but they won't attack unless provoked."

The gray wolf growls, and I surmise that it must be the alpha of the pack checking us out. I can see the keepers eyeing each other as they wonder if they should cut our visit short. A moment later, another wolf with tawny fur appears next to the alpha. She brushes up against the incensed wolf, and the growls stop, replaced by a whine. The wolves rub their heads together before the tawny wolf cautiously approaches. She walks between Thorin and Khalil and

I see her gaze on me, head tilting as if she can tell the difference between me and Zeke.

"Hey, it's you," I greet when Meera jots close enough to brush against my jeans. The keepers gasp when I reach out a hand and boldly scratch behind her ears. "What?" I ask when the keepers gape at me. "We're old friends."

Aurelia grins at me over her shoulder, and I wink. Meera does the same to Aurelia, nudging her thigh with her snout, and I lean over to whisper in her ear.

"I dare you."

"Seth."

"Double, triple, quadruple dare you."

Thorin looks over his shoulder as if he can feel the mischief in the air and narrows his gaze. "Don't you fucking dare."

But Aurelia is already reaching a hand toward Meera, her fingers running through her rough coat a second before the alpha barks a call and Meera walks away. She returns to the wolf, and they walk to a spot under a tree.

"And I think you remember these two," the keeper says as two smaller wolves wander over.

"Oh my God," Aurelia gasps. "Is that Rom and Remy?"

"Yes, yes," the keeper answers enthusiastically. "It's them."

"They've gotten so big!" she squeals.

Emboldened by their mother's presence, the pups sniff at Khalil's and Thorin's shoes and legs and then Aurelia and me before losing interest and running back over to the rest of the pack to play.

We stay for a little while longer before we leave, and as we're walking to the truck, something lands on Aurelia's cheek and she swipes at it. Inspecting her wet fingers, she frowns. "Is it raining?"

"No," I say as I stare at the white flakes falling down. "It's snowing."

"Already?"

Thorin snorts. "Prepare yourself for it to happen often. It shouldn't stick for another month though."

The four of us hop in the truck and we drive off, stopping in town for some food and supplies. We're walking through the aisle of the grocery store picking up mostly junk food and liquor, to Khalil's annoyance, when Aurelia stops by the stand of magazines.

I only glance her way before I search the store for any lingering gazes. Keeping our heads on a swivel is what we do whenever we bring Aurelia into town, which we don't do often for this very reason. She—who is supposed to be dead—is still at risk of being recognized, so whenever we see someone looking too closely her way, one of us will kiss her senseless to block her from view. It really sends them scattering when we take turns.

Scandalous, they whisper.

Aurelia was annoyed at being judged at first, but now she thinks it's hilarious, and so do I. What can I say? She breathes, and my heart sings.

When I finish my scan and notice her still over by the magazines, staring at the front cover of one, I wander over and cage her in with my hand braced on the wall. "Anything interesting?"

She turns slowly, and the crestfallen look on her face immediately puts me on edge. She doesn't say anything, but the hand holding the magazine trembles, so I take it from her and read the cover.

The Estate of Aurelia George sued—Lawsuit reaches $40 million

"It says my uncle is refusing to pay a penny to the families who lost a loved one in the crash because of the contract they signed

when they were employed waiving indemnity. They lost their—"
Her voice catches as tears build in her eyes before falling uncontrollably. "Some of them were *fathers*, Seth. They had *children*, and my uncle doesn't care. He still won't pay."

"Shit, Sunshine." I pull her into me, and she sobs into my chest.

"He can't get away with this."

"He won't."

"I'm going to fucking kill him."

"You will." I promise. If she can get to him before I do.

"What's up?" Khalil asks as he walks over. "What happened?"

"Later."

Aurelia turns without a word and grabs every magazine from the stands before handing them to Thorin, who stares after her when she leaves the store. He walks over to the cashier to pay. Khalil and I follow her back to the truck, and then we drive back to the cabin in silence once Thorin catches up.

The moment we're inside, Aurelia begins poring over every magazine looking for more information about the lawsuit. As it turns out, not only is her uncle trying to get the courts to waive the seven-year-rule for the presumption of death, but he's also ignoring the cries of the victims' families while silently selling off her catalogs to the highest bidder.

When she's done, Aurelia doesn't say a word for the rest of the night, but I can see the silent fury sliding over her features as she plots her vengeance and more. It's a few more hours before she tucks it all away. I'm sitting on the front porch staring at the moon—for some fucking reason—when the front door opens behind me. I know it's her by her soft footsteps. She lowers herself onto the step next to me, and we sit quietly for a few moments before she speaks.

"Are you ready?" she whispers.

I peer down at her with my brow raised. "Are you sure you're up for it?"

"We made a promise."

"That we did," I agree even though I'm more than a little reluctant to keep it. But if I don't, why should Zeke? I stand and help Aurelia up, and then we walk away from the cabin and out of the clearing together. We walk in silence until we reach a precipice not far away that has a clear view of the moon. It's so close that it feels as if I could reach out and touch it. But I don't, because I'm too busy drinking in the sight of Aurelia in the moonlight. She's the real breathtaking image.

Aurelia steps closer to me and rests her soft fingers on my forehead just above my brows. It's something we've been practicing and perfecting these last three months. Feeling her one last time helps to calm me. Helps me to say goodbye, to let go.

"I love you," she whispers.

"I love you more, Sunshine."

Softly, she trails her fingers down my face and whispers, "Chrysalis."

CHAPTER THIRTY-SIX

EZEKIEL

She's the first thing I see when I wake up, and just like all the other times, I feel my racing heartbeat slow a lot quicker than it would if she hadn't been there.

"I'm here. You're safe," she says. "We're still in the Cold Peaks, not far from the cabin. It's only been a day since you were last awake. Khalil and Thorin are fine, and everyone's safe."

Her lips trembles and I shake off my own anxiety to pull her close. "But you're not fine. What's wrong, princess? Did something happen?"

As we've been doing for the last three months, she quickly runs down the day, ending with the news that her uncle was, surprise, surprise, a heartless piece of shit.

"I'm sorry, princess."

She laughs, but it's humorless while a tear streams down her cheek. "Kiss me, please. I've missed you."

I give in to her demand and kiss her senseless before picking her up and wrapping her legs around my waist as I walk us back to the cabin. Khalil and Thorin are lounging around the living room, pretending they aren't tense and waiting for our return, but I see the collective sigh they release when they see us unharmed.

"How did it go?" Khalil asks as he sets aside one of the many magazines spread around the living room floor. "All good?"

"Yup. So how was Meera?" I ask as I take a seat in the recliner with Aurelia in my lap.

"She seemed happy. Healthy. The pups are *huge*."

"Yeah, so big it doesn't really feel right calling them pups anymore," Thorin points out.

Aurelia gives him a withering look. "Khalil, be a dear and hand me that apple so I can throw it at Thorin's head."

Khalil hands it to her and as promised, she tosses it at Thorin, who raises a hand at the last minute and catches it in midair. He then leans back with a cocky grin and takes a bite out of the apple.

"Thanks, songbird. I was starving."

Aurelia fidgets in my lap. I can tell she wants to go to him, so I sigh and unwind my arms from around her waist. Aurelia smiles softly at me over her shoulder and then crawls from my lap and into his. Thorin grips her thigh possessively, and she rolls her eyes at him.

I don't get those two and probably never will.

"You ever thought about cutting your hair?" she asks him after examining the unbound strands falling around his face.

"You don't like my hair?"

"I love your hair. I'm just thinking about how much hotter Brad Pitt was with shorter hair in *Mr. & Mrs. Smith* after seeing him with long hair in *Troy*."

"Yeah, but I'm a lot fucking hotter than Brad fucking Pitt."

Aurelia groans and tips her head back. "Yes, of course you are, but that wasn't the point."

Thorin sighs and leans his head back on the couch to stare at Aurelia from under his lashes. "If you want me to cut my hair, then I'll cut it."

Aurelia doesn't miss a beat, swiveling her head toward Khalil. "What about you, handsome?"

Khalil pauses, looking like a deer caught in headlights with a beer frozen halfway to his lips. Clearing his throat, he sets the bottle down. "Actually, I was thinking about loc'ing my hair. I should have done it years ago."

Aurelia's expression becomes thoughtful as she taps her chin. "You know, that's such an interesting thought. Let me see…yeah, *no*."

Khalil sucks his teeth while Thorin and I snicker.

"You really want them to cut their hair?" I ask, noticing she hadn't asked me about mine. She's already seen me both ways since Seth doesn't do well with haircuts.

"No. But I was thinking we should probably consider disguises. By now, my uncle will have done background checks on all of you, and we shouldn't underestimate him. You'll all be a lot less easily recognized if you alter your appearance. Just a little."

"What about you?"

Aurelia plucks one of her longer curls from her shoulder and studies the gold giving way to her natural brown before eyeing Khalil. "I hope you're not too attached to calling me Goldilocks."

"Your hair wasn't the only reason I called you that, so changing it won't change who you are to me."

Aurelia leaves Thorin, who looks like he was nodding off before being jarred awake by the loss of her warmth. He scowls at Khalil when he finds Aurelia curled in his lap now and then scrubs a hand over his face as he leans forward.

"We're still no closer to figuring out what to do about Isaac," he reminds us.

"What about drawing him out?" I suggest. It was the plan I'd come up with months ago, but I couldn't bring myself to go through with it because it felt too much like a betrayal. I realized it the moment Bane started uttering warnings of the cabin not being safe. He'd known what I was thinking, what I was planning to do, and was trying to warn them. When all three sets of eyes turn to me, I know I can't take the words back, so I gather the courage to press forward. "We bring him to us."

"And if we fail to kill him? What then?"

"If we fail, we die, so I guess we won't have to worry."

Khalil snatches his beer from the table and sits back as he swigs from it. "Not necessarily. We could be blowing our cover for no reason. We'll end up on the run again."

"Then we don't fail."

Thorin shakes his head, already shutting down the idea. "It's too dangerous, Zeke."

"More dangerous than sneaking into his compound and fighting our way out? That won't work a second time, and you know it. It'll be the four of us versus his *thousands*."

"Zeke's plan has merit," Aurelia says after quietly watching us argue. Khalil and Thorin both glare at her, but she pays their scowls no mind. "But what if we find somewhere far away from here to draw him out? If he gets away, we retreat to our hidey-hole to lick our wounds in peace and then try again later."

"But not immediately," Khalil amends while considering her plan. "Just in case we're tailed."

"Didn't Thorin mention Aruba? I could use a vacation."

The room falls quiet as we all look to Thorin, our unspoken leader. He's staring at the floor as he contemplates the pros and cons.

"We can't wish him dead, Thor," Aurelia says gently to urge him into the decision we all made minutes ago.

Thorin's head doesn't move, but his gaze cuts her way while his lips remain firmly shut. Thorin is no coward. He simply has too much to lose, especially now with Aurelia, the girl of our dreams right here within our grasp. We're safe here, and there's no reason to believe we won't be for another ten years and another ten after that. We're inviting chaos into our lives by choosing vengeance over peace, but a man like Marston George should not be allowed to live.

And neither should my father's other son.

If it all goes wrong, Thorin will blame himself, Khalil will blame himself, I will blame myself, and Aurelia will blame herself. None of us will be blameless, but at least united, we can all share this too.

"Okay," he mumbles finally. "We do this."

My heart thuds against my chest. "The only question left is *how* do we do this?" I ask to distract myself from the nervousness trying to fester into terror. "We need to get back on US soil without Isaac being aware of us. A decade ago, he had *cops and federal agents* under his thumb; who knows who else he's brainwashed into his cult since then. Someone with enough pull to have the airlines monitored no doubt."

"Um…" Aurelia raises her hand. "I can help with that." When we blink at her, she scoffs. "I'm rich and famous, remember? I guarantee I have more pull than Isaac."

"Are you forgetting that your uncle is in control of all of your assets?"

"Uh…*no*? Believe it or not, I have my own connections outside of Uncle Mars. Someone who tried her best to help me once. Before I knew the monster my uncle would turn out to be."

"And she's willing to stick her neck out for you again?"

Aurelia nods. "I know she will. I uh…" She begins to fidget in Khalil's lap, twisting her fingers into a knot until he wrestles them free and kisses her palm to give her courage.

"You what?" he whispers. "It's okay, Goldilocks. You can trust us."

"I um…I called her. A few months ago. After the avalanche when the sheriff came for us."

It's an effort for Khalil, Thorin, and me not to react.

"Why?" I ask, remembering to keep my tone gentle.

Aurelia makes a gruff sound of frustration. "I don't know! Because I wanted to prove to the sheriff, and that *fucking* smug therapist, and I guess myself, that even if I had a way out, I wouldn't take it?"

"And if you changed your mind later, the sheriff was supposed to get a message to her, wasn't he? That's why he insisted on the daily check-ins."

Aurelia nods with her gaze on the floor.

"Okay, so how fast do you think your contact can arrange a plane?"

Aurelia looks surprised at how quickly we're moving on, and Thorin laughs when he sees it. "You could have left at any time," he tells her. Aurelia narrows her gaze like she doesn't quite believe him. "We weren't teaching you how to hunt and survive out here for shits and giggles."

"We're not saying we wouldn't chase you," Khalil amends when Aurelia still looks skeptical. "It's not in our nature to let you get away. You'd just have to be faster. Smarter." He trails the back of his fingers down her bare arm. "But we've been working on that too, haven't we?"

Aurelia looks shell-shocked, and we're quiet as we wait for it to finish sinking in. For her to remember everything we've demanded of her these past months in an effort to make her less dependent on us or anyone for that matter. I see the moment it clicks; the tension coiling inside her muscles suddenly unravels and her body relaxes as she covers her face with her hands and then drops them again once she's collected herself.

"Let's call the sheriff," she says.

CHAPTER THIRTY-SEVEN

KHALIL

Alone in my bedroom, I stare at the old and worn photo of my parents. I never allow myself to pull it out too often and only ever give myself a second to look at it—to reaffirm the memory of their faces—before I tuck it away under my mattress again.

It's been ten years since I've seen or spoken to them. I know they're alive, but they can't say the same for me, which makes the possibility of facing them again that much harder.

Will they forgive me? Will I ever forgive me?

The four of us spent the night coming up with a plan to draw Isaac to us and making it as airtight as possible. The plan is to lure Isaac to our hometown in Six Forks, Nevada, since he'll be less likely to suspect the trap if he thinks Zeke is just coming home after all these years in hiding. It's only when I'm alone in my bedroom that I realize what it would mean if we succeed. We wouldn't just be free, my parents would be too. Free from the pain I've caused them all these years.

I'm still staring at the photo when the door creaks open, and I know it's her without looking up. She pads softly over to the bed and sits next to me. I can smell the sweet scent of her soap from her shower and feel her arm brushing mine as she peers down at the photo in my hand.

"Are those your parents?"

"Yeah," I answer, my voice hoarse.

"You look just like your mom," she says to no surprise. Everyone's always said how I'm her twin. "I see a little of your dad too. You have his ears."

I cackle at that. "He'll be happy to hear that. He's always saying how his genes could have fought back a little."

Neither of us speak as we stare at the photo of my parents together on their anniversary.

"Have you thought about what you'll say to them?" Aurelia asks.

I laugh, but the last thing I feel is real mirth. "Many times. Nothing I come up with to apologize for being the world's worst son seems good enough though. How do I give them back the last ten years? How do I take away that pain?"

"You can't. All you can do is everything in your power to make sure they don't spend the next ten years believing the worst. It'll be hard, but they've endured worse not knowing your fate, and so have you. You can't live with this guilt forever, Khal. It's drowning you. You try to hide it, but I can see."

"I don't regret choosing my brothers," I say as I tuck the photo back in its hiding place. "Zeke needed me, and Thorin couldn't have done this alone. They would have killed each other, and they don't have anyone else. They only have me. I don't regret being here for them."

"I don't think anyone is asking you to," she assures me gently.

"Then you don't know my parents," I say with amusement.

"Well…" She stares at her toes as she swipes them back and forth across the floor. "They raised you, Khalil. Would they really be all that surprised at how much you love your friends or how loving and loyal you are? Don't you think in some way they might be proud?"

I stare down at her while she blinks up at me, waiting for my answer. "Maybe."

I want to tell her how lonely it's been, how lonely I've felt sometimes, keeping Thorin and Zeke from falling apart on my own. And how I'm glad she stayed because I haven't felt that way since she arrived, but Aurelia then leans her weight against me and I let the urge fade away because I don't want her to stop. I don't ever want the day to come when she no longer thinks I can be strong for her.

She won't. Tell her.

"And at any rate," she says in a light tone, "you'll always have us, and I'll be right there with you if you want. I'll even let you hold my hand while your mom and dad cuss us both out."

"Yeah?" I feel a smile slowly splitting my face. "You want to meet my parents, pretty girl?"

In classic Aurelia fashion, she gives me a dry look. "You planning on taking some other bitch to meet them?"

Leaning down, I take her lips and kiss her nice and slow before pulling back to stare into her eyes. "Only my future wife."

"I'll tell Seth to pick out his dress."

Standing, I scoop her smartass up and carry her to the head of the bed while she squeals. I toss her down and then rip off my shirt before diving on top of her. Aurelia is still trying to untangle herself from the sheets when I begin tickling her sides. "What was that shit you was talking?"

"I'm sorry!" she screams as she twists and turns and contorts her body while laughing uncontrollably.

"What?"

"I said I'm sorry!"

"Nah, I can't hear you. You're what?"

"I'm sorry!"

"Not good enough. Say you'll marry me and maybe I'll stop."

"Are you crazy?" I tickle her ribs a little harder, and she damn near breaks her back trying to get away from me. "Okay, okay! I'll marry you! I'll marry you!"

Lifting my hands from her body, I lean over and kiss her forehead while she shyly peeks up at me from underneath the twisted sheets covering her nose and lower face. "Glad to hear it," I say as I join her on the bed. "It's a date, Goldilocks."

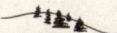

I stare at the table full of weapons and wonder if it will be enough. Normally, this time of year, we'd be prepping for the winter by canning, stocking up on nonperishables, resealing any drafts, insulating the pipes, emptying the septic tank, and filling the water tank…among other things.

Instead, we're counting bullets and arrows and making bombs.

We even let Seth near the flamethrower we hid.

He's fiddling with it now, and Thorin keeps casting nervous glances at him. We still don't know which of us he tried to set on fire that day. He *claims* it was an accident, which we know is a goddamn lie.

I don't point out the fact that this is all pointless. It's not as if we can bring any of this with us back to the States, not without a whole lot of red tape and paperwork when the key to succeeding is to stay under the radar. Besides, most of the shit here is illegal as fuck. I don't point it out for the same reason none of the others do. Preparation makes us feel better. It makes us believe we actually stand a chance.

"We've got enough bullets here to start our own army," Aurelia says as she sits back with her feet propped up and pretends to help. She's already restrung her bow and counted and organized all of the ammunition twice. "I've even got a few ideas for a name. Aurelia's Awesome Army. The Triple As. The Aurelites."

"You never miss an opportunity to toot your own horn, do you?" I ask as I wipe down the barrel of a shotgun. Thinking about it, I pause my cleaning to stand from my seat next to Thorin and move to the opposite end of the table.

Aurelia's gaze shifts to my face once I'm seated and then becomes unfocused as she stares at me for a few seconds like she's thinking. "The Aurelians."

"The answer," Thorin says with a chuckle, "is *no*. She doesn't. And she doesn't give a damn."

A plume of fire suddenly shoots out over the table, and I quickly drag Aurelia down with me who shrieks as Thorin and I duck under the table.

"Shit, shit. Sorry, sorry," Seth says as he releases the trigger and the flame winks out.

"Goddamn it, Seth!" Thorin shouts as he stands and storms over to the fire extinguisher to put out the curtains hanging over the back door's window.

"All right. That time it was definitely aimed at you," I say to Thor as I reclaim my seat. When he looks at me, I point to his shirtsleeve that's on fire.

Seeing it, he curses as he rips off his shirt and throws it in the sink before running water over it. Aurelia giggles and then throws a hand over her mouth when Thorin sends her a dirty look.

"That's your own fault," I tell him. "You should know better than to insult her in front of Seth."

Thorin's eyes widen. "It wasn't an insult, and you're the one who brought it up!"

I lift a brow. "Why do you think I switched seats?"

Seth winks at Aurelia, Thorin scoffs, and I shake my head as I go back to cleaning the weapons. Thorin shoves the back of Seth's head as he passes to return to his charred seat, and Seth pops the top on a cool beer before sliding it down the table toward him. Thor accepts without hesitation and then tips his beer to Aurelia who blushes prettily.

I spend a minute searching for a word to define our group's unique dynamic until I finally arrive on the perfect one: dysfunctional.

My gaze travels around the table as everyone goes back to their contented silence and individual tasks.

I wouldn't have it any other way.

CHAPTER THIRTY-EIGHT

SETH

I think this is it," I say as I haul the last of the plywood out of the hardware store. I place it into the truck bed with the others, and Khalil begins tying them down for the journey. It's the day before we leave Canada, and we, minus Aurelia, made a last-minute stop in town to grab wood to board up the cabin.

"All set." Khalil hops down and joins me on the sidewalk.

"Good," Thorin says as he slams the tailgate closed. "Let's hurry up and get back. It looks like it's going to storm, and Aurelia isn't answering the damn radio."

"She probably fell asleep. She's been doing that a lot lately." Probably storing up her energy for all the murder. Or maybe she just doesn't want to think about it. The three of us hop in the truck with Thorin in the driver's seat. "Do you think she'll really do it?" I ask from the back seat as Thorin starts the truck.

Khalil peers at me over his shoulder. "Do what?"

"Get on a plane again after what happened. I wouldn't blame her if she couldn't. I don't think I would either."

"I don't know," Khalil answers after considering it for a moment. "I guess we'll see."

Thorin takes off toward home, but we don't get more than half a mile before the red and blue lights of the sheriff's truck in our rearview stop us. Thorin swears and pulls over, and moments later, Sheriff Kelly is standing at his open window.

"I'm glad I caught you boys," he greets as he removes his hat. "She said I'd find you near here."

Thorin frowns. "Who?"

"Your gal. Aurelia."

"You talked to her?" I lean forward to get a good look at the sheriff who looks even more haggard than the last time I saw him, and notice a deputy I don't recognize standing a few feet behind him. Must be new. "When?"

"'Bout an hour ago, I'd say. I went looking for you boys at the cabin first, and she answered the door. Said I'd find you here." I think the three of us breathe a collective sigh of relief at the confirmation that our girl's fine and probably fell asleep like I'd guessed.

"Who's he?" I ask, referring to the silent deputy.

"Ah, this is Deputy Green. Brought him on two weeks ago after Plocher decided on an early retirement. His first week was nothing to write home about, but I'd say he's had an exciting second week, wouldn't you, Green?"

"Definitely, sir."

Fascinating. I roll my eyes.

"Listen," the sheriff says. "I know you boys are getting ready to hightail it out of town, and this is highly inconvenient, but I have a favor to ask."

"What's up?" Khalil's friendly ass asks.

"We got some out-of-towners who went camping, and a couple of them got separated from their group last night. No one's seen or heard from them since. I've got the new SAR team out there looking, but they aren't familiar with the terrain and haven't found diddly-squat. With this nasty squall coming, I don't want to waste any more time. You three know those mountains better than anyone. Maybe you'll see something they can't. What do you say? Help this old man out one last time?"

Frowning, I sit back and cross my arms, choosing to keep my thoughts to myself.

The search could only take a few hours, or it could take a few days. It's been a month since we decided to go after Isaac, and it feels like now or never. A delay could make us all lose our nerve, not to mention search and rescue is a dangerous job. If one of us gets hurt, we're *fucked*. We're already wildly outnumbered, but that's okay because we only have one target. Anyone who gets in our way will simply be collateral damage, but we have a way around that too.

I watch Khalil and Thorin glance at each other, and then they both look in the back seat at me, and I raise my brows because we're obviously going to do it. Why? Because Aurelia told the sheriff where to find us, which means she thinks we should. So we will.

Our girl's got a sharp tongue but a soft heart. She knows what it's like to be lost out there and wouldn't be able to live with herself if she allowed us to ignore someone else in need.

"We'll do it," Khalil says. "We just need time to grab our gear."

"No need," the sheriff states. "Your young lady already took care of that. She packed your gear, and we put it in my truck."

Thorin blows out a breath and then waves a hand. "Lead the way."

It's fucking snowing. And worse, it's late enough in the season that the shit is actually sticking and being a goddamn nuisance. I shiver in my leather jacket for the third time and pull the fur-lined collar up to protect my nape and ears.

It's just my luck that this shit show landed on my day instead of Zeke's.

I'm tempted to force the fucker awake so he can deal with this cold instead of me. I'm already grouchy that I won't be able to hold Sunshine's hand during the plane ride tomorrow. *Zeke* gets to. It's not fucking fair.

A helicopter flies overhead and I glare at it as it goes.

We've been searching for hours and haven't caught a single lead yet. For one, the dickheads who radioed for help can't seem to keep their story straight about the last time they saw their friends or where they were going when they disappeared, which makes it harder to establish a searchable grid.

And two, their camp doesn't look lived in. It looks more like it was staged to give the impression of camping, which also doesn't make any sense. I get lying about your friends going missing if you murdered them. But why would anyone drag all of this shit out here just to *pretend* to camp?

Nothing about this makes any sense, and I can tell by the matching scowls on Thorin and Khalil's faces that they're thinking the same thing. We have no reason not to trust the sheriff though, so we stay and hope that the alarm bells that have been going off in our minds for the past hour are wrong.

And then there's Aurelia.

We still can't get ahold of her, but it's probably the storm interfering with the signal. Nevertheless, I'm getting ready to bow out and head back to the cabin to check on her when the sheriff walks over to where the three of us are searching an abandoned wolf den.

"So the witnesses now think their friends might have gone to explore a system of caves near Maia. I'd send some volunteers out there, but they're all pretty weary and spread out checking the other leads. You boys think you're up for it?"

"Sheriff, how sure are you that this is legit?" Khalil barks. "It doesn't seem off to you that their story keeps changing? I mean, what the fuck?"

"I've had those thoughts myself, but we can't take that chance. Either a terrible accident occurred or a terrible crime. Either way, I'm not leaving until those hikers are found."

"Fine," Thorin says. "We'll go and let you know if we find anything."

"Take Deputy Green with you, will you? Show the new kid the ropes?"

I glare over at the creepy fucking deputy who keeps staring at me like he has an eye problem. I can't actually see his eyes behind those dark shades, but I know he's watching me and has been ever since we arrived.

"Nah," I snarl. "I don't like him."

The sheriff's brows raise at the unprovoked hostility in my tone, but I ignore him and walk off to stand near the ATVs. I hear Thorin murmur something to the sheriff, and then he and Khalil join me with deputy fucking Green.

I straddle my ATV and try again to radio Aurelia.

To my immense fucking relief, she finally answers, sounding like she was asleep. "Seth?"

"Sunshine," I greet with an exhale. "Where were you? We've been calling you."

"Sorry. I fell asleep. How's the search going?"

I press on the receiver. "Shitty. We haven't found a thing. Not even a set of footprints."

"Really?" Aurelia sounds surprised. "Why?"

"My theory? We've been using the wrong M. I'm thinking *murdered*, not missing." I release the receiver, and Aurelia's tone changes.

"That's…disturbing."

I grin and press the receiver. "Aren't you glad you told us to come?"

"Be careful, Seth. I don't like this."

"Is that Goldilocks? What's she saying?" Khalil asks before I can reply to her.

I turn my head toward where he's sitting next to me on his own ATV and smirk. "She wants us to come home."

Thorin snorts and shoves his helmet over his head.

"Seth?" Aurelia calls over the radio when I take too long to reply.

"I'm here, baby." The deputy walks by, and I watch him climb into one of the pickups. "We'll be careful," I promise her. "Gotta go, but we'll be checking in. Don't fall asleep."

Her response comes through immediately. "I won't."

The snow is coming down even harder by the time we reach the caves on the far east side of Maia. We're so far away from the rest of the search team that even the helicopters searching from the air are a distant *thump-thump-thump*. They'll have to give up the aerial search soon once the visibility becomes too limited and to avoid the blades from icing over.

The knowledge soothes some of the agitation that's been riding me since we started and injects some urgency in its place. Before we head inside though, I radio Aurelia one last time to check on her, since we'll probably lose signal. Once I'm satisfied she's safe, the four of us head inside the first of the caves.

I make sure to keep the deputy within my sight at all times as we search high and low for the missing and possibly dead campers.

CHAPTER THIRTY-NINE

AURELIA

I promised Seth I wouldn't fall asleep, and after what he told me, I don't think I could, so I set aside the book I'm reading and rise from the bed Khalil built for me and stretch. Leaving the room I've been sharing with Zeke and Seth, I walk out onto the lower deck for some fresh air. I haven't been out here since the guys locked me out to freeze to death that first night. I push the memory away and focus on everything I've learned about them since.

It's snowing now, but the cold doesn't deter me.

My guys are out there, and the worry stirring in my gut still won't abate even with the cool air filling my lungs. I head back inside when I can no longer feel my toes and I get to work lighting the fires in all of the wood-burning stoves.

I want the cabin warm when they return.

Hopefully, in one piece.

Feeling like I need to do something, I recheck all our packed bags waiting by the door to make sure we're not missing anything from the list. We packed pretty light even though we'll be gone for months.

We have no way of knowing how long it will take Isaac to take the bait, and then there's my uncle and cleaning up the mess he's making of my name. After we deal with them both, the four of us plan to lie low in the Caribbean for a few weeks until we're sure it's safe to return.

It's a good plan, but somewhere in the back of my mind, there's a loose thread taunting me. One that I can't seem to grasp no matter how much I try. A blemish in an otherwise flawless plan.

At night, it makes me toss and turn, so now I sleep whenever I can, which is usually at random times during the day.

Oni will be arriving with the plane tomorrow, and the idea of boarding one again makes me nauseated. I groan miserably as I shuffle into the kitchen with my hand clutching my cramping stomach under Khalil's shirt. I grab the kettle to make tea and stare out of the window at the whiskey barrels and the strawberries I planted months ago, when I thought there was time. They aren't mature yet and would have gone dormant soon, but I'll never know now if I succeeded in growing the fruit, since I won't be here to care for them.

There's always next year.

If I live.

As I wait for the water to boil, I'm considering radioing the guys again to check on them when I jump, hearing a knock on the front door. Immediately, I'm on edge since the guys wouldn't knock and the sheriff is no doubt busy with the search. And then my blood goes cold when I wonder if he came to tell me something happened to Khalil, Thorin, or Seth.

Shoving away from the counter, I run to the door and snatch it open only to rear back when I see a lone robed figure standing on the porch. *Interesting choice for outerwear. Maybe he's a priest.* His head is bent like he's praying, so I can't see his face, but priest or no priest, I'm officially creeped the fuck out.

Remembering there are lost hikers out there, I ignore that

paranoid voice in my head whispering *danger* and reach for empathy.

"Can I help you?"

Finally, the visitor's head lifts at the sound of my voice, and I'm met with a scarred black mask and familiar green eyes. Before I can react to the strangeness of it all, movement across the clearing catches my eye, and I squint as I try to make out the dark shapes taking form. The hand of the stranger in front of me slowly raises toward his mask just as more robed and masked figures slowly drift from the trees like a plague. I count at least twenty carrying lit torches, and that whispering voice in my head starts screaming.

"On second thought, *nope*."

I only get a glimpse of the man's charred face before I slam the door shut and lock it without an introduction or an explanation. I run to the kitchen where I left the radio. The kettle is whistling now, but I don't stop to remove it from the stove or radio my guys. Instead, I make a mad dash out of the kitchen and down to the basement where the weapons are stored.

As I ransack the weapons locker, I try repeatedly to reach the guys to no avail. It doesn't take many guesses to figure out who the creep is, which means Seth, Zeke—*all* of them—are in danger.

Isaac is here in the Cold Peaks somehow, and if he and his cult want inside, there's not much that can stop them. This cabin wasn't built to be a panic room. It's not a fortress than can survive a siege. Khalil, Thorin, and Zeke's entire defense system rested in never being found, and now their walls are crumbling, and they don't even know it.

If Isaac had them, he wouldn't be coming after me, so I don't have to wonder if they're safe. And the only hope of them staying that way is to make damn sure Isaac doesn't get his hands on me.

He's already used the girl Zeke loved against him once. I'll die before I let Isaac do that to him again.

It's not until I smell the smoke and return upstairs armed with my bow and a handgun to investigate that I realize Isaac never had any intentions of coming inside. With burning lungs and stinging eyes, I run over to the windows in the kitchen and see flames licking around the porch railing and smoke curling from the shed.

A moment later, I hear a window shatter, and I run out of the kitchen to see the couch and Bruce on fire. Before I can grab the extinguisher and put them out, more windows shatter one after another. I scream and duck and scramble for cover from the flaming objects as fire erupts all around me until the message from Isaac is clear.

Come out or *burn*.

CHAPTER FORTY

SETH

"Y ou got the line ready?" Thorin asks as he peers inside a hole that's little more than a slit. It's exactly the kind of dumb antics tourists would risk their lives exploring for shits and giggles. "We need to get down there to look around."

We're in our fourth cave in a system that has at least twice that after searching the first three with no sign of the campers.

"I don't know about this. We should wait for the divers," Khalil suggests. "It looks tight as fuck. What if you get stuck?"

But Thorin is already shaking his head. "We can't wait. You heard the sheriff. Everyone's spread thin, and if they're trapped, they might have limited oxygen."

"Which means *you'll* have limited oxygen."

"I'm going, Khalil. We agreed to this. Let's just find them quickly and get the job done so we can get back. I won't go in far. Just enough to look around."

"Let me go," I offer before Khalil can argue further. "I'm leaner than both of you. I won't get stuck."

"You're also claustrophobic, so no," Khalil denies.

Ignoring him, I glance over at the deputy, who is standing outside the cave at the edge of the cliff, looking through some high-grade binoculars. That eerie feeling returns when he lowers the binoculars and turns his head toward me with a creepy smile I don't return.

"Can we at least ditch this dude? I told you I don't like him."

"You don't like anyone," Thorin absently retorts as he assists Khalil with hooking him to the line that we'll use to safely guide him back out.

"Yeah, but I *really* don't like him. He doesn't feel right."

Both of them pause, and their heads turn at once to frown at me. "What do you mean?" Khalil asks in a low tone so that Green doesn't overhear. "How off does he feel?"

"Like I need to go take a piss."

Khalil and Thorin stare at me and I feel the temperature inside the cave plummet a few degrees, and it has nothing to do with the snow falling outside. Thorin tilts his chin toward the mouth of the cave, telling me to go. I don't waste time and spin on my heel, passing the deputy who is now smoking as I go.

I make sure to walk far enough from the caves to become irresistible bait. And since I really do have to go, I don't have to make a show of pulling out my dick and relieving myself. Once I'm done, I do make a show of poking around the bushes as if I'm looking for the campers. I'm buying time, but it only takes two minutes before that eerie feeling of no longer being alone skips down my spine.

I keep walking though, as if I don't sense I'm being followed. I lead him farther away from the caves as I wait for him to make his move.

"You can stop pretending not to know I'm following you now," he finally calls out after five more minutes of our cat-and-mouse game.

Turning around, I don't bother feigning surprise as I give the deputy a dry look. "I thought you were enjoying the ambience. I didn't want to be rude."

"Hello, Ezekiel." The deputy's head tilts as he considers me. "Or is it Seth?"

"Does it matter?" I retort as I slowly back away, playing my part of the cornered prey. "What do you want?"

"I am Undying Daniel. A disciple of the Savior, and I want you to come with me."

"I'm not going anywhere with you. You can tell Zeke's brother that he can go fuck himself."

"Ah, so it is Seth then. I don't believe I've had the pleasure. Now, about that message. Are you sure you wouldn't like to tell the Savior yourself? No?" When I don't respond, Daniel frees the binoculars from around his neck and offers them to me. "I want you to take a look through these and reconsider."

"Why would I do that?"

"Because she'll die if you don't. What was her name again? Ah, that's right. *Aurelia.* The singer who's supposed to be dead but isn't."

Swearing, I can't snatch the binoculars out of his hold fast enough, and then I dance out of reach again as I lift them to my eyes. Automatically, I pan them toward our mountain in search of our cabin where Sunshine should be. I stop when I see fire. It's eating away at the trees and climbing down the hillside. But the wild fire isn't what sends my rage and terror colliding. It's the origin.

Sunshine…

Reluctantly, I lower the binoculars as if keeping my eyes on the destruction will stop it from spreading.

"What the hell does he want with her?" I force past the knot in my throat.

"The girl? Nothing. He only wants you, Seth. Surrender, and she'll be free."

"How did Isaac find me?"

Daniel's eyes harden at me using Zeke's brother's name. "The *Savior* has searched long and hard for his most precious sacrifice. No stone was left unturned."

"Bullshit! Someone tipped him off. Who?" As in, who do I have to kill after I rip out Daniel's intestines and wear them like a lei?

"I am not at liberty to discuss that information, but if you come with me, I can take you to the Savior."

"You're unable or unwilling to give me answers?" I echo for clarity as I glance behind him.

"I am forbidden."

"What you are," Thorin snarls, "is useless."

The twin shadows converging behind the deputy split apart and then take form on either side of him. Khalil shoves Green onto the ground until he's kneeling, and the deputy doesn't try to fight or beg for his life.

Why?

Because he believes Zeke's brother's lies. He truly believes he cannot die.

"Who the fuck are you?" Thorin demands as he moves to stand in front of the deputy. "You're not a real cop."

Deputy fucking Green smiles. "I am Undying Daniel. A disciple of the Savior. A child of the Seeds—"

"Good enough for me." Khalil sends a punch so vicious into the jaw of the deputy that I hear the bone shatter with a sickening crunch. The deputy's screams are enough to turn stomachs when Khalil lifts him up by his broken jaw until they're almost eye level. "You want to try telling us what the hell you want with him now? No?" *Squelch.* I don't see the knife in Khalil's hand until it's already lodged to the hilt in Daniel's lower stomach. Khalil's eyes are cold as he holds the deputy's gaze and slowly splits him open from gut to sternum. "Aight then."

Everything ugly inside the deputy tries to spill out of him like toothpaste in the tube when you squeeze it hard enough but change your mind at the last minute.

Wrong angle, I guess. That's disappointing. No necklace for me.

"For someone who's supposed to be undying, he sure looks dead as fuck to me." Khalil stands and spits on Daniel's twitching body and then lifts his gaze, which softens when it finds me. "You okay, Seth?"

"No," I answer as I steal the deputy's gun from his holster. "We need to go. Sunshine's in trouble."

"The fuck are you talking about?"

"Isaac has her." I don't bother handing them the binoculars so that they can see the fire since that would waste time. I just start running for the ATVs and feel them hot on my heels as I pray we get there in time.

CHAPTER FORTY-ONE

AURELIA

Y ou're going to have to do a lot better than that, asshole!"
Coughing immediately proceeds my shout with my voice
barely rising above the roar of the fire. It doesn't matter. Anyone else
would have run from the cabin when they had the chance, which
means Isaac is already learning how badly he'd overestimated my
will to live.

If living means giving up Zeke and Seth, and even Bane to that
monster, consider me one deader than dead bitch. He can't have
them. I won't let him.

After shoving on my boots and tying my wet shirt around my
nose and mouth, I crawl in sports bra and shorts underneath the
flames licking the walls and ceiling and head toward the basement
stairs. I tell myself not to look back at the destruction, but I don't
listen. My gaze, like my heart, is drawn to the dining table where we
shared all of our meals—some rife with tension but most of them
pleasant and filled with laughter.

The worn books that I never got to finish reading.

The loft and the first piece of this cabin that I claimed for
myself.

And then there's the view of the wilds that I never came to fully appreciate but hoped one day I would—in time.

Now there is no time left. It's all gone. Or will be soon.

The fire has nearly engulfed the cabin, and even though I can't see them anymore, I know that they're still out there.

So I crawl toward my doom rather than run for safety.

The fire hasn't reached the basement yet, but I only have minutes until it does, if I'm lucky. Strategically, it's the worst place to be in a fire, but it's also my only way out of the cabin undetected.

The front wall of the cabin is engulfed, so I'm forced to crawl down the stairs, ignoring the way the hard edges dig into my hands and knees, bruising them as I go. Finally, I reach the bottom where I stand and look around, but my relief at seeing the den unharmed is short-lived.

Wood groans and debris from the ceiling rains down on my head. Something explodes above me, and I hear more glass shatter before a plume of fire sets the top half of the stairs aflame, barring my only way back. I feel the heat rising even faster down here as the smoke quickly builds inside the enclosed space, burning my eyes and limiting visibility.

I quickly locate one of the battery-powered lamps and start for the cellar door when I stop after a few steps, my gaze catching on Khalil's open door and the bed of twisted branches. Flames have already made their way inside the room through the shattered window overlooking the cliff, and while my head screams *no*, the plea in my heart is relentless.

"Fuck." I divert from the cellar and dash into Khalil's room.

One of the four posters holding up the canopy is already on fire, and my heart breaks a little for the inevitable destruction of the beautiful bed, but it's not what drove me in here. It's not what I risk precious seconds to save. Falling to my knees, I shove my hand under the mattress and blindly feel for the reason. The fire is getting closer, and when I nervously glance over my shoulder, I can see it curling around the doorframe. Less than a foot from my face, I scream when a piece of the canopy falls onto the bed and the burned bark singes the comforter.

"Come on, come on…"

Finally, my fingers touch the smooth film of the photo, and I free the picture of Khalil's parents from under the mattress. Rising to my feet, I fold and tuck it into my shorts and then head for the door. As soon as I run out, the ceiling of the den collapses, and I feel the heat of the flames that burst through the hole it created. I watch with my heart in my throat as the fire spreads across the ceiling. More of it spills from upstairs, completely engulfing the basement stairs.

I run for the cellar door, my only avenue of escape now, and pause long enough to confirm that the handle is cool before I rip open the door and disappear into the dark.

The cellar door slams behind me, cutting off the stream of light and plunging me into total dark. Yanking Khalil's still-wet shirt from my face, I kneel and shove it against the seam under the door to keep the smoke out for as long as possible. I don't bother feeling for the light switch once I'm standing again since the power will be out. Instead, I activate the lamp in my hand before creeping cautiously down the stairs while keeping one hand on the rough surface of the wall. I'm halfway down when I freeze, hearing what sounds like the entire cabin collapsing on top of me.

Well and truly trapped now, I take a calming breath and force myself to keep going toward the trapdoor and my salvation, ignoring the way my heart thuds relentlessly against my chest. I never did learn where the door led. With a sense of cold dread, I realize too late that it could be nothing or it could be exactly what I need.

Too late for second thoughts.

The more I think about my mountain men though, the more confident I grow that I'm right, and my pace quickens. Khalil, Thorin, and Zeke are too smart and keyed into their survival to build their home on the edge of a cliff with no way out except the front door.

Trapped is exactly what they'd want their enemy to think.

The fringed edge of the thick burgundy rug comes into view, and I set the lantern aside as I kneel and toss the rug aside to reveal the door.

"Argghhhh!" I scream out in frustration when I see the secured padlock barring the hatch from opening. "Goddamn it, guys!" Standing, I let my temper get the best of me as I bring my booted foot down on the metal door over and over. "You goddamn paranoid overbearing fucks!"

Through the walls, I can hear more of the cabin collapsing around me and the roar of the fire getting closer as my sweat-slicked skin becomes unbearably warm. The air down here is already becoming thick with smoke, and I feel myself getting dizzy as the coughing returns.

Defeated, I lean against the wall and close my eyes, but my head doesn't get the message. It pushes me to keep fighting.

Think, think…

In the event the guys are separated or taken by surprise and have to get out quickly, they would have stashed the key somewhere close.

Somewhere…but where?

I've been down in the cellar plenty since it's where they store their produce and the meat inside a walk-in locker in a separate room. I've never come across a key.

Khalil, Thorin, and Zeke built this cabin themselves, brick by brick. Metaphorically speaking, of course, since only the cellar walls are made of brick. Only they know all of its secrets, but they aren't here. In one final goodbye, I lovingly scrape my fingers across the rough surface of the wall holding me up while it still can.

Except...

My eyes fly open. Brick doesn't burn.

Lurching forward, I spin around to study the wall, running my hands over every inch of the surface I can reach before moving on to the opposite side like a mad person.

But I'm not mad.

They *hid an escape inside the floor*, for fuck's sake. There's absolutely no reason to think they wouldn't hide the way *in* inside these walls if they wanted to keep the key close but undetected.

So I search and search and search with my heart thudding in my ears and the cloying smell of smoke filling my nostrils and singeing my lungs. In my peripheral, the door to the cellar is now a wall of flame as black smoke wafts toward me.

I've almost reached the last of the wall when I finally feel it.

A loosened brick that yields too easily at the tug of my fingers. I toss the brick away and hear it shatter as I stare inside the gap in the wall.

Resting inside is a small brass key.

"Yes!" Snatching it, I race back over to the hatch with the key clutched in my palm and waste no time inserting it into the lock. The shackle springs free, and I yank the lock off.

The door is heavy and creaks loudly as dust and dirt fall from the top and disappear inside the hole. I'm still fighting to get it open all the way when the cellar door behind me blows open.

"Fucking shit!" I scream when I see the door flying toward me followed by a wave of fire, wild, angry, and eager to consume me.

There's no time for me to second-guess dropping into the hole or how far the fall will be. Holding the hatch open with one arm, I throw myself inside the gap and pray that I know my mountain men as well as I think I do.

CHAPTER FORTY-TWO

SETH

Abandoning the ATVs in the foothills, the three of us race toward the cabin, ignoring the trees falling down all around us and adding to the hazard the wildfire already creates. I can feel the heat of the flames, but all it reminds me is that Aurelia might be feeling them too. We'd already glimpsed the cabin on fire once we were high enough. Had she gotten out in time?

We shouldn't have left her.

Our paranoia over keeping her safe might just be the reason we lose her forever.

A helicopter flies overhead, no doubt alerting the sheriff and emergency services of the fire destroying everything. I expected no less of Isaac than to burn down Zeke's refuge and any feeling of safety. Rabbits, squirrels, wolves, deer, and even a family of bears forced to leave their homes race by us in the opposite direction, toward the safety of Maia and Little Bear while the three of us head into the thick of the danger.

For her.

Isaac is up there waiting for us, waiting for us to fall into the trap he's set. But we were already too far away. There will be no time to plan, no time for caution, so we keep running at full speed up the fiery hill toward home, knowing that it might cost us our lives.

Finally, we're closing in on our clearing, so Khalil, Thorin, and I slow our run to a creep, keeping our footsteps silent. It's a few more feet before we see them. The robed figures scattered throughout the trees.

Jesus, there's a fucking lot of them.

A few of the disciples are gathered in the clearing watching the cabin burn, and I search among them for Isaac. It's not hard to spot him in the crowd of his disciples. The prick always had to be the center of attention. The crown jewel. He stands among them silent and unmoving.

Until someone screams.

The attention of everyone, including Isaac, turns toward the woodshed in time to see the body of one of the hooded disciples drop mysteriously to the ground.

"She's out of the cabin!" a voice shouts.

"Where is she?"

"Does someone have eyes on her?"

"There she is! Get her!"

The air is thick with more than smoke, and I feel like I can't breathe until I spot a small figure with golden curls darting away from the woodshed and into the trees on the other side of the clearing.

Aurelia.

She got out.

She must have found our secret tunnel and the key we hid in the walls.

Good girl. My relief is palpable, mingling with Thorin's and Khalil's as we watch our girl disappear from sight. It's all I can do not to rush after her when I see three or four disciples give chase.

But that would be foolish and counterproductive since there are about twenty more of them armed and standing in between us and Sunshine, not to mention the ones hiding in the trees with us.

"We need to get over there," Thorin barks under his breath. "Now."

"Come on. We'll go around," Khalil suggests.

We skirt the fire and hug the dark, killing as many disciples as we can without detection until one unknowingly puts himself in our path. We see his eyes widen with recognition through the mask, but then Thorin reaches out and snaps his neck before he has a chance to call out.

Hearing the body fall, another disciple nearby whirls around. "What was that?"

Khalil is already circling his position, getting behind him and closing in until he's able to wrap a thick arm around the disciple's neck and squeeze hard until the man slumps in his hold. Khalil lets his lifeless body fall to the ground.

When we left the cabin hours earlier, we only expected to make a quick run to the hardware store, so we went unarmed, something we *never* do. It figures the one time we let our guard down in ten years, this happens. I still have the deputy's gun, the only weapon between the three of us, but there aren't enough bullets for all of Isaac's men, so I won't use it until there's no other choice.

I only need one for Isaac.

We're still searching for Aurelia among the flames consuming the forest when we're suddenly surrounded by twelve hooded figures.

"Ezekiel," the sole masked disciple greets with his eyes locked on me. There's something about him that's familiar but before I can poke at the memory, a massive branch engulfed in flames breaks off from a bent tree behind him. The tree with its trunk aflame had been split in half from the fire and propped up by another tree with a burning crown. The branch falls to the ground with a *boom*, but the masked disciple doesn't flinch because he doesn't fear death. "The Savior is eager to meet again. Please. Come."

There's nothing we can do with their weapons trained on us, so we don't fight them as we're led out of the trees and into the clearing. Our home is little more than flames now, with only some of the structure remaining.

Gone.

The cabin is *fucking gone*.

"Savior, we have located the sacrifice," the masked disciple announces. "We've found Ezekiel."

Isaac turns and tilts his head, his gaze too discerning even behind the mask. "But that isn't Ezekiel at all, is it?" The disciples surrounding him immediately tense as they look to each other in confusion and worry that they've failed him.

"Savior?"

"This is Seth. I remember him well. There's a certain wildness to his eyes that can't be hidden. Zeke begged me to stop. Seth laughed through the pain."

"Yeah," I say with a sneer, "but you screamed. Like a bitch if I recall. How's your face, little bitch?"

Isaac reaches up and removes his mask. The charred skin around his lower jaw and cheekbone seems to split apart when he smiles. "Just fine, thank you. You've helped me more than you know. Because of your...*intransigence* I was able to show all of Death's children that he will not forsake his most devout if we believe."

Great. I blowtorched his face and made him a goddamn living martyr. And I'm sure that's when the masks became a part of the uniform. To protect Isaac's vanity at being a fugly piece of shit now.

"You mean if your sheep convince someone who loved and

trusted them to kill themselves so your followers can live forever. I'm just curious. What happens if one of you does die?"

"They'll rise again of course."

"And let me guess, if they don't, you just tell your sheep they must not have been a true believer. Kind of a convenient pile of horseshit, don't you think? Your retention rate of followers must be *through the floor*."

Isaac's smile wavers a little as he holds out a hand rather than answers my question. "Come with us, Seth. *Quietly*, and we'll let these nonbelievers flee unharmed. You were so close the last time I had you on my table. I'm sure it will all be over soon."

"Well, that would be a mistake," Thorin says. "Since he isn't going anywhere, we don't *flee*, and we have every intention of harming *you*."

Isaac turns toward one of the unmasked disciples and gives a short order. "Convince him."

Thorin immediately shifts into a fighting stance as the disciple moves to obey, but he isn't the only one. Two of them grab Khalil before he can react. They throw him to the ground and pin him there with knees on his back and feet on his arms while six others descend on Thorin and proceed to beat the shit out of him. Of course, Thorin fights back and even gets the best of a couple, so more of the unmasked disciples join until there are so many I can't see Thorin anymore.

I run forward to help, only managing to pull one of them out of a *dozen* off Thorin before I'm yanked back and shoved away. The disciples don't restrain me though, and that's a mistake. Instead, they create a wall between Thorin and me.

"Interfere again and that one will get the same treatment." He points to Khalil, who is struggling and screaming obscenities and threats into the dirt. "Your friend is strong, but he isn't one of us," Isaac taunts. "He isn't an Undying. He's another lost soul for Thanatos."

A disciple kicks Thorin in his jaw. The blow snaps his head to the side, and blood spews and hits the ground in a wet splatter. He doesn't move after that.

"Stop! Stop! Stooop!" Feeling helpless, I crumble to my knees as I'm forced to watch Zeke's friend—*my* friend—brutally beaten to death.

But Isaac doesn't call them off, and he doesn't lift a finger to end it. He watches me with that unwavering smile as Thorin is beaten long after his grunts of pain end and he falls quiet and then deathly still. Over the sound of my blood rushing, I think I hear Thorin's ribs shatter and Khalil crying for him to get up.

Thorin doesn't so much as twitch as he lies face down in the dirt.

"I said stop!" I don't remember pulling the gun hidden in my waistband or shooting one of them in the head. There are still too many, but I can't give a shit anymore. It's Thorin. The disciple drops, and the rest of them quickly move away from Thor with wary eyes trained on me.

"You didn't search him?" Isaac shouts.

I don't see who he directs his ire at because my gaze is pinned on Thorin, waiting for him to get back up.

He doesn't.

I don't even think he's breathing.

His face is mangled and blood coats his hair, and I'm pretty sure one of his arms looks broken.

Rage that tastes like ash and blood in the back of my throat rises up and I re-aim the gun. Something akin to fear flickers in Isaac's eyes once I have him staring down the barrel. It's gone in a flash when he remembers he's not supposed to fear death, and his calm mask of control slips back into place.

"I can see that you won't be moved so easily, Seth. That's unfortunate."

The masked disciple who captured us suddenly reaches for his mask and removes it. When his face and salt-and-pepper goatee come into view, I feel the edges of my vision turn black.

Not now, not now…

"Come with us," William Brantford urges. "Come with us and you can be with Tatum again. You can be with my daughter like you've always wanted."

My lip curls, and even though I'm not Zeke and never fell for the bitch, I feel his burning hatred for the girl who betrayed him curling in my gut like a disease. Need to cut it out. Once and for all. I'm going to kill this fucker. "Fuck Tatum," I spit out in her father's face.

He startles like he's shocked, and his weathered face turns red at the disrespect to his dead daughter's memory. If Brantford's one of the masked ones, then it means he's completed his sacrifice. Isaac would certainly want to separate the true believers from the sheep as another exercise of mental manipulation.

But who did Brantford sacrifice? His youngest daughter? His wife? Someone distantly related who he pretended to give a shit about long enough to use them like Isaac did me?

"Fuck," I grumble, knowing my mind's made up and there's no turning back now. I re-aim the gun and shoot Brantford between the eyes. His blood splatters Isaac's face, and a few of the disciples cry out in horror as the man's lifeless body falls to the ground.

"That," Isaac snarls as he removes a handkerchief from his robes and wipes his face, "was a mistake."

"Why? According to you, he can't die, right?"

Isaac doesn't answer my question. Instead, he points a finger toward Khalil and coldly orders, "Kill him too."

Too?

No…

My heart sinks as my gaze moves to Thorin lying lifeless on the ground.

One of the disciples presses a gun to the side of Khalil's head and time slows as his finger curls around the trigger.

No….no, no, no. I can't. Not again. I won't.

With tears running down my face, this time I press the gun underneath my chin. Isaac's eyes light up as he steps forward. "Yes, Seth. That's it. Do it. Your friend is dead. You can join him. Pull the trigger. Pull it and let Thanatos ferry you to the other side."

If I do, Khalil will live. Sunshine will live. I can make it all better if I go. It used to be Zeke. Now I'm the one who wants to die.

"SEEEEETH!" I stop breathing when I hear her furious roar rise above the trees and the flames claiming them. "DON'T YOU *FUCKING* DARE!"

Sunshine?

Something flies by my ear, and a strand of my hair rises from the wind it creates and then falls back in place at the same time I hear the *thunk* of a familiar yellow arrow finding its target. The throat of the disciple aiming a gun at Khalil. The other two holding him down quickly fall to more of the arrows, and then Khalil is free and bounding to his feet. I see him swipe a gun from the dead disciple, and then he's aiming, but he doesn't shoot.

We're still woefully outnumbered.

My eyes search for Aurelia in the dark as more bodies fall one by one all around us. Half of the disciples are dead before they even realize what's happening. I'm almost relieved that I can't see her, which means they can't either, but my relief is short-lived because suddenly there she is. I watch as she sprints into the clearing with her golden curls flying behind her and her bow aimed like a goddess of the hunt.

She looses an arrow and then another before I can blink and two more disciples fall. She's thinning the herd and giving us a chance, but will it be enough? Isaac brought with him a small army, and we still don't know if there are more hiding in the trees.

Aurelia moves closer with her bow still aimed at the remaining disciples until she's standing next to me and then Khalil backs up until the three of us are standing shoulder to shoulder in a straight line.

"Ah, yes," Isaac says with the false confidence of someone who thinks he's won. "There she is. The pièce de résistance."

"What the hell are you talking about?" she inquires coldly. I see her glance toward Thorin, so quick I might have imagined it if not for her flaring nostrils and her lips trembling before she lifts her chin and forces it all to fade away.

"Your uncle," Isaac supplies. "He's the one who sent me. Told me where to find my dear brother. The deal was I kill you after I'm done with him, so I guess you can say that this entire night is really for *you.*"

"Yeah?" Aurelia pulls back on the arrow. "Well, try it, Freddy. I dare you." Isaac's brows slam down at the reminder of his disfigurement, and I smirk. "Khalil?" she calls out softly without taking her eyes off the group in front of us.

Isaac is down to only six disciples out of the dozens he came with, but we're still outnumbered two to one, and we're also down one when Thorin is easily worth a dozen of them.

Don't look at him. Don't look at him.

"I'm here, Goldilocks."

"Can we do this?" she whispers.

Isaac raises a brow, enjoying her doubt. I growl in response, and his grin spreads. Khalil inhales sharply, and we have the answer we need.

It'll be close.

Aurelia is quick with her bow, but not quicker than their guns. She has one holstered to her thigh, but reaching for it is too risky.

"Seth."

"Sunshine," I answer.

"I need him. I need Bane."

I swallow past the knot in my throat. I tamp down the possessive part of me that wants to say no. I don't want to leave her. I want to be here to protect her.

But she doesn't need me.

She needs Bane.

"Do it," I say with tears in my eyes. "Call him."

"Chrysalis," she whispers without hesitation.

None of us are prepared for three of Isaac's disciples lunging for her at the same time. Their hands grab at her and yank her forward while Khalil dives at another before the disciple can shoot. I growl, rushing forward for Aurelia and the dead men who dared touch what's mine, but a step is as far as I get when the world suddenly tilts and shifts and I black the fuck out.

CHAPTER FORTY-THREE

BANE

The fog that usually comes with an awakening doesn't linger for long when I hear Mine scream. She's swearing too—as viciously and colorfully as Zeke's friends whenever I try and... regrettably fail to kill them.

If they're hurting her, I won't fail this time.

There's gunfire and the crackle of wood giving way to the flames all around us, but the sounds dull to a silent roar when I hear Mine scream, "Bane!"

I shake my head to clear the last of the fog only for my vision to bleed red when I see some dead fucks with their hands on Mine. Khalil is fighting to get to her, but dodging bullets delays him too much to make him useful. He's clutching a dead body in front of him as a shield while two other robed men fire rounds in a panic.

They don't notice me, and I don't hesitate to dismiss them all.

Khalil isn't my concern.

Only Mine.

Currently, she's being dragged away from the burning cabin while another robed man leads them, and I don't hesitate to give chase. The sound of the gunfire mutes my footsteps so I'm able to get the drop on them before they get too far.

The one in the rear twists at the last moment and his eyes flare behind the mask, but it's too late. I already have my hands around his neck and with a vicious twist and a sickening crack, he drops to the ground. I step over him to eliminate the other threats to Mine when I'm suddenly grabbed from behind. I don't falter and drop my weight, becoming a tree rooted to the ground while my prey grunts in his desperate attempts to lift me. I thrust the back of my skull into his nose and ignore the signals that tell me to feel pain as I roll out of his hold before he can recover.

Sweeping his foot out from under him, I pounce and grip his hair in my hands as I lift his head. His scream is cut off when I slam it down onto the ground but I don't stop even when the snow and charred ground is covered in his blood and occipital lobe. I can feel the flames from the cabin licking at my sweat-slicked skin, but I can't stop making more red.

Zeke's hands are covered in it.

My hands are covered in it.

We're all covered in it. All of us.

Khalil, Thorin, Zeke, Seth…and Mine. She's covered in it too, but she doesn't have to be. She's got me.

I rise slowly as I seek out my next prey. The two remaining disciples that have Aurelia are no longer rushing to escape. They're standing with her between them, their hands that I plan to remove from their bodies clutching her arms as the four of them watch me. My chest burns with fury as I move toward them. "Mine."

I don't hear the word leave my lips until the leader reaches up to remove his mask and I'm greeted with the scarred face of the Savior. I growl and the Zeke's brother smiles at the sound. "Interesting. Bane, was it?" My gaze narrows on the man responsible for causing Zeke so much pain. I'll kill him first. "You must be one of Zeke's, which means you must want to protect him. Something tells me you're the only one who can. I have no doubt that you can kill me, Bane. Because I'm not the real threat, am I?" The bloodlust thickens as the Savior's words feed the fervor. "There's another predator trying to take what's yours and you know who he is."

My gaze flicks toward the men doing their best to kill each other in my peripheral vision.

"Don't you dare listen to this whack job," Mine says with a furious growl. "Khalil is safe. Khalil is part of the group. He's Zeke's friend. He's your friend."

I frown at that as a hot bolt of confusion twists through me.

Friend? No. Competition…yes.

The Savior returns calmly, "You have to kill him now, Bane. You'll never get the chance again and they'll never let you near her." Something inside me reacts violently to those words. "All you have to do is pick up one of those rifles and pull the trigger. Kill him, Bane, and this pretty little thing is yours. All yours."

As if the Savior's promise was a release, I suddenly turn to find Khalil on the offense this time. Every part of me—the part that Zeke's afraid of—urges me to go in for the kill now that he's distracted. Mine wouldn't approve. She and Zeke would never forgive me, but I can't turn away from the bloodlust.

As I move away from Mine and closer to Khalil's unsuspecting back, my gaze snags on one of the rifles. I kneel to wrestle it free from the lifeless hand still clutching it. The gun feels foreign in my hands.

"That's it, Bane," the Savior praises. "Now aim and pull that lever in the middle."

I raise the gun.

"Bane." Mine gasps when she realizes my intent. "Bane, no!" And then she yells in a panic, "Chrysalis! Chrysalis, Chrysalis, Chrysalis!" But the trigger word fails to penetrate the bloodlust.

Not when it means I can keep her and Zeke safe.

"KHALIIIIL!" Mine screams again when she comes to the same conclusion. He finally has the throat of a disciple trapped inside the crook of his elbow, but he looks over in the direction of Aurelia's voice. "Ruuuuun!"

Khalil's gaze immediately searches for the threat and finds me holding the rifle pointed at him. My finger curls around the trigger at the same time he curses and drops the disciple. My shoulder smarts from the recoil as bullets spray from the muzzle in an uncontrolled spread.

Khalil makes a break for the trees.

I can't see much beyond the spark from the rifle, but I shoot until there's nothing left. I'm distantly aware of Aurelia fighting off the disciples' hold and breaking free. In my peripheral vision, I see her run down the secret path and the disciples giving chase.

CLICK. CLICK. CLICK.

I drop the rifle immediately when it ceases to fire and I turn away from the trees where Khalil disappeared to go after Mine instead, but I'm suddenly brought to my knees by invisible chains coiling around my wrists and ankles. Throwing my head back, I roar my fury into the night sky and then I am no more.

CHAPTER FORTY-FOUR

EZEKIEL

I'm yelling when I come to. My ravaged throat quakes with a hoarse gasp when I stop abruptly to look around. My vision is blurry, and there's ringing in my ears, but that's nothing new with a switch. What I don't expect is to find myself surrounded by flames. The first thing I notice is that the cabin is gone. It's nothing more than charred wood and ash as the last of the fire consumes what remains. The second thing I notice is that I'm alone.

My gaze moves around, and my stomach sinks at the dead bodies everywhere. All of them robed, all of them except—

"Thorin?" I stand from where I'm kneeling and rush over to him. He isn't moving, and it doesn't look like he's breathing either. "Thorin." I touch his shoulder gently and then move to try to check his pulse, but I pull my hand away immediately to study my now wet palm. It's caked in blood. "Shit, Thor." My bloody hand trembles. "You better not be fucking dead," I choke out.

Tears fall from my eyes, joining the ones already drying on my cheeks.

What the hell happened? Did I do this? Did Bane?

"Shit!" someone shouts, drawing my attention to the woods or what's left of it. "I found her! I found her! Someone get over here!"

A moment later, I hear a scream and a gunshot, and my blood chills when I recognize that scream.

Aurelia.

Finding one of our radios among the carnage, I call the sheriff and tell him to send a medevac before shoving the radio in my back pocket.

"I'll be back, Thor. Help is coming. Hang on for me, brother. *Please.*" Grabbing the first gun I see, I pause only long enough to check the clip before running off around the side of the cabin and down the only drivable path.

I'm barely fifty feet when I spot a body lying on the ground, another robed man wearing a mask with his neck twisted at an odd angle. I feel my own burn as I disregard him and keep pushing down the hill.

"Fuck! Hold her down!"

Looking over the side, I spot them below on the precipice where I've been waking up every other night for the last three months. With her.

Now Aurelia is the one who needs me, and she's alone with three others, all of them robed, but only one wearing a mask.

Two of them have her pinned down as she struggles to get free.

Where the *fuck* is Khalil?

I finally reach the first sharp turn and sprint down the path leading to the precipice. To the cliff that I share with Aurelia. I'll be damned if I let them hurt her on our spot or anywhere else.

The leader finally removes his mask to say something to her, and my steps slow as everything comes to a screeching halt inside my mind.

That face.

I know that face.

It's haunted my memories.

"ISAAC!" I roar when I spot my father's other son.

He turns, spotting me on the path, and smiles like he was expecting me all along. "Ah, Ezekiel. So it's finally you."

"Let. Her. *Go*."

"Now, why would I do that when I have you right where I want you?" He crooks a finger, and because Aurelia is there too, I go.

I step onto the cliff jutting out from the mountain face and walk right past my brother as if he doesn't exist. I feel his surprise and then I feel his fury, but none of that matters as I kneel to check on Aurelia.

She's lying parallel with the edge of the cliff now, her head facing away from the rest of us, and when I turn it with gentle fingers, I see blood pooling from her temple. There are bruises all over her body, and she looks like she's been through hell.

She's also unconscious.

It's a far cry from the last time I saw her less than twenty-four hours ago. She'd been soft and sweet, and high on endorphins.

Rising, I turn to face Isaac. "I'm going to kill you."

Isaac finally drops the false charming persona and lets his anger show. "Do not forget who your master is."

"She is," I say, pointing to the unconscious girl at my feet, and then I let my crooked smile free. "When I let her be. She's also the reason I'm no longer afraid of you, and you hurt her. That means you die."

"Take a good look, Ezekiel. What do you see?" Isaac pushes the hood off his head, and I'm startled to see that he's bald now. His hair is completely gone, which doesn't make any sense given how much he used to be obsessed with it—always claimed it was his best feature. His vanity would never so much as allow him to dye it, and he'd rage for hours if his barber cut an inch more than he liked. There's no way he'd ever shave it willingly. No way. And then I notice everything else I missed before—the sallow skin and lost weight.

Holy. *Fuck*.

He's sick.

No. Not just sick.

Isaac is dying.

I wonder what his followers thought of that. No doubt he found a way to twist the truth and blame me. And that's when I realize how much I do not care. From the looks of it, Isaac has been getting his due for a while now.

"When did you find out?" I ask curiously. Not that I give a shit.

"A month after you were kidnapped."

Ten years. He's been sick all of this time. "You mean rescued," I correct. "*From you*."

"Your life finally had meaning when you were with me, Ezekiel."

"What do you want from me, Isaac?"

"I want you to take that gun, and I want you to shoot yourself. I am meant to live forever. *You*"—he points a finger at me—"were never even meant to be *born*."

"Yes, I know. Our father cheated on your mother with mine, and she killed herself in front of you when she found out about me. That's all very sad, but I stopped giving a fuck the first time you strapped me to that table. You stopped being a victim when you broke apart families and manipulated *thousands* into suicide because you just couldn't accept that sometimes life isn't fair. You're a murderer, Isaac. A serial killer with an LLC. And I'm done with you."

Behind me, I hear Aurelia begin to stir just as I see a lone figure stagger from the woods while clutching his side.

"You will never be done with me," he snarls. "Not until you're delivered unto Thanatos and I am delivered from Death. It is your duty as one of my blood."

"You know," I say when I hear the rapid whir of helicopter blades as the medevac approaches. "I was going to beat the shit out of you and maybe torture you for some karmic retribution, but it looks like fate already has that covered. And as for family, I've got that covered too. Every second I spend on you is a second less I have with them, so enough chitchat. Goodbye, Isaac."

I lift my gun, and his disciples raise theirs.

"Do you really think this will end well for you, Ezekiel?"

"I don't know. You tell me."

Two shots ring out, each one from opposite directions, and the disciple to his left drops followed by the one on his right. Khalil emerges from the shadows, clutching a gun in his hand, and behind me, Aurelia groans as she rises into a sitting position while holding her own gun.

Isaac looks around, finally realizing he's alone.

There. That look. The fear of death finally enters his eyes. There are no more disciples, no more sheep to hide it from. There's also no cage to throw me in or a table to strap me to.

It's just him and me.

Khalil kicks Isaac in his back and sends him to his knees while I turn to help Aurelia up.

"You okay?" I ask her while leaning down to brush the tip of her nose with mine.

"I'll live," she answers. "You?"

I smile down at her. "I'll live."

Those two words carry a heavier meaning for me though, and I see the moment she realizes it too. "Good."

"Ayo, Zeke. I really liked your speech about not needing to torture him and all, but there's no reason why we can't kick the shit out of him for a little bit."

Aurelia raises her hand. "I'm down for some stomping the motherfucker out."

"No," I answer firmly. "There's no time for that. Thor needs us."

The reminder sobers the two of them as they nod and get into position. We aren't taking any chances of this bitch surviving.

"Ezekiel, please," Isaac begs when all three of us lift our guns to his head. "I'm your brother."

"You were never my brother," I say.

And then we fire. I'm numb as I watch the light leave Isaac's eyes and then his body slump to the ground. It's quiet except for the wildfire and the helicopter arriving. The three of us glance at each other, and I can see the silent question in their eyes as we consider Isaac's insane belief that he'd *rise again*.

"Just to be sure?" Aurelia asks.

Khalil blows out a breath and grunts. "Fuck it."

All at once we lift our guns once more and empty our clips into Isaac's lifeless body. I then grab him by his bloody robe and drag him toward the cliff's edge, painting a trail of blood as we go. Once there, I drop his body and lift my boot before kicking his ass over the side.

Just to be sure.

CHAPTER FORTY-FIVE

AURELIA

The steady hum and beep of the machines surrounding the hospital bed is the only confirmation that Thorin's alive, but the real question that plagues my heart is if he's still in there.

Coma, they'd uttered after he was finally brought out of surgery. Among other things like skull fractures, brain injury, broken ribs, a ruptured eardrum, and a shattered left arm. Thorin may never walk again. He may never talk. And his doctors won't know a thing about how bad it is until he wakes up. If he ever does.

Isaac didn't do this.

My uncle did.

He's the one who told Isaac where to find us. He knew what would happen. He'd banked on it.

I cannot allow him to get away with this.

I can't.

It's been three days since Isaac burned down the cabin and nearly killed Thor. Three days of sitting by Thorin's bedside, wishing he would open his eyes and call me songbird or wolf and being disappointed every time.

Right now, I'm alone in the room. Khalil and Zeke left a little under an hour ago to go for a run and quell their aggression, which rises to new heights each day that Thorin doesn't wake up. But there was no way for me to dull mine, which was quieter but no less furious. I refused to leave Thor's bedside for longer than a few minutes, so I sat and I thought of nothing but revenge.

Khalil and Zeke will be back soon, which means I don't have much time left to say goodbye.

Tucked inside the overnight bag next to my feet are the results from my own doctor's exam, but I can't bring myself to look at the damning sheet of paper for longer than a glance. Instead, I shift forward in my seat next to the bed and I take Thorin's hand in mine, wishing I could feel him squeeze it or link our fingers together like he always does.

"I love you," I whisper through my tears as I rest my cheek on his lap and rub the blanket covering him. "I love you so much. And when you come back to me, I pray that you can find what's left of me in your heart to not hate me. To forgive me for not being here when you wake up. I don't know what else to do since I can't forgive *him*. Not for hurting you. Never for hurting you. I can't."

Sobs rack my body because I know it's a pipe dream. I'm already imagining the look in his eyes when he wakes up and finds me gone. I can feel his hurt and confusion and the hate that will inevitably come since I promised, I swore I'd never leave.

And to them, I know it will look like I'm choosing vengeance over being here for them when all I can think about is how long before my uncle tries again. How much will he take from me this time until he's stopped? I'm constantly watching the doctors and nurses like a hawk, wondering which of them has been paid off, which of them will finish the job. We've never been more vulnerable than we are right now. My uncle is a calculating man. He knew there was a possibility Isaac wouldn't succeed. How long before he tries again? Not long. I know that. This paranoia festering inside of me is whispering that my men will never be safe as long as I'm here. Even if I fail, Uncle Mars will have no reason to come after Khalil, Thorin, and Zeke. All he wants is me—back under his thumb or dead. It makes no difference.

"I have to go back, Thor. I have to. And I'm sorry it has to be without you. Khalil and Zeth need you, and you need them. Take care of each other. Forget me if you can."

Sniffling, I grab my bag and rise from the chair I've barely left in three days, and I force myself to walk away before I lose my nerve. The beep of the machines keeping him alive follows me to the door, and then I look back one last time before I walk through it.

Five minutes.

It's all the time I have before they return, and this gets a lot more complicated. Not to mention *hard*. I won't deny that I'm a coward, but I also know that if Khalil and Zeke ask me to stay, I will. And then my uncle gets away with what he did to Thorin. Marston George's wrongs against me and everyone else fade into the background. Every day he's left unchecked, my uncle grows more powerful.

It has to be now.

The elevator comes and I ride it down. Thorin wasn't taken to the hospital in Hearth. His injuries had been too severe, so he was flown to the nearest city with a hospital equipped to deal with them.

In a weird twist of fate, it's also where the airport is.

Down in the lobby, I keep my gaze forward as I walk toward the automatic sliding doors and the chauffeured car already waiting at the curb. Standing next to it is sharply dressed woman in a tailored pantsuit and high heels with dark hair, brown skin, and a phone in her hand that she's typing furiously on.

Oni Sridhar, former A&R rep at Savant Records. The same label my uncle used to work for before he quit to manage me once my name meant something. Now Oni has her hands full co-managing the biggest band in the world, but just as she promised me all those years ago when she saw the vise grip my uncle had on my life, she came when I called.

"Oni," I greet once I walk through the doors. "Sorry to keep you waiting."

"Nonsense." She waves me off and then looks me over but doesn't remark on my bruises, dark circles, and tearstained cheeks. "Ready to go, my dear?"

"Yes, I——" My ears pick up the sound of rapid footsteps pounding the pavement, and when I follow it, I spot Khalil and Zeke running an easy pace side by side on the sidewalk leading up to the porte cochere.

Their faces are tense as they talk with one another, but they haven't noticed me yet.

Go! Go! Leave before they do.

But my feet are rooted to the ground, and I can't move. Oni is saying something to me that I can't hear. I'm stuck staring at my most volatile mountain man and my most loyal.

I can't move because my heart that bleeds for them won't let me.

Khalil notices me first. His brows inch down, and he slows to a stop when he sees me standing there. Zeke, realizing Khalil isn't running next to him anymore, stops too.

"What's up?" I hear him ask. When Khalil doesn't respond, Zeke frowns and follows the direction of his gaze until his own lands on me. "Princess? What are you doing out here?" And then he notices my bag, the car, and the chic exec, who doesn't look like she belongs within a thousand miles of here, and his chest expands with a deep inhale that he releases with a shake of his head. "No."

"It's like that, Goldilocks?" Khalil shouts with a sneer.

I turn my head.

Out of the three, Khalil is the least likely to understand me abandoning them when they need me most. And I don't blame him when I remember all he's sacrificed.

At my nod that I'm okay, Oni rounds the car with a curious but wary look thrown at Khalil and Zeke and then climbs inside the car.

"I'm sorry," I say once it's just the three of us.

"What did we do?" Zeke says as a wild look enters his eyes, and he reaches up to grip his sweat-slicked hair with both hands. "What did we do? What did we do?"

For a moment I could easily mistake him for Seth, but the alter hasn't been awake since the night of the fire. He won't wake, and I think I'm the reason why. Seth's heart just barely finished mending when I unwittingly broke it all over again by asking for Bane.

Maybe I'm not built to love.

It's a flaw that I can't blame my uncle for. No, this one has me written all over it.

"You didn't do anything, Zeke. It's what I have to do."

"We can do it together. Please. Don't go. Not now."

"Nah. Don't beg her," Khalil says with hard eyes filling with tears trained on me. "If the bitch wants to go, let her go."

Even though he's already looking like he's regretting those words, something shatters inside of me at hearing them.

"Goodbye." Head down, I step toward the car and Zeke explodes.

"You promised!" I hear him shout as I climb inside. I'm immediately taken aback by the lavish interior. "You said you wanted to bleed!" Khalil grabs Zeke when he tries to run after me, and I force myself to close the door. I don't look back, but I can see their reflections in the glass of the hospital windows. It's taking all of Khalil's might to hold Zeke back as he wrestles to get free. The car jolts forward, and I hear Zeke's heart-wrenching scream once more as I leave. "YOU PROMISED!"

Those two words clang around inside my mind, heart, and soul the entire drive to the airport, and they don't leave me as I climb the steps onto the private plane that ferries me back to reality.

ACT II

AURELIA GEORGE...ALIVE? THE MISSING AND PRESUMED DEAD QUEEN OF POP GETS FLAGGED AT IMMIGRATION

33 mins ago

By Hannah Leigh | America's Daily News

While attempting to enter the United States, celebrity singer Aurelia (27) was waylaid by an alarming lack of passport. Though no one can deny her identity—hello, she's *the* Aurelia George—it seems to have caused quite the kerfuffle at Canadian customs when the international superstar, who went missing earlier this year, arrived at a private airfield in Vancouver without a scratch. You might recall the devastating plane crash that claimed the lives of seven and critically injured one—her head of security, Tyler Westbrook. Though one cannot help but give thanks that the rising legend is alive and well, it does leave everyone scratching their heads and asking one very important question. Where exactly has she been all this time?

CHAPTER FORTY-SIX

AURELIA

The news that I'm alive breaks before the plane lands in Portland.

And yet, all I can think about when I step off the plane is how different the air smells. I don't know why it's the first thing I notice, but I try not to fixate on the differences as I'm quickly ushered into an SUV with tinted windows under the cover of several umbrellas.

It isn't raining. The umbrellas are to shield me from anyone with a powerful enough telephoto lens to capture me from outside the private airfield.

No one is supposed to know I'm alive yet, but that plan quickly went to shit hours ago once I found myself seated in front of a slack-jawed immigration officer who stared at me like he'd seen a ghost. Valid. When he stumbled to ask for my passport, I remembered that I no longer have one.

But Oni and her assistant were on it, having already filed the necessary paperwork and skipped past the red tape for a limited passport. By the time we landed in Portland an hour and a half later, I'm once again making headline news.

It's only a matter of time before someone lands a picture of me to confirm, which is the reason for the long line of twenty identical black vehicles as we leave the airport.

Even though I'm staying local, the car ride is a long one since the driver was given explicit instructions to loop around several times to shake any tails. It doesn't help that I have no idea where I'm going.

Oni hadn't been too forthcoming with the details, and I hadn't cared enough to ask, but by the time we finally arrive at wherever I'm going to be hiding out, I'm more than a little curious. Especially when I look out the window and get an eyeful of the towering spires reaching toward the moon, the elaborate tracery in the arched windows, and the decorative masonry draped with vines. The Gothic-style abode is more castle than house.

It's haunting and beautiful.

It's the small garden of purple lilacs losing their leaves to the fall in the middle of the circular driveway where my gaze lingers though.

I'm still frowning in confusion when the SUV rolls to a stop.

"Where are we?"

"Somewhere safe with people you can trust," Oni says ominously next to me in the back seat. The exec never even looks up from her phone. She's been working nonstop to scramble a team together for me to deal with the fallout of being alive.

Because apparently when you're famous even *living* is scandalous.

I start to tell her that I don't trust anyone that isn't them, my mountain men, when a shadow falls over the window and the words die unspoken. It doesn't matter. While nothing has changed for me, I know they will never trust me again. Never…let themselves love me again.

The back door is yanked open before I can tumble down that heartbreak hill.

"Relly!" Before I can get a glimpse of the culprit or even be properly startled, I'm pulled out of the SUV and lifted into a bear hug. The cologne is rich and smells expensive, and the burgundy silk shirt is smooth against my smashed cheek. "Holy shit. It's you. It's really you. You're alive. What the fuck?"

I finally get a glimpse of my host when I'm set on my feet and he pushes me to arm's length to get a good look at me. I gape at the blond man with black eyes and a magazine-cover smile. And I do mean his face and smile have literally been plastered on the front cover of several magazines around the globe. "Loren?"

The hands still holding my shoulders give a comforting squeeze in answer. "In the flesh, baby girl." He goes back to looking me over in that assessing yet platonic way of his. "You look like shit by the way."

"Thanks."

"You're welcome. Come on," he says while taking my hand. "Let's get you inside and settled in."

"Wait… I'm staying here?"

"Of course," he answers easily. "Where else are you going to find a better hideout? And with the single most interesting group of people on the planet."

I can think of one place, but that's gone now. It's over. I walked away knowing I could never go back, so I force the cabin that's no more, the Cold Peaks, and them from my mind as I follow Loren James, the bassist of Bound, around the SUV.

The ornate front doors of the mansion are thrown open, and the space is filled with three other bodies. I take in the grim smiles of Houston Morrow, Jericho Noble, and Braxton Fawn, and I want to weep.

Oni could have stashed me anywhere—some ridiculous villa or penthouse in the sky where I'd be alone with only the paid staff to keep me company, but instead, she was perceptive enough to bring me here. To make sure the first faces I see on my return home are friendly ones. And probably the only ones I'd see for a long while.

I send her a grateful smile that she once again waves away like she's just doing her job and it's no big deal. Maybe to those accustomed to basic human decency, but for me, it's a very big deal.

"Just so you know," Braxton says when her doe eyes land on my trembling smile. "If you cry, these guys will cry, and then I'll have to spend the rest of the night reinflating their manly egos."

I start crying, and the broad-shouldered man next to her with brown hair and green eyes that reminds me of a certain horde shifts uncomfortably like he wants to comfort me but doesn't know how. "Welcome home," Houston greets.

"We're so happy you're alive," Rich says as he shoves a set of drumsticks in his front pocket.

"For the record," Loren says. "I never doubted *for a second* that she was still alive."

Rich rolls his eyes. "You literally cried for a week when we all got the news, plastered her pictures all over your Insta, called her the second baddest bitch to ever live, and ranted at anyone online who talked shit about her."

"I was *grieving*," Loren defends through gritted teeth.

"We had to call in a PR crisis team after you told a fan he should walk off a cliff for calling her overrated," Houston reminds him.

Loren cringes at the reminder, and then his cheeks warm when he catches me gaping. I have a feeling I wasn't supposed to hear all of that. "Don't look so surprised, Relly. I told you the day we met that I'm a huge fan."

"But are you sure you want me staying here? If it gets out that I'm here I don't want to bring that kind of heat on you."

"Da!"

It's only then that I notice the infant in Braxton's arms, who is currently staring at me and trying to eat a fistful of her hair. He has the same red hair, though his is a more muted shade than his mother's fiery red.

"Oh my God. Is that…?"

All three of Braxton's husbands slash bandmates start beaming with pride. "Yup," Loren answers. "This is Coda, our son and prince of the castle. And he says it's okay, so get your ass inside."

Loren drops an arm around my shoulders and steers me into the house when the rest of them back away. The moment we're inside, I crane my neck to gape at the rib vault ceiling that looks like it belongs inside of a church.

"Oh, I almost forgot," Oni announces as she finally looks up from her phone to address the rest of us. She digs inside her green Hermès bag and pulls out a new iPhone still in the box. "I got you a phone. It's already activated, with my number and a few others saved to your contacts."

"Wow," I say as I stare at the device like it's foreign. I haven't held a cell phone in nearly a year, and I'm only now realizing how easily I acclimated to life without one when I used to consider it a lifeline. "Thanks."

"Don't mention it. I should warn you though. It's a real shit show out there, Aurelia, and it's only going to get worse. I'm sure you're curious, but I would caution against making any statements for now. Of course, you're a grown woman, so that's just my advice. I've already started setting up interviews for your new team. If there's anyone you trust enough and would like to retain from your old one, let me know. When you're ready, I'd like to talk logistics and start prepping you for your return. I should be back in a few days. And don't worry, Aurelia." She sheds the efficient exec role long enough to smile warmly and squeeze my arm. "You're in safe hands."

"The *best* hands," Loren garbles around the mouthful of the burger he's now clutching. When the hell did he leave?

"Dude," Rich says like he's disgusted. "Can you not talk with your mouth full?"

"That's not what you said last night." Loren winks.

Um...what? Rich and Lo? I glance at Braxton and then Houston for confirmation, but she's too busy clutching the baby's ears dramatically like he can understand, and Houston is pinching the bridge of his nose.

"And on that note." Oni chucks a deuce and turns on her heels to strut to the door.

She leaves, and the six of us travel away from the front door and down the long hall. I catch Rich and Loren flirting with their eyes, but all it does is make my own longing worse, so I look down to admire the distressed black and gray harlequin floor tile. It's still gleaming from a recent wax and partially covered by a narrow blue rug that looks worn but still plush.

There are even thick stone pillars creating an internal arcade with light from the windows streaming through the natural arches. The walls are all dark, and so is the decor, which fits my current mood and state of mind perfectly. Everything is in tones of black, silver, and dark blues.

When we reach the wide spiral staircase to the second floor, I smile at seeing that it's barred by a baby gate that looks out of place with the rest of the interior.

Houston unlatches the gate and I follow them upstairs, but at the landing, they all start to go their separate ways. Braxton and Rich disappear down the hall with the baby while Houston swears viciously as he struggles to re-latch the baby gate.

"Good. It's just us now. Let me show you to your room, and then I want to hear everything, because I will say it again, *what the fuck, Relly*? I'm glad you're alive, but like, *how* are you alive, you know?"

"Leave her alone, Lo," Houston orders in a tone that makes it clear he's the boss. "Don't make her relive that shit if she doesn't want to. That's not why she's here."

Loren pouts but doesn't argue or push once he gets me alone inside one of the rooms and out of earshot of Houston. I'm grateful for it. I'm not ready to tell my story, and I'm not sure that I'll ever be. I want to keep the cabin and my mountain men and my memories of them for myself just a little while longer.

"So this is you," he announces once we step inside a room with periwinkle and gold wallpaper. There are more arched windows and dark purple drapes and a chandelier to die for made of crystal and faux wax candles hanging from the room's black lacquer ceiling. The four-poster bed is made of black iron and reminds me of another beautiful bed that's no more. "It used to be Braxton's, but she never uses it anymore and the others are still being renovated."

"It's beautiful. Please tell her I said thank you."

"You can tell her yourself. She's putting the baby down for a nap, but she'll be in here soon to check on you. I'm sure you want some time alone, but she won't be able to resist. Brax is worried about you. We all are."

I sigh as I sink onto the foot of the bed. "I'm fine, Lo."

"Uh-huh." When I glower at him, he begins to fidget in agitation like he's torn between his chivalry and curiosity. "Look, Houston is right. I shouldn't push, and I won't, but if you need me—if you need *any* of us—know that we're here for you."

"The stories I have to tell would probably give you nightmares, Loren. I don't want to burst the happy bubble you have here."

"Try us," he says as he leans against one of the arched windows with a shrug. "I think you'll find our *bubble* is made of stronger stuff than you think."

I feel a flare of hope in my chest that I extinguish immediately before it can get out of hand. Bound might have survived the worst, but that doesn't mean we will. Not after what I've done.

I left them, and even though I believed them when they said I could walk away anytime, I left them when they needed me most.

It's…unforgivable.

"So, speaking of bubbles, did I read the room right?" I ask. "You and Rich? When did that happen?"

"It *happened* a long time ago," Loren answers with a smirk. "And then it happened again a few years ago after we met Brax, only this time, we didn't stop." He shrugs.

"Wow," I say, feeling jealous for a different reason now. I brought the possibility up with my guys once, but all three shut that ever happening down immediately. "Braxton is a lucky girl."

"We're the lucky ones."

On cue, there's a knock on the door and Loren saunters over to it like he's on a runway. When he opens it, Braxton is standing there with the baby. "What's up?"

"Coda. He won't go to sleep until you do the thing."

"What thing?" I blurt. I'm not even bothering to pretend I'm not eavesdropping.

"No, don't—" Loren says when Braxton's full lips part to answer.

"He pretends to be a dolphin, and Coda laughs so hard that it tuckers him out and he falls right asleep after."

"Aww! Does it come with sound effects?"

Braxton's eyes light up, and Loren groans. "It *absolutely* comes with sound effects."

Coda whines and holds his arms out for Loren. I feel my fingers flex toward my stomach, but I ball them into a tight fist. *No.*

"And on that note," Loren says, sounding like Oni. Loren takes Coda from his mom, and they both disappear down the hall while Braxton ducks inside the room to join me at the foot of the bed.

"You should know," Braxton says, breaking the silence first, "I'm trying really hard not to ask how you're doing. I'm sure you're tired of hearing it, but I may slip up a time or two. Is that cool?"

"I'll survive," I reply with a dramatic sigh, and she snorts.

"I missed you." Braxton nudges me with an elbow.

"Missed you too."

My friendship with Bound wasn't well-known to the world. In fact, it was no better than a dirty little secret to keep it hidden from my uncle who didn't like me involved with anyone he couldn't control or buy. There wasn't a whole lot I knew about the band outside of the profession, and we only communicated through infrequent texts, but I've felt a strong kinship with all of them from the moment we met backstage at an award show three years ago.

It wasn't a habit of Bound's to frequent them, but Braxton had won her first Grammy for Best New Artist and her guys had all but dragged her there for her chance to shine. I was the one who got to present the award to her, and I still remember being in awe of the way all three of them beamed at her with pride. She'd been glowing, and I had the strong feeling even then that Houston, Loren, and Jericho were secretly responsible.

"So… Whose is he?"

Braxton's smile is coy when she retorts, "Who?"

"Don't play dumb, girl. *Coda.* Who's his father?"

Brax tosses back her head and laughs. "I honestly couldn't tell you. We decided it was better that way."

I couldn't hide my surprise if I tried. "And you're okay with that? Truly?"

"Yes. Coda is as much Houston's son as he is Loren's as he is Rich's, regardless of what his biology says."

"And if, God forbid, there comes a time when it's necessary to know or Coda wants to know?"

"Then we'll cross that bridge when we get there," she answers easily. I consider if I could stand not knowing before deciding it's a moot point. There's no chance I wouldn't know exactly. "Oh, I almost forgot." Braxton reaches into her shorts to pull out a small case containing noise-canceling earbuds. "For you. In case you have trouble sleeping at night." When I look at her strangely, her cheeks warm, but all she offers in explanation is a grumbled, "Thin walls."

I take the earbuds at the same time there's a knock on the door. "Um...come in!" I call out when Braxton doesn't say a word, waiting for me to say it's okay.

The door opens, and Houston peeks his head inside before pushing in with the rest of his body. There's a large suitcase in his hand that he leaves by the door. "Oni said you might need this," he explains. "It's got clothes and toiletries in it."

She really thought of everything. It's only been a few days, but I'm already indebted up to my eyeballs to the woman.

"I guess I'll leave you to it," Braxton says as she stands and joins Houston, who holds up his arm for her by the door. I feel my nape grow warm when I watch them embrace. "Let us know if you need anything, okay?"

Suddenly, I feel Houston's piercing green stare and Braxton's warm brown focus on me, so I nod. "Will do."

As they leave together, I hear him whisper urgently to her, "Did you give her the headphones?"

Braxton tosses back her head in exasperation and groans. "Yes, Houston. I gave her the headphones."

The door closes behind them, and I'm alone.

Standing from the bed, I drift over to the window like a specter doomed to haunt this plane without a real existence. The curtains are parted to show me the full moon in stark contrast to how incredibly fucking empty I feel being here without my mountain men. I'm back in the States, back in my reality, but I feel far from home.

I don't allow myself to dwell on it, and instead, I turn to stare at the phone I left on the bed.

They're only a phone call away, but I don't feel brave enough to call yet, so I ignore the phone and walk over to the suitcase before ducking inside the en suite for a long, hot soak in the clawfoot tub.

When I emerge an hour later, I'm too nauseous and exhausted to eat, so I crawl into bed and fall asleep immediately only to be jarred awake sometime during the night by the carnal sounds coming from down the hall.

Cursing, I lunge for the earbuds left on my nightstand and shove them into my ears, and then I shove a pillow over my head for good measure.

Thin walls, indeed.

The next morning, I'm sitting cross-legged on the bed in the fluffy robe Braxton loaned me with my new phone in hand and the number to the hospital room in Canada keyed in.

All I have to do is press call.

But I've been sitting here for thirty minutes, and I haven't pressed call yet.

My hand is trembling, my heart is racing, and my skin is fire hot.

I'm a coward.

I'm a coward, I'm a coward, I'm a coward.

I've already tried calling the ICU's nurse's station for an update, but since I wasn't an authorized contact, they refused to give me the status of Thorin's condition.

What if he's already awake? What if he needs to hear it from me why I left? Don't I at least owe him that?

Exhaling a long breath, I press call and shut my eyes tightly as if it might shield me from the incoming pain.

The phone rings three times before it stops.

At first, I think it might go to voicemail, but then I hear a gruff and exhausted male voice say, "Hello?"

I don't speak.

I stare across the room as my vision becomes blurry and my body trembles so hard the bed begins to shake too.

After a few seconds, Khalil tries again, but this time he sounds annoyed. "*Hello?*"

My lips move, but no sounds come out. In the background, I hear another male voice murmuring a question that sounds like, "Who is it?"

Zeke.

He's still awake.

Khalil's voice suddenly sounds muffled, like he pulled his mouth away from the phone to answer. "I don't know. They're not saying shit."

I hear footsteps growing louder on the other line, and then I swear I hear Zeke utter, "Let me try."

There's shuffling from the phone changing hands, and then his voice is clear but not as close as Khalil's was previously.

Speaker.

They'd put the phone on speaker.

"Hello?" Zeke says. Like before, my only reply is silence, but it doesn't matter because everyone Thorin has is already in that room. Everyone except me. "Princess, you there?" My head falls as I squeeze my eyes closed. "Princess… I know it's you. It doesn't have to be this way. Just come back. Come back to us."

"I…can't." A moment later, I jump when I hear a loud thump on the other end of the line—like someone angrily putting their fist through a wall. Losing my nerve to say any more or ask about Thor, I drop the phone on the bed and quickly end the call.

I cry for an hour before I pick up the phone again and dial another number. It rings only one time before someone answers.

"Y-hello!" Sheriff Kelly answers cheerfully.

"Hi, sheriff."

"I know that voice," he says without an ounce of animosity. "That's the voice of someone who's caused quite a bit of trouble on my mountain this summer."

My smile is small but genuine as I retort, "We both know who those mountains really belong to, Sheriff."

He chuckles heartily. "That we do. That we do. What can I do for you, honey?"

"How's the investigation going?"

"As far as I'm concerned, it's an open-and-shut matter. Some out-of-towners came looking for trouble and got more than they bargained for. Case closed."

"Good," I whisper distractedly.

"But that's not why you really called," the sheriff guesses wisely.

A sob breaks free as I shake my head like he can see. "*No.* How is—" My voice breaks. "How is he?"

"He's fine. He's fine. Still asleep, but *strong*. You just remember that, darling, hear?"

I can't answer as I unleash all of my emotions on the poor unsuspecting sheriff. He doesn't complain or stammer uncomfortably.

He just waits for me to get my bearings. When I'm finally done crying, I ask with a sniffle, "Can you…can you let me know the moment he wakes up?"

A long silence follows, and then the sheriff sighs. "Aurelia… I don't enjoy telling you this, or being put in the middle, but I've been given explicit instructions not to give you any information about Thorin if you call. I'm sure I've already said too much."

My jaw drops with a gasp at the news that I've been shut out.

He wouldn't.

Would he?

"Why the hell not?" I snap.

"Well." I hear the creak of the sheriff's chair in the background as if he's sitting back in it. "He said if you really cared, you'd be here," the sheriff reluctantly relays. "Simple as that."

"Who?" I ask, even though I know the answer.

"Khalil."

Ending the call, I stare at the wall, feeling my fury and pain boiling me alive from the inside even as the happy, contented sounds of Braxton, her men, and their son float up the stairs from where they're all having breakfast together.

A moment later, I'm making a mad dash to the bathroom to empty my guts into the toilet. I brush my teeth once I'm sure there's nothing left, and then I crawl back into bed, and I don't get out again for the rest of the day. I call my mountain men again the next day and every day for a week, but I'm met with the same resistance and the same demands each time.

Come back to them or forget they ever existed.

Khalil most of all was adamant that I couldn't have it both ways. And at the end of that first week, they stopped answering the phone altogether.

CHAPTER FORTY-SEVEN

AURELIA

The thick velvet drapes are shut, plunging the gorgeous room into total darkness. It's for that reason that I have no idea what time it is, but I'm still in bed when the door creaks open. It's not unusual for Braxton or one of her guys to bring me food or try to coax me out of bed, but I hardly eat and their encouraging words always fall on deaf ears. Sometimes, it's Oni who struts over to my bedside, with the click of her thin heels, to speak to me sharply, but the tough love doesn't work either.

I don't react to their presence as I wait for whoever's turn it is today—Rich's, I think—to leave the food, say a few words, give up, and go.

It's been our routine for weeks now.

What I don't expect is for Bound to throw out the entire playbook and start from scratch.

I hear the curtains being drawn open and wordlessly turn away from the sun now streaming through the windows. It's not the first time they've tried that tactic. The next time I'm forced out of bed to shower and vomit, I'll just close them again.

I close my eyes, waiting for them to go already.

Instead, I feel the bed dip and then confusingly, footsteps

quickly retreating from the room until they fade. I assume it's a tray of food, which they usually leave on the nightstand, so I keep my eyes shut until the bed dips again and they fly open.

I feel the sheets shift and still at the realization that someone else is in the bed with me. Slowly, my gaze travels down the length of the bed as my heart pounds and I hold my breath. My eyes are the only part of me I allow to move as I search the now-lit room.

The door was left open, either in invitation or a firm command, something they hadn't tried before.

"Bah bah!"

And neither was this. My gaze finally lands on the one-year-old currently crawling up the bed toward me. He shrieks happily when he notices my attention and then sits back on his bottom once he reaches my thigh.

"Hey, buddy," I sit up and pull the baby into my lap. "What are you doing here, huh?"

"Ba-ba-ba-ba-ba-ba-ba."

"Sure, sure... I was just feeling sad. That's all. It's really not that weird." He pauses and looks up at me with his little lips open. "Okay, maybe it was a little weird."

"Oooooh-ah," Coda coos.

"Yes, I do think Khalil was being a jerk, but it's kind of my fault. I hurt him. You see, I left them behind for a reason, and even though they can't see it now, I still think it was the right thing to do. It was the only way to protect them. My uncle is an evil man, and he must be stopped."

"Vrrrrrrrrm!"

I nod at the car-like sound. "When you're right, you're right, little man. I got to get up."

Coda squeals and kicks his chunky legs excitedly.

Gathering the pillows, I quickly build a pillow fort around him before I grab my phone from the nightstand and turn it on. I ignore the messages that come in—mostly from Oni—and text her the name she asked me for the day she dropped me on Bound's doorstep before I climb from the bed and shuffle into the en suite. I leave the door open though, since I can see Coda on the bed from here, and then I get ready for the day.

I'm too nervous to leave the baby alone for too long so I forgo the shower for now and dress in a pair of tight jeans and a loose pullover, and then I pick up Coda from the bed and we head downstairs.

"See, I told you that would work," Loren boasts when we walk into the dining room. "No one can break someone out of a funk like a baby can, and our son happens to be the cutest, smartest fucking baby there ever was."

The long table is full of every breakfast food you can imagine, and I have a feeling it's all for me. I say good morning to everyone and seat Coda in his high chair on the other side of Rich. I even get a glimpse of the possessive hand Loren has on Rich's thigh as I walk around the table and take my seat next to Brax.

"Stop saying *fuck* around the baby," Rich scolds. "For fuck's sake, he'll be fucking talking soon."

"Not to mention your theory only works when you can give the baby back to the parents after," Houston dryly retorts.

Braxton, who is currently buttering a bagel with a *very* sharp knife, pauses to flick sharp eyes toward their lead singer. "Are you saying our kid doesn't cheer you up?" Braxton inquires softly.

It's fucking comical the way Houston's eyes flare as he drops his fork to gape at his wife.

Something tells me that out of the three, he frequents the doghouse the most. Sadly, I can't help but think how much he reminds me of Thor.

"Of course, he fucking cheers me up, Bambi. He's my *son*."

Rich and Loren snicker at their best friend in the hot seat, and Houston quickly redirects his ire on them. "And did you seriously throw our son in her room like a smoke grenade and run out?" he asks Rich.

"What? It fucking worked, didn't it? She's out." Jericho glances at me like he wants me to back him up. I stare at him over the rim of my glass and take a sip of my orange juice without saying a word. I'm enjoying seeing them give each other a hard time too much. It reminds me of happier times in the wilds. "Wow," he says, catching on with a chuckle. "Fuck you too, Relly."

Loren immediately points his knife at him. "No. Relly is mine. Get your own nickname."

"Please," I object while holding up a hand. "No more nicknames. I have quite the collection already."

Loren's knife drops from his hand and clatters onto his plate as they all sit forward at the first hint of finally learning something about what happened to me. Even Houston, who I can't imagine engaging in gossip at all. "Oh? Do tell. What are these nicknames and who gave them to you?"

At first, I hesitate, and then I remember these last weeks and how they never gave up on me. I'd say it's earned at least a little of my trust.

"Well… There's Sunshine," I utter, thinking of Seth. "Princess and Goldilocks." I get choked up when I think of Thorin. "Songbird. Wolf." Without thinking, I relinquish the most damning one of all. The one I never fully claimed until now, when it's too late. "Mine."

Under my lashes, I see the members of Bound glance at each other.

"And the who?" Braxton presses.

"That," I say with blurry eyes and a strained smile, "I'll save for another time."

She nods, and they all go back to eating. I force myself to get something down since I've been puking my guts up every day, sometimes twice a day, for weeks. Soon, they're all done eating, which means I'm done pretending I want to eat.

"Hey, superstar," Houston says to me after they're all gone from the table, and I contemplate what to do with the rest of my day. I'm out of bed. That's as far I've planned. "You're with me. Come on."

I stand and follow him downstairs like a mindless drone, but I perk up unexpectedly when I step inside their huge practice room slash recording studio. The red padding on the walls was no doubt soundproofing now that they had a baby in the house. There are guitars of every kind all over the place along with a drum set, keyboard, a few microphone stands, and a worn leather sofa pushed against a wall.

And there are awards and certifications too. A fuck-ton of them. I have more, but their number is quickly catching up to mine. The real difference is that I've never felt like I deserved mine. Not a single one. I could sing and dance better than the rest of them, it was true, but the part that's always been missing from it all is me.

Houston takes a seat at the table with the mixing board, so I join him. On the other side of the glass is a sound booth, and I think about how long it's been.

Suddenly, I'm itching to get inside one now, but there's just one problem.

There's no song in my heart that doesn't include them.

It's been weeks since my return, but Oni still wanted me to lie low while she finished putting all the necessary pieces in place. She's already released a written statement on my behalf requesting grace and time for healing and yada yada yada, and it seems to have cooled the rising flames for now, but I didn't have to check online to know that time was running out. I won't be able to hide for much longer—not from my uncle and not from the world.

"What am I doing in here?" I finally ask as he pulls over a fresh legal pad and plops a black pen on top of it before sliding it in front of me.

"You're going to take whatever it is you're feeling in here"—he points at my chest—"and put it on here. And then, you're going to release it all in there." He points at the sound booth.

"I don't know if I'm ready," I whisper while staring at the pad.

"We're never ready," he answers simply and businesslike.

I have a feeling he runs a tight ship, and I'm reminded once again of Thorin. Instead of pushing the mountain man from my mind as I've been doing for weeks anytime I'm conscious, I hold on to him like a lifeline, and I pick up the pen.

Houston and I work in silence for hours.

I jot down lyrics on the pad, and he critiques them with constructive red slashes and short and to the point notes that hurt my feelings and wind me up at the same time. Houston's brutal in his assessments, but I can appreciate that. Each time he pushes me to dig deeper, the song becomes stronger until it's hair-raising enough to reach the far ends of the world.

Maybe even the wilds of Northern Canada.

CHAPTER FORTY-EIGHT

THORIN

I don't know where I am, but I'm weightless. I'm floating untethered in an open space with endless dark, and I'm alone. Other times, I'm sprinting toward a light that, no matter how hard I push, winks out the moment I reach out for it, whispering that I'm not ready.

"Hey, Thor. I'm back," Khalil whispers. I hear the rustle of a bag, the scrape of a chair, and his tired sigh as he falls into it, but all of the sounds—like his voice—are a distant echo. "I finally found that shaving cream you like, and not a moment too soon. You're starting to look like you're auditioning for a role in *Sons of Anarchy*."

You sound like shit, brother. You should get some sleep. But like all the other times they talk to me and I answer, my lips don't form the words and I'm sprinting again.

Racing toward them.

Khalil and Zeke and…Aurelia. Where is she? It's been too long since I've heard her voice. Before it was a constant, always there to keep that floating feeling away, but lately nothing. Khalil and Zeke talk to me sometimes, but not as much as before. They barely even talk to each other now. I know Zeke's somewhere close. I can feel him close by, but he's quieter than I've ever known him to be, even after Isaac, but why?

Is it because of her?

Aurelia? Where are you, wolf? Why aren't you here? They need you. I need you.

I'm not sure how much time passes before I hear water running and then feel something warm and cool at the same time lathering my cheeks and jaw. I reach up to touch it, but my arm and hand don't move from wherever they're resting. Once my entire lower face is covered, I feel the familiar scrape of a razor shaving a stripe through my lathered skin.

"I know your brain needs time to heal, but I'm begging you, brother. Please wake up soon. I miss you. Zeke misses you. And the food in this hospital tastes like shit."

Hearing the devastation in Khalil's voice and fearing that this time I might push him beyond repair, I start sprinting again, running toward that light that will take me back to them, only this time… I don't give up.

CHAPTER FORTY-NINE

AURELIA

I'm in the studio for the fifth time this week recording a new track with Houston and Rich's help when Loren comes in and signals for me to come out. Since I'm almost done and I'm in love with the take, I finish the recording before I remove the headphones and leave the booth.

"What's up?" I ask once I'm standing in front of him.

Houston already has Braxton on his lap, and they're making out like I'm not even here. They're kissing like they're two seconds from fucking.

"You have a visitor. Oni's here too, but she's meeting with Braxton first as soon as Houston takes his tongue out of her mouth and remembers that we're working. You're up next, kiddo." Overhearing, Braxton ends the kiss and curses before rushing out of the room. Technically, Oni was Braxton's manager. Houston, Loren, and Jericho already had their own powerhouse in Xavier Gray when Brax joined Bound, so Oni and Xavier decided to shake hands and join forces, sharing custody of the band.

"Who is it?"

"I'm not allowed to say," he says with a sniff. "It would ruin the surprise."

Rolling my eyes, I follow Loren out of the studio with a frown and up the stairs until I'm on the ground floor, staring down at a familiar face that I never thought I'd see again. On the outside, he looks the same—deep dark skin and military stance complete with crew cut and disconnected goatee. But his eyes are different. My former bodyguard used to have expressive brown eyes filled with warmth. They're shuttered now.

"Tyler?" I gasp, seeing but not believing that my old bodyguard is really there. He looks good. Different, but good. He looks like he made it out in one piece even though I know that isn't true.

"It's really you," we both say at the same time.

"Aww, how cute," Loren says with a sarcastic smile.

Ignoring the bassist, who quickly makes himself scarce inside another of the many rooms, I take one step toward Tyler before I give up the pretense to rush forward and throw my arms around his neck. "You're alive," I say tearfully.

Even though I can see that he is, I still need Tyler to confirm it.

I feel his large hands fall on my back, one of them caressing my spine consolingly. "I'm alive. And so are you. I heard but I didn't believe it until now. When I saw the news, I thought it was a cruel joke, especially when no one had reported seeing you since."

"Bound took me in. I've been hiding out here."

"All this time?" he says, sounding slightly hopeful.

"No," I let him go and take a few steps away. "I've only been back for a couple of months."

Now he just looks horrified, imagining all the horrors I've endured. I almost tell him about them. About the cabin and the men who gave me a home, but I don't because I can't talk about any of it without spiraling.

Loren returns to the hallway where Tyler and I are still standing and I almost laugh when I see him awkwardly holding a platter of sugar cookies. Loren was a trust fund baby who decided to forsake his family's money and make it on his own, but he was still a silver-spoon kid at his core. He's also ridiculously pretty and groomed to the *gods*. I've even heard Braxton call him princess a few times.

"Come along, children. I have refreshments."

We follow him into the living room where he sets the cookies on the table. There is already water, tea, milk, and coffee waiting. He quickly leaves us alone when he hears Coda awakening from his nap with a cry.

"So are you okay?" Tyler inquires softly.

"Am I o Tyler… I should be asking you that. I am *so* sorry about your leg. About everything. If I could take it all back—"

"But you can't, Aurelia," he interrupts before covering my hand with his. "And I don't need you to. The crash wasn't your fault, and neither was the avalanche. You can't carry that with you forever, even though I know you'll try. Besides, it's just a leg, and this new one isn't so bad." He pats the prosthetic hidden under his jeans with a grim smile. "It could have been a lot worse if search and rescue hadn't found me when they did." Tyler swears and shakes his head as if warding off the memories. "I just wish they could have found you too."

They did, I say to myself. *In their cabin.* But unlike they were with Tyler, my mountain men weren't so eager to get rid of me.

"Has it been hard for you?" I ask. My stomach turns with dread as I wait for his answer, so I quickly grab one of the waters waiting on the table and take a healthy sip.

"It was at first," Tyler answers. "I'm still waking up most mornings in a cold sweat. And when I rip back the blanket, I have to relive the moment I first woke up in the hospital all over again."

"I'm sorry," I say again when nothing else comes to mind.

"Don't be." Tyler chuckles and then glances down at his hand, but my gaze is still stuck on his face and that wistful smile. "It helps that I'm not waking up alone anymore now."

"I'm sorry, what?"

"I'm...married now."

I choke on my water when he shows me the gold band on his finger that I hadn't noticed before. "Holy fuck! Really?" I snatch his hand to get a better look at it and then drop it like it's on fire. "Already? What the hell, Tyler? It's only been a year since the crash!"

He shrugs and chuckles again. "When you know, you know."

All I can do is gape. I'm both happy for Tyler and flabbergasted. "Who is she? How did you meet?"

"Her name is Shauna, and I met her in physical therapy."

I stare at him and notice he can't quite meet my gaze, so I try to hear everything he *isn't* saying. "Was she your therapist, Ty?"

When all he does is blush, I cackle while feeling my respect for him grow. Tyler pulls out his phone and shows me a picture of her and then another and another. Most of them are of her sleeping. Boy is *whipped*. "She's beautiful," I say when he finally tucks his phone away. "I'm impressed, Ty. Look at you bangin' the pretty doctor like a good little patient. You're always so straitlaced."

He makes a sound like he's insulted. "*We've* fooled around, Aurelia. I don't know why you're so shocked."

"Yes, well." I swallow nervously. "I think it's best if you never mention that again." When Ty's eyebrows jump and I see the question forming in his head, I quickly change the subject. "You should know that I only came back to confront my uncle. He's doing and has done awful things, and he's been using my name to do it. I have to stop him."

Tyler's body is strung tight as he sits up and swears. "How are you going to do that?"

"I don't know yet. I can't just return to my uncle's side like nothing ever happened. I need to figure how to get close to him without tipping him off to what I'm up to."

Tyler is pensive for a few moments before he speaks. "Your uncle always felt like you couldn't survive without him. You need to create a scenario in which you need him. You need to make him believe he has complete control again."

"How the fuck do I do that? He knows I can't stand him. He'll see right through me."

"Not if you give him a crisis he can believe. Make him think you've fallen back into your old ways and you're drowning without him there to fix it. People love to be proven right."

"You mean another scandal."

"You're rife with them, princess."

I bite back the urge to ask Tyler not to call me that, but instead, I'm stuck recalling how differently Zeke sounds when says it. He always whispers it like it's a secret between us, like I'm precious to him, and he doesn't want anyone else to have me.

"You make me sound like the Wicked Witch of the West."

"Have you been online? You might as well be. People think you faked your death to garner sympathy." I did fake my death, but the last thing I cared about was their fucking sympathy. "The scandal is already brewing and has been for weeks. You don't even have to start the fire. You just need to fan the flames."

I drum my fingers on my thigh as I give it some thought. "What about Allesi?"

"The *blogger*?" Tyler immediately exclaims. "No. *Hell* no. Allesi is a fucking psycho. I don't think we need to go that extreme."

"I've met psychopaths," I say, thinking of Isaac. "Allesi isn't one of them. He's a pest, but he can make waves. The bad kind we need. And he can make it believable since everyone knows he hates me. We need to get the job done quickly, and Allesi is nothing if not a sweeping plague." When Tyler still doesn't look convinced, I add, "We'll only create just enough of a scandal that it *feels* like the perfect storm but nothing that I can't bounce back from." But then I remember how it was the last time the whole world was against me, and I begin to lose some of my nerve. "Fuck."

"Fuck," a small voice echoes. Surprised, I twist to see a partially nude Coda ambling into the room, wearing only a diaper and clutching his father's drumstick. He loses his balance and then rises to take more unsteady steps toward the couch where we're sitting. "Fuck. Fuck. Fuck."

I clap a hand over my mouth while Tyler and I stare at each other with guilty eyes. Coda stumbles over to me and then uses my knee to stay upright, so I lean down and lift him onto my lap. I see Tyler frowning down at my stomach when my shirt pulls tight over it from the movement. I've always had a bit of a belly, but it's rounder and firmer than before. When his questioning eyes snap up to meet mine, I shake my head, silently telling him I don't want to talk about it.

I take the drumstick from Coda before he pokes his eye out, and a moment later, there are multiple footsteps rushing toward the room. Rich enters first. And then Braxton, Loren, and Houston taking up the rear.

Loren stops abruptly when he sees that Coda's fine, which causes Houston to collide into his back. Coda, seeing all of his parents together, rises onto his feet excitedly while I hold him steady. He's back to babbling again as if he'd never spoken.

"Did he just speak?" Rich asks with a mixture of excitement, confusion, and dread in his gray eyes at his son's first word and possibly missing it.

"Nope," I immediately lie with a shake of my head. "I don't think so."

The members of Bound all give a collective sigh. Braxton takes her son and the five of them leave the room until Tyler and I are alone again.

"Oni said you wanted me back as your bodyguard," Tyler says before exhaling shakily. "Are you sure that's what you want?" His voice cracks. "I'm still not at a hundred percent."

"Of course I'm sure. There's no one else this side of Canada that I trust to keep me safe. But only if you're willing. You don't owe me anything, Tyler." I take his hand, and he squeezes mine in return. "It's me who owes you everything."

"I'm here for you, Aurelia. For however long you need me."

"Are you sure you're ready for this?" Rich asks a week later. His brows are dipped with concern as he and the rest of his family stand together in the front door of their home facing me. "You don't have to go so soon."

But I do. I've already lost too much time. Now that I'm alive and the world knows it, according to Oni and her investigators, my uncle has been selling off my property and stocks without my consent, using the proceeds to fund his own businesses and portfolios, and slowly hiding as much of my wealth as he can before I have a chance to reclaim it.

He nearly killed Thor, and now he's *stealing* from me.

"She's ready," Braxton answers when she notices the look in my eyes.

"Then good luck," Houston offers.

"You know where to find us if you need us," Loren says with a salute.

"Thank you. For everything."

Tyler and my bags are already waiting for me in the car, ready to ferry me back to Los Angeles, so I turn to go.

"Relly!" Loren calls out before I can climb in. I turn my head to silently regard him. "You're still the second baddest to ever live," he says with that magazine-worthy smile.

"And let me guess, you're the first?" Climbing in, I slip my shades over my eyes and shut the door to the sound of Bound's raucous laughter.

EXCLUSIVE | AURELIA STUNS IN FIRST OFFICIAL SIGHTING

2 hours ago

By Allesi | The Tea Sip

And there we have it. It's no longer a rumor. After making us hold our breaths, the infamous Aurelia George has finally made her first public appearance. It's been months since the singer was rumored to have been returned to our loving, adoring arms, and while previous statements from her team have already confirmed her status, the lack of proof has left us all feeling jaded.

Theories that her return was just another publicity stunt from her uncle and manager, Marston George, have already begun to rise, but now we can lay them all to rest. The girl with the golden voice is back and chic as ever, dazzling us all in her custom couture.

If not for the tragic deaths, one might believe she never left. And while Aurelia's clearly alive, it does make one wonder if she was ever truly lost or sunning on a private beach. She certainly doesn't look the part of someone who's been through hell. Thoughts?

And right alongside her is the ever-faithful bodyguard Tyler Westbrook, who was critically injured in the plane crash. Apparently, despite his newlywed status, he's still loyal and dutiful enough to return the moment the gorgeous superstar snaps her fingers. Is that a scandal I smell? Already? It certainly would be true to form for the twenty-three-time Grammy winner.

I, for one, cannot wait to see what drama the entertainer has in store for us next.

CHAPTER FIFTY

THORIN

C an you please take it easy?" Khalil gripes as he helps me back into the hospital bed after my shower. He's always standing over me these days, clucking like a worried mother hen. I want to deck him, but I kind of love him, so I don't.

"You beg me for weeks to wake up and now you want me to take it easy?" I bark back. "What did you think would happen?" I've been in a sour mood ever since waking up from a coma, confused as fuck, barely able to speak, and with no memories of how I've sunk so low. It's no surprise that I'm impatient to get back some normalcy for myself.

And now...

Now I'm in a rehabilitation center trying to learn how to fucking walk again. Or whatever the hell the doctors said—*regaining the strength in my legs*. In three months, I've gone from bedridden to wheelchair-bound to short shuffling steps after getting frustrated and purposely snapping the cane they gave me in half.

Once I'm settled in the bed again, Khalil returns to the recliner in the corner while I glare at the red heart-shaped balloon one of the volunteers left in my room for Valentine's Day.

Fuck love.

Love isn't real. Love doesn't lie. Love doesn't *leave* you when you're fucking fighting for your life.

The door to my room opens, and a hooded figure walks in. I don't have to see his face though to know his mood is as bad as mine. The three of us have been scowling and snapping at each other for weeks with no sign of our moods improving.

"Where the hell have you been?" I grunt.

Zeke doesn't answer though, as he collapses on the couch pushed against the wall across from me. He's got a secondhand Android in his hand that he bought used off eBay. He stays on that damn thing searching for signs of *her*. Khalil's got a similar one that he rarely touches, except for keeping track of Zeke when he disappears during the day for hours.

Despite the cramped room and lack of bed, the idiots still refuse to get a room at the hotel next door when it means leaving me alone. Instead, they take turns sleeping on the too-small couch at night.

"She's back in Los Angeles," Zeke says, his voice hoarse from disuse. He hasn't spoken a word to us in days. "She's back with *him*."

"Who?" Khalil asks when he forgets to pretend not to care. "Her uncle?"

"The bodyguard."

Tyler fucking Westbrook. "So what?" I grunt despite the jealousy running through my veins. "We have to move on, Zeke. She left us. She made her choice."

"She left us, but that doesn't mean we have to let her go."

"Shy of kidnapping her, I think it does." Khalil stretches lazily and then pulls his phone from his pocket, and I narrow my gaze on the device when he starts to fiddle with it, likely looking up whatever news article that riled up Zeke.

"When the fuck did you get so soft?" Zeke snaps at him.

Khalil looks up from his phone to stare at him blankly. "Since *Aurelia*."

The two of them start to bicker, and since I can't run away, I pull my pillow from behind my head and try to smother myself with it. A moment later, the pillow is yanked from my grip, and Zeke scowls down at me from under his hood as he tosses it away.

It's the first time I notice how much the tables have turned.

I watch Zeke return to the couch and then pocket his phone inside his hoodie to glare out the window at the darkening sky.

"Shit, yes!" Khalil shouts before looking up from his phone with bright eyes. "I just got the email. Our passports have been approved. We can go home."

"Yippee."

Khalil's excitement doesn't deflate from my lack of it though. He's the only one who ever had any reason to go back. My home, my real home, burned down months ago.

I have no home.

Khalil stands and walks over to the bed before picking up the paper that I glanced at once and never again from the night-stand. It's a list of recommendations for physical therapists in the States to continue my outpatient treatment. Khalil places it on the swinging table overlapping the bed, and I look away to stare at the ceiling.

"The doctors said you're recovering well and should be out of here in a couple of weeks. You need to choose which therapist you're going to see once you're out."

"Pass," I say immediately.

Khalil's eyes become hard. "It's nonnegotiable, Thor. You still have a long road ahead of you. You need to take this seriously."

"I. Am."

"Are you? We have to go three rounds with you every day just to convince you to get up and do the therapy *here*."

"What do you want from me, Khalil?"

"I want you to try! I want you to stop acting like you died. I want you to start living again. And I want you to forget about her." He snatches the paper from the table and slams it against my chest. "She isn't. Coming. Back."

"Fine." Snatching the paper from him, I scan the list of reputable clinics that's over a dozen long and all scattered around the West Coast, and I grit my teeth in frustration as I mentally cross them all off.

Seattle. Portland. San Diego. Las Vegas. San Francisco.

Finally, my eyes arrive on the city I want, and I relax against the remaining pillows. "This one," I say, pointing at the clinic listed third from the bottom. "I want this one."

Khalil picks the paper up to read it and then looks at me over the top of it when he sees where it's located. I stare back at him, and he swears but doesn't argue as he yanks his phone from his pocket to make the arrangements.

Three out of four wishes ain't bad.

I'm released from rehab a couple of weeks later and with enough medication to start a pharmacy. I threw them all in the trash on my way out, much to Khalil's and Zeke's annoyance since I'm even bitchier when I'm in pain. Not even being back in the States after a decade away is enough to cheer me up.

I feel like a fish out of water, and I know Khalil and Zeke feel the same way.

It's...*loud* in Los Angeles, and the air isn't as fresh as the wilds. It's not a detail I ever noticed before we took Zeke and his horde and fled to Canada, but it sticks out in my mind now and tugs at my desire to return to our lonely cliff.

And the people...

There's too fucking many of them. They're always talking and rushing to one place or another, and snapping fucking photos as I try to see what the hell they see that's so picture-worthy.

Now the Cold Peaks...that's picturesque.

As for our current lodgings, Khalil managed to get in contact with his cousin Gary, who used to be his manager during his boxing days. Gary's girlfriend has a few rental properties around the city, and she agreed to put us up in one of her furnished condos for a few weeks while we figured out our next move.

It's where we are now as Khalil, Zeke, and I lounge around the living room staring at the TV, not talking and barely breathing as we focus on a live talk show.

In between pretending we aren't here for one thing, I keep my promise and go to the physical therapy sessions, which become less of an exercise in will the stronger I feel myself getting. Khalil helps a lot with that too when we do some light exercises together. It's good for him too since he hasn't been eating, and he's lost a lot of muscle tone keeping a constant vigilance over me.

I'm not going to be running any marathons anytime soon, but I can cross the room and stand long enough to shower on my own without getting winded.

The closer I get back to myself though, the more the dark circles under his eyes fade, so I push past the heartbreak and hopelessness because it feels like I'm healing him too. It's not easy to see on the surface unless you really know him, but Khalil took Aurelia's leaving the hardest. Most days, I barely recognize my best friend. He's quicker to anger and completely closed off when he's not focused on piecing me back together.

He thinks about her. Often. Always.

We all do.

But Khalil isn't ready to face his feelings, so we bide our time and fill our days cyberstalking our girl. Unfortunately, her sightings are few and become rarer as time passes. And whenever her public appearances are unavoidable—usually of her dashing from her penthouse apartment to a chauffeured car surrounded by security—she's always dressed in the most outlandish outfits. One day it's baggy denim and oversize sweaters, and the next it's flowy tunics and voluminous tulle.

Layers upon layers, as if she's trying to hide.

But there's no hiding for Aurelia, so it's an effort in futility.

I knew she was famous, but I didn't really get the full measure until these last few weeks after I left rehab.

"So, Aurelia," the host of the talk show says with a gleam in her eye, "Are you ever going to tell us what happened to you? Where you've been all this time?"

Aurelia is in another one of her ridiculous getups for the appearance, and she still looks fucking beautiful. I hate that. I cross my arms and pretend I'm not half hard after noticing that her tits have grown. Fuck's that about?

"Well, I would, Avery, but I've been advised by my agent that I should save it all for the book. I'm told it's going to be a real page-turner, and I wouldn't want to spoil anything."

The crowd laughs, and Avery Shaw chuckles, but I can see even through the screen that the hostess is searching for a way around Aurelia's well-rehearsed answers. "Well, how much have you written so far?"

"Oh, about a page. Yeah, I've been really giving it my all. The publisher is optimistic. I think my agent is already talking to directors about developing the screenplay."

Avery feigns surprise. "Just from the one page?"

"Well, it's a really good page, Avery."

The crowd laughs again, and the discussion moves on once Avery realizes she won't get Aurelia to crack. I feel the corner of my lips tugging with pride before I remember to shove it down.

She's not mine anymore.

When the show goes off and Aurelia is gone, Zeke changes the channel and Khalil turns his head to regard us with impassive eyes. "What do you guys want for dinner?"

I run cold fingers through my shorn hair—the length long gone—as I pretend to give a shit, since me not eating becomes a big fucking deal around here these days. I'm still getting used to my hair being short since it hasn't been in the ten years since I was discharged from the Marines, but it's not so bad. At least, it's not a fucking buzz cut. It's long enough to spike when it's tousled, brush my nape, and curl around my ears.

I make the mistake of wondering if Aurelia will like it before I banish the thought of her from my mind. Khalil still refuses to cut his hair, but it's braided now with the ends tucked inside the blue durag he's wearing.

"Chinese?" Zeke suggests.

Khalil pulls out his phone and begins to look for a spot. It's a few minutes before he looks up from his phone. "This one looks good, but it's a bit of a drive."

"Where is it?" Zeke asks absently as he scrolls on his phone.

"Beverly Hills."

Zeke's head pops up while all of my muscles become coiled like a snake. I'm feeling ravenous all of a sudden, but it's not for food.

Beverly Hills.

Where Aurelia lives.

Where she'll likely be heading right now.

"Well, I guess there's no time to waste," I say as we all stand and dash out the door. The three of us hop inside the rental with Zeke in the driver's seat, and the drive to Beverly Hills seems to be over in a flash despite the traffic. Once we reach our destination, Zeke parks on the street with the neon sign of the Chinese restaurant Khalil found online flickering next to us, but none of us get out of the truck as we wait for the arrival of the black SUV with dark tint. There are already a few paps and overzealous fans waiting outside as if they had a similar idea.

"Fuck, there's a lot of them," Zeke growls while he strangles the steering wheel. His rage at seeing all of those people waiting to ambush Aurelia and the lingering possession that demands we do something about it feel like a twin to my own.

But there's nothing we can do because the SUV carrying Aurelia, including the lead and tail, are already pulling up. We watch with gritted teeth as they all clamber to raise their cameras and get closer to the vehicle. Aurelia's security steps out first, led by Westbrook, and they work to push the crowd back to make room for Aurelia before she even steps out.

Once there's a clear path to the door, Westbrook returns to the SUV and opens the back for her. Aurelia takes his hand as she steps out, and then she waves and signs a few items, but doesn't stop to pose for a photo or revel in the attention.

She's there and gone in under sixty seconds, and I'm left with a craving that's ten times worse than before now that I've seen her. It's all I can do not to get out of the truck and force my way inside. To return the favor of when she ambushed our lives like a shiny wrecking ball.

Aurelia George ruined my fucking life, and if I had the chance to choose, I'd let her do it all over again.

"She looks good," Zeke says, breaking the silence that feels stifling inside the car.

"She's also a liar," Khalil reminds him.

Zeke has no rebuttal for that, and it sobers all of us, putting a damper on the desire and obsession that drove us to come running like fucking stalkers. Aurelia's right. We are creeps, but at least once upon a time, we were her creeps.

We sit for an hour more before we feel the tether leashing us to her slacken enough that we're able to drive away, but it's not long before it's pulling taut again and we find ourselves back on that street night after night.

We return for Chinese food many times. In fact, we can't seem to get enough of the addicting cuisine.

CHAPTER FIFTY-ONE

AURELIA

A week after my interview with Avery Shaw, I'm being ushered through a familiar heavy set of marble doors on one of the high floors of a downtown office building. It's the end of the day, and I know the suited man sitting behind a gargantuan glass desk is moments away from leaving to visit the condo of whichever one of his kept women was his favorite this week.

He barely looks up or acknowledges my presence as I enter the spacious office.

My heels sink into the plush carpet as I cross the room and reluctantly take a seat in one of the stylish chairs that I know will be a killer on my back by the time this unpleasant meeting is over.

"I have to admit," Uncle Mars drones as he signs his signature on the top sheet of a stack of papers before slamming the folder shut, "I'm surprised you requested this meeting, but it's good to see you, Aurelia."

"Oh, I wish I could say the same, Uncle, but that's nice to hear." While I'm way past feeling simple resentment for the man, I know showing how deeply I want my uncle dead will only make the dream that much harder to obtain. I also know that playing the part of an adoring niece will be just as damaging to my cause, so I settle right in between burning hatred and familial love.

"If that is the case, then why are you here?"

"Because I need your help. Things aren't going the way I thought they would. They're worse than ever, and this new team…" I purposely let my voice trail off to assess just how much he knows. Oni being my manager was not widely known yet but easily confirmed for anyone who dug hard enough.

"Oh, you mean *Oni*, right?" My uncle smiles like he just slammed down the Draw Four card in an Uno match. "Yeah, she's aight, but she's no me." I resist the urge to roll my eyes as Uncle Mars sits back in his high-backed wing chair. "So what is it you want, Aurelia?" he cuts to the point when I don't take the opportunity to inflate his ego.

It's obvious deception and a trap. I can't appear too friendly or he'll see right through it.

"I want to put the past behind us. I want to be a team again."

"And what makes you think I want that? I wasn't kidding when I said I could make a hundred of you, Aurelia."

"Then why haven't you? You've been trying for months, and yet you haven't scratched the surface with any of them."

"Okay, Aurelia. You've convinced me." I'm careful to hide my surprise and suspicion over how easy it was as he continues speaking. "I'll be your manager again and save your ungrateful behind, but under one condition." He holds up a finger.

"What's your condition?"

"That." Uncle Mars's gaze drops to my belly, and the disdain there has me wanting to cradle it, but I know I can't, so I sit frozen in the chair even though I want to run for the door. "I know you're pregnant, Aurelia. You've done an okay job trying to hide it, but not well enough. It's obvious to anyone with eyes that you're knocked up."

"I don't know what you're talking about."

"For how long?" he tosses back.

I'm startled by the question. "What?"

"How much longer can you pretend not to know what I'm talking about? Another week? A month? You're well into your second trimester. It will be impossible for you to hide it soon. You're barely concealing it now. It's a good thing you were already on the heavier side or else everyone would know as soon as they looked at you."

Suddenly, I am picturing my uncle with his head tipped back, an arrow in his eye, and the wall behind him splattered with his blood.

"Okay, even if I was pregnant—*which I'm not*—what does being my manager again have to do with my baby?"

"I want you to get rid of it," he demands with a curl of his lip.

I flinch as if he just slapped me. "Excuse me?"

"I need you focused on the music, and that baby will be nothing but a distraction. It's obviously too late for an abortion, but adoption is still an option. Privately and anonymously, of course."

I feel sick.

I feel violent.

I feel like taking that letter opener and slicing my uncle's throat open. He wants me to give up my baby, and even though I could be as duplicitous as him and agree, since he won't live long enough to even see my baby born, my heart won't let me reject the little one for even a moment.

"You know I can't do that, Uncle Mars."

I'm pretty sure he was banking on it, which explains his easy capitulation. And while it's no secret he's been underestimating me, I realize that I've been overestimating my worth to him. Uncle Mars probably feels he's already squeezed every penny out of me that he can. I can give an Oscar-worthy performance in contrition and obedience, and he still won't buy that it will be like before. Uncle Mars knows that I won't be as easy to control now.

"Then I guess there ain't shit for us to discuss." He turns to his computer in dismissal and begins typing.

I sit there for a few moments in stunned silence. And then I eye the letter opener on his desk.

I could do it. I could kill him right now. It would be so easy, even with this bump of mine.

I could stab him in the heart and make it quick, or I could slice his neck open and enjoy watching his blood spill all over the glass desk and his fancy suit.

I can't believe this is the man my father once called *twin*.

Yes, my dad was older, but only by a few minutes. And the worst part of all is that the two were identical. I used to think I was lucky because it meant I would never have to forget my father's image. But then my uncle showed his true colors, and over time, I came to hate the face of my father, which only dug the knife of losing him that much deeper. Just another thing my uncle has taken from me.

"Actually, there's just one more thing," I say, ignoring his dismissal. "I want to know why you won't pay the families who lost someone in the crash."

"Because it was an act of God and out of our control, which means we aren't liable. Those people are grieving and understandably looking for someone to blame, but we don't control the weather."

"Does it really matter who's to blame, Uncle Mars? You weren't there. Harrison, Susan, and everyone else on that plane spent their last moments screaming and fearing for their lives. And Cassie... She got it worse than anyone because she didn't get to die quickly. She was *torn apart*—"

"Enough, Aurelia." Uncle Mars holds up his hand. "I'm sorry for what happened to Cassie, but she signed a contract—"

I pound my fist on the desk, sending a few of his knickknacks toppling. "Who the fuck cares about a contract! I'm sure if they knew it was even remotely possible they'd die, much less like *that*, they would have reconsidered that predatory permission slip to screw them over! It's *my* money, and I'm ordering you to pay them *whatever the fuck they want*."

My uncle stares at me as if despite all the scandals, he's never been truly disappointed in me until now. "I knew you were naive, and I have no one to blame but myself for keeping you so sheltered, but I guess I'd hoped you'd learned something while you were out there playing house with those cavemen." He makes a sound of disgust. "This world—the *real* world—is going to eat you alive. It's a shame we aren't a team anymore so I can protect you from it."

"And you still can't see that it was you I needed protection from all along."

"I'm sorry you feel that way," he retorts, not sounding sorry at all.

"If the money helps their families move on, they should have that. End of story. Settle the lawsuit and pay the money." My uncle glares at me, but it doesn't have the same effect that it used to. "And by the way, I know what you've been doing," I say as I rise unsteadily from the uncomfortable chair. My back is screaming, but I ignore it to keep my posture straight as I stare down my nose at my uncle. "I know that you think you can take what's mine. You couldn't wait for the presumption of death to inherit everything as my next of kin, and you couldn't kill me to prove that I was dead, so now you've resorted to embezzling to get what you want."

"Aurelia, you're hormonal and not thinking straight," he replies in a monotone. "I've been the safe keeper of everything you own since we began this *partnership*." I chuckle dryly at that. Partnership my ass. He sounds like he's reciting the lies he rehearsed in the event he were ever questioned about it. "And I've always had your best interests at heart. It's true I've been making some risky investments lately, and they haven't all panned out, but it's business." And then he shrugs as if that's all the explanation needed for the sudden disappearance of more than a quarter of my billion-dollar net worth.

"It's also *fraud*."

His eyes are cold when he looks up from the stack of papers he's reviewing. "Can you prove it?" I don't respond, and the arrogance in his demeanor quickly returns. Let him think I'm too dumb or weak to get the best of him. "I didn't think so. Now please." He gestures toward the doors. "Get the fuck out of my office. This meeting is over."

My phone rings the moment I step off the elevator and onto the first floor of the office building, so I stop to answer once I see that it's Tyler. He's on a much-needed vacation this week after I caught him limping from the strain of following me around and made him take one.

"How did it go?" he asks as soon as I answer.

"About as expected. Not great. My uncle agreed to be my manager again, but only if I give up my baby. He says it's a distraction." I roll my eyes.

Tyler falls quiet for a moment and then he asks, "And what did you tell him?"

"Well, I said no, obviously." The line falls quiet again. "Don't tell me you think I should?"

"I'm not really sure what to think since I still don't know how you got pregnant in the first place. I mean what the fuck, Aurelia?

Everyone, including me, thought you were dead, and then you pop up out of the blue, alive, intact, and pregnant as fuck. We've all been trying to give you time, but you got to start giving us some answers."

"I really don't think I do."

"And you still don't realize that's what scares us all the most. The fact that you're so close-lipped about what happened to you. I'm trying to fill in the blanks, and I got to be honest... I'm coming up with some really dark shit here, Aurelia."

I stop walking abruptly, and one of the men from my security team curses as he narrowly misses bowling me over. Before Tyler left, he put the fear of God in his men to stay on my ass at all times. It's...really sweet and only kind of annoying. "Like what, Ty?"

"Like someone took you," he growls into the phone.

"Okay," I say as I walk over to the windows by the lobby's lounge area. Once I'm staring out onto the busy street, I make the decision to try him. I know I can trust Tyler to keep my secrets, but I don't know if I can trust him to handle the truth. While his head might have gone to dark places, that doesn't mean his mind is ready to accept them. "Let's say someone did take me," I whisper since I'm not alone. "Would that change anything?"

"What the fuck, Aurelia?" I picture Tyler squeezing his eyes closed and rubbing his brow bone. "Are you serious?"

I chew on my lip. "Maybe."

"Who was it? Who took you?"

"It doesn't matter." I sigh as I scan the crowd of people walking to and from. "I left them, and now I'm here, and I'd like to—"

"Wait a minute," he interrupts. And he shouts, "*Them*?"

"Oh, shit," I swear under my breath. I didn't actually mean to reveal that much.

"What the hell do you mean *them*? As in more than one?"

"Ty... Untwist your panties. I told you it's not important."

"Goddamn it, Aurelia."

I lean forward and rest my forehead against the cool glass. "I know."

"I don't like this," Ty grumbles, and I roll my eyes.

"Hence why I didn't tell you."

"But what did you mean by you left?" he prods in a whisper like he's afraid of someone overhearing. "You didn't escape? They just let you leave?"

"Pretty much, yeah."

The line goes quiet again and then, "What are you telling me, Aurelia?"

I haven't even begun to reach the tip of the iceberg, so I straighten and whisper, "Everything."

Tyler asks yet another question, but I don't hear a word of it as my gaze catches on a figure with broad shoulders encased in a white T-shirt and towering at least a head above everyone else moving through the crowd.

My stomach clenches when a feeling of recognition washes over me, and I immediately press myself against the glass to get a better look. It's not unusual for me to see my mountain men everywhere I look, but after a week of feeling insane and like I'm hallucinating, I've learned to ignore it.

But I can't brush it off this time because while the accelerated heart-beat every time I think I see them is like an old friend, the tingling sensation down my spine that tells me they're near is very much new.

But it can't be him.

Because Thorin is trapped in a coma in a hospital in Canada with long tresses that I miss seeing cascade over his powerful shoulders and frame his face whenever he fucked me senseless.

This man's hair is much too short, barely more than two or three inches long, showing off the strong column of his neck. He also doesn't have Thorin's panther-like gait, walking with less control and a slight limp as if the simple act is sapping too much of his energy.

Despite the rationale, my gaze doesn't leave him until he turns the corner and disappears from view.

Gotta get it together, bitch.

I force myself to walk away from the window, but once I'm outside, I stop short when I see a disheveled White man in his early thirties with an overgrown beard and haunted, bloodshot eyes lurking in the darkened alley next to the building. No one else seems to notice him, immediately dismissing him as another of Los Angeles's seventy-five thousand homeless, but no one else seems to be the center of his focus either.

He watches the comings and goings of the building closely, and a cold feeling sinks into my bones when he straightens at the sight of me, but somehow, I don't think he's a fan.

No, that's deep-seated hatred pinning my feet in place.

I'm so stunned by the look in his eyes, searching frantically for the word to define it, that I don't notice the gun until it's too late.

The sun glints off the metal, drawing my eye, and then there's no time for me to react before I see the spark flash from the muzzle and hear the gunshot followed by a glass window shattering behind me. There's screaming and shouting, but I all I can think to do is throw my arms over my head and spin away to protect my baby from the flying glass. The second shot comes too quickly before I can run for cover, and it hits the ground by my feet. A moment later, I'm thrown to the ground and a body covers mine protectively. The shooting eventually stops, but I'm stuck inside my head as chaos erupts around me.

Grief.

That's how I would define the pain in the man's eyes.

SHOTS FIRED—GRIEVING MAN SEEKS REVENGE AGAINST AURELIA GEORGE OVER DEAD FIANCÉE

6 mins ago

By Rachel W. | Pipeline

While Aurelia certainly could, it looks like not everyone has been able to move on since her private plane went down deep in the Canadian mountains this past winter. Sources report that earlier today, a lone gunman, who has been identified as Logan Abbott—fiancé of Cassie Holloway, Aurelia's former and *deceased* assistant—opened fire on the singer.

According to speculation, Abbott was allegedly waiting for Marston George, Aurelia's uncle and former manager, to leave his office for the day when he encountered the music mogul's niece instead. We have no news on the condition of Aurelia, but our prayers are once again extended to her.

Is it just bad luck, or does trouble seem to follow the singer wherever she goes?

CHAPTER FIFTY-TWO

THORIN

"Thor." I'm in bed, lying on my stomach and in a deep sleep. I'm dreaming about being back at the cabin and in the wilds with Aurelia when I feel someone shaking me awake so hard my goddamn teeth gnash together. "Thor! Wake up. Wake the fuck up!"

"Khal, I swear to God," I warn inside my pillow. "I'm going to break that fucking hand if you don't get it off of me and get out."

Ever since the coma and the TBI, nothing comes easy to me these days—first and foremost sleep—so I'm as grouchy as a bear in hibernation when disturbed. I rarely feel like myself when I'm awake, and the only relief I get is when I'm asleep, so I'm less than one second from tackling Khalil to the ground when he says, "Someone tried to get at Aurelia. We need to go."

I lunge from the bed and I'm on my feet before he can finish speaking. "What the fuck are you talking about?" I've got his shirt in my fists, and I'm slamming him against the wall before I can remember that he's not my enemy. "Who touched her?"

Khalil shoves me off of him and then grabs my discarded clothes from the floor before shoving them into my chest. "I'll tell you in the car. Let's go."

I get dressed in record time while Khalil paces angry steps across the floor. I then follow him out of the room and the condo. Zeke is already waiting in the driver's seat of the rental, and I barely get the door closed before he's speeding away.

It's the wee hours of the morning as we race all the way to the apartment building that's become our regular haunt. It doesn't matter that we already know there's no way to slip inside undetected. There's a doorman. We park in our usual spot across the street from the building and try to figure out how to get inside to check on our girl.

"We should try that thing we discussed," Zeke suggests. "I can pose as a pap and see if we can get any information."

"Did you bring the camera?" I ask as I watch the front entrance.

Zeke nods and reaches under his seat to pull out a high-grade camera that we purchased for this purpose. "I'll go," he says. "He might not be an easy sell, and I'm the only one with the temperament to pull this off convincingly."

True. With the way I'm feeling right now, the moment the doorman refused to answer a question, I'd try to put him through the cement.

"The only identity you mean," Khalil remarks.

Because if Zeke were Bane or Seth right now, they'd be just as bad. Seth would have just walked right up to the doorman and stuck his knife under his chin until he told the alter where his Sunshine was.

Zeke flips Khalil off and hops out of the truck. Khalil and I hold our breath as we watch him cross the street and approach the doorman. The portly man doesn't seem to want to give Zeke the time of day as soon as he notices the camera Zeke makes sure to flash around.

They don't speak for long, but it seems like an eternity before

Zeke climbs back inside the tinted truck and shuts the door with a vicious curse. "Remind me to inform Aurelia that she's never fucking returning to this place. The doorman didn't care if I was a pap or not. He sold her out for twenty bucks."

My gaze snaps toward the window, returning to the doorman as I contemplate beating the shit out of him. *Too many cameras*, I remind myself.

"What did he say?" Khalil presses impatiently.

"He said that Aurelia checked out of the apartment an hour ago, but he overheard it mentioned that she was returning to her permanent home not far away."

I frown at that, even though I'm relieved to know she's close. If Aurelia lives nearby, though, why the hell didn't she just go there instead of the apartment?

"Did he tell you where it was?" I ask.

"No need," Zeke says as he shows me his phone and the Google search he has pulled up. There was drone footage of a sprawling mansion and an address underneath along with the hefty price tag that the home had come with. Like her apartment, it was that fucking easy to get her location, and learning that after hearing she was attacked today—or I guess yesterday—puts me in an unbearably black mood.

"Let's go."

Even with a map, we have a hell of a fucking time finding the place since the GPS stops directing us about a mile away from where the home is actually located. And blocking our way in is a guarded gate. We find somewhere discreet to park so we can remain inconspicuous while surveying the area.

I can see several homes in the distance scattered around the rolling hills, and my gaze snags on the highest one. I can't make out the details from here, but I know in my tightening gut that it's hers, sitting above all the rest like the king of the hill.

Getting in won't be easy, and while that eases some of my agitation, I'm still restless to get inside and find her.

"All right, so how do we do this?" I ask.

"We kill the guards."

Khalil and I startle at the telling shift in Zeke's voice, and he grins as we gape at the man now in the driver's seat. "What the hell—*Seth*?"

He shoves Zeke's hair out of his eyes and winks. "In the flesh."

"When the hell—*how* the hell are you awake?" Khalil demands.

Seth wiggles his fingers and says, "Magic."

"What happened to Zeke?"

"He said he wasn't ready to see Sunshine, so he bailed." Seth playfully rolls his eyes toward the roof of the car. "What a pussy."

I snort, but Khalil says, "Leave him alone, Seth. You weren't there when she left." And then he turns his head to direct the last part at me. "And neither were you, Thor, so cut him some slack."

I nod and clasp Khalil on the shoulder.

"So are we doing this or what?" Seth asks as he pats Zeke's body down in his seat, looking for his favorite knife.

"We're not killing them, Seth," I decide. "They're the ones keeping people out. That's a good thing."

"Sunshine doesn't need them. She has us."

"We're not killing them."

Seth glares at us both before muttering under his breath. "Pussies."

Ignoring him, I climb out of the car to get a better look at the surrounding area, and my gaze snags on the mountains behind the entire community and the smaller hills at the base. "That's our way in," I say. "They didn't bother to block it off because no one will be crazy enough to try to climb down from there."

"No one but us," Khalil agrees.

The sky is a soft blue and pink, and I can even see the bright dot of Venus winking at me when the three of us creep toward the patio doors overlooking the pool. My legs twinge in pain since I pushed myself too hard climbing up and then down the mountains nestled behind the community. And because Aurelia's house—a classic château that reeked of old money—sat on the highest hill, we had to hike up the pretty steep incline.

By the time we reached the property, we were covered in sweat and dirt and scrapes and bruises. Khalil was bleeding near his elbow where he'd lost his grip and subsequently some of his skin, but he paid the wound no mind as he picked the lock on the door.

I'm ready to say fuck it and just knock out a panel of the glass when he pushes the door open and walks inside like he owns the place. I'm right behind him, with Seth taking up the rear.

"This is niiiiice," Seth says as we all look around. The cavernous room we entered bounces his voice around, and I cringe.

"Keep it down, Seth."

"Why? She's going to know we're here soon enough."

"Because we don't know who else might be here," I tell him.

We dip in and out of all the rooms on the ground floor, looking for signs that anyone else is here before we make our way to the second floor, where we do the same thing, stopping in front of a set of ornate double doors cracked open, but not enough to see inside.

No one else is here.

Good.

After what happened yesterday, Aurelia will be feeling fragile and paranoid and will want to be alone—something we've banked on.

This time, I enter first as I push inside the room that's easily the size of the cabin's ground floor from wall to wall. The chandeliers in the ceiling twinkle in the soft light of the rising sun as if welcoming us inside and the sleeping form on the bed catches my attention immediately.

I don't let myself go to her though and skirt the edges of the room instead while looking around.

The paneled walls have ornamental molding—except for the single window overlooking the mountains. It's large and arched, with smaller, thin panes built in. The window takes up the entire wall, and for a moment, I'm stuck admiring the mountainous view that reminds me of home. Here, they look super close.

I feel Khalil and Seth join me at the window and feel their awe and shock.

"Now I see why she didn't come back here instead of the apartment," Khalil remarks.

I turn away from the window and creep over to the bed in the center of the room. It's a taupe color with a simple headboard and sheer white drapes hanging from the ceiling and draping the ground.

Her bedroom is exactly how I pictured it, I muse as I part the drawn curtains and crawl onto the bed. I care not about the dirt and debris I leave on her pristine white sheets as I go either. We'll be dirtying them up soon enough.

Slowly, I pull the blanket down her body when I reach her to check for wounds, my gaze catching on her breasts cradled inside the short nightgown and the enlarged veins that give me pause. The material is sheer, allowing me to also see her puckered nipples from the cool air in the room.

I'm straddling her body while sitting on my heels so when I shift, my knees catch on the edges of her nightgown and I realize there is a split going up the middle and stopping between her breasts where the bow is tied, keeping the bodice together.

The panels of the nightgown part, and my breath catches painfully in my chest when I notice her swollen belly peeking out.

"What the fuck," I whisper hoarsely. "*What the fuck.*"

Khalil pushes through curtains on the side of the bed just as I cradle Aurelia's belly with both hands just to be sure my eyes aren't playing tricks on me. "What? What's wrong? What happened?" His gaze drops when he doesn't get an answer from me, and then he stumbles back a step when he sees.

The curtains on the other side of the bed are ripped open, and Seth appears holding one of Aurelia's perfume bottles. He sniffs it distractedly and then grumbles something about liking Aurelia's pussy better.

"Seth," I say, my voice cracking a little. I grab his hand, and the perfume bottle falls out of it, dropping onto the bed as I yank his hand forward and rest it on her belly. "Do you feel that?" I demand, unable to trust what's real. My head still doesn't feel right sometimes. I need to know.

"She feels different," he says with a frown that's confused.

"She's pregnant, Seth."

His eyes widen and then dart back and forth between my face and Aurelia's belly before settling on our girl. "I'm going to be a daddy?"

The three of us are quiet for a while as we let in sink in. *I'm going to be a father.* I'm not sure how long we sit there in silence before I break it. "How far along do you think she is?"

Khalil's hand inches forward, and then he places it reluctantly on her belly above where mine and Seth's still rest. It's warm despite the rest of her skin feeling cool. "At least five or six months."

It's the last time any of us touched her.

"I don't understand," Seth says with a wrinkle in his brow. "Why isn't she waking up?"

Khalil removes his hand and turns toward the nightstand. "I think this might explain why," he says as he shows us the small bottle of Benadryl.

Seth's frown only deepens. "Is that safe?"

"Don't know," Khalil answers as he replaces the bottle on the nightstand. "But I trust that she wouldn't take it if it wasn't."

More light spills into the room, and I turn my head to gaze out of the window at the sun creeping higher into the sky. Aurelia will be waking up soon, so we leave the bed and blend into the remaining shadows to wait for her.

We only have to wait an hour before she starts to stir. I watch through the sheer curtains as she rolls around for a while as if trying to get comfortable but can't so sits up with a sigh that makes my cock hard when I see the strap of her nightie slip off her shoulder.

I watch her pause when she notices her ruined blankets and then the perfume bottle that wasn't there when she went to bed.

She doesn't react at first, and then she speaks.

"I know you're there," she calls out calmly. "You can come out now."

Khalil and I look at each other, and he looks mildly impressed, and then I'm turning my head toward Seth, who smiles with delight. He's practically fucking giddy at seeing her again—at least while conscious.

Seth leaves his corner first and approaches the bed. I hear Aurelia gasp, but before he can say a word, Khalil reveals himself too, and Aurelia shifts like she wants to go to him, but the hard look in his eyes warns her to stay away.

She shrinks back and then fists the sheets. "Thorin?" I hear her inquire after me. "Is he?"

Leaning my head back against the wall and closing my eyes, I try to quiet the voice that keeps whispering, *she left you*. She could have chosen anytime to walk away, but she did it when I was at my most vulnerable. I'm angry and itching to get even, but at the first opportunity we had, we came running instead.

And I know I'm not the only one feeling this way. Khalil is still angry, and apparently, so is Zeke. He split the moment we found her rather than face her again. Seth is the only one who doesn't feel some type of way, but then again, he's Seth. Aurelia could say she wanted to let the world burn, and Seth would light the match.

It's hard to blame her after seeing all of this and all that she has to lose, but it still hurts, and I don't know when it will stop.

I finally walk over to the bed and watch her eyes widen when she sees me standing there. Her hands cover her mouth, and then she shakes her head to ward off the tears in vain. They spill uncontrollably over her hands like a waterfall.

Finally, she drops her hands to choke out, "You're awake."

I tip my chin down and coldly greet, "Aurelia."

She gulps and then she takes turns looking at all three of us standing in her bedroom like thieves in the night. Or morning. It feels like déjà vu. Like we've come full circle.

"You're here. You found me."

"Don't flatter yourself," I retort. "We're here because you have something we want."

Misunderstanding me—or perhaps knowing me better than I know myself—her hands rise to cradle her belly.

"I—"

"Your uncle tried to kill me," I explain and watch her brows slam down in confusion when I don't acknowledge the obvious elephant in the room. "We want him dead as bad as you do, and you're going to help us get even." I let my gaze trail her body that's ripening like freshly bloomed fruit and let my anger show. "It's the least you can do."

"The *least* I can do?"

I step closer toward the foot of the bed. "You heard me, wolf."

"Thorin, what is your problem?"

"Did you seriously just ask me that?"

Her breathing quickens, and then her gaze climbs, and her lips part when she notices my hair. I see the question form in her eyes and her pleasure at my new look, but she doesn't allow herself to act on either. "Well, if you hate me so much," she asks instead, "then why are you here? You don't need me to get at my uncle."

"We saw the news that someone tried to hurt you. We were worried you might need us, so we came," Seth answers honestly before I can think of a lie.

I roll my eyes when Aurelia's gaze softens. A moment later, she thrusts out her hand for him in invitation, and Seth wastes no time accepting, letting her pull him onto the bed. "Hi, Seth," she whispers softly once he's sitting next to her on the bed.

"Hey, Sunshine."

"Are you okay?" she asks since he hasn't been awake in months. Not since the night Isaac came.

"I should be asking you that," he retorts. I nearly swear when he tentatively reaches forward to rest a hand on the swell of her belly. "You're having a baby."

"Mm-hmm," she confirms noncommittally. "I am."

"Are you scared?" he asks while Khalil and I stand there like we're furniture. It's our own stubbornness getting in the way, but tell that to my heart because it won't budge either. The jagged, broken pieces lie at her feet and to reclaim them would mean cutting myself open again.

Aurelia makes a sound caught between a laugh, gasp, and a sob. "I'm terrified."

"Don't be," Seth says immediately as he rests his chin on top of her head. "We'll help you."

"*Seth*," Khalil growls in warning.

Aurelia peeks up at him and then her face crumples before she pulls away from Seth and angrily swipes the tears from her face. Her eyes and the skin around her nose are both red from crying. She's so fucking beautiful, even when she cries. "What's your problem, Poverly?"

"I don't have a problem. You clearly didn't want us involved," he says, waving at her stomach. "I don't want Seth getting reattached if you're just going to leave him in the lurch when things get too hard."

"Oh, yeah?" she challenges. "Is that what happened? Is that what you think I did?"

"Aurelia," I interrupt before things get out of hand. We didn't come for this. I still don't know why we came, but we're here now, so down to business. "Are you with us or not?"

"With you?" she echoes.

I could be wrong, but I swear there's a tiny spark of hope in her eyes that I waste no time snuffing out. "Are you going to help us with your uncle?"

Khalil's right. I was told the doctors examined her too when I was brought into the hospital, which means she had to know she was pregnant when she left, and she still did it anyway.

Aurelia was having our baby, but she didn't want us to be a part of this.

The wound she left gaping just keeps getting bigger.

"Fine," she says while rising from the bed unsteadily and passing us as she heads for the bathroom. "I'll help you but not for free. If you want to stay, you'll have to earn your keep, boys."

She walks into the bathroom and slams the door before we can ask her how.

CHAPTER FIFTY-THREE

KHALIL

I'm blowing it.

But the realization doesn't help because then I get pissed at myself for caring.

Aurelia made us her new security team, which is serendipitous since Tyler apparently canned the men guarding her yesterday. Aurelia then made it perfectly clear that the fuckwad was still in charge of all security matters and that we'd be reporting to him.

I honestly thought she cared about the little shit, but maybe she secretly wants him dead because fuck that. Thorin, Seth, and I don't answer to anyone, especially when it comes to protecting what's ours. Aurelia should have learned that by now.

Thorin and I left briefly to clear out of Gary's girlfriend's condo, but this time we were able to use the front gate when we returned. After that, for the first few days, we did nothing but lie low since the press and online gossip blogs were all over the story, wanting to know what happened with the shooting and how Aurelia is faring.

On day four, we finally meet the illustrious Oni.

She seems more perturbed than surprised to find us here. Oni takes one look at us filling up the chic mansion like a trio of sore thumbs and drags Aurelia into a room where they yell at each other for an hour before she leaves.

"What was that about?" I ask after I follow Aurelia into the kitchen. She's wearing a knitted white two-piece short set with the long-sleeved crop top showing off her belly.

Aurelia cuts her gaze toward me. She's drinking from a glass of orange juice after taking her prenatal vitamins, but she lowers it and gives me a look. "Oh, you're talking to me now?"

"For the moment."

"Hmm." She abandons her juice and leaves the kitchen, making it clear that she has no desire to talk to me.

I last three seconds before I chase after her.

Aurelia walks in the living area and grabs the thin yoga mat and bolster pillow waiting there before laying it out on the hardwood floor. She then grabs the remote before turning on the TV and loading up a program.

"Yoga?" I ask when I see what's playing. There's a woman on the screen with a man, and I realize belatedly that it's meant to be a couples' exercise, but Goldilocks had been forced to do it alone.

Aurelia wordlessly nods as she pulls off her top, revealing her tan sports bra underneath. "I'm told it helps with the discomfort of growing another human inside you."

"You need a partner?"

Her gaze flicks uncertainly toward me, and then she avoids my gaze as she gives a small shrug. "If you want."

I ask myself what the hell I'm doing as I take her hands when she tries to sit and help her lower onto the mat. Facing Aurelia, I sit next to her while she crosses her legs and places her hands on her knees. The moment she closes her eyes though, she starts to sway and my hands reach for her automatically, settling on her stomach and back to keep her steady. Aurelia's lack of balance and coordination reminds me of Thor and how he said his body didn't feel like it belonged to him after the coma. The therapist suggested yoga on his own time, but the jackass would never do it.

"Thanks," she says softly before pulling in a deep breath and slowly releasing it.

I've lost my excuse for following her in the first place, so I flounder for something to say since it's clear she's not going to tell me what she discussed with Oni. Fortunately, Aurelia beats me to it before my presence and hands on her body can become awkward.

It's a big enough house that we've been able to avoid and ignore each other without issue. It would feel awkward as fuck moving into her home if we hadn't already lived together in the cabin where we couldn't avoid each other.

"Have you seen your parents yet?" she asks with her eyes still closed.

My fingers flex involuntarily, and I find myself pulling in a calming breath with her. "No. Not yet," I answer once I exhale.

"Why not?" Her tone is soft and curious rather than accusatory.

I wait until she inhales deeply again and exhales. "Because I'm a coward."

A laugh bursts free when Aurelia nods her agreement and then looks apologetic when she realizes. "Sorry."

"Don't be. It's true."

"You should call them," she suggests. "If you're going to be my bodyguard, you'll soon find out that privacy and hiding are impossible, even when you're rich. You don't want them learning you're alive from social media."

Fuck, she's right. That would almost be as bad as letting them think I was dead in the first place. I did it to protect them, but they won't give a fuck about that. My parents would rather die *for* me than live with the pain of losing a child.

I feel a bit of anxiety rising, so when Aurelia inhales again, I mimic her until the nausea dissipates. "There's another reason I haven't gone to see them," I admit before I can stop the words.

Aurelia's brown eyes pop open, and she turns her head to meet my gaze. I don't realize how close our faces are until her lips are right there. "What?"

"You," I confess slowly. "You promised to be there when I go to see them, remember?"

She quickly looks away and chews her lip. "I didn't think you'd still want me to keep that promise."

"Why wouldn't I?" I retort quietly.

"Because you hate me…for being a bad girlfriend."

"Neither of those things are true, Goldilocks."

She looks like she wants to say something but bats the urge away and reaches her arm nearest me up as she leans over toward the opposite side. "Khalil, can you—" She gestures toward her arm and I quickly catch on, placing my hand on her bicep above her armpit and helping her lean into the stretch.

"Feels good?"

"Yes, thank you."

The conversation grows stale again after that as we try to avoid all the things we're too afraid to say. This time I break the silence after shifting to her other side to repeat the stretch. "So why are you here all by yourself?"

"Because the fewer people who know I'm pregnant, the safer I feel," she softly confesses with a worried pinch of her brow. "My security team didn't even know. No one except Tyler."

"Where is he anyway?" I grouse. I've never felt so much dislike and envy for someone I've technically never met. When we found Westbrook in the Cold Peaks half buried alive, he was barely conscious and only mumbling Aurelia's name.

Aurelia flicks her gaze toward me, and a small smile she won't let free plays on her lips at my jealousy. "He was pushing himself too hard, so I made him take the week off. He should be back in a couple of days. He's married, by the way." She blurts that last part out, likely picking up on my jealousy.

"Happily?" I ask unmoved.

"*Very*. I met his wife. She's lovely."

"I'll take your word for it," I say as I help her move into a new position.

Aurelia takes the bolster pillow and sits on top on it before placing the soles of her feet together and letting her knees open. I'm sitting behind her as I wait for her to tell me what to do. I can't even bring myself to listen to the instructor on the TV because it means taking my focus off of her.

"Put your feet on my back," she finally tells me. I glance down at my sneakered feet before removing my shoes until I'm left in just my socks. And then I lean back on my hands to place my feet on her back. It's comical the way my big-ass feet dwarf her back. "Lower."

Obeying, I slide my feet down until they rest on her lower spine. "Like that, baby?" I let slip.

I feel Aurelia's muscles tense under my feet like she's just as startled, but then she relaxes just as quickly. "Perfect."

She doesn't thank me this time, and it feels like a step forward from the polite distance she's been keeping. After she's done breathing some more, she tells me to move one of my feet to her upper back.

And that's how Thorin and Seth find us.

"What the hell are you guys doing?" Seth asks as they walk in through the patio doors. All morning they've been out doing their rounds patrolling the grounds while I stayed inside to look after Aurelia.

Thorin already scolded Aurelia for not doing better to keep people out, to which Aurelia gaped at him and made a very good point that only someone insane or with a death wish would attempt to scale a mountain just to gain entry to her backyard.

"Yoga," I grunt when Aurelia ignores him. She's busy pulling in her deep breaths again.

Thankfully, Thorin and Seth don't stick around, but I can feel Thorin's eyes on us as they cross the room to reach the door leading to the kitchen. When I look up, he lifts a brow before disappearing through the doorless entryway.

I stay with Aurelia, helping her through her poses and assisting with her stretches, and then I help her stand when she's done while I roll the mat and tie it.

"How are you feeling now?" I ask once I set the mat aside and toss the pillow on the couch. "Do you need anything?"

"Fries," she says immediately while staring longingly out the window. The landscaper is out there mowing the massive lawn, and I wonder if she thinks about her garden back in the Cold Peaks.

"Okay," I say even though it's ten in the morning. "Easy enough. I'll get you some fries."

"And ice cream."

My brows raise as I hope she doesn't mean together. I've heard about pregnancy cravings from my aunts and cousins back in Six Forks. "Any particular flavor?"

Her nose wrinkles as she gives it some thought. "Pistachio," she finally decides.

"They make that?"

She shakes her head while looking like she's caught in a trance. "I have no idea."

"I guess we'll find out then. I'll be back." It feels like I'm running when I rush the door.

"Khalil," she aims at my back. The tremble in her voice makes me pause even though I don't want to. I turn to see tears welling in her eyes. "For what it's worth, I'm sorry for—" Her voice catches. "I'm sorry for leaving you too. I never wanted you to feel alone."

I don't realize my feet are moving to return to her until I'm already standing in front of her, cupping her cheeks and using my thumbs to wipe away her tears. I stay with her until the rush of hormones settle and then I kiss her forehead when she quiets. "It's cool," I finally say before I let her go to leave and hunt down her fries and ice cream.

By some miracle, I actually find pistachio-flavored ice cream, and then I return to her hilltop mansion to watch in horror as she sprays cheese on top of the ice cream like whipped cream while shoveling fires inside her mouth.

"I don't know what's happening, but I'm scared," Seth says after he and Thorin join us by the pool where Aurelia was sunning herself when I returned.

She's got on a two-piece bathing suit now, and her hair is pinned in a high bun as she lounges on one of the patio chairs. I'm sitting on the one next to her with my legs thrown over the side and my arms braced on my thighs as I watch her dip a fry inside the cheese and ice cream and then devour it one bite.

"It's so good," Aurelia moans.

"We'll just have to take your word for it," Thorin retorts as he watches her stab the ice cream with a spoon and then lick it clean. Aurelia grins like she knows she's grossing us out, and it brings her even more joy. The baby seems to like it too if the way her stomach changes shape, the skin rippling and bubbling from his excited kicks, is anything to go by.

His...

It's when I realize I don't even know the sex. There are a million questions I have, but my broken heart won't let me ask any of them. *I don't want her back*, I whisper to myself. *I don't want her back, I don't want her back, I don't want her back.*

Maybe if I say it enough times, I'll start to believe it.

The door to the guest bedroom creaks open the next night, and not one to be caught slipping, it wakes me immediately, but I pretend to still be asleep as I listen to the soft footsteps pad across the room until the visitor is standing by my bedside.

I peek an eye open with one hand under my pillow, but when I see Aurelia standing there wearing nothing but a gray grunge graphic T-shirt from Thorin as if we're back at the cabin, I release the gun hidden there.

"What's up?" I ask groggily as I roll over and rub my eyes. "Why aren't you sleeping, Goldilocks? Something wrong?"

My room overlooks the pool on the first floor, so the light from the pool casts a soft glow inside the room allowing me to see her shattered expression.

"I need your help again," she says shyly. Before I can ask her what's wrong, she reaches out in the dark and fumbles for my hand. I close mine around hers the moment I feel her soft, slender fingers in mine, and then she's tugging my hand toward her.

I think she's about to tell me something's wrong with the baby until she not-so-shyly slips my hand between her thighs, forcing me to feel the juices gathered there. "Aurelia… Where are your panties, baby?"

"I lost them," she whispers as I play with her pussy. She's fucking soaked.

"I know you hate me," she sobs as I explore her lower lips with my fingers. "I know I don't deserve it, but please. Just this once. I need you."

Grabbing her waist without a word, I pull her onto the bed, twisting to plant Aurelia on her back inside the cradle of the pillows and blankets. "Are you sure?" I ask, knowing it's the hormones that brought her to me. "You might regret it in the morning."

Aurelia places her hand on my cheek. "The only thing I regret is leaving you."

My gaze drops down to her stomach, and I place a trembling hand on the side when I realize I want to believe her. "So what are we having? Do you know?"

"A boy," she answers immediately. I crack a grin that makes her smile too, like my excitement is infectious. "Yeah, I thought you might like that."

"A girl would have been cool too."

She rolls her eyes, her tone disbelieving. "Yeah right."

"Nah, I'm serious," I say honestly. "It wouldn't have mattered because she would've been mine."

Aurelia beams at that. "That's cute. Thorin said the same thing when I told him."

"Wait…" I stare down at her accusingly. "You told Thorin about the baby and not me?"

Goldilocks gives me a dry look. "*He* asked."

"And let me guess, Seth knows too."

"Of course," she answers lightly. "Seth asked the first night you guys arrived."

Damn, I was the last to know, and it's my own fucking fault for being stubborn. I'm stuck in my head when Aurelia starts squirming impatiently. "Khalil," she whines. "Are you going to fuck me or not?"

"What do you want me to do?" I ask as I bend to kiss her naked thigh. "I don't want to hurt you." I already know what I want to do to her. I've known since that first night, but I need to know how far she's willing to let me go. It's not like at the cabin either. Here, she holds all the cards, and I know it gives her a little thrill ordering us around for a change.

"You're not going to hurt me," she grumbles. "You're going to piss me off if you don't get your dick in me."

I'm pushing up her T-shirt when I pause to kiss her hard on her lips. "Don't tell me what to do with my dick," I warn.

"Fine. I'll go to Seth's room." She pushes me away and swings her legs over the bed. I watch in amusement as I let Aurelia think she's getting away before I give chase. I catch her at the door and then pick her up before carrying her through it.

"Fine," I growl into her neck. "Let's go to Seth's room."

Realizing she might have bit off more than she can chew once again, Aurelia squirms to get away while I carry her down the hall to the alter's room and push inside. Unlike me, he doesn't wake up, because he crashed from a sugar coma. He and Aurelia gorged themselves on sugar and fried snacks for dinner rather than the balanced meal her chef arrived to prepare before leaving.

After eating the chef's cooking, I finally understood why Aurelia never bothered learning how to cook.

Seth is lying on his back on top of the covers when we enter. His head is turned and his arm is hanging over the side of the bed. He's still wearing his clothes and shoes.

I carry Aurelia over to the bed and set her down. Seth jerks awake when he suddenly feels her weight, but then I see his confusion clear when he sees that it's her. Since he doesn't like the dark, the lamp next to the bed is already on, so I dim it until the room is mostly dark but still cast in a soft glow.

"Seth," Aurelia says breathily as she reaches for the button on his jeans while I pull off Thorin's shirt, revealing her naked body underneath. "Seth, fuck me."

He isn't hard when she pulls him out, but that quickly changes as the sleepy edges fogging his brain recede and she leans down to put her lips on him. I can hear his groan and her suckling him in the dark as I shed my shorts and join them on the bed.

"What brought this on?" Seth struggles to ask while Aurelia deepthroats his dick.

"She's horny and too impatient for pillow talk, so I brought her to you."

"Yeah? You want to be fucked, sweet girl?" Seth forces her to release his dick and Aurelia lets him go with a wet pop. "I'll try not to take it personally that I was your *second* choice for a human vibrator," he mumbles as he flips her onto her back to get a good look at her.

"I promise you'll be my first choice tomorrow," Aurelia says and then squeals when he bites her.

Seth shoves her thighs apart and then takes his now-hard dick in hand to plow into her but quickly realizes it's awkward with her belly in between them, so we carefully arrange Aurelia on her side until she's trapped between us with Seth at her front and me behind her.

I'm eager to watch, so I let Seth go first, and it's all I can do not to hit him when he fits his crown at her hole and plunges inside her.

"Shit, yeah. Missed this," he groans. "Missed you, Sunshine."

Aurelia lays a hand on his cheek like she did to me while he works himself inside her. "I missed you too, Seth." Her hand leaves Seth's cheek and I feel her grab mine, bringing it forward to cup her breast. "You too, Khal."

"You fucking better have," I say as I kiss gently down her arm. Her skin is already becoming slick with sweat, and I wonder briefly if we're overheating her before she pushes her ass back against me and my attention shifts to that part of her body while Seth fucks her.

Damn, I want it bad.

But I'm woefully short of lube and I'm too fucking impatient to get creative, so I grab her thigh and seize Seth's thrusting dick at the base. I feel him snarl when he catches on to what I want and then glances at Aurelia who's tense now, before reluctantly pulling out of her. I'm there in an instant, replacing his dick with mine, and Aurelia begins to moan once more. When I feel the tightening in my balls, I pull out and Seth takes over fucking her pussy.

Aurelia moans loudly from the sordidness of it all, and I grin down at her. "Oh, you like that, do you? You like the way we take turns, Goldilocks?"

We make it so speaking is impossible, so she nods eagerly. Seth pulls out again and grunts like it pains him, and I start fucking her again. We continue this back-and-forth, driving Aurelia and ourselves crazy until I slap a hand over her clit and work the engorged nub until she's coming while clinging to Seth.

Once we're both at the brink and there's no turning back, Seth and I take our dicks in hand, stroking furiously until we erupt. We paint our girl in our cum, re-staking our claim so that there's no question left that she never stopped being ours.

After we're spent, Seth and I lie there fighting to catch our breath. It's a few minutes before the room finally quiets and only a few more before Aurelia lifts her head to whisper one word.

"Again."

Aurelia makes us ride her through the night, dozing off just to wake up half an hour or an hour later to roll over to one of us to slake her lust. The sun is coming up when she finally falls asleep for good, so I climb from the bed, careful not to disturb them as I redress and step outside the room with my phone in my hand. I return to mine and stare at the number dialed in my phone before I take a calming breath and force myself to press call.

The line rings three times before a gruff voice answers. "Poverly Construction. How can I help you?"

My next breath shudders out of me at hearing my father's voice for the first time in a decade. And then I speak. "Hey, Pops."

Later that morning, I'm still reeling from speaking with my parents, who were happy to know that I'm alive but disenchanted with me for staying gone for so long. The conversation had been short but emotional, ending with me promising to come and see them soon.

It went better than I imagined and worse than I imagined at the same time.

Thorin, Seth, and I are crammed together on Aurelia's couch, sitting shoulder to shoulder with our arms crossed as we stare down the uncomfortable man next to her who looks like he's not happy about our presence.

The feeling is more than mutual.

The disturbed look on his face tells me that Tyler Westbrook knows exactly who we are and he doesn't approve of us being here to take back our girl. Like we give a shit.

Aurelia's glaring at us since none of us say shit to his ass after she makes the introductions, and he offers a reluctant, "Nice to meet you."

Seeing Aurelia upset at the chilly reception, though, Seth's soft ass is the first of us to crack, giving a reluctant, lazy wave. "'Sup, Tyler. I'm Seth. That's Khalil and Thorin." He throws a thumb at each of us. "Don't worry about them. They just don't like you very much. You'll meet Zeke later, he's sleeping right now. But if you're a very good boy, you'll never have to meet Bane."

"Bane…" Tyler says before his voice trails off. "Wait, there's five of you?" He glances at Aurelia, who just awkwardly rubs her nape.

"Yup," Seth says without elaborating.

Westbrook will figure it out soon enough.

If it didn't mean scaring the shit out Zeke—or Aurelia—I'd wake him up now just to see the smug fuck run in the other direction. I'm told he's a pretty decent guy, but I don't like anyone I wouldn't die for sniffing around, and I just *know* that fucker used to have feelings for her.

How could he not?

Aurelia's beautiful, smart, talented, and fearless…

I feel a little nudge inside my chest when I hesitate on her final quality that made me fall head over heels in love with her.

Loyal.

Aurelia's loyal.

AURELIA'S NEW BODYGUARDS CAUSE AN ONLINE TRAFFIC JAM

3 days ago

By David Earnest | Off the Press

It's no secret that Aurelia's security—like the rest of her team—is a revolving door of new faces. After the shooting a few weeks ago, it comes as no surprise that she's already flanked by new bodyguards, but when it comes to this new set, I think I speak for everyone when I say...*meow*. The trio are hot enough to incinerate a sidewalk, and if I had to choose anyone to guard my body, it would be these three, no question about it.

And while questions of who they are ripple across Aurelia's internet, one can only hope that this new team is here to stay.

CHAPTER FIFTY-FOUR

SETH

The three of us are still sitting on the couch when a team of people walks in carrying bags and boxes and talking among themselves. I memorize each of their faces and the sounds of their voices before dismissing them to return my gaze to Sunshine.

She's talking with Oni, who led the pack, about something, and I really wish I could read lips because I don't like the furrow in my girl's brow. That shit gets deeper and deeper the longer they whisper heatedly about something. I'm getting ready to go over there when she sighs and mutters something that looks like, "Fine."

"What's up?" I ask the moment she's within earshot.

"No more hiding," she starts with, and it sounds ominous. "I've got meetings with lawyers and the label and then a maternity shoot. I won't actually announce that I'm pregnant until after the baby is born," she assures us when we all tense. "But my fans—what remaining I have—will want to see and I'd like to share this with them."

"Okay," Thorin says, taking it all in stride. "What do you need from us? When should we be ready?"

"Well… First, we have to talk about appearances. If you're going to be my bodyguards, you have to look the part. That means uniforms."

"I'm not wearing no damn tight-ass collar shirt and khakis like a jackass," Khalil immediately fusses with a scowl.

It's definitely a dig at Westbrook.

Aurelia glares at him for already forgetting her order to play nice, and he stares right back at her like he's not sorry at all. "You'll be wearing suits. Very nice tailored suits that the stylist did a great job picking out for you."

"Not doing that either," Thorin grunts.

"What's wrong with our clothes?" I ask, worried she might be ashamed of us.

"Nothing," Aurelia quickly assures us. "It's just protocol. Most of the events I attend are closed to the public. They need to be able to tell you're actually part of my security team and not—"

"Criminals," Tyler coughs into his fist. "Stalkers. Psychos," he coughs again.

"I'm so sorry to hear about your wife," I respond with a tilt of my head. "Widowed so young. Such a shame."

Tyler rolls his eyes at my thinly veiled threat. I'd omit the veil entirely, but Sunshine would only get upset.

"As I said, it's protocol *and* temporary." She gives Thorin, Khalil, and me a pointed look, reminding us that we won't be her bodyguards forever. We're just playing the part long enough to get near her uncle.

And then we'll kill him.

"Here are the suits," the stylist says as she lays them out. "Will the other two be joining us?" That's when I realize there are five.

My gaze connects with Sunshine, and she winks at me. I don't really want a suit but knowing Aurelia was thoughtful enough to make sure each of us—even Bane—have our own makes me want to do things to her that I've been told I'm not allowed to do when other people are in the room.

"Not this time. You can just match the measurements to Seth's."

"Ooookay."

In the corner, I see Tyler frown. I don't like the way he hangs on our every word. Aurelia is ours to look after, not his. I don't appreciate another man pissing all over my territory either.

I barely tolerate Thorin and Khalil, and I love them. They're my brothers as much as Zeke's. Actually, come to think of it, it annoys me when he gets her too.

But I don't want to kill *them*.

I want to kill Tyler Westbrook. Or at least seriously maim him. Cut a finger off or two…

"Stop thinking about murder," Khalil leans over to whisper.

"I wasn't thinking about murder. I was thinking about maiming."

"Stop thinking about maiming. We're supposed to be *nice*," Thorin says.

"Nice is for Sunshine. Maiming is for everyone else."

"You'd maim us?" Khalil asks curiously.

"Only when you're not nice to Sunshine."

"What are you guys talking about?" Aurelia asks as she walks over with three black garment bags thrown over her arm.

"You," I say.

"And maiming," Thorin tattles.

Aurelia frowns and mumbles, "I'm afraid to ask."

"Don't be," I coo as I pull her into my lap. "We'd never maim you."

"You're not allowed to maim my friends either," she decrees since she knows us so well.

"You're not allowed to have any friends but us," I tell her as I nuzzle her neck. "We're your BFFs forever."

"BFF *means* best friends forever, Seth."

"I know," I say as I pepper her shoulder with kisses. "But when forever's over I'll want another go."

"Aww. That's sweet. But I don't have sex with my friends," she informs dryly.

"Oh." My head pops up. "Well, then never mind."

Snorting, Aurelia tries to stand from my lap, but she struggles to regain her feet so much that Khalil has to stand and help her. She then goes about freeing the suits from the garment bags and laying them in our lap. "I just need you to try them on, and then the tailor will take your measurements."

I glance over at the bespectacled man wearing a sweater vest and eyeing Thorin like he can't wait to get his hands on him.

"Can we have the room, please?" Aurelia calls out, and everyone except the tailor, the stylist, and her assistant leave. "It's only temporary," she promises again when she sees we're still sitting.

Khalil and Thorin stand and start to undress while I eye the suit in my lap.

I've never worn one before. What if I look silly? What if Sunshine doesn't like me anymore because I look silly?

"You're enjoying this, aren't you?" Thorin says after he's stripped down to his boxer briefs and is shoving a leg inside the black pants.

"Very much," Aurelia answers, her brown eyes gleaming with humor.

I slowly get up from the couch and try to ease out of the room, but Sunshine's commanding voice stops me in my tracks.

"Stop right there, Seth." I stand still as she walks over to me.

"I was just…" I scratch my head for an excuse. "Going…to the bathroom."

"Please?" I feel her belly brush my arm as she reaches out to take my hand. "For me?"

Feeling myself cave, I raise our joined hands and kiss the back of it. "Of course for you."

As soon as she turns away, I roll my eyes and reluctantly let her lead me back over to the couch. I undress and climb into the suit that looks and feels nice but makes me want to tear free of my own skin.

The urge is stomped under her cute little heel though when Aurelia turns around from grabbing the boxes of shiny shoes and her jaw drops.

I know it's a genuine reaction when the shoeboxes tumble out of her arms. She tries to bend and grab them but doesn't get very far, so I step forward and crouch to retrieve them. I turn and shove them into Khalil's hands before facing Aurelia again. "Like what you see, Sunshine?"

"Do I?" she says, hyping me up. "I didn't think it was possible for you to get any hotter, Seth Cura."

Forgetting we're surrounded by people, I bend and kiss her neck.

I hear a few gasps, but Aurelia doesn't push me away. Unbothered by their stares, she just smiles and adjusts her head to give me better access.

Our debut as Aurelia's bodyguards happens a week later.

First, we trail her to meet with her lawyers and label. The following week, we watch over her while does her maternity shoot, which happens in two locations.

The first is in Washington state, starting by a waterfall and ending on the edge of a rocky cliff that makes us swear and grit our teeth while overlooking the evergreens wrapped in fog. She's naked in those photos, her front covered in a simple white wrapping that becomes sheer from the pool created by the waterfall.

The second shoot takes place in a Los Angeles studio with far more dramatic outfits and poses and glamour.

It's not until it's over and Aurelia is in her dressing room getting redressed that it dawns on me why she did two.

One shows the haunting truth that will forever remain ours alone.

The other a pretty, digestible lie to fawn over.

"Why do they keep looking at me?" I lean over to ask Khalil when I notice for the third time a group of women whispering to themselves while stealing glances at me. I think they were the ones who did Aurelia's hair and makeup.

Khalil still has his head on a swivel as we guard Aurelia's dressing room when he answers tonelessly, "They want to fuck you."

The women turn to stare at me openly when they notice my attention.

Suddenly, I feel like I'm about to be eaten alive. "No. No, they can't. I won't let them. They're not Sunshine."

"Seth, it's all right," Khalil attempts to console me. "Just don't pay them any mind."

"No, I don't like it." I shake my head as I back up against the door, grabbing the knob and twisting until I'm stumbling into the room and out of sight. I slam the door closed and lock it for good measure.

I hear a sound and turn to see that Aurelia is naked and pinned on the couch with Thorin's hand over her mouth to keep her quiet while he kneels between her legs, eating her pussy and wrinkling his new suit.

I sigh with relief and lean against the door, resting my head against it and closing my eyes.

Much better.

When my heart calms and it no longer feels like I'm about to have a panic attack, I open my eyes to find Aurelia watching me. A moment later, she comes against Thorin's mouth. Her skin is glistening from the body oil and gold flecks they painted her in for the shoot, and my gaze catches on her brown nipples that are puckered obscenely.

Thorin stands and wipes his mouth as he moves to the cooler and retrieves a bottle of water. He drinks one, washing out his mouth, and then grabs another before taking it to Sunshine.

"What's the matter, Seth?" Aurelia pants as she takes it from him. "Something happened?"

"No," I say, not wanting to upset her. As with all of us, I still see the wilds in her from time to time, and I don't want to chance her going out there and painting herself in their blood next. Although it would be a delight to see. "I just wanted to see you."

She holds out her hand to me, and I cross the small room to grab it and help her from the couch. "Thanks. I can't wait to get home and shower all of this off me."

"You looked beautiful today."

"I could say the same about you," she says as she straightens my tie. "You look so dashing."

I hold her waist as I kiss her lips. "I'm glad you approve. I feel like your boy toy."

"My dirty little boy toy," she teases as she kisses me back.

"Wait until I get you home," I promise even as I'm backing her toward the couch. "You're the one who's going to be dirty." On second thought, I'm not sure I can wait until then.

"Guys, I'm still here, and this is getting a little cringy," Thorin says, sounding annoyed.

I don't take my lips from Aurelia as I glare over her head at him. "Then *leave*."

Thorin doesn't leave though, choosing instead to lean against the vanity table. Aurelia tumbles onto the couch, and I reach for my belt as I climb on top of her. She gaps her legs open for me, and I stare at her glistening pussy as I work my belt free. I'm just shoving my pants down over my ass when a knock comes to the door.

I ignore it, and so does Thor as I work my cock into Aurelia while kneeling between her legs.

The knocking continues, but I don't hear it as I focus on Aurelia's moans instead.

"Oh, Seth," she moans, "fuck me." A moment later, Sunshine reaches up and grips my tie before yanking on it hard. Thorin swears while Aurelia whispers, "*Harder*."

Goddamn. Of course, I obey and start fucking her hard enough to make the couch skid across the hardwood floor while she tosses her head back and takes it.

But then the knocking turns into pounding until I think the door might break down. Or that someone is breaking in. Luckily, I feel Aurelia coming around my cock, and it's a few seconds more before her tight pussy releases me enough and I slip out. I stuff my still-hard dick back inside my suit pants before throwing the blanket on the back of the couch over Aurelia and then storming over to the door and snatching it open.

"What?"

"We got a problem," Khalil says with a hard look in his eyes.

"Well, what is it?" Thorin snaps grouchily. I think he was enjoying watching us a little too much.

Khalil doesn't answer and instead steps aside to show us an official-looking person standing there in business attire. Before I can ask who he is and what the fuck he wants, I'm elbowed aside as Aurelia, now dressed, comes to stand in front of me.

"Aurelia George?" the visitor asks.

"Yes?"

He holds out a yellow envelope to her. "You've been served."

CHAPTER FIFTY-FIVE

AURELIA

A conservatorship.

Last week, I completely severed ties with my uncle, cutting him out of everything.

So Uncle Mars retaliated by petitioning the probate court to appoint him control over my personal and financial affairs, claiming I was the victim of psychological abuse.

Stockholm syndrome.

He's claiming I have Stockholm syndrome and am currently under the influence of my kidnappers, and now the court is ordering me to an evaluation to prove that I'm not.

There is no hope of winning. It doesn't matter if it's true. It only matters what it looks like.

It would be easy enough to prove that Thorin, Khalil, and Seth were the search and rescue team tasked with finding me. From there it was only a matter of connecting the dots. They show up here as my new bodyguards after I went missing for months and reappeared out of thin air. It would be impossible to convince the world, much less a judge, that they weren't involved.

And then there's the fact that I'm pregnant and clearly conceived before my return to the States.

The only thing I can do is tell the same story that I gave the sheriff. That my uncle hired men to kill me—which he did—and my bodyguards heard my plight and saved my life by shielding me from him—which was only partially true.

The only problem is I have no proof.

The men he hired are dead, and my uncle could easily claim that he sent them there solely to find my body and bring me home for burial. We'll still end up looking like the bad guys and my uncle the hero.

I'm screwed with a capital F.

"We can't wait until after the baby is born," I tell my guys once we're alone. We're in the apartment instead of the house because I couldn't stand being in the car long enough to make it there. I'm pacing the length of the living room, my toes sinking into the plush carpet, the city lights through the large windows winking at me, and my hand on my aching belly as my mountain men watch me from their seats with worried frowns. "I have to kill him. I have to kill him *now*."

"We actually *can't* kill him now. You've already been served the papers. Marston George being murdered hours later will only land you the number one spot on the suspect list."

"What about Logan Abbott?" I say.

Thorin sighs with impatience, and I pivot to face him looking so out of place in the white tufted chaise with shaggy throw pillows all around him. "Yes, I know what you're thinking. There are probably dozens of Logan Abbotts out there who want him dead and no one who will mourn him, but you're the one with the most compelling motive, wolf. It'd be an open-and-shut case."

"Other than firing him as your manager, no one knew of the rift between you," Khalil points out, "and even then, he had more reason to hurt you than the other way around. This petition will have everyone looking at *you*."

"I don't care. I don't care, I don't care, I don't care. He can't do this to me. I can't—aaaaargh," I groan as I bend over to relieve the cramping in my stomach. "Gaaah, I can't wait."

"Aurelia, sit down," Khalil demands.

"No." I start pacing again, but wince when I'm hit with another cramp.

"AURELIA, SIT DOWN!" Khalil roars.

I jump and then feel tears immediately welling in my eyes. "Don't yell at me," I wail. "I'm *scaaaared*."

"Fuck." Khalil jumps up from his seat and takes me in his arms. "I'm sorry, Goldilocks. Hey, stop that. Please stop crying," he begs when I sob harder.

I couldn't stop even if I wanted to. "I don't know what to do anymore. He's already taken everything, and he still wants more."

"He hasn't taken us," Thorin reassures me as he comes to stand behind me and rub his hand across my back. "We've got you. We'll fix this. Marston George will die."

"In the meantime, how can we make this better for you? What can we do right now?"

I sniffle and lift my head to see Khalil, who asked the question. "Cheeseburger."

Once the guys bring me the fattest, juiciest cheeseburger they can find, and I fill it with fries and chocolate sauce before devouring it in a handful of bites, it feels like I'm thinking clearer.

Enough to say, "I know what to do."

Khalil and Seth, who are sitting on top of the counter together, staring at something on Seth's phone while I eat, look up. Thor is sitting next to me with his fingers linked on his abs and his head tipped back as he naps sitting up. His blue eyes pop open, and he regards me with a steady patience.

"What do you mean?"

"I know how to deal with my uncle without breaking a single law."

"How's that?"

"My uncle has been misappropriating the funds I entrusted him with, and he's likely been doing it for years, but on a much larger scale since learning how hard I am to kill. If we can find the proof, we can hand it over to the Feds and ruin him for good. He'll be facing prison time, and no judge on earth will grant him a conservatorship after that."

"How do you plan to get the proof?" Khalil questions. "I doubt he just leaves the evidence of his misdeeds lying around."

I hold up a finger. "Actually, he would. My uncle is greedy and arrogant. He knows that I know he's been stealing from me, but his ego will never allow him to believe that I'm smart enough to follow the money trail. And he's right. I wouldn't know where to begin to find the proof. But I'm also disgustingly rich, which means I have a lot of resources at my disposal. I can end him with a phone call, and I wouldn't have to lift a finger beyond that."

"But all that does is put him in prison. I thought you wanted him dead," Thorin says with a narrowed gaze.

"I do. And he will be. You just have to trust that I know my uncle better than anyone." I don't say more than that though because if my mountain me knew just how badly my uncle will react to being bested by his "dumb little niece" they'd never take the risk of me getting hurt.

So I make the call first thing in the morning, and I set the wheels in motion.

A few days later, the news of my uncle's petition gets out, and the curiosity and enchantment people once had for my mountain men turn into half-baked theories and suspicion. The paparazzi have been even more relentless than usual.

"Aurelia! Aurelia! Can you comment on where you were last year?"

"Aurelia! What is the relationship between you and your bodyguards?"

"Aurelia! Blink if you need us to call the police!"

One even manages to sneak into the apartment building and catches me coming from the gym after yoga. Thorin snatched his camera, and I barely managed to stop him from using it to bash his face in. Instead, he broke it and then told the man to bill him.

Meanwhile, my uncle is living it up in Vegas, no doubt celebrating his impending win and control over me once more. It's been a stressful few days, and when my blood pressure spikes, Khalil has the bright idea for us to get away. There aren't many places I can go where I can hide, but the guys know of one that would do everyone some good.

They decide to take me home.

Home—where Khalil can finally see his parents again, and I can hide somewhere for a few days of peace. A town that almost sounds too good to be true.

It's how we end up in Six Forks.

The town of Six Forks is tucked within the desert landscape of Nevada. I'm instantly enchanted with it when I slide out of the rental and onto the driveway of the one-story bungalow. The couple standing together on the porch give me pause though, and I glance up at Khalil to see him just as uncertain, so I shove down my own anxiety at meeting his parents and I take his hand. Khalil lets me guide him toward the house and up the wide front steps.

I feel his parents' curious gazes on me, but when I try to step back out of view and join Thorin and Seth at the bottom of the steps, Khalil's hand tightens around mine and I remember my promise to be right there with him.

So I stay, and we face off against his parents together.

His mom, who resembles Khalil so much, even down to the coloring, is the first of us to move or speak. I feel Khalil tense up beside me as she comes to stand in front of him, her head only reaching his shoulder as she lifts a hand up toward his face and rests her palm on his cheek.

"Hey, Ma."

His mother's eyes are pained but warm as she stares up at her son, taking in everything that wasn't there the last time she saw him. "Did you get it done, son? Whatever it was you needed to do?"

"Yes," Khalil answers on a broken whisper. "It's done. It's over."

His father, still dressed in a dusty white T-shirt and worn jeans from his construction company, is even taller than Khalil. He's a commanding and burly man with a salt-and-pepper beard and focused eyes. He steps forward and pulls his son into his arms, and they do the manly clap thing before the older man leans in to kiss his son's cheek. "Then welcome home, boy."

"I don't want to drive the knife in deeper," I say later that night as I shuffle on my knees toward the head of Khalil's bed, the mattress springs squeaking loudly as I go, "but your parents were definitely more excited to meet me than they were to see you."

Khalil cackles but doesn't deny it as he finishes snapping on his skullcap to protect the fresh stitch braids I gave him before we left LA. He then gently pulls me down to sit next to him while I lean into him and lay my head on his strong shoulder. His scent wafts over me, immediately calming me. Khalil always smells so good—a little sweet, a little spicy, and minty.

"Well, *you* didn't disappear without a word for ten years, so you have that going for you. And also, you're famous. I think they were a little starstruck. My mom and pops are happy to see that I'm alive, but they're not too thrilled with me right now."

I stare at the wall of posters Khalil collected as a teen. "I've never seen anyone get cussed out for that long." It was truly a sight to behold. After the warm welcome, his parents immediately went in on Khalil's ass—cursing their grown son out six ways to Sunday, and when one got winded, the other took over like a well-oiled parenting machine. "You think they're weirded out about you being in a four-way relationship?" I ask. "Honestly, they didn't seem all that surprised. *Confused*, but not surprised."

"Thorin, Zeke, and I have always been weirdly close, and I disappeared with them for ten years. My parents probably don't feel like they even know me anymore."

"They're your parents," I remind him. "No one knows you better. They're probably just worried that if they show too much concern, they'll drive you away when they just got you back. You should talk to them about it. Ease their minds and help them understand so that they don't have to worry about you any more than they already are."

"When did you get to be so wise?"

"I think it's all the baby juice I've got pumping in these veins. I think it's altering my brain."

Khalil snorts, and then his eyes widen slightly when I stare up at him seriously. "Really?"

"I don't know." I shrug. "Probably. Where are Thorin and Seth?" I ask as I yawn. I haven't seen them since dinner, before I left to shower off the day.

"They're bunking together in the guest room across the hall."

I start to sit up. "You think your parents will mind if I…?"

"Go 'head." Khalil tips his chin toward the door and then slides down on his bed, getting comfortable with his shoulders resting on the pillow and his head still propped up by the headboard. My gaze catches on his abs bunching and flexing as he moves and the impression of his semihard dick pressing against the front of his loose athletic shorts. Khalil starts laughing, flashing his straight white teeth when he sees me having second thoughts. "You might as well go because my parents might be cool as a fan, but there's no fucking under their roof unless it's them." He shudders at that last part.

"Fine," I grumble as I scoot down the squeaking bed. When I get to the foot, I look over my shoulder as I bounce up and down rhythmically, smiling like a villain when I see the panic in his eyes.

"You better stop before my mom comes in here and pops you," Khalil warns.

I laugh riotously as I head across the hall, glancing at the open door of the hall bathroom when I do. I don't bother to knock on the bedroom door as I push inside to see Thor sleeping soundly on one of the two twin beds crammed inside the bedroom. There wasn't much room for any other furniture except for the old chest in the corner. Khalil already told me that Zeke and Thorin would often spend nights here growing up when life got too hard at home, so his parents had created a safe space for them to use whenever they needed.

I look over at the other bed by the open window with the curtains blowing in and see that it's empty, so I walk over to Thorin's bed on the opposite side and I reach out for his shoulder to shake him awake, but he catches my wrist before I can. His blue eyes pop open, and then he releases me and immediately tries to pull me onto the bed with him as he rolls over.

"Where's Seth?" I ask as I go willingly, letting him spoon me with his hand on my belly.

"Bathroom?" Thor guesses.

I shake my head as I stare at the empty bed that looks like it was never slept in. "He can't be. It was empty when I came in."

Thorin tenses behind me and then he's cursing as he lunges from the bed, nearly toppling me over the side in the process. "Shit. Sorry, songbird." He helps me sit up and then dresses before dashing from the room.

I hear him burst inside Khalil's, and it takes me a minute to stand. *Not much longer now*, I think as I waddle across the hall after him. I'm in my third trimester and more than ready to evict this little invader of mine.

"Why the fuck would he go back there?" Khalil barks at Thorin when I walk inside. Khalil is already up and shoving back into his clothes.

"Not him," Thorin clarifies. "*Zeke.*"

Zeke's awake? My heart falls. When? Why hadn't he said anything? Why would he just leave?

"What's going on?" I finally ask when it's clear they don't notice me standing there.

Thorin turns to me wearing a stormy expression. "We think coming back here woke up Zeke, and he's gone back to his mother's home."

"Okay... Other than him doing it secretly, why is that a bad thing?"

"Because even though he never talks about her—never even allows himself to think about her—his mother's house is where it all began. She's the reason Isaac was able to mold his mind like Play-Doh. Going back there will not be good for him."

"You don't know that. Zeke is stronger than you think." But my words fall on deaf ears because Khalil and Thorin are already moving for the door. "Wait," I say since it's clear they can't be convinced that Zeke doesn't need saving. And if I'm honest, I'm more worried than I let on. I still remember how easy it was for Isaac to manipulate Bane when he'd never even met him. He's dead now but that doesn't mean he isn't still dangerous. "I'm coming with you."

Neither of them argue because they know what I know—Zeke isn't a danger to me, and neither are Seth and Bane. We leave Khalil's parents' home and drive across Six Forks to a rougher part of town that fills me with unease when the buildings become dilapidated and the people we see roaming the streets this time of night become more frequent. I immediately try to piece together the fragments that have become Zeke's mind like a puzzle, but it's not until we're pulling up to a gray house with the roof caving in and the front door hanging off the hinges that I finally see the whole picture staring back at me.

CHAPTER FIFTY-SIX

EZEKIEL

It looks the same. Worse, but it was never much to begin with.

I stand inside the one-room shack feeling the cold draft spilling through the massive hole in the roof.

It wasn't always that big. I used to stare up at the ceiling from my mattress on the floor and count the cracks spidering from the hole that was a fraction of the size it is now and wonder when it would finally cave.

I walk the house like it's a museum housing the worst of my childhood memories.

The small square kitchen table where I'd sit and wait for a meal that most nights wouldn't come. The iron still plugged into the wall from the last time *she* made me hold out my wrist until I told her the name she wanted me to have and not the one my mother gave me. The dented walls inside each of the rooms that she'd throw herself against whenever she was caught in one of her rages and I managed to trap her inside.

And then there were the warm hugs and smiles. The assurances that she didn't regret having me. The home-cooked meals. The songs she'd sing to me when I was sick. Those are the memories I cling to.

My mother had DID too—Bianca and Mara.

Bianca was my mother's name. Mara was her alter who tortured me, screaming about me taking her baby away. The first time my father met Bianca's alternate identity, he fled and ran straight back to the family he'd abandoned for her. Isaac's family.

A sound behind me, the crunch of glass under a shoe, has me looking over my shoulder and seeing a very pregnant Aurelia walking in while looking around with an unreadable expression. "Princess?"

Slowly, Aurelia's eyes turn to me, and she gives me a warm smile that I don't return because the shame of her seeing this place has my skin crawling.

I turn to fully face her as she walks deeper inside, carefully stepping over the debris littering the floor. I rush over to meet her and take her arm to hold her steady. "What are you doing here? And *what the fuck*?" I say as I touch her hard, round stomach. "You're pregnant? When did this happen? *How* did this happen?"

"Well, you see, Zeke. When two people love each other, they sometimes express that love by—*ow*," she says when I bite her cheek.

"Smartass." I rub her belly and try not to freak the fuck out at the news that I'm about to be a father. The last time I saw Aurelia, she was getting into the back of a car and I was screaming at her not to leave. Did she know then? Is that why she left? "How are you feeling? Thorin must be insufferably happy," I ramble when I can't find the right words.

"Well, there's the mood swings, heartburn, and swelling in weird places, but yeah, Thorin's thrilled. Look, we don't have long," Aurelia warns, skating right past the fact that she's pregnant in only the way she can. "I convinced Khalil and Thorin to wait outside, but they're very nervous and worried about you. I figure we have about two minutes before they come rushing in here to make sure you're in one piece."

We have so much to talk about—her leaving at the top of the list—but I guess that will have to wait.

"I don't think I've ever been in one piece," I say. "Not for as long as I can remember."

"What do you mean?"

I take a deep breath and fight past the urge to bury the truth I came here to find. But one look in Aurelia's warm eyes and I know I can trust her with it.

"I want to show you something."

She nods. "Okay."

Walking over to the filthy, mold-ridden mattress, I crouch and peel the corner back. A mouse scurries out from underneath where it chewed a warm home into the underside, but I pay it no mind as I stare at the name written on the floor in crayon.

"*Seth*," she breathes out when she sees it. "*How?* How is that possible? I don't understand."

"I think Seth manifested long before Isaac ever got me on that table. I think after my mother died and she couldn't hurt me anymore, he stopped waking up and I forgot about him until—" I try to swallow past the knot in my throat.

"Until Isaac."

Letting the mattress go, I stand, towering over Aurelia, who tilts her head to look up at me. "I don't think he even remembers existing. I was so young when she died. My memories barely stretch back that far, which means Seth can't remember either. He thinks his life began in that cult, and the alternative isn't much better."

"Why?"

I tell her about my mother having DID. I tell her about Bianca and Mara. Two sides of the same coin, one who had the warm embrace of a mother and the other who wore her face but never wanted anything to do with me.

"Why do you think she hated you?" Aurelia asks softly, referring to Mara.

"I don't think she hated me. I think she knew I didn't belong to her. I think she was jealous of Bianca having a child and wanted one of her own. I think everything she did to me was to create Seth. A child of her own."

There were gaps in my memory from childhood, but I always chalked it up to my young age, never once considering those gaps were coming from Seth's presence. At the time, whenever I'd wake up to find I'd lost a few hours or even days, all I could remember was feeling afraid and not knowing the reason why.

Aurelia's lips part, and her eyes shimmer with tears. "So Seth has a mother?"

"Seth had a mother," I softly correct.

Because when mine died, it meant Seth's did too. And one day, when I go, it means Seth and Bane will too. And even though Seth having a mother in Mara meant I had to be in pain, I don't begrudge him that. The real question is how do I tell Seth he had a mother he doesn't remember? He might get curious. He might go digging in places where neither of us belong, searching for memories closed off by time to both of us forever.

I already owe him a lot more than I thought. I owe him a life without pain.

"What are you talking about, Zeke?" Aurelia questions, sounding nervous when I tell her that.

"I'm talking about giving Seth that chance," I say as I take her hands in mine, trapping them between our bodies. "I'm talking about going to sleep one last time...and never waking up again."

"What?" Aurelia snatches her hands from mine and backs away with disbelieving eyes.

"I can let Seth have it all," I say. "My body, the baby, and you. He deserves it. You deserve someone who can always be present for you, not just sometimes."

"And what about what you deserve? It was your pain too. It's your life too. You can't just give it up because you think it will be easier. And don't tell me you're doing this for me without even asking me what I want."

"Aurelia, what if the cycle repeats itself? What if one of us hurts our kid? I know Seth won't, but Bane is *dangerous*. I can keep him away like Seth did, but for good this time. Seth obviously figured out how, which means there's a way. I can keep you and the baby safe."

"You can't assume that because you and your mom had the same disorder that it makes you the same. That's bullshit. You are not a danger to our child. Bane isn't going to hurt me. He isn't going to hurt the baby. You have to stop being afraid of him. Bane isn't the monster you think he is. You just have to trust me and give this a chance. We can have it all. You just have to believe it."

"Are you sure?"

"Sure that I love you and don't want you to leave me? Of course I'm sure."

"I love you too."

The front door creaks open, and I look over Aurelia's head to see Thorin and Khalil sneaking inside. They don't bother to look around. Their focus is on Aurelia before shifting to me and seeing that I'm okay too.

"Everything okay?" Khalil asks.

I don't expect Aurelia to spin around and tattle on me, but that's what happens. At first, they're distracted by her puffy face soaked with tears, and then their worried faces turn into deep scowls and vicious curses when her words finally penetrate.

"Don't worry, songbird. Seth would never have allowed it. At first, he would have been ecstatic at never having to leave you, but the moment he knew how sad the loss of Zeke made you, he would have done anything to make it better."

Khalil, who had been quiet until now, hauls off and punches me out of nowhere. Pain explodes in my shoulder, and I glare at him as he lifts a brow. "Next time you start talking that crazy shit, it'll be your face. We are a family, and the family isn't complete without you."

I glance at Thorin who's staring at my other shoulder. Aurelia must notice too because she suddenly throws herself in front of me. "No more hitting Zeke. Use your words. We want him to *want* to stay." And then she waddles for the front door, grumbling under her breath, "I've attached myself to idiots."

"Foreeeeever," the three of us chorus as we follow her out of the house.

CONGRATS ARE IN ORDER! AURELIA GIVES BIRTH TO THE CUTEST BOUNCING BOY

2 months ago
By Allesi | The Tea Sip

Singer Aurelia stuns the world with a recent Instagram post after confirming that she's just given birth to a healthy son. Among the outpouring of congratulations and well wishes to the new mother, some are happy to finally have their suspicions confirmed while others, like myself, are simply in shock.

It begs the question: Why the secrecy?

One might wonder if the public claims made by Aurelia's uncle and former manager in the upcoming conservatorship hearing are true and that the pop singer's relationship with her bodyguards/boy toys is more than what it seems. Her fans certainly hope so despite the concerning rumors of how the relationship started. Votes and hopes are already underway regarding which of those stunning specimens is the biological father to baby Nico. Everyone certainly seems to have their favorites.

So, is it possible?

Does the gorgeous, talented, mega-rich, and widely adored Aurelia George have a harem of hotties? While that term and its usage may spark debate as well the question of its validity and social acceptance, one fact remains indisputable.

Some girls...have all the luck.

CHAPTER FIFTY-SEVEN

AURELIA

So when does he become fun?" Seth asks as he stares inside Nico's crib that Khalil built for him, along with the rocking chair that I often sit in when feeding our son.

Our son is eight weeks old today, and I'm still reeling from actually giving birth to a little human. My days are filled with cuddling, nursing, and changing diapers and then living in between more cuddling, nursing, and changing diapers. I'm most surprised by how much it doesn't bother me. I am *obsessed* with the little guy.

"Fun?" Khalil echoes distractedly as he adjusts the blue cap over the wisps of blond hair on Nico's little head.

I watch through the camera in the nursery as Seth gestures to the baby, who's asleep even now. "He kind of just lays there all day like a potato. I want to play with him."

Thorin sighs from the rocking chair where he's flipping through one of the baby books. "Babies aren't toys, Seth."

"I know that, but how are we supposed to get to know the little guy if all he does is sleep, shit, and hog Sunshine? I mean, what do we *really* know about this kid? Except for the fact that he's a titty hog."

"You know that he's yours, Seth. That's enough for now."

Seth thinks about it for a moment before blurting, "I'm waking him up."

He reaches inside the crib, and Khalil quickly puts him in a headlock. "Don't," he whispers. "We just put him down. Goldilocks will kill you."

"Fine, fine."

Khalil lets him go, and Seth deflates as he stares longingly at Nico. It's been two months since Nico was born, but he's still upset that he missed the birth—along with every other day of Nico's life since we've resumed the schedule we had in the Cold Peaks.

Today is Seth's day. Tomorrow will be Zeke's.

Seth's been worried that he'll miss another important moment of Nico's life, including all of the unimportant ones, so whenever Nico's asleep—which is all the time—Seth becomes restless and agitated.

"Seth," I call through the built-in microphone. His head snaps toward the camera. "Can you come here, please? I need you."

Seth rushes out of the baby's room, keeping his steps light, and moments later, he bursts through our bedroom where I'm supposed to be napping before my first appearance since giving birth at the Stardust Gala this evening. It's just like the Met Gala in New York, but in Hollywood. "What is it? What happened?"

"Nothing," I say calmly as I hold out my hand. "I can't sleep, and I was thinking maybe it was because I needed you close. Will you lie with me?"

"Oh." I see him visibly relax. "Okay." He takes my hand and lets me pull him onto the bed with me, and then I crawl between his legs and rest my back against his chest. His scent envelops me immediately—juniper and leather.

"Is everything okay?" I ask when I realize he's quieter than usual.

"I'm worried Nico won't know me. What if he prefers Zeke or the others to me?"

"He won't," I confirm with confidence.

I hear Seth's heart thud against his chest, and it amazes me how differently the rhythm seems compared to Zeke's and Bane's. Even their breathing. "How do you know? I'll only be around for half of his life. Khalil and Thor will get all of him. It's not fair."

I'd say Seth sounded petulant if he wasn't completely right. It's not fair. Seth was already robbed of a childhood and a mom he doesn't remember. Finding out about Mara had been hard for him, but it mostly left Seth feeling conflicted and frustrated. How do you mourn a mother you don't even remember having? How do you feel robbed of a childhood you never knew was possible?

And now there's Nico, who has more parents than most who are all ready and willing to love, live, and die for him if need be. But for Seth and Zeke they can only be around some of the time and that reality makes Seth feel left out and unneeded, even though he's never not once doubted that Nico was his.

"Because I think our baby is so special and so sweet that he has enough love in his heart for all of you. And I think that when you're gone, he'll miss you just as much as you miss him. Don't you agree? Don't you think our baby is the most loving little being on the planet?"

Seth reaches up and caresses my jawbone with his callused finger. "I think you might be, Sunshine." He drops his hand to my thigh. "But Nico is a close second. He's pretty fucking awesome. And so are you."

"You'll be there for the next one," I tell Seth. "I promise."

"I know." He kisses the top of my head. "Are you ready for tonight?"

It's a loaded question since I know he isn't talking about the gala. My uncle will likely be there, and it will be the first time we've been in the same room since he landed under federal investigation for fraud. Whether he knows I'm responsible is a mystery, but I have a feeling I'll find out tonight.

"Ready," I answer.

My arrival on the red carpet draws a lot of attention—more than even I'm used to, because for once the focus isn't entirely on me—or my stunning red gown.

Everyone's looking at the four of us together. At the way Thorin, Khalil, and Seth flank me as I walk up the steep steps into the venue under the flashes of cameras.

My stylist chose the glittering red to give the people what they wanted and feed the whispers of the shameless seductress who dared defy societal rules, and she chose the ball gown style with a basque waist to remind them all that I'm still the people's princess.

A blend of the old and the new me.

I think the biggest shock of all came from the shedding of my trademark. My hair is no longer gold or blonde, and the soft curls meant to invite are long gone, replaced by a provocative black and styled in a wet, slicked-back look for the night.

Despite the confidence I force myself to display on the long walk, my breath leaves me in a rush the moment I'm out of sight of the cameras, and I hold my now flatter stomach as if it can quell the queasiness I feel. Even the swish of my dress is loud in my ears. I hear the soft footsteps of my guys behind me, but they won't comfort me.

I made them promise not to.

For now, in order to keep our son safe, we can't confirm anything. The public can talk, they can whisper, they can judge, and they can point, but at the end of the day, no one really has anything except a rumor.

And we're going to keep it that way.

The amount of ironclad, life-ending NDAs my lawyers had to distribute to make sure no one on my team talks could make a stairway to heaven.

Oni and my new assistant are walking ahead of me in simpler red gowns of their own, and I follow them into the ballroom where there's already a crowd gathered, the cheers of the crowd outside fading with each step.

There's music playing, and I realize like an afterthought that it's mine—the song I wrote for my mountain men with Houston's heavy-handed help. I should call and thank him. It turned out to be a huge hit. It wasn't my goal at the time other than hoping that it would reach my mountain men.

I should have known they wouldn't wait nearly that long before coming after me.

I smile to myself and hear a throat clearing behind me, our signal that one of them wants my attention. I'm still smiling when I glance over my shoulder, and Khalil looks pleased as he traces the edges of my grin.

"Now that's more like it," he says.

"You could tell I was smiling?" I ask incredulously. "How?"

"Because you glow when you smile," Seth answers, and I shift my gaze to him. "You're sunshine."

I'm robbed of my chance to respond when a woman calls out my name. I shift my attention to the voice and see that it's none other than Tania fucking Bradshaw. She's wearing a green dress that clashes horribly with her skin tone and has a lot of fucking feathers. She's wearing a blond curly wig cut into a bob that doesn't quite mesh with the dress, and her makeup looks as if the artist was commanded to make her skin paler since it's about three shades lighter than her neck or chest. My mood sours instantly, especially since I know she's now being managed by my uncle. I'm pretty sure he's screwing her too—if the rumors are to be believed.

"Aurelia, hi! I'm so glad we finally had a chance to run into each other."

"Why?" I ask dryly, feeling like this exchange is a mirror of the one that started all of this a year and a half ago. The one that turned Tania and me into enemies and landed me on a plane to Canada.

She blinks her big, round eyes, playing the part of stupid perfectly, and I immediately see why my uncle signed her. Other than the fact that it would piss me off. "What do you mean?"

"Why are you glad we ran into each other? I don't like you. I thought I told you that."

I feel my mountain men close in on me, and Tania's gaze rises to meet them and sparkles with interest. "Is that them?" she whispers in a hushed voice as she tries to inch closer. "The photos do not do them justice. Way to go, Aurelia." I stare at her. "Unless, of course, the rumors *aren't* true. In which case, are they single?"

"Let me introduce you," I say as I shift a little until she can get a better look at my guys. "This is Khalil, Thorin, and Seth."

"Why, hello," Tania greets with invitation in her tone.

None of my guys speak or even glance her way as they scan the room. Some of Tania's confidence wavers, so I quickly say, "Seth likes entrails, did you know that? He's fascinated with them. Hopes to see some one day."

The color leaks from Tania's face. "Um...okay."

I tilt my head to hold her gaze when she starts looking around for an avenue of escape. "I was thinking later you can join us somewhere private and I can show him yours. What do you say? Are you still glad you ran into me?"

"I think I'm going to go."

"Yes, you do that." She starts to walk off, but I stop her after only a couple of steps. "And hey, Tania?"

She reluctantly turns to face me while frowning nervously. "Yes?"

"Make that the last time you try to take anything of mine."

Nodding quickly, she hurries away, and I hear several throats clearing behind me, so I turn to face my guys who are all watching me with amused eyes. "What?" I say with an innocent shrug. "I'm not sorry. She had it coming."

"Indeed, she did," Thorin says.

The rest of the evening happens uneventfully with me mostly dodging questions about my security team. Halfway through the night, an emergency alarm sounds, drawing everyone's attention, and I use the cover of the commotion to break away to head to the bathroom. It's likely a pap or an overzealous fan of one of the countless celebrities in attendance. When I reach the bathroom, I manage to convince my guys to stay out in the hallway and *not* follow me in since my uncle still hasn't shown his face.

And he won't now since the gala has a strict late-arrival policy.

I'll stay another hour and then I'll go, I think as I look around the fancy bathroom. There's another door at the other end that I dismiss as a supply closet while I head inside the largest of the three stalls. Once I'm inside, I lift up my dress, but the heavy material strains my arms, and I can't seem to get it all over my hips at once. This is the reason why relieving yourself is not an option when attending one of these things, but I recently had a baby, so…nature calls. After several failed attempts of trying not to ruin the custom dress I got on loan, I call out for one of my guys, and Seth appears inside the stall in a flash.

"What's up?"

"Help me, will you?" I indicate my dress, and he wordlessly

walks over to hold it out of the way for me while I squat over the toilet.

"How did they even expect you to go in this thing?"

"They didn't," I answer dryly while I pee.

Once I'm done, Seth carefully rearranges my gown around me and then backs out of the stall. I follow, and he hangs around while I wash my hands and check my makeup. As I'm reapplying my lipstick, I hear the creak of the door opening and look toward the one I came through only to see that it's still firmly shut.

I'm still frowning at it in confusion when I hear a thud and grunt and turn in time to see Seth slumping to the ground and my uncle standing behind him with the gun he used to knock out Seth pointed at me.

The look in his bloodshot eyes tells me that Uncle Mars is long past familial bonds, and frankly, so am I. I open my mouth to scream, and he aims the gun at the back of Seth's head. "I wouldn't do that."

"What do you want?" I ask coldly.

"Lock the door." When I don't move, he fires off a shot into the tile an inch from Seth's head, and I hurry over to the door to lock it before Khalil and Thorin have a chance to burst through. I hear them pounding on it and calling my name as soon as I turn the lock. "Now come over here. Get over here!" he roars when I don't move fast enough.

"You look like shit, Uncle Mars. Is something wrong?"

"I know it was you who told the Feds." Before I can deny it, he grabs my hair the moment I'm close enough and forces me through the door he came in.

The door I assumed was a supply closet.

Thorin will scold me about that later after he tortures himself for not checking out the bathroom and all entry and exit points before letting me inside.

Right now, I stumble into what looks like another hallway, and the first thing I notice is the red exit sign at the end of it marking my doom. If he gets me through it, I'm toast. He'll likely have a car waiting close by.

My uncle presses the gun to my spine to get me moving faster since it's only a matter of time before Thorin and Khalil break through the bathroom door.

"There's no point in killing me, Uncle. If I die, my son inherits everything."

"And who do you think will inherit your son after your boyfriends are in prison where they belong?"

A cold fury sweeps through me, but there's nothing I can do with a gun pressed to my spine, so I do what I do best.

I keep poking the bear.

"Maybe one of them will be your cellmate since I hear that's where you're heading too."

"You think I'm worried about that?" Uncle Mars snaps back. "I have the best lawyers money can buy."

"Oof." I feign a wince. "I sure hope you didn't buy those fancy lawyers with my stolen funds too. I'm told by *my* fancy lawyers that each count is worth a pretty good chunk of time."

"Shut the fuck up already!"

There.

That's it.

The opening that I've been waiting for when he lifts the gun to strike me. I spin using the speed Khalil drilled into me and grab his raised arm before he can bring the gun down on my head. It goes off during our struggle for control, and when Uncle Mars tries to slap me down with his free hand, I block the blow and send the heel of my palm into his nose, feeling it break.

He shouts as he stumbles back, and the shocked expression on his face would be comical if he weren't still holding the gun. My uncle seems to remember that it's in his hand a moment later, and he swipes his bleeding nose as he regains his composure. "I see you weren't just out there lying on your back. Too bad it won't do you a damn bit of good." He raises the gun again.

Behind him, I see the door to the bathroom open slowly and a figure cast in shadow filling the entrance. The utter stillness is a dead giveaway, and I take one last look at my father's twin, memorizing the lines of his face since it will be the last time I ever see it.

"I think," I say slowly as I back away, "that you should really rethink hurting me."

"The only thing I regret is telling my brother's enemy where to find him," he says. "If I'd known what a fucking headache you'd turn out to be, I never would have had him killed."

"Killed," I gasp more than say as the room begins to spin. "It was you? You're the reason?"

"Your father didn't give me any choice. I *begged* him to let me turn you into a star, but he didn't care how much money you could make us, so…" My uncle shrugs. "He had to go. Your father was no saint, Aurelia. He had it coming, and now so do you."

My mouth opens and I think I'll scream, but instead, all I do is say his name. "*Baaaane*," I cry out when my rage reaches its tipping point. My vision is blurred by tears now falling freely down my face, but I can still make out the alter's indistinct shadow looming over my uncle.

I hear a sickening crunch and then the gun falling to the ground as my uncle's chilling screams fill the dark hallway. I blink the tears away and my vision clears enough to see Seth's hunting knife embedded to the hilt in my uncle's wrist, but that's not all. Uncle Mar's bare arm has been split open from shoulder to wrist in a gory display of violence.

Bane removes the knife just as my gaze drops to the discarded gun. I could go for it, but shooting my uncle after what I just learned would be too good a death for him.

"*No*," I say to Bane when he moves to plunge the knife into his chest.

Bane's eyes rise to meet mine in the dark, and he almost looks like he won't stop until he drops his hand and shoves my uncle into the wall. He holds him there, and with my eyes on my struggling uncle, I reach under my gown and quickly free my own knife strapped to my thigh.

"*You*," I say with rage riding every letter as I come to stand before him, "will *never* take another thing from me, Uncle. And I will never give you a single thought after tonight. Not one."

"You—"

Whatever venom my uncle was ready to spew is cut short when I drag the knife across his throat. He chokes on his own blood before falling to his knees, and when our eyes meet one last time, I release a guttural scream and drive my knife through his eye. Filled with grief and sorrow and hatred, I stab his face over and over until he's unrecognizable.

Until I'm bathed in his blood and my rage, and he no longer looks like my father.

CHAPTER FIFTY-EIGHT

BANE

S he kicks and screams as I lift her away from the bloody pulp staining the floor now. The bathroom door bursts open a moment later, and Ezekiel's friends burst through, stumbling to a halt when they see me—or rather the crimson scene we made together.

Mine and I.

"Seth…" I growl, and the one Ezekiel calls Khalil swears. "Bane?" I don't respond, and his gaze flicks back and forth between Mine, who is still now and staring, unseeing, and me. "What happened?" he questions as he keeps a healthy distance. "Bane? What happened? Did he hurt her?"

"No."

"How the fuck are we going to explain this?" the one called Thorin barks before kicking the one who tried to hurt Mine.

"Self-defense?" Khalil throws out.

"Believable before she turned his face into ground beef."

"Who cares? He's clearly not dressed for the gala, and he brought a gun. He was here for one reason, and we all know what it was."

Thorin still shakes his head. "It's too risky with the conservatorship hearing coming up. We need to get rid of the body."

"We'd have to make sure there is nothing left of Marston to find, and even if we did, his DNA *and* hers are all over this place. We can't pull off that kind of cleanup with two hundred people down the hall. We have to risk it."

"What about cameras?" Thorin volleys. "It could prove she was in danger."

"There aren't any in this hall. It's the first thing I checked. This hall is a blind spot and likely the reason Marston chose it."

Thorin swears and then nods his reluctant agreement and looks at me warily. "Bane," he huffs out. "I need to check Aurelia. I need to make sure she's not hurt."

I tighten my grip on her and give him a look to stay away.

"Bane," Mine croaks a moment later. "It's okay. *I'm safe.* Thorin and Khalil are safe."

Safe.

Ezekiel thinks so too. And Seth.

I eye the men as they wait anxiously for me to allow them near her. It's what Mine wants, so when Thorin steps forward, I don't kill him. I stand motionless, holding Mine close as he gently turns her cheek and inspects her bloody nose. "What happened?" he asks her.

And then Aurelia recounts everything from before I woke up on the bathroom floor to after I pulled her off her uncle. Thorin and Khalil hang on her every word, their eyes filling with rage until the story is over and they're silently wishing they could kill him all over again.

"We have to play this one by the book. We need to report this. It's our best chance of walking away from this. Do you think you're up for it?"

"I can do it," Mine swears with a determined nod and then swings her brown eyes my way. "Bane, let me down."

I slowly set her down, and then the four of us leave the hallway and return to the ballroom, where the screams of the guests rent the air once they see Aurelia painted in her uncle's blood.

CASE CLOSED! AURELIA CLEARED OF ALL CHARGES

1 week ago

By Erica Danes | America's Daily News

The Stardust Gala was a glittering assembly that ended in panic and chaos as Aurelia George, known to bring the drama wherever she goes, emerged shaken from a violent backroom encounter with her uncle, who reportedly barged into the women's bathroom and attempted to kidnap the singer at gunpoint. You might have heard that Marston George is currently facing several federal indictments for fraud and that his niece may have been the one to blow the whistle. Luckily, Aurelia's bodyguards were there to save the day. And though the reports of the scene are unnecessarily grisly, we appreciate the dedication to keeping America's former sweetheart safe.

CHAPTER FIFTY-NINE

AURELIA

Scorched earth.

That's what our lonely cliff looks like when the four of us step onto it again more than a year after the fire. The few trees that are still standing are blackened, the ground is charred, and the vegetation is sparse. The cabin, which used to mean home, is nothing but a ruin at the edge of the cliff.

Decades.

It's what the forestry team that escorted us up told us it could take before the cliff and the forest surrounding it are back to what they used to be. The fire didn't take it all. The night Isaac burned everything down, at least a dozen helicopters carrying water arrived to quickly put it out. The walls of water falling down from the sky were the last I saw of the cliff and Big Bear as we were being flown away.

But there's life here too.

Because clinging to the charred trunks of the trees are spots of fuzzy green. Wildflowers are already beginning to spring from the ground along with some herbaceous plants and other green shoots. It's going to be a long recovery, but we've been doing everything we can to help it along and return this home to the wildlife.

"We should get going before it's dark," Zeke suggests after he walks over to stand next to me at the edge of the cliff.

"You think he's still down there?" I ask.

"Must be," Zeke mumbles as he peers over the edge. "We would have heard about it if anyone had found the body."

"Maybe some bears got him," I muse. "I heard they like porridge."

It takes Zeke a second to draw forth the image of what Isaac's corpse must have looked like after a fall like that, and then he snorts at the storybook reference. He drops his arm over my shoulders, and I let him steer me away.

Thorin and Khalil are already waiting at the top of the hill for the hike down to where we left the ATVs. From there, we head to Little Bear where we plan to camp for the weekend. Nico, who is almost one, is back at the ranch with Khalil's parents, who we also invited up with us for our return to the Cold Peaks. It took them a minute to get used to our quad plus the addition of Zeke's alters, but their love for their son helped them push through their shock and discomfort. It also helps that they adore Nico and me.

"I never thought I'd see this place again," I confess over the roar of the water once we reach the hidden waterfall and drop all our gear. My gaze immediately travels to the cliff where Zeke first kissed me, and I see him glance at it too out of the corner of my eye as he responds.

"Neither did I."

We make quick work of setting up camp. Well, they do. I get led away by one of them to a rock to sit whenever I try to help, so I get started on dinner instead and end up eating it without them when they're still cursing and fighting with the tent an hour later.

"Don't tell me I've spoiled you and you forgot all your survival instincts."

Thorin throws me a glare over the top of the collapsing tent while Khalil fusses at him to pull. I keep my smile small to avoid laughing, and Thorin's gaze narrows before he turns his head and barks something back at Khalil.

It took my mountain men some time to acclimate to life back on the grid, but having the best of everything money can buy helped a lot. Thorin's been complaining that all my *frills* are making them soft, so I loaded them up on my private plane and surprised them with a trip back to the Cold Peaks so that my big burly brutes can rough it for a little while.

The tent is finally up a few minutes later, and my guys join me around the fire I started.

"Why are your clothes still on?" Thorin asks me with his focus still on his food. My heart thuds against my chest as goose bumps spread over my skin, and then his blue gaze slowly rises to meet mine when I don't move.

I jerk to my feet at the unspoken command, feeling my skin flush from the fire and the weight of all their attention as I lift my thin T-shirt over my head. I feel their eyes tracing my exposed skin as I drop the shirt and move my hands down to my denim shorts. I see Khalil's eyes glowing even brighter in the firelight when I peel them off my hips and over my ass. The shorts drop to my feet and I kick them away before unhooking my sports bra from the front and discarding my thong.

"Turn around and put your hands on the log," Khalil commands softly the moment I'm naked. "Let the birthday boy see you."

My gaze finds Zeke's, and I smile softly as I hold it until I'm forced to let it go when I turn around and bend over for his gaze. And because I'm me, I give a teasing wiggle and hear several groans chorusing around me.

"Fuck, princess." I start to tremble when I hear Zeke stand and then walk over to run a hand over my ass appreciatively. "You make me want to devour you when you're like this, did you know that?"

I don't have a chance to respond because he's kneeling and shoving his face between my thighs.

Zeke's tongue is a hot brand on my pussy as he tastes my arousal while creating more, like the never-ending waterfall just a few feet away. My cries as he licks me from behind mingle with the rush of the falls, the crackling of the fire, and his thick tongue swirling through my wetness.

Zeke is an insatiable eater, and I so love feeding him.

It's over too soon though because the moment he flicks my clit after teasing me to the brink, I'm coming with a whispered curse on his tongue.

"Mmm," Zeke moans with a smack of his lips. "Best birthday cake ever." It reminds me of how he wouldn't let me bake him one the first time we met two years ago.

He stands, and then I hear the rustle of him dropping the shorts he's wearing before he's lining his thick crown up with my entrance and plunging inside with a groan from us both. Zeke's dick is long, so it feels as if he's tunneling inside of me forever before he reaches the base. It feels exactly like the invasion it's meant to be and I'm helpless against the power of his thrusts as he uses me roughly to get himself off.

Suddenly, his thumbs are digging into the base of my spine hard enough to make me wince, so I twist my upper body to get a glimpse of him. From this angle, all I can see is his head and shoulders partially cast in shadow from the glow of the setting sun behind him, but the eerie feeling I associate with only one of Zeke's alters ripples through me and I gasp.

"Bane?" I whisper so that Khalil and Thorin don't overhear. If they knew it was the violent and unpredictable alter inside of me right now, they'd freak out. "Oh God. Is that you?"

"Mine."

My lips fall open to scream for Thorin and Khalil, but rather than a cry of alarm, I let out a long moan as I feel my pussy tighten and flutter around him in excitement. It feels like a dirty little secret when I prop a foot onto the log and open myself up more for Bane's ruthless pounding. Despite the undercurrent of danger, I can't take my eyes away from the stillness in his expression even now, my cries growing sharper and higher as we lose ourselves in the forbidden fuck.

I swore to them all after the gala, when they saw for themselves how possessive Bane was of me, that I wouldn't take the risk of calling for him, and the promise seemed easy enough to keep until now.

"Ohhhh," I cry out when his unskilled pace quickens. "God, *fuck me*. Fuck me, fuck me, fuck me, fuck me."

And as if I'm not being screwed within an inch of my life mere steps away, I hear Thorin and Khalil talking among themselves about hunting later, adding to the humiliation and the fantasy of being used.

Bane comes inside me and then whispers *Mine* again before going still.

A moment later, Zeke is back, and he looks confused until I give him a tremulous smile, and the question in his eyes clears as he realizes what must have happened. I shake my head, silently begging him not to ruin this, and he swears before hooking his forearm around my waist and roughly lifting me from the ground. He walks me over to Thorin, who immediately ends his conversation with Khalil about their plans for a new cabin and grabs me when I move to crawl into his lap.

"I don't want to wait," I say with a kiss as I reach between us and rip open his shorts—just in case he has plans to tease and torture me first. "I want it right now, okay?" He's already hard from pretending not to watch Zeke and me, so I have his thick crown fitted against my tight little pussy in no time.

"Such a good wolf," Thorin says as I eagerly lower myself down. "Taking all of our cocks like a sweet little slut."

My nipples harden even more at the degrading pet name, and then I'm throwing myself against his chest, wrapping my arms around his neck as I kiss him deeply. Thorin groans in my mouth while he uses his hands on my ass to bounce me in his lap. I'm so lost to the feeling of him moving inside me that I barely notice when he shifts his body on the wide log, turning us both while I take over bouncing on his dick. Thorin lies down, and I feel another set of hands grabbing my hair and forcing my head back.

Khalil.

His thick, pretty dick is suddenly in my face, and I open my mouth for him immediately. I feel my lips stretch wonderfully when he stuffs himself inside. My head is already bobbing by the time I hear the top of a bottle pop open and the lube undoubtedly being squirted on Zeke's fingers and dick.

Like a well-rehearsed dance because we've done this so many times, I hold on to Khalil and lean into Thorin when I feel Zeke straddle the log behind me.

"Show me that sweet little hole, Princess."

Releasing an excited moan muffled by Khalil's dick, I reach behind me and spread my ass for him, feeling my anus pucker from the exposure to the warm spring air. A moment later, two of Zeke's slick fingers are pressing inside and Thorin is holding me still for the invasion when I start to squirm.

Every time he pushes his fingers deep, I tighten around Thorin, and he swears while letting his head roll around on the log like he's being tortured. Meanwhile, I'm gazing up at Khalil and his dark coily hair, loose around his shoulders. He still refuses to cut it, and in moments like these, I'm glad for it as I drink in the way it frames his gorgeous face while he feeds me his dick.

"Shit, Goldilocks. You're going to make me come looking at me like that."

I attempt to respond around his length that just comes out like a wet garble and ends on a whine when I feel Zeke carefully remove his fingers and immediately replace them with his slick crown. He doesn't push inside though until I relax from the natural reaction of tensing.

But when he does...

I think my eyes roll back in my head, but I can't be sure because Khalil, Thorin, and Zeke start moving as one and all I can remember is floating on a cloud wrapped in darkness and sin as they grunt and curse and groan and lose themselves to the pleasure of having me trapped between them.

After, when I'm painted in their cum inside and out, I'm picked up by Khalil, and the others soon follow as he carries me into the water. We stop when the water is waist deep, and then he sets me down. I'm surrounded immediately by my men who are just as wild as ever despite following me back into my world of glitz and glamour, and I wouldn't have it any other way.

Feeling content, I close my eyes and bask in the praise they shower me with as they use the sponges and soap Thorin and Zeke brought with them to bathe them from my body.

This is the part I enjoy the most—my men carefully piecing me together after brutally ripping me apart.

"I love you, Goldilocks."

"Best and most terrifying, songbird," Thorin reminds me.

"You make me feel whole, Princess."

I'm bawling and whimpering like a baby and swearing through

my ragged cries that they do it just to make me cry. I hear their chuckles and then feel their lips on my shoulder, forehead, and breasts as they attempt to console me and apologize for making me feel so happy and cherished. I have no way of knowing which mouth belongs to who. All I can do is tip my head toward the darkening sky when I feel their hands began to roam again with more purpose and give thanks that it was in these wilds I fell.

I'm still feeling raw about them splitting me open and stuffing their feelings inside, but luckily, I know the perfect way to get even. After we'd fucked and bathed once more before leaving the pool, I manage to sneak over to the path leading to the top of the waterfall.

I'm almost to the top of the cliff when I hear Zeke call after me. "Princess, what the fuck are you doing?"

Ignoring him, I find the exact spot where he jumped, and then I begin to back away with an evil grin when I hear him yell, "Holy fuck, she's going to jump."

Thorin and Khalil look up from the knives one of them is sharpening and the knot the other one is tying in a rope and when they see me, those overbearing assholes drop everything and start sprinting toward the path. Only Zeke remains as if he can't look away and since I know Thorin and Khalil will be up here in a flash, I quickly judge the distance I put between me and the edge before deciding it'll have to be enough when I see Thorin's head crest the path.

I start sprinting toward the edge to their combined shouts, and at the very last second…I leap.

I instantly regret it, but it's too late now as I plummet with a scream toward the surface of the moonlit water.

My ass is still stinging hours later after we're all piled inside the tent for the night. After my big leap, I was forced to flee the hidden oasis when I took one look at the dark scowls on the faces of my mountain men and ran the other way.

They chased, of course, and it ended with me tossed over a tree stump, my hands bound with rope, and my mouth gagged with Thorin's shirt as they took turns stripping my ass raw.

"Sunshine's been a naughty girl," Seth says into the quiet dark of our tent. I'd woken him up a couple of hours ago once Zeke's time was up, and he immediately dared me to do it again after accessing all of Zeke's recent memories.

And I do mean *all* of them.

"He's right," I confess with a yawn and a stretch as I get comfortable inside the bedroll I share with him. Feeling sated, I let my eyes drift closed to the sound of Seth's heartbeat, and I'm already falling sleeping with a smile on my face when I mumble, "I fucked Bane."

The tent immediately explodes with Seth's loud cackles and Khalil and Thorin's combined roar, "*You what?*"

EPILOGUE

AURELIA

THREE YEARS LATER

C*abin* doesn't quite feel like the right word to describe it. The massive rustic structure slowly taking shape blocks out part of the sun from this side. It's been three years since we broke ground, but with only a small window every year to build before the snow falls, it's taken some time to even get this far.

I will admit my excitement has made me a little impatient.

We've been staying for part of the year at the ranch, but it's not the same as the cabin.

Although this log cabin won't be the same as the old either. It's bigger, grander, and most importantly, it will come with modern appliances. It's also being built on one and a half acres overlooking the lake with Big Bear towering behind it like a massive shadow. We chose not to build it as high for easier access to town, but the guys are already talking about building a smaller hunting cabin somewhere more secluded.

The guys have been working around the clock to get it ready before the fall comes, so that we can finally spend our first winter inside, but I haven't been allowed anywhere near by decree of my very protective, very obsessive mountain men, and I've obeyed until today.

Seth has been texting me pictures nonstop until my curiosity finally drove me up from the ranch.

"Let's go see your daddies!" I say to my son and daughter as we leave the car.

Already, I can see traces of Khalil in the details with the roaring bears and howling wolves etched into the narrow support beams in the extended overhang. The natural awning shields the front door and the steps leading to it, and I start toward them when one of my mountain men barrels through, having received my text warning him that we were on our way.

"You. Stop right there," Khalil orders with a point of his finger when he sees me walking toward the construction site with our daughter on my hip and Nico clutching my hand. He's wearing a hard hat, dust-covered boots and jeans, and a loose muscle shirt that shows off his sweaty arms and makes my mouth water.

"Daddy!" Bliss squeals with a wave when she sees him, looking just like his ass.

Khalil softens even more when he sees his little princess, and he takes her from my arms when she reaches for him. Nico abandons me too to run over and grab his pant leg, and Khalil bends to lift him until he's got a kid in each arm, and they're talking his ear off.

"I thought I told you to keep your mama in line," Khalil says to Nico the moment he gets a chance. "We had a deal. What's up?"

"We wanted to see you, Dad," Nico responds with a mischievous grin.

"I'm happy to see you too, Nic." Khalil kisses his cheek, and when I try to slip by him now that he's distracted, Khalil says, "You can't go in, Aurelia, and you know why. It's not safe for you and the babies."

As in, baby number three…and four.

"I'm barely showing, Khalil. It's fine. I'll be careful. Please?"

Before he can tell me no, Khalil's father comes ambling out of the cabin in a hard hat, and my babies get hyped and start yelling for him at the same time. "Pops," I say to the large man when he comes over to gently steal the kids from Khalil, "do you mind doing me a favor and watching the kids while your overbearing son gives me a tour?"

"Yeah, yeah. Go on, go on," he says distractedly as he showers his grandbabies with affection.

"See?" I say to Khalil. "Problem solved. You can be right there to protect me."

Sighing, Khalil gives in and takes my hand, stopping by a workbench to grab a spare hard hat for me. The massive Douglas fir support beams on either side of the front steps catch my attention as he carefully arranges the hat on my head, and I make a mental note to goad one of my mountain men into fucking me against it later. Khalil whisks me toward the double pane glass doors, and I take one last look over my shoulder at the kids with their grandpa before Khalil pulls me through the door.

The sound of hammering, sawing, and drilling fills my ears as we walk inside, our steps on the reclaimed pine floors echoing up to the thirty-foot ceiling. Directly across from the entryway and perpendicular to the front doors is a switchback staircase leading up to the second floor.

I glance to the left when we reach the wall propping them up and see a huge open space with a chandelier already installed, and I know from the plans that it's the living room. Khalil keeps me close to him, tucking me into his side as he leads me to the right toward the kitchen where the majority of the noise downstairs is coming from.

I take a moment to take in the plaster walls held up and framed by more massive logs and the antler tiered chandeliers everywhere we go.

"It's all so beautiful," I say tearfully and feel Khalil squeeze my hip as we enter the kitchen.

Immediately, I spot Thorin with his shirt off, and my gaze narrows when I realize he's standing with his dirty-ass boots on my custom and *very* expensive granite table as he attempts to fix the chandelier hanging above it.

He glances over when we walk in and then double takes when he sees me before swearing viciously. "What the hell, Khal?" He jumps down and rushes over to me. "Wolf, what are you doing here?"

"I wanted to see."

Thorin immediately touches the barely there swell of my stomach. "It's not safe," he says.

"Neither is ditching your shirt in a construction site," I whisper as I trail my fingers down his glistening abs. "But that didn't stop you from turning yourself into a little thirst trap, did it?"

His abs twitch from my touch, and then he presses forward when his mind shifts gears before he remembers where we are. Thorin then blows out a harsh breath and shakes his head. "Seth's going to lose his shit."

"Where is he?" I ask as I look around.

"He's working on something in the bedroom. Come on," Thorin invites as he takes my hand. "Let me show you."

The two of them flank me as we head back the way Khalil and I came and toward the stairs that are crafted out of logs sawed in half. Their dedication to every detail nearly brings tears to my eyes again because I know they didn't really care about the frills but did it all for me anyway.

This time, they had some help, and we pass a few of Papa Poverly's crew that he brought up with him as well as a handful of locals to help get the job done since we are now sitting on a 14,000-square-foot house.

The three of us travel through a few winding hallways before we reach the master suite at the back of the house. As soon as we walk through the double doors, my jaw drops at the view of Big Bear through the panoramic window behind the massive bed. The house still isn't furnished yet besides the dining table, lighting fixtures, and the bed.

"Oh my *God*!" I squeal, startling Seth who hadn't noticed us come in.

Something falls out of his hand, and he curses as he scoops it up before tossing it on the bed and rushing over. "Sunshine," he greets with a sigh before crouching to kiss my stomach. "Plums." He glances up at me with a frown. "What are you doing here?"

I rub my belly with a smile. "What do you mean? The babies and I missed you."

"Nice try," he says as he stands and scowls. "You wanted to snoop around, didn't you?"

"Yes. Now where's my tour?" I demand eagerly.

"Come on." Seth takes my hand and shows me around the room before leading me out with Thorin and Khalil, pointing out things and explaining all the rooms we weave in and out of on the second floor and then the first.

There's a recording and dance studio for me, a boxing one for Khalil as well as a workshop for his woodworking, and a library for Seth and Zeke who like to read—one of the few things besides the group they have in common. Thorin is the only one who doesn't have a special room for himself because most of his hobbies took him outdoors, but I know somewhere on the property is a detached garage with every piece of sporting equipment known to man.

"The house is beautiful," I say as we leave the living room with a view of the lake and walk toward the front doors. "Thank you for making it a labor of love."

For a while it felt like we'd said goodbye to the Cold Peaks forever and that we'd never reclaim our home. But once we learned it didn't matter where we were, and that the only place we truly belonged was with each other, we realized there was nothing stopping us from coming back. At least, for part of the year.

I'm still *the* Aurelia George to everyone else.

But first, I'm mom.

Wolf. Songbird.

Goldilocks.

Sunshine.

Princess.

And...*theirs*. Yup. I even taught Bane how to share.

As we walk toward the front doors that have been thrown open to an unobstructed view of the lake, I can hear and see Nico and Bliss playing outside. I can almost see our future laid out for all of us too.

Their first winter in the wilds.

The snow fights after a storm.

The warm nights cuddled up by the fire.

Teaching Nico and Bliss how to hunt and survive in *and* out of the wilds and giving them the best of both worlds so they can decide for themselves which one they prefer.

"Now I *really* can't wait for the wedding ceremony," I say and we all have matching smiles as we leave the unfinished cabin.

AUTHOR'S NOTE

And now we've reached the end of this tempestuous journey. The original concept of this retelling began as a quick and shameless read that would take one of your darkest fantasies and turn up the heat. I should have known I was full of shit when I decided that a great title for this "smutty, casual novella" was *The Chrysalis of Aurelia George*.

My inspiration comes from the many bodice rippers I grew up reading as a teen hellbent on defying her mother's rules. The kind with Fabio on the front cover, long hair blowing in the wind while he clutched a busty heroine whose bodice was…well, ripped. In some ways, I still think I achieved my wish of writing one of my own, but I don't regret for a second letting this world and these characters become more.

Each of them surprised me in their own way but none more than Aurelia George.

Aurelia was a welcome change from the heroines I typically write. I adored her. She was thorny and mean and spoiled. She was a villain who got her happy ending. Aurelia didn't always say or do the right things, but she was also soft, sweet, and selfless on her terms. Hate or love her, Aurelia made for a compelling character to write (and hopefully read). Even though she wasn't always easy to like, she made me feel a range of emotions that never made for a dull moment. I often find myself thinking about some of the things she said or did even when I'm not immersed in the story and all I want to do is dive back in.

Character development is important to me because there is nothing that bores me more than a flat character—who they are when you meet them is exactly who they are when you say goodbye. When that happens, we don't get to experience their growth and feel those tingles that follow from watching them yield and soften for the people they care about. For me, not shying away from showing characters at their worst is crucial. It makes for a truly relatable character because we've all had cringeworthy moments that we wish we could take back but can't. All we can do is embrace our chrysalis when it comes.

The second biggest surprise was Zeke. My decision to give Zeke DID came from the frustration of writing him in the beginning. I needed him to be too many things. His personality literally kept changing based on the scene and it made his character far too inconsistent. Rather than resist it, I embraced what he was showing me, and I got Seth and Bane out of it, who will forever be some of my favorite characters. Bane was my third and final surprise. His evolution did not start until I began writing *Chrysalis* and I finally got to fully meet him. After that, I was hungry for him. He's sort of unique. He was never meant to be more than a side character and even now, I would not categorize him as a main character, though he is part of the group and an official love interest of Aurelia's.

As for the cult—I went back and forth about diving deeper before deciding against it. Cults are intricate and compelling and naturally carve a world of their own, which leaves the risk of yanking on too many threads and deviating from what this story actually is—a Goldilocks retelling. I felt that I would do cult-hood a disservice by limiting that part of Zeke's story to flashbacks. I'm a "do it right or don't do it at all" type of gal.

And of course, this story of Goldilocks wouldn't be complete without Thorin and Khalil—or—Papa Bear and Mama Bear.

Thorin's brute force and Khalil's nurturing presence elevated this retelling from just a girl with golden hair and a cabin in the woods.

Thank you so much for reading my twisted version of Goldilocks. I hope you enjoyed it as much as I did. I hope you come back to visit these characters as often as you need, and I can't wait to see which retelling I do next...*wink*

ACKNOWLEDGMENTS

Without these people I would be just a girl with a story and no one to tell it to. Thank you to Christa Désir and Kylie Hagmann for braving the trenches with me and helping me mold this retelling into one that I can look back on with no regrets.

Georgana Grinstead, you are my champion, and because of you I actually sound like I know what I'm doing.

Thank you to Madison Nankervis for working so hard to get this story into as many hands as possible. Thank you to Almeda Beynon for helping me get the perfect cast for the audiobooks. Let's scorch some headphones and make some bookworms blush. Thank you to Kimberly Hunt and Susan B for untangling the chaotic thoughts that my too-fast fingers and sleepless nights would have inflicted on the world.

Thank you to Julie at Books and Moods for helping me with *Chrysalis*'s original covers. Thank you to Amanda Simpson at Pixel Mischief for being there always when I need someone reliable.

And of course, thank you to my Sirens, whose allure and generosity are unmatched.

ABOUT THE AUTHOR

B.B. Reid is a bestselling author of several romances, including *Crucible*, the imaginative retelling of Goldilocks. She's most known for her dark and contemporary romances but began her career writing new adult. B.B. currently resides in Atlanta with Ivan, her moody tuxedo cat. When she's not being a nomad, she enjoys gaming, white chocolate mocha, home decor, and retail therapy.